ANGEL AND APOSTLE

ANGEL *and* APOSTLE

DEBORAH NOYES

UNBRIDLED
BOOKS

Unbridled Books
Denver, Colorado

Library of Congress Cataloging-in-Publication Data
Noyes, Deborah.
Angel and apostle / Deborah Noyes.
p. cm.
Summary: Pearl, the daughter of Hester Prynne from Nathanial Hawthorne's "The Scarlet Letter," tries to make sense of her life and her self while a young girl in 1649 Boston.
ISBN 1-932961-10-0 (alk. paper)
[1. Self-perception—Fiction. 2. Mothers and daughters—Fiction.
3. Puritans—Massachusetts—Fiction. 4. Massachusetts—History—
Colonial period, ca. 1600–1775—Fiction.] I. Hawthorne, Nathaniel, 1804–1864.
Scarlet letter. II. Title.

PZ7.N96157Ang2005
[Fic]—dc 22

2005015903

1 3 5 7 9 10 8 6 4 2

Book design by SH • CV

First Printing

For Elizabeth Jones

The angel and apostle of the coming revelation must be a woman indeed, but lofty, pure, and beautiful; and wise, moreover, not through dusky grief, but the ethereal medium of joy....

—NATHANIEL HAWTHORNE, *The Scarlet Letter*

ANGEL AND APOSTLE

*W*ith Mother slumped in the stocks, he settles before her, circling his knees with long arms. He lays palms together as if he would pray, but instead the words come tumbling again like petals from a failing rose: "As a young man in London—I beg your hearing once more—I oft lurked in playhouses, a frustrated scribbler. That instinct has lately returned, and to speed my nights I'm writing your story, our story, from which I am removed for your sake.

"How will I tell it? Shall I grant you a nobler lover? Shall I let you have, for posterity, your sainted minister? And why not, too, a twisted demon of a husband—an old cripple, perhaps? Few in more tolerant times than ours will fault you then.

"I can do this much if it's all you'll allow, or at least act the roles in turn, for I will try anything, be anything but this merely"—he finds his feet again, swiveling in a fool's bow—"outcast from your heart."

When she will not suffer a glance for his antics, his voice rises like floodwater. "Will you not take passion over loathing? Would your pride not affix better to that?" He paces, and his long shadow plagues her. "I confess the quill falters in my hand. But history, at least, should revenge you. Tell me," he commands, "cannot life become art—to save itself?"

Now she lifts her head with effort, and she is lovely, this muddied muse, my mother. "Spare me more words," she says. "They spray from you like water shaken from a dog. Leave me. Please."

For a moment more he stands on the damp grass, gathering resolution, and then he lopes away. "Pray," he calls back, over and over in memory, into the silence of a vanished morning. "Remember me . . . who looks out from your child's eyes."

1649

New England

SIMON

When I tell you that I honor my father, you will think me false. "The lies of an infant witch—" Simon once teased, "none but the prince of Hell has time for."

Believe what I say, I shouted in jest, seething with disappointment. *Whatever I say, or see me curdle your butter. It's all sport to me.*

Simon only laughed, as well he might. If it were true that I knew dark arts, I would have saved him while I could. I would have restored his sight and turned time back at the cellar door. Instead, at the inquest, I became invisible. When Nehemiah's eyes looked for me there on the public floor, they found only my grief, puddled like his brother's blood—a deeper color than ever Mother wore embroidered at her breast.

But before death there was a garden. There were children taunting, for I served as well as any Quaker the amusement of Boston's godly youth.

It was the Lord's Day, and we were idle—I with the sting of stones at my back, they shrieking like brats possessed. Because I knew that no pack of holy pygmies would brave the wood without master or mother, I ran and ran, willing myself be an otter and the shade be water. How cool it was and dark, my wilderness. How sweetly it repelled them. With their brat-threats dying in my ears I crashed through a thicket and found in a clearing, as stark as any miracle, a gabled house with a skinny lad in its kitchen plot.

How do I fashion him in your thoughts?

Let us say this boy was still, as still as marble, and riveting for it. What's more, he was as stately in his solitude as the townsfolk I daily spied on (blasphemers and nose-pickers all) were shrunken in theirs. I would come again and find him on a little three-legged stool, milking his cow with deft hands, and again, when he would be whittling by the wall in the sun. But on this day he was sitting, just sitting on a house chair in the green-specked mud of the garden, with his strange, pale eyes shifting in their sockets. His hands were beautiful birds chained to his lap.

He must have heard me, but I stood and caught my breath, watching him. When it came my voice was still ragged from the chase. "Why have they planted you there in the shade like a mushroom?"

He looked not before him but straight up, as if my words came from beyond.

"Here," I called. "Past the fence. By the beech tree."

"I won't find you there."

"Why not?"

The boy I would come to know as Simon turned to my voice that Sabbath day, and I considered how much deeper his was than I might have imagined, a man's voice, though he looked to be no more than a scrawny boy. Were I old enough to know better, I would have blushed. Instead I crept closer and scooped a handful of dry leaves from the ground. Leaning over the fence, I showered his boots with them. He did not look down.

"Have you no sight?"

"Who is it wants to know?" he demanded. "A girl pursued hither like a sow?"

"*I* do." I caught my breath again. "Pearl."

"And who is your father?"

"I have a mother." I murmured her name, courting the barely perceptible nod, the gossip's grin. It didn't come. Then he was deaf, I mused, as well as dark. "And you," I pronounced, arms crossed, "are a stranger here."

"I'm new to this plot but not these shores. We come south from Cape Ann. My father's at sea. My brother will be here yet."

"And your mother?"

He tilted his head. The palms of his hands kneaded his knees. His every movement was slow and measured, nimble as a fox crossing a streambed. "Your voice travels," he said. "First here." One hand made a sweeping arc. "Now over there. Are you moving?"

"I am not."

"Are you a pixie?"

I draped my arms over the fence rail, eyes narrow as a cat's. "I am too old for games."

"Are you a pity?"

"Indeed."

He sniffed the air. "Come here, then. Let me smell you."

I snorted, but this was grievously immodest, so I clapped a hand over my mouth. His answering smile was a miracle, and I giggled to hold it fast, though the giggling smacked of greed. Why he didn't make haste to dismiss me then (we're some of us overwilling and run our best chance ragged, trample it underfoot), I'll never know.

He said: "A pretty pity too, I wager. With a pretty laugh."

The hand at my mouth was raw with cold and streaked with blood from my stumbling flight through the woods. I licked a knuckle clean and pulled my cloak tight, backing away from the fence. Moving a few steps through crackling twigs (how thunderous the world became, listening with Simon), I hugged the smooth beech for balance and peered at him from behind it. The moment seemed suspended, and when his empty gaze did not release me I gave what payment I could: "You wondered how I smell?"

Well, then, mused the upraised chin. *Tell.*

"Mother says like rain."

Still on his chair, the blind boy with the man's voice nodded gravely, sweetly, and my legs felt free again.

*M*y earliest memory is of Mother's strong hands holding me under water. It's no proper memory, I know, but my young life's unrest contained, at last, by her confession.

Embattled, my mother came like a sleepwalker (she revealed on a night when I was bedeviled by dreams—a night years after the fact and one year or so before this story begins) to the water's edge with the same infinite pragmatism that once prompted her mother's kitchen servant to drown kittens or wring the necks of hens. Killing her bastard would mean sure and swift punishment. A noose round the neck, God willing.

"Didn't you love me even a little?" I asked, shocked but not shocked enough, apparently, to leave it be though I was in my seventh or eighth year at the time (I don't know my count exactly) and content, as children are, with the here and now. Mother nestled closer under the bedcovers. She stroked my sweaty hair, kissed my brow, and wished all watery nightmares gone. What she did not do was answer my question.

In the coming days her silence lingered, and my dread grew. Did not every mother love her babe? Though my own failed to reply, she filled my hands and hours with dainty shells, with stones made smooth by the sea, with salty crab claws and the strange, spiny remains of fish. She held my fingers as the waves sighed their ceaseless sigh at our feet, beckoning, and in time as we gazed forth together without fear into the emptiness, I felt safe again.

This earliest of memories, then, is a figment. But in this memory (let us call it that) my mother's hands, like her face with its startled look, are prison-bleached and jaundiced. She cannot hold them steady. Kneeling, she lays the infant me on wet sand, her body quaking uncontrollably with the urgings of the waves and the vast glare of life outside prison walls. She believes (Heaven and Hell were snuffed like candles in that dank jail) that peace will come with a shroud.

Froth tickles, folds soaking over me, and though the cold shock of the surf little resembles the womb, its mild rocking does. So my infant brain has scant cause for alarm until I feel the crush of her cheek against my chest. Rigid with despair, Mother is counting my heartbeats, *one two three four five six* . . . and then she is a fog moving away with hopes the tide will have me. When the tide won't or won't hurry, she reaches out, and in her thoughts, her mother's onetime kitchen maid is singing.

It is only when I cease to hear my mother's mad humming, when my ears and lungs fill with airless, fractured light, that I make out another voice. This voice is muffled and aggrieved, reproachful but tender (as Mother's shaking-strong hands had been, holding me under). And I am plucked like a coin from beneath the tongue of the sea.

*J*t was days before Mother finally answered my question: "Did I love you then? I loved no one, Pearl. No soul on earth." Though she said no more, her dark eyes spoke for her. Had she courage, I understood, she would have walked into the water *with* me that day—long before our Puritan minister wandered into that remote bay from some faery realm, striding to my rescue and into his life's mission to right the wrong of my existence.

My father (though I knew him not then) has in his notebooks over the years made fanciful much of Mother's courage, though he never named her in those pages as he did me. Had she the courage he claims for her, both Mother and I would have perished in the surf. Instead we retreated to our little cottage by the bay near Boston, there to endure a thousand petty persecutions, outlast our wary love, and bide our time until he could return to claim what was and wasn't his. Even now, as a woman grown and with the mystery of my father solved, I cannot unpuzzle my mother. But in those days it was *my* heart and history that consumed me.

"What was it like up there?" I would demand, brushing Mother's dark hair, which with its wave and furtive gloss seemed to me a living thing. "On the scaffold?"

If she considered her answer, her face concealed it. "I felt as a friend to the breeze."

Even I, at best indifferent to society's rules, being fatherless and scorned by all but her, could not forgive this woman—who wore by law the letter "A" on her dresses for *my* sake, she was not above reminding me—her upright carriage, her terrible calm. It was an affront. "This fine noon," I countered, letting my voice grow mighty like the minister's, "I was nearly stoned to death by cretins." Words hot and relentless as the noon sun must have been that June day years before, scorching her prison-pale cheeks. I thrilled always (and this shamed as punishment never could) to imagine it: Mother exposed on the weathered platform of the pillory while the governor in finery, flanked by sergeants and ministers, scolded from the meeting-house gallery. Was it weeks or months afterward that she thrust me on the sea? Days?

I'd attended my share of public stripings and shamings—idle bond servants, Antinomians, vagrant Indians turned lewd by the white man's spirits—and could well picture the greedy masses milling at her feet, snickering over apples and gnawed cheese rinds. What I couldn't see was my own small self wailing in her arms with no history, no memory. Her shoulders had cried out from holding me that long three hours, she had confessed once in a rare show of self-pity. "My arms quaked like rushes in the breeze."

This night she waited till I'd had my fill of brushing and then stood, shaking her mane and padding barefoot in her nightdress to her stool at the spinning wheel. The heavy thump and whir began, a savage rhythm I despised. Mother's hands were never at home at the wheel as they were with needle and silk threads. In the light of the fire she looked at peace, but what mother would see her child stoned? The world would have me sewn up in my burial cloth, Mother oft accused, before I learned to master my tongue.

An owl called from the meadow west of our cottage, and I felt my blood tug toward the flames. I went and sat at her feet by the hearth, contrite, and rested my cheek against the warmth of her leg. I thought of tiny mice scattering for their nests as white wings beat the grass to a froth. And then my mind fixed on the boy Simon, imagining him at his table in useless candlelight or, like me, propped beside the popping flames, content to stare at nothing.

I roamed west to spy on my quarry the very next day, and the next, and another. On the third day, the house servant—a red-faced woman Simon called Liza—was balanced high on the roof cleaning the chimney. Her stout frame struggled with a rope that held fast what sounded to be a goose. As she lowered the great bird, she called out to Simon on his chair in the yard to aid her. He didn't mind her overmuch as a rule, I soon noticed, though there was nothing imperious in his bearing until she started to scold. Now, as before, he kept his hands imprisoned on his lap, as if they might fly away. Once he even sat on them, but he seemed to know it was no proper posture and set the hands free in his lap again.

The March day was grayer than those previous, and more raw. Liza struggled, and the goose echoed in the chimney, honking and flapping inside the brick well. Liza both cooed to it and cursed it (though once I saw her look up and round with stealthy eye). Enjoying the sun on his face, Simon seemed not to know he was being watched.

Liza let go the dancing rope, and as she wiped her hands on her apron, there was a muffled thud and a great squawking from inside. "There, old girl, keep your head about you. Simon, run, open the door and let this infernal mother loose——"

Simon stood and walked with a hand brushing the wood and casements at the rear of the house. He was bony but sure, and I knew he would run and leap in the meadows if only his eyes would let him. I wished he might be my companion. I wished for him.

"Simon! I hear the just arse in there flapping soot all over!"

An instant later, he pulled open the door and out waddled the disoriented animal, black and indignant, trailing a soiled rope from its ankle. I could see the bird had once been white. Up on the roof, Liza clucked and brushed her hands together. She looked as if she might leap in one stout, easy motion through the air, but instead she disappeared from my sight huffing and sweating to where a ladder must have been propped on the other side of the house.

I'd had little sign of the man of the house, nor anyone but Liza pegging her old gray shift to the line or stooped over a kettle in the backyard brewing soap and Simon whistling among the hens, whittling (how I feared for him, but his hands knew the knife, it seemed, as they knew the worn knees of his breeches or the downy stubble on his chin) and trying, when his hands were empty, to tame them. Often he cocked his head to the side, as if listening to music only he could hear. I well understood this posture, this stillness. There was endless conversation in the spring air, but for Simon, I realized, sound must by all rights be like streaks of paint on his world's canvas. Where was his mother? Where was the brother he had spoken of? He seemed so alone, yet content to be.

I couldn't resist. I took an acorn husk and flung it. It landed at Simon's feet and he started. With my hiss, a vague smile spread across his face. "It's you," he said.

"That was a goodly dance you did with that goose, Master Simon."

"Now you have my given name. What's yours, pixie? I won't give you the advantage."

"I told you, I'm Pearl."

"I shan't forget again."

"You best not do."

"And how long have you been hidden, Mistress Pearl?"

"I've been here three days or so. How long have you been without sight?"

"I've lost count—seven or eight year, I guess." He toyed with a weed he'd plucked by his chair. "I still see shadows. Sometimes. Come, stand closer. Clear the fence."

"No, I won't. Your mother's servant will skin me."

"She's harmless enough. Unless you're a goose."

We both laughed, and I moved out from behind the beech tree to the edge of the fence. I hung on it and studied him. "Why did a shadow pass your face just now when I spoke your mother's name?"

"You didn't speak it." He was silent a moment before revealing, with weary candor, "She is Mistress Weary of this World."

I said no more but tugged at the brush by the fence, weaving leaves into a length of vine I'd pried from the bramble. I fit them into a crown, my fingers moving fast, knowing the work well. But I felt Simon's empty gaze and the shadow of the house like a specter in the corner of my eye.

"I'm weaving you a crown. Your dwelling is very fine. Is your father a great man?"

He considered a moment. "Maybe," he said at length in a level, nearly cheerful voice. "He's of the middling sort, a merchant. But his travels serve him well. And where is your father?"

Had he seen me, Simon would have kept mum, but he couldn't know. He couldn't see. "Mother says I have only a heavenly father," I relented in a voice neither kind nor cheerful.

"My mistress will be gone before the Indian corn is ripe." Simon settled back on his chair and cleared his throat like one ending a grim sermon.

"Well, then," I rallied. "Now that's done, I'll tell you my story."

"What story is that?"

"Of the sinner's brand at Mother's breast. She wears a red letter on her dress." I lowered my voice for effect. "I would tell of her walk through the prison gates with a babe in arms."

"What is all that to me?" he asked, but I could see that I had grown in stature in his estimation.

"Don't you know they call me the devil's spawn?"

He grimaced and leaned forward, speaking very low. "Then is my mortal soul in danger?"

"Oh, yes."

"I don't believe you." Simon tilted his head to one side as if to listen for a change in me.

I looked left, right, and then climbed deftly between the shorn logs of the fence, my heavy dress trailing behind like the great tail of the peacock from the horn alphabet. I crept toward him and felt the drama of play fill my lungs. I had less play even than other Puritan brats in my early life and craved it exceedingly, even in that late hour of childhood. I wanted to fling my arms full round his thin neck and bury my face there. His icy eyes stared past me, his head still tilted like a fishing crane's.

"Believe it," I whispered and with great clumsy ceremony settled the crown on his tousled head. His nose twitched like a rabbit's and his face looked pained, but I was off at a trot before he could speak. Every grateful part of me, every nervous inch of skin and blood-beat of my small heart, knew this strange boy for a promise. Life, at last, had made me a promise—how to account for it!—and I could not bask in him more that day for fear of being scorched by my own bliss.

As I whirled under the blurred canopy, I saw Master Simon in my mind's eye. He would remove the crown cautiously, having never seen one. But he was not half afraid of me, like the others, and he would know this talisman of mine. He would touch every part of it, leaf and bark. He would hold it to his freckled nose, perhaps his tongue, as I would see him do with many objects in days to come. He would know every edge that my hands, or Other hands, had made.

ALL LIFE IS BARTER

*C*hance soon brought my mother and me to Simon's father's door. Or I should say Mistress Weary of this World brought us. As we walked along the forest path my restless gait more than once nearly knocked the basket from Mother's arm. She moved as ever with a stiff grace, a certainty that had been my comfort over the years. I could always retreat into her colorless skirts or call her hand to my shock of hair when I needed such soothing, and I fought still and viciously to call that right my own.

The air was full of chatter. Cardinals sang, and pigeons thickened the trees. The dappled air rang with portent. I found an oriole's feather on my walk and twirled it round and round my cheek, enjoying its silky scraping, then tucked it behind my ear. I hoped very much to have a glimpse of the dying woman, for Simon had assured me that a physician newly arrived from England, a Dr. Devlin—whom I had lately glimpsed from one hiding place or another on the Milton property, leaving with his physician's bag, but whose name and aspect I had not hitherto encountered in my charitable travels with Mother—had already been and gone from her side with his herbs and potions. Now it was her loosening soul men would care for as best they could. Servants and neighbors, able volunteers like my mother, would tend the wasting frame and failed flesh.

Mother hesitated outside the door, intent as ever upon society and its hostilities, her milky hand raised to knock. She shooed me as always and bade me keep close to the house, but she didn't close the door behind her; I saw not Simon or Liza or the father inside, but I heard a woman's weak voice cry, "Enter," and watched my mother, basket on arm, glide in like a gray mist and vanish.

Mother always left the door ajar, as if she might need its opening for a hasty retreat. The shadows called to me, and I found myself carried in past pegs with coats and cloaks hanging, on into the large hall, larger than our entire cottage, not lavish but unusual in that it was not entirely dedicated to implements of work and hard-won comforts. There was an explosion of color on the table, where a pristine rug with an exotic design had been draped, and a lovely carved desk on which rested a pewter tray with an inkwell and pounce pot and a hole full of quills. Above it hung a worn, ornate map penned with all manner of colored inks. I studied this at some length, noting serpents and other exotica in the far-flung seas.

There were many pewter plates, and there was more glassware than I had ever seen in one place. Even the light streaming through the leaden panes of the window casements held a silvery promise because there was more of it. The room where I lived with Mother was ever dark, even on the brightest spring day. Here was little dust to speak of, and no sooty film on everything. And on a shelf were books! Ten or twelve leathery volumes of different thicknesses, some with lettering of lovely engraved gold. One I knew, as the dame teacher used its dreary contents to help those of us who had outgrown the horn, but the others, like the great rug and the shimmer of glass and pewter, seemed to speak in a voice full of secrets.

I did not see his image until I had been staring a long while at the paintings on the wall at the back of the great hall. Even in the gloom I could make out the face closest to the hearth and appreciate its similarity to Simon's angular mug (though I suspect it was, like the others, a sickly likeness). There was a drawn melancholy about this face, a darkness in the forthright stare that made it both fearful and fascinating to look at. The jaw was even harder than Simon's, the nose sharper, and I wondered at this family's greatness that its sons were objects of an artist's brush. I couldn't look away. Who had made this painting, and the others in the hall, and why waste them here on the dark rear wall?

Now and then I heard in the room beyond rustling or my mother's soft voice, the voice reserved for the infirm.

Near the small feather bed in a corner where Simon must have slept so as not to disturb his mother in the room beyond, I found a flock of carved figures, crooked little beings from another world, neither animal nor human nor faery. I nearly made off with the smallest and finest—had it in my itching hand and would have slipped it into my stocking were I not afeared to find my fingers in the stocks. It seemed part dragonfly, part fox, and I wondered was the skewed shape of this and the other carvings because he couldn't see his handiwork, or did his mind, like mine, leave this world when it could? I put the fox-fly back and touched gently every surface in his house. My two quick hands roved over the pottery and the trenchers he ate his meat and pudding from, the blankets that covered him at night, the hearth by which he warmed himself, even the pallet on which Liza surely slept. But I returned often to glimpse that fine visage on the far back wall of the hall. He had not Simon's luminous, scarred beauty but the sun-browned strength and sternness of a man; he was older, perhaps sixteen, I guessed, to Simon's twelve or thirteen years, and he was more sure, with eyes that beheld the world if not his place in it. I thought then that I would have liked to be the artist who painted him, who sat that long in righteous study.

My mother's voice in the room beyond the stairwell washed over me, coaxing, gentle, punctuated by the occasional startling groan or angry but ineffectual outburst of Mistress Weary of this World. There was nothing like it—pain—to stoke a body's rage. Some stayed pious and stern till the end, but most didn't. Many an ill-mannered invalid lashed the well with ugly mutterings. It was a wonder women like my mother endured, but they did, washing and stretching the limbs that seized up in resignation, scraping furry tongues and peeling soiled linen from beneath bodies limp or spotted with sores. As I stood that afternoon, furtively measuring the shape and state of my new friend's home life—and the face on the wall that would haunt my future as surely as the letter "A" had my past—I felt curiously calm. I hovered at the corner desk, pulling the wooden chair out as quietly as possible to sit like a lady intent on addressing a letter to her beloved lord, and though I dared not search out and soil a sheet of paper, I schemed to leave behind some trace.

Instead of writing, which I did poorly, I skulked round the room and, having little else, laid the prized oriole feather from behind my ear on Simon's canvas mattress. The little carved sentinels seemed to watch me stooping there.

It was then the door slammed with a great flourish, and I flinched.

"And what hath the cat dragged in?"

Before I could retreat, I found Liza's hot breath on me and was made to witness the black of her back teeth when she spoke. "I know you. I know all about you. What right have you here?"

I gestured weakly toward the rooms beyond. "My mother is there, ministering to the sick."

"Your mother might have left her woe at the threshold."

I felt defiance build in me like March wind, though I tried as best I could to contain it for Mother's sake. "I'll go, then."

"You right will go, child. And don't let me see you sniffing round Master Simon's feet anymore. You think yourself a stealthy little mongrel?"

"No."

"He is a good boy," she said, her voice falling flat. "Let us keep it that way." She looked as weary as her whining mistress in the room beyond sounded. But there was a growing delirium in the other woman's voice that tugged like a cord at Liza's attention. She shooed me and strode down the narrow hallway holding her skirts, past the stern young eyes of the painting, and her leather soles slapped on the wood. By the time I fled into the light, the lady of the house was shrieking to high Heaven, as if her very soul had been offended. Only my mother could rouse such passions in a body.

．　．　．

*I*t was a relief to flee into streaky sunlight, but I was restless there and longed to hear the mistress's voice. Faint though her presence now was, she had borne Simon, and I was grateful to her. But with gratitude forming a sick knot in my stomach, I wished her dead and gone too. I crept along to the rear of the house, crunching old snow. The lady's own window was sealed fast and draped inside with cloth, but faraway voices came floating through the casements of the window facing out from the adjoining room. Perhaps there was an inner door open between them, for with little effort of concentration I heard Liza's hoarse instructions, low and impatient. My mother's voice was strained and haughty. The invalid spoke not at all. Perhaps she had drifted off to sleep. Liza grunted as if under a weight, and I understood that she was struggling to draw the bed linens out from under the sick woman. "You might make yourself useful. I've changed that basin already."

Mother said, "Command me, then. I've not come to be idle."

"No, misspence of time is not your crime, I'm told."

There was no reply, but more heaving and grunting. I felt provoked on Mother's behalf. It was usual for perfect strangers to take a knowing, nasal tone in our presence, to own us with their verdicts.

"I see you've made yourself at home among our local gossips. And your hands are ever clean?" Mother challenged. Though I could scarce hear her low voice, its familiar edge—normally reserved for me alone—unnerved me. "I've not met a servant with clean hands yet."

"You could eat off my hands," said Liza. "What part of *you* hasn't the devil had his touch to?"

"That may be," Mother said in a monotonous tone of affliction, and then, hotly, "But I've not come here to suffer your abuse. I neither seek nor offer apology. They've had their due. I've paid my debt with years."

Liza, like a horse, blew a great blast of air through her nose. "Your debt. In England—here too, for that matter—they might hang you for like offense."

"They might do me a service."

"Mind that tongue." Liza's lilting voice had snagged on disbelief and something else, pity perhaps; whether it was for Mother or the sick mistress she manhandled I know not. She huffed and murmured, "And you still a young woman. I hope the child won't take your view. Damp this cloth," she said. "What sinner won't thank God for the life she's given? Wring it, please. We want to cool her, not drown her."

I waited for Liza to speak again but heard instead the drops of water in the basin as Mother squeezed the rag. I heard the buzzing of a fat bumblebee by my thumb and watched my breath come in foggy blasts against the boards. My cold hands were flat against them now, and my neck was cramped. After a grudging pause, during which Liza no doubt roughly shifted Mistress Weary's ruined body on the mattress, her muffled voice told me that she and my mother had exchanged something in their silence—a look, an understanding. "Rest easy, miss. My hands are not so clean," she said, "as to wave back mercy."

"*I* know not," Mother said as I begged to be told what had made the lady shout. "Death throes. She is far gone."

"Did you kiss her hand? Did you damp her brow?"

"Yes, yes. I always do."

"Did the house servant come screeching?"

"Yes," Mother sighed, "like a harpy. But she helped me ease the good woman to her afternoon's rest."

"But why—"

"I know not, Pearl. Now go." She rubbed her temples and slipped into our cottage. "Let me rest." Mother closed the door lightly. I kicked it.

I kicked the door again and again, feeling wrath shoot through me. When she did not reopen the door, I pitched sticks and broken shells from the garden rim at the walls. Still she did not return to me. She wouldn't, I knew. She would only when others were about and to placate me was to protect us both. Otherwise she let me rail. Often she threatened after these episodes to place me in service with a stern and godly family—the custom for older girls—but I think she knew not whom to ask. Though she and her infamous "A" were no longer so reviled, she would sooner do a favor than ask one.

I felt foolish in my violence and huffed and stomped down to the water beyond our cottage. I knelt on the ground and scowled at the rushes and clumps of scrubby trees that did little to conceal our humble cottage—though we were far enough from the nearest homestead not to want concealing—and rubbed cool sand on the tender flesh above my wrist until a red slash appeared. Then I fell into a heap on the little beach, curled like a restless infant to watch a distant sloop chase the sliver of pale moon. The sun was low behind the forest-covered hills of the mainland across the basin. The water shimmered. I shivered and sucked my sandy middle and forefingers and watched that boat, as if it carried my life and might soon crash against the rocks. Then I turned away from the tedious sea and surveyed the clearing beyond.

I may have sensed him before I saw him, but my eye soon fixed on a man stooped in a meadow west of our inlet. He had been collecting new herbs and now brought himself tall, regarding me. The basket swung at his elbow as he strode near with alarming purpose. The wind-blown grass made his lower half appear fogged, as if he did not walk so much as float forward.

As one forced by standing to loathe most everyone I knew, I was more than usually enamored of strangers, not cowed as one my age and size ought to have been. In fact, the striding figure was none other than Dr. Devlin.

The learned physician had come too late to ease Mistress Weary's struggle, but Simon often parroted his older brother's sentiment that Devlin was a thoroughly modern man of science. The community would do well to value him above the barber-surgeons, as he might effect a cure with his store of herbs and the treatments stored in the pages in his mind . . . *before* he bled you silly. Just now he looked quite mad, and the closer he came lurching, the madder he looked. His skin was sun-brown against the blackest hair I'd ever seen, blacker even than Simon's, but just as unkempt and far too long for Puritan Boston. Surely some worthy would hunt him down with scissor and razor. The doctor had deep squint lines around the eyes that would have given him a perpetually merry look had the eyes themselves—strange hazel flecked with gold—not been so violently sad. These mournful eyes were older than he by far and seemed, at close range, awed at the mere sight of me. I frowned and pushed blown hair behind my ears. *Like a bear lumbering stay back don't step more or I'll scream murder.*

His pace did not change, though I brushed the sand from my skirts and rose, haughty before the ocean. The water now seemed distant and drowsy in the late light, calmly sparkling, but it was the one calm thing in this windy world, and I was poised and ready *don't come closer.*

"There," he barked cheerfully. "That will be our line." He pointed with his staff to a half-visible nest in the tangle of last year's shore grasses. "I won't cross it if you in turn won't scamper off like a rabbit."

"Well, sir," I braved with raised brow, "rabbits do not scamper. I believe they bound or spring."

He sucked in gaunt cheeks, set down basket and staff, and settled hands behind his back. I trusted this humble posture not at all. "I see words matter to you, Pearl. I confess this pleases me."

I did not ask why it should. Grown people were forever saying such things, and were like to mean almost nothing they said. "Goodman Baker would not wish to see you collecting his weeds," I scolded. There were few on this earth I had license to scold, few who would not peer down at me with a rage of flared nostrils or produce a hazel switch, and I expect I recognized and loved those few instantly. "He does not like me on his beach or in his meadows. He spits his juice on my Sabbath shoes and calls me idle. He does not like even old Belle, the Prices' mule, to tread over his lines—"

"Nor the birds to sing, I wager. But you are a famously idle girl, aren't you, Pearl." It wasn't a question. It was his second challenge. He wanted a question from me, and I would not grant it *how do you know my name how do you know me pearl pearl it is my name.* Elders often knew things, took things I had not offered. His familiarity was of no concern to me. His uncanny stare and restless gait, though, were. He did not cross the bird's-nest marker but seemed to hover at its border as a horse will before moving water. "Do you wonder what I want, Pearl?"

"Do you wish me to?"

He laughed through his nose. "You're a clever child, but do you know that many fine feelings will desert you if you're ruled by cleverness?" He took one step, not over but onto the line, where the nest should be. I backed away, imagining the eggs smashed and working up a fury for it when he squinted through the fingers of one hand raised against the glare. The lines radiating from his eyes bunched together and darkened like storm clouds, and his formerly playful voice now better matched the expression in those eyes—high-sorrowful and cloying. I can't say the change suited me.

"Is that your mother's cottage there, round the bay? Why does she live no more in her father's big house in town, Spring Street I think it was? I've been gone some years, Pearl. I've only lately returned to these lands."

"Spring Street?" The words were bland in my mouth. "No, she doesn't live here or there. I have no mother."

He smiled and looked bemused. "You must have a father, then?"

"Not in this world."

What a hearty laugh, his. I did covet that laugh—the eyes were truly merry then—and it made me forgive him the despair that had come straying, stamping over our discourse as his heel had doubtless trodden the bird's nest.

"Can you keep a secret, Pearl?"

"Not very well," I said, "but I'll rally for love of one."

He dropped to one knee near his edge of our invisible line. "I know him—your father."

My narrowed eyes cupped the sun and watered. I did not, would not, gnaw on my lower lip as blind Simon claimed of late to know I was doing whenever Liza happened near and frayed my nerves. How he knew, I can't say.

"He sent me to you," the doctor persisted.

Don't invoke him. "You crushed them," I cried, and my hand, eager for diversion, shot out toward the nest hidden in the grass.

He stood and plucked something from behind his ear, where nothing had been before. It was a single splendid oriole's feather. He held it aloft on his palm.

"Are you a sorcerer?" I demanded, thrilled to my core, for it looked to be the very feather I had left behind for Simon.

"Take it."

I did, nodding with slow delight and not a little irritation that Simon was now deprived of my offering.

"And come again at this time tomorrow with one morsel of life as it has been with you," he paused, bringing a finger to whispering lips, "and your mother. Come here to our line, and we shall barter. But do not bring me untruths. In time you'll have more than you can measure, a new bauble each day if you like—"

I did not ask what manner of morsel he meant but only skipped away, happily bewildered, and slipped the feather up my sleeve.

Inside I found Mother refreshed. I don't know why I held my tongue about the doctor, but I did. It seemed no more proper or necessary that I sacrifice him to public scrutiny than if I'd glimpsed a doe in the wood with her fawn, or a nymph from my fancies stepping back through the bark of an oak (after which I would press my ear to its trunk to hear her heartbeat). These fleeting favors I would not share, even with Mother; they were mine, and too precious to part with, and now again some gracious instinct commanded me; I felt a proud discretion.

My parent—not the only one, it would seem, if the doctor were to be believed—had lit the reed lamp and was chopping turnips for stew. I put my head on my arms on the table to watch the blur of her knife. Her hands were able, like Simon's, like my own, yet I never shed tears at my work.

"What hurts?" I asked, and she smiled dimly and shook her head.

"I shall kiss it," I announced. She stopped her chopping and held out her knuckles. I traced them, the peaks and valleys, with my little finger and settled on one. "This one?"

Mother nodded, and I stooped with great ceremony to kiss the imaginary wound.

"Thank you, Pearl." She was a clever player, for my sake. She smiled as if by all rights she was happy, and I took up another knife and quartered the onion. When my eyes teared, I made a great show of it, and even ceased chopping to give Mother time to repay a sweetness. But she did not. Instead she brushed the turnip chunks onto a trencher and carried them over to the kettle. She knelt by the fire. I fingered the feather in my sleeve, and my play pain burned on like a lonely candle.

That night and all the next day it rained and rained, and the ocean roared. Mother made me stay indoors and spin, but by supper I was half mad with captivity. When she nodded off over her embroidery by the fire I escaped west toward the woods and there reveled in the violence, the water streaming into every rivulet, branches bending under the weight, spring rain sliding from bowed and swaying leaves. My dress was wet through before I noticed, my cloak like a heavy shroud, but I kept going until I reached the now familiar fence. I stood behind the great beech and studied the rear of Simon's house. I wasn't there long, shivering and feeling every bit the fool I was, when a muddy carriage drew up out front. I didn't see who got out, as the house blocked my view, and in minutes the transport drew away again, the horses sputtering and shaking their manes in complaint.

I crept forward, holding my hood closed. It was hard to hear a thing, even with my desperate ear pressed close to the house. The window was shut tight and the rain pounded out its rhythm, but I knew the weather had changed inside the house. The muffled voices were not merry exactly, but there was something new in the current of them.

I pleaded in my mind for Simon to come out to the privy, but instead, after a time, Liza came and caught me by surprise, hissing and shooing at me with a stick, calling me a wretched little dog. She shook her head in utter disdain at the sight of me—dripping, my hood plastered against my cheeks. "You must be quite mad, child! Look at you, drowned!"

My voice died in my throat. I stuttered something incomprehensible and heard a man shout through the rain behind us, "Who's there?"

"It's that little dog I spoke of come sniffing again about my master's door. I do think she's smitten with your brother, sir." She let go an undignified snort.

"Liza, your comportment lacks charity."

In nary an instant his hair had been pasted to his angular face by the rain, his damp shirt molded to his chest. Oh, but he was beautiful, even wet; like a prince. My every limb felt locked. I wouldn't have known how to differ when Liza chimed, "Be it so, young master, but this one has no business among christened infants. Her own mum bears the mark of the fiend at her breast."

"The Good Father would not wish to hear you speak so, and pray you remember, Liza, your eyes are not His own. We are all born to sin."

The servant blinked at his pious words and fixed her misty gaze on me. She bowed with mock gravity, a fuzz of gray hair dangling from her drenched cap. "Christ's sake, there's dye running in my eyes. Good sir and lady, I take my leave."

Astonished—whether by the whole muddle, or her blasphemy, or the young man's indifference to it, I know not—I found I was sucking on my fingers as I had as a babe and sometimes did still. I willed my rigid knees to unlock, but because of my twisted stance it was to the forest I curtsied, his presence a weight at my back. I fled to the safety of the trees, snagging my soaking cloak on the fence as I squirmed through. He called after me, and I looked back. Holding a hand above his eyes to shield them from the torrent, he urged me to come inside and get dry, but I kept running.

Raw to the bone, I tripped and splashed and stumbled all the way home, where Mother undressed me by the fire and rubbed me dry and wrung out my clothes and hung them. She begged me to be civil just once and let her soothe me, but instead I raged. I'd flourished on a diet of scorn all my young life, but this, a stranger's sympathy, had caught like a bone in my unworthy throat. "Will they come and take me away and lock me in the prison for spying?" I sobbed, repelling her caresses. "Will they put me on the scaffold alone?"

But Mother, who had seen storms worse than this one, shook her head. She caught me close and sang into my hair, and we rocked by the fire. She blamed herself for my ways but without conviction, and I knew on that rainy night that my life was my own. It was the second priceless gift she gave me.

My realm

*P*itching stones at the water's edge the next morning, I heard voices back at the cottage. I raced to see who was there, for no one ever came to our little shore and a visitor other than our neighbor, Goodwife Baker, was cause for alarm. Maybe I was to be hauled away to the scaffold after all. Mindful of it, I came to a cringing halt halfway up the hill when I saw Liza at the door in her old gray smock and cranberry cap.

"I'll put her to work if you won't," she was saying with her back to me. "Such a child should not be idle."

"What such is that?" Mother wondered from the threshold, and went on sweeping last night's rain from our sunken floor as if she didn't see me.

"I'll not mince words, miss. It's well and good that our betters spoil their children, but she'll not gain from it. She won't be small forever, nor will such idle sneaking seem quaint in a maid."

"No," Mother chimed. "Her future's bleak, as you say."

Liza seemed stumped by that. She hadn't expected Mother to agree so cheerfully. "She might marry up. I've seen it done." The old woman parked hands on ample hips. "You *speak* pretty, I dare say. And you've dressed her well. What's more, your needlework's quite the fashion in town. I hear the quality wet themselves to wear what a sinful hand will craft, sumptuary laws be damned."

"Marry up?" Mother had refused the bait. "Here in the seat of my shame? I think not."

"Then train her for service like my own mum did. Send her away. Meanwhile, let me put her to good use. My master's still at sea, his eldest came last night with his list and went again this morning, and I've got my hands full with a blind child and his sick mother. It'll plump up her character."

Mother smiled and swept, swept and smiled. "Will it, now?"

"It will."

"And what will you have her do?"

Liza whirled and made as if to lurch at me, roaring, "Ha!" I nearly leapt out of my flesh. She straightened and turned serenely back to Mother. "I'll stop her sniffing about, that much I know. She has a sneaking nature, I observe. Come, child." She stuck her arm out straight as an arrow, palm up, and her fingers beckoned.

I stepped slowly forward and took that dry old hand, looking back but once. Mother shook her head, eyebrows raised as if to say, "Well, then," and blew me a tepid kiss.

*L*iza worked me all right. Day after day for weeks till I knew that fine house, that garden plot and fieldstone cellar, better than my own snug cottage. She did her best to pry secrets from me too. "Have you seen your father lately, dear heart?" and "Is it true your mum's badge glows full of hellfire at night? A lass I met last Lord's day said you can see your mum well off, burning like a demon lantern. Tell poor Liza where she walks to at night, love. There's no harm in it."

"Tell her nothing," Simon cautioned, smiling, "that you won't have the whole marketplace know, Pearl—and quickly too."

"Bah, I wish you deaf and dumb instead of blind some days." She turned to me. "He's a good boy, he is. Keeps me honest."

One early morning Liza fetched me to the house and then sat with her feet up, swigging from a little flask she slipped from the kerchief tucked behind her bodice, below which I fancied her old breasts drooped like withered peaches. She sat and laughed at me for working so hard, for my ready fawning. "Simon, look here," she bellowed. "Ah, well, you *can't* look, but your girl's scrubbed the very skin off the planks."

Whoever would imagine it—me, someone's girl? Good thing he couldn't see me blush. Though I spent little time on the receiving end, I had sense to know how exasperating gratitude can be. He spoke softly in his deep voice. "Hush, Liza. You'll wake Mother. And what *would* you have Pearl do, now she's here enslaved to you?"

"Oh, today," fretted the old woman with a blithe wave of the hand. She pulled on her flask again, swiping dribble off her chin. "Your dour brother may be ashore again, but it's May Day, after all. We should be merry."

"Do you really think him dour?"

"Well, no." Liza relented. "Sober, more like—and too fine for his britches. A good boy, though. You're both good boys."

I was still taken with the notion of May Day. I crawled nearer Liza's chair on hands and knees and rested my chin in her lap. She didn't fault me for it. "Show me how it's done," I begged, "the May games." I knew a show like that would be banned right quick in Boston.

"You don't need my teaching. A little bird told me you weave a faultless garland in your own right." She gave my head a lazy pat and sighed. "In old Norfolk such and maypoles were no heathenish vanity. Even in my day there was piping all night in the barns, feasting and dancing. We had wakes and ales on Lord's day, fools and bells and bonfires in summer, hot cockles and thrashing of hens at Shrovetide." She slumped back on her chair so the legs squealed on the wood. I felt sure she would tip over in her zeal, but she leaned in when Simon shushed her again, whispering conspiratorially, "We had carols and wassails at Christmastide with good plum porridge too—and not a spoonful of it profane."

"You needn't long so for it, Liza," soothed Simon. "There's little chance to be merry in England now. Dr. Devlin says they've closed the playhouses.

My brother's heard you're not to be caught whistling in Covent Garden lest some saint hear you."

"Well, the mistress sleeps, and the sun shines; the floor here's clean—" she patted my head—"and May is the mischief in me. Come, you," she commanded me, "and let's crown the King of May." Liza plucked Simon off his chair, and we headed out toward the woods behind the house. "And you'll be his bride."

We trekked a long while, humming in our throats like bees, then settled in a secluded clearing. Warblers and sparrows darted in treetops as Liza and I gathered columbine, trout lilies, and trillium; we snapped off evergreen fronds and carried it all to Simon while Liza sipped from her flask. Simon hoarded our stash on his lap, breathing in armfuls, running his hands over hemlock and juniper as if they were heirloom silver. I wove him a brand-new crown while Liza wove one for me, singing hoarsely:

> A garland gay we bring you here,
> And at your door we stand,
> It is a sprout well budded out,
> The work of our Lord's hand.

"What cruel church is it won't let us nail a birch branch over the door for luck?" she sighed when she'd finished, tousling Simon's long, dark hair and crowning us both with great ceremony.

He was our king all that bright morning, and I his queen. Bawdy Liza bade me kiss the groom, and he only winced a little. I felt like a bird pecking at seed. His lips were as smooth as the inside of a cat's ear, and I believe he thanked me afterward, under his breath.

"Now dance," cried Liza. "Dance!" But she was drowsy now (perhaps she'd been at her flask all night, it being a holiday) and slumped against a birch with her mouth open, drifting off to sleep in our May palace far from the trodden path. We obeyed our dancing master well—spinning, more like—round and round, elbows linked, till Simon cried dizzy and we collapsed in a heap. We lay on leaves and crushed wild onion with our arms touching till I got up to paint his face with the morning's last dew.

"Queen Pearl," he said solemnly, his blind blue eyes peering right through me, and he caught my painting hand, circling my wrist with long fingers as if to measure it. I yanked it back, unused to such an easy touch, used to being in charge. We were awkward a moment, faced perhaps with our two ideas of what grown horizontal brides and grooms do to amuse themselves. After a bit of squirming, that scrap of shame wore off. We lay all the morning listening to catbirds and to Liza's swinelike snore, until poor Mistress Milton back at the house began shrieking for cider.

I never saw Simon's mother, who lay shut up in her chamber the weeks I labored in that house. She was an imperious figure of ever-increasing proportions, and sometimes I imagined her beyond the door on her haunches like a great sphinx, ready to devour those who ventured un-prepared into her airless chamber. She was indeed weary of this world, and as her state worsened that month, Liza came to fetch me less and less of-ten. Soon she came not at all, and I reverted to my feral state, wiser and lonelier for it.

When I made my old spying rounds now, I never found Simon on his chair in the garden but saw only the new vegetable plot overtaken in the sun. Wondering how people could be so grand as to neglect such a task (neglect me, for that matter) I slipped in and weeded as best I could (though none had asked for me), the feel of earth a familiar pleasure. More and more, though, pride kept me away from that house. And then one day when my chores at home and my lessons were done, I wandered down-town with heavy heart to spy on saints and ladies and found instead a fu-neral procession.

Mistress Weary of this World had been in state for days, said a strange child who claimed to be a cousin, holding out her gloved hand and her ring, a gaping skull, for me to envy. I saw Simon and, beside him, his brother, Nehemiah, the face from the painting and the rain. For a moment I couldn't take my eyes from that face, but when I looked again at Simon, I felt a thrill of fondness, and something like remorse, for grief had settled in his aspect.

Before them, behind the pall and coffin bearers, stood a tall, rugged but finely dressed man who must have been their seafaring father. I could see both Simon and his brother in the man, whose neat black-and-silver hair was combed back in a becoming way under a stately hat. Many others snaked down the street in murmuring pairs behind them, and I slipped into the line as it passed. I saw ahead at the church gates the minister, standing with clasped hands and a mild smile of welcome.

We snaked behind the church, and the coffin was placed on a bier by the fresh grave. I kept near the back and vanished in a sea of cloaks as mourners flowed inside the gates for the eulogy, coughing and whispering and even laughing under their breath—funerals were as often as not a chance for socializing. I knew his manner of oratory well enough, but this minister— unlike our own, who had of late been ill and under Dr. Devlin's distin- guished care—had a dull tone with no music in it.

Prayers were muttered, and the eager procession shifted again for the in- terment. I kept away as the crowd positioned itself by the grave, and I roused myself again only when Simon and his brother stepped forward toward the gaping earth to cast their sprigs of rosemary. The elder held his brother's wrist, guiding the slender hand to release its fragrant twig. Then there was the light hiss of earth on the coffin, and the group began to disperse. I heard Liza's voice, overloud at some distance, crying for Simon to come to her.

"I have him, Liza," spoke the brother, who walked always with his wide hand at Simon's elbow and seemed to give him little way. "Here."

Liza bustled through the crowd and embraced both boys heartily, de- spite the elder's embarrassed looks. Simon only looked lost, and while Liza bounded to the father and the elder son stood by the gravedigger's elbow, I slipped to Simon's side and whispered in his ear, "I've missed you, Master Simon."

His face filled with the light his eyes lacked. But it drained away as quickly as it had come. He shook his head. "Go now, Pearl, before Liza scolds you for the world to hear."

"I will, but can't you come out one day? When your heart is able?"

He dragged at the ground with his heel. "Nehemiah won't have it. He's had an earful from the town fathers and wants you not under our roof."

"Is he your keeper?" I looked for the elder boy, fearful suddenly.

"Yes," said Simon. "He keeps us well. He's in more ways father to me than Father."

"Then I'll come to the edge of your garden and speak like a sprite in the trees. Your turnips and peppermint need affection."

"I'll weed at sunup. My brother will be gone again to Cape Ann. Go now," he said.

"Farewell then." I nodded pointlessly toward the grave. "May she rest well with the angels."

He looked down toward his boots, though not at them, I knew. His silence terrified me. "I can't help what he says," Simon whispered. "He says you must go home and stay there. With your fallen mother."

Before I could understand, I saw Nehemiah turn from the gentleman he had been conferring with. I'd been watching the tall man's back—his familiar carriage—from the corner of my eye, and when he turned I turned, as if we were dancers separated by space, and I recognized Dr. Devlin. I looked wildly from him to Simon, and my eyes blurred with heat. I ran out of the churchyard and crisscrossed quiet lanes and meadows and marsh until I was sick and stooped with running. I didn't stop until I dropped to my knees by the bay, and I wondered, sobbing for breath, if I would ever know a life without this sinking.

*M*ost every year at this time there were anxious rumblings around town when great flocks of birds blackened the sky in their passage south. I once overheard a farmer at the inn tell of a roosting site near Virginia to which families came from hundreds of miles away, driving their hogs, to camp and wait. The men met the birds' deafening arrival armed with poles, guns, and pine-knot torches, with iron pots full of sulfur, while the besieged women plucked and salted. All around, branches sagged and snapped, the farmer said, and none could hear a rifle's report a yard away nor his own voice whooping, and when they went, the flocks left a snow-white sea inches deep. The pigs had their fill and were fattened, the wolf crept forth and the lynx, the polecat, the possum.

But in Puritan Boston, such plenty was ungodly. It was the devil's work, all glut and gloat, and worse than suspect. "Where are they going?" I asked Mother as the year's first stragglers came. She looked up from the crimson thread and her deft fingers embroidering. "I don't know, Pearl. Some say they bear dark tidings, but I think there is too much evil in the world to be carried on the wings of pigeons."

I paced the cottage and finally, weary of her concentrated stare that did not include me, slipped outdoors again. I thought the rhythmic pumping of their wings, the rippling wave of noisy birds, was the most comely sight I'd ever seen. The pigeons had a slow grace as a whole that they lost once they settled in fields and on branches, from which boys netted and clubbed them, stuffing them into sacks.

I ran and twirled under their shade into Goodman Baker's meadow, imagining myself aloft with them until I was too dizzy to stand. Collapsed on the grass, I watched the travelers surge past while the sun broke their ranks as light from Heaven pierces clouds. I mourned their going and wondered a while about Heaven, and would my mother be there to greet me at my turn. If, as the godly wise claimed, this life was but preparation and atonement, my short stay on Earth was doomed enough. Mine would not earn the hottest room in Hell, though Mother's surely would.

Simon had called her fallen. He had spoken like the others. But he couldn't, like them, look daggers at me from on high. I shook to think of his face, his empty eyes searching for me, finding nothing, only the dark. Who had schooled him? Nehemiah only? His recently arrived father? Now that they wore the black bands I couldn't hate them, but it was hard to see these people—who had seemed so promising a diversion—now as any different from the others, like Dame Ashley, who just this morning as I was murmuring the Lord's Prayer had snapped my back with her hazel switch and said, "Even your temptress mother sits straight, child, and she with every reason to stoop."

Temptress. The word, like many words, had a certain roundness, a gleam about it. I wagered it was no great task to skirt Heaven, and perhaps Simon would help me do it. If Mother wouldn't be in the beyond to hold me, there was no point in going there at all.

As promised, he was in the garden at sunrise. Though Mother wondered why I'd mastered my chores so soon, and would I be late for Dame Ashley's lessons, I'd reassured her, kissed her cool cheek, and proceeded to my post by the beech tree. "I shouldn't have come!" I called coyly.

He gave a solemn nod over his fist full of weeds.

"I never saw you weeding before. How do you know a carrot from not?" I challenged.

"I feel them. Some I won't pull, if I'm not sure it's waste."

"I shouldn't have come." I nestled the toe of my shoe into a curved tree root.

"I know. I'm sorry."

"'Sorry' is a fool's gift."

"Come here. They've all gone for the morning."

"I won't," I sniveled. "I always come to you. Now you must come to my realm."

"I dare not ask what that realm is, pixie."

"Come again to the woods."

"No."

"Why not?" I challenged. "Because of savages and wolves?"

"And other things."

"The fiend."

"He sleeps by day, I expect."

"I doubt that truly." I saw in mind a rippling field of new grass, a bird's nest, and the physician who was by now a constant confusion of bright and dark in my thoughts. Like the dappled forest he attracted me, but for fear of him I had not honored his compact these many days. I couldn't think what I might barter for his baubles, what "morsels" he might favor, and the longer I delayed the more forbidden his game appeared—and the more inclined I felt to keep my strange encounter with him private, though he'd only requested secrecy in relation to my father. I even kept the doctor from Simon, to whom I now pledged, "I will be your sight."

"It was different with Liza there." Simon raised his head, like a bear testing the air. "Still, I wish you would."

"Then come." I scaled the lower fence rail, tugging at my dress, and took his hand. He rose slowly, as one in a dream rises, and I led him back to the fence, raising his foot. "Climb through."

He struggled, gripping my arm. "You don't believe in throughways?"

"I told you . . . my realm. We have our own outs and ins."

Once across, Simon resisted, standing still and alert.

"Do you know what sort of day it is?"

He shrugged and grinned but with half his heart, I saw. "A chill one. The sun shines and then retreats."

"But do you know the look of it?"

He frowned with impatience. "Don't mock, Pearl. Tell me if you must."

"Everything," I began in a lofty tone, "is past straining. There is new life under every surface. You feel it in the garden, don't you?"

"Of course," he sighed.

I took his hand and led him to the beech tree. "You know this beech tree?"

"I don't know it. You spoke of standing by it."

"This is a grand tree. If you look up in the early morning—that is, right now—there's a green light that sears the eyes. It's like a burn, it's so bright. The new leaves are wide open and laced, like this—" I wove his fingers and mine together.

I reached up and plucked a leaf for him. "Its leaves are coarse but soft, like the touch of fingers." I rubbed his face with the leaf, but he didn't smile.

"Don't look so grave, Simon. It's a good thing."

He rubbed the smooth bark. "How does this surface look whole? I've forgotten."

"Have you groomed a horse? Your old cow will do. This trunk is like the bone and muscles of their legs, firm and curved and strong. Like the great haunch of a beast of burden, only wider and tall as two houses. There are hundreds and thousands of trees here of all sorts, many much taller than this. But her branches are like outstretched arms. Her bark, the outside, isn't green like the leaf but gray . . . do you see it yet?'

He laughed. "What is gray?"

"That will do," I said, tugging him further into the woods, "for now."

It was slow moving with Simon, who tested his footing and came so carefully. "Don't you trust me?" I asked once. "Do you think I'll leave you?"

He considered, and I watched his jaw tighten. "You might."

"And you would well remember it." I let go his arm and moved away stealthily.

"Pearl?"

"Yes."

"Don't, Pearl."

"Why did you say it?" I begged.

"The world spins." He spread his arms wide like a preacher, but they soon settled safely at his sides. "I hear a roar of birds and leaves in wind. I know what those things are because I know how they sound, but they have no shape now, except here." Simon tapped a finger to his temple. "When first you stood at my fence, you said you were like the rain. Do you know why I pray for rain?"

"No," I allowed him. "Why?"

He stepped toward me, and I stepped back. "Because it gives a shape to things. It falls on the roof and slides down the walls. It pounds on the old stump outside where father cuts wood. It brings the earth its edges. Without it the world's like a big, soft pudding."

I determined to listen no more, fixing fast on my question. "Why did you say it?"

He sniffed thoughtfully at the air. "I don't know."

"Because he told you about Mother?"

"He did. My brother has always told me. I have no eyes, Pearl. I depend on him."

"But are you blind *inside?*" I asked cruelly, and skipped a few yards in a mad little dance, slapping at the brush with relish.

He started at the sound of me, considering a moment. "Perhaps."

Simon seemed small and alone there in the clearing, and I admit I enjoyed it. His graveyard voice echoed again and again in my mind as I danced round him. *Go home.* I let my silence wash over him. *To your fallen mother.* I let him seek for the edges of the world and find them not, hands hanging idly at his sides. I let him wonder at green leaves laced like fingers, at hundreds and thousands of trees like the still legs of beasts. He was afraid to bring those watchful hands of his to bear on these savage woods, I saw, but I knew also that it wasn't really me or my negligence he was afraid of. *Go home.*

"You bade me go home, Simon, to my fallen mother. I can't go home," I said softly, and he lifted his head. "Any more than you can."

He stood half bewildered in that clearing as I settled silent as a cat on a mossy rock. I told him it would not be long but that he must be patient. I waited, without a word more, for forgiveness to come.

*A*fter a time, he relaxed. He settled on a crisp bed of last year's curled chestnut leaves, pulled his knees up, and rested his chin on them. He let the sounds of the woods wash over him with my silence, and we were alone in all the human world. Gradually, his hands took in his surroundings. He lifted pods and shells laced with winter rot, held them between thumb and forefinger to feel the tiny teeth marks, and dropped them. A squirrel whirred and clicked and complained in a branch above, and as the sun climbed the coo and twitter of birds stilled. I came closer until we sat together without touching.

"Do you feel me here?"

He nodded, no longer contrite or fearful. The teasing light returned to his face. "I should slap you."

"You may then if you like." I lifted his hand, placing it palm down on my smaller palm. He gave it a halfhearted slap and laughed nervously. We sat a long while in the woods, and once I fled to a nearby meadow. He didn't look frightened exactly, when I returned, but rather grateful to hear my light step. I wove still-dewy wildflowers into his shaggy hair and made myself a chain, or half of one, before I lost interest and began to flick away the petals. My singing voice was shrill and off key, even to my own ears. Mother cautioned me all the time to restrain it, and my laugh with it, on the road to Sunday meeting.

Simon sat very still, and sometimes let his hands ride lightly on my wrists or forearms as I worked, following each movement to its end. We worked thus, and I told him of the streaming light and gave him a strip of white birch peel to hold, explaining that it was the skin of one kind of tree. I prattled on about the bluebird's bright dress, the pigeons perched like foolish sentinels in every branch, the crystal gleam of the spider's web. I bade him listen for the brook that traveled from his home to west of my own, and once we sat as still as rabbits in our concealed clearing when a man went by whistling on the path. Simon heard him before I did and clutched my wrist as the man approached, leaves crunching under his boots. Traders, town leaders, and men of the church took that path often to the Indian settlement.

When the walker was some distance away, I led Simon back the way we had come. I felt how surely now he belonged to me, and when he stumbled in the brush, I spoke gently, with more patience than I felt. I planted him back among the needy turnips, and went away smiling to endure my travails with Goodwife Ashley. Simon did not look after me, of course— why should he? But I felt him listening, and now he knew where in the great pudding of the world my footfalls carried me.

Some days later I returned to the grave of Mistress Weary of this World. Carved below the grinning skull on the marker were the words:

Reader beware as you pass by
As you are now so once was I
As I am now so you will be
Prepare for death and follow me.

Here Lies ye Body of Mrs. Caleb Milton whos sol took its flight from
Boston to ye Heavenly mansions on May 26, 1649.

It was no thanks to Dame Ashley that I could read this epitaph. Mother,
who had been raised by wealthy parents from Nottinghamshire and Holland, took pains that I understood the language well, and I knew my letters long before she bartered for my education with Goodwife Ashley,
who let me under her roof with the others in exchange for fine embroidered cloth or a new pair of gloves when it suited her (and it often did; she
was as vain as a cockerel). Though I could scarce write my own name, I
could read well enough, and the portent on the grave, so like others in the
churchyard and like the sermons I was well accustomed to, interested me
little. Mistress Milton was no puzzle but an ordinary woman who'd fled
an unremarkable life.

Simon had characterized his mother as a pious Puritan. It was she, he
said, who initiated their journey to the New World. His father, an adven-
turer with precious little religious feeling, repaid her by spending most of
his life between ports. Perhaps, in the end, she regretted her decision. Her
eldest, Nehemiah, was learning his father's merchant trade. Simon, who
could go nowhere, had been her only consolation. She was at best a cold,
babbling woman from the sound of it, babbling over her scriptures by the
fire as the world flowed past her door. The cries of wolves far off in the
wood made her back stiffen each night against the hard work that was expected of it by day.

As for Simon, Liza was his only comfort. She was kind to him, he said, if
brisk and impatient, and though he occasionally had to listen in the night,
he hinted, when she took a furtive lover to her bed, Liza was a voice to follow and a relatively cheerful one at that. She was noisy at her work and let

him be idle just often enough without forgetting that he could complete most any task if someone brought it to him or him to it.

I stroked the cold stone and sang a little parting song to Mistress Weary of this World, who had borne me a friend. Though the public festivities surrounding her funeral might be deemed colorful enough—with rum and cakes and trinkets for all—hers seemed to me a lonely end. Thinking thus in the damp churchyard made me long for my own mother's arms and know, for an instant, the worth of that embrace, though her mind often wandered from me.

I didn't go to her, of course, because I am as lazy as a cat and knew Mother was stooped over her needle and thread or churning butter, and that I would purchase her affections only with an hour's work or more. Instead, I walked along the edge of the quiet churchyard hitting pebbles with a stick. I crept through the tall grass that swayed by the dappled tree line, a tiger in darkest India. I scrambled up a pine as far as I could go before the middle limbs, or lack thereof, blocked my ascent. I tugged at and arranged my dress and sat on a sturdy branch, legs swinging, high above the dead. I heard cows lowing on the distant Commons, a dog barking, wagon wheels grating the earth to the rhythm of horses' hooves. I heard also the laughter of children, a sound that at one time would have haunted me. I felt the sap on my palms and—hoping, for Mother's sake, that it was not on the skirt of my dress—listened to the taunts and playful shrieks grow distant. I felt not rage or melancholy, as I might have before, but a detached calm. Someone in this churchyard, and in this world, belonged to me now. I sat still and smiling above the dead.

I was not long in the tree when I heard a squelch of boots in the damp leaves and the light swish of vestments.

"Pearl," said a voice I knew well from Sunday meeting, "come down from there."

"No."

"You mustn't give the magistrates added cause to doubt your mother's fitness. You don't want them calling her teachings into question again, do you?"

"What teachings are those?"

"Exactly," the minister said with a light laugh. "Come down, and walk a while."

I studied his thinning hair, his pale, trembling hands. One of them found its way, as always, to his breast, as if he had run a vast distance. He was as thin as a sapling, but his voice at least was strong.

I pouted and crossed my arms, resolutely silent.

He strolled a moment among the graves, hands now clasped tight behind his back. This gave him an appearance of calm forbearance, but I knew better. I knew from years of observing him at the pulpit that those fingers, that palm, were itching to rest over his heart, which organ was, rumor had it, frail and faulty. I wished I could be one of the squirrels that sailed from branch to branch, tree to tree. I would escape into the woods without his pity.

"Why do you hide among the dead, Pearl?" His voice, for a moment, rang with hopeless wrath. "What draws you here? Do you wait hoping I'll come out, as I did today, and speak to you? Do I seem a haven to you? I would wish it—and yet I wish you away, too, like any bright light that shines on failure."

There was no denying that because he was a man, and kind, he brought me a degree of comfort. I'd even on occasion imagined him as my father— tried him on as it were, as I would a friend's or cousin's dress had I friend or cousin to speak of—but like the other townsmen I auditioned in mind, he fit ill. He would tie my morning bonnet with pale, fumbling fingers, I suspected, and because I made him nervous, I would feel forever nervous in kind. "I come to be among the dead, minister." It was wicked, I know; mayhap I was a prophet unawares and teased him to ward off terror. "Are you dead?"

"Not quite yet, but in any case, you are alive. Haven't you a friend to sport with?" His jaw clenched. "Chores to do? Life is hard for your mother, as you know. You might be a helpmate to her."

"I am her helpmate," I murmured, only half believing it. "And I do have a friend to sport with."

"Then go to her. Don't lurk here among the graves. It pains me to think of it."

"I've come from him, just this morning, and I said the catechism with Dame Ashley after, and so my soul is safe for today."

He looked up, alarm in his eyes. "It's a finer knowledge than you imagine. Don't discredit it, Pearl, nor let your mother's damaged nature defeat you. You have a life and light of your own. Be true to it." The minister shook his head distractedly and walked away from the tree in which I sat. His vestments made an angry swirl round him as he walked, hands clasped tight behind his back. "You are a lamb, Pearl, a lost lamb, and I have failed you and your good parent from the beginning."

"Your sermons serve my soul well," I said weakly, looking round for something or someone to draw my attention from his stern brow and twitching mouth. His pacing made me understand, for a moment, how hard my restless nature must have been on my mother.

"How," he asked mysteriously, "have I kept his bitter secret thus long, only to find it lodged under my very roof?"

Even as he spoke, nodding with a kind of grim exuberance, I heard again the sound of boots squelching in the leaves. Both the minister and I looked to it and found a disheveled Dr. Devlin, hands behind his back, leaning over the fresh grave of Mistress Weary of this World. "A strange little bird," he mused, peering up at me through his sad squint, "has lighted in our churchyard, minister."

The good man appeared far more startled by this address than I was, and that was a puzzle. I had been given to understand—had overheard on my spying rounds—that the physician was an old friend of the minister's, now boarding at the parsonage. Were their relations always so strained? Now the man of God hovered below my branch with bullish posture, and

I saw from my vantage point the rosy bald spot on his crown perspiring. He thrust out his cleft chin, a pudgy infant's chin in a man's face, and I felt the stirrings of mirth at the unspoken bristling below me.

But then the doctor looked up and at me with those perilous gold-specked eyes, and called in a voice humorless as the night, "He might be a bloodless shadow, Pearl, for all the use he's been. What other flock has suffered so dull a love?"

My body began to hum with the feeling it sometimes had in the woods, when an unseen presence unnerved me and bade me run. I was not afraid exactly, but there were things that came there, I knew, that could seize or overwhelm or slice me, the swipe of a panther's paw or the current in the air before a storm, or a harpy from my own musings. It was a danger that for me, as for the doe or grouse, manifested itself in physical terms. I needed to run but had first to climb down.

The two men had drifted some distance apart, and perhaps in another time, had they been other men, they would have treated me to a duel. Instead they smoldered. I shimmied down the tree in rapt confusion, feeling my wool stocking tear underneath my dress. I could not remember such urgency, even as a young child in the presence of the governor when Mother, delivering to his grand house a pair of embroidered gloves, the most beautiful I've ever seen—guarding, I fancied, a lavish spell in their stitches—begged to keep custody of me. It was the minister, finally, who had convinced him. I looked at him now, so small and stung without his fine words, and feared for him.

The men didn't speak but stared at one another, each glancing round from time to time to find me in the corner of his gaze.

"Is our little bird alone, Arthur?" the healer asked in a hopeless tone, smoothing his black hair back from the elegant forehead. "Or does the mother perch nearby?"

"Pearl is wayward," said the minister, and that seemed to end the impasse, for the two men nodded as if in agreement. The distance between them diminished, and soon the physician had caught the pastor in a hearty embrace and they tolled with false laughter like rival schoolfellows. "Pearl!" called the minister. "Come here and meet my old friend, a sometimes wise physician."

"I have had his acquaintance," I called, dropping to a defensive crouch on the ground.

"Here, young lady. Right your posture. Come hither."

I went and felt again the doctor's winking gaze upon me. "Pearl," he said simply, almost tenderly, nodding as if he knew me well. "I have had the pleasure of her acquaintance, Arthur, to be sure."

There followed an interminable pause. "Yes," I told the silence. I looked from one mute man to the other. "Why do you stare at me like cattle? What do you wish of me? A dance, perhaps?" I curtsied as low as I could and then stood again, waltzing a slow turn. "Mayhap a song?" I seized on my favorite verse of a tune Liza had taught me, "The Clarke of Bodnam," and loosed my voice in a wailing frenzy:

> Yet though my sins like scarlet show,
> Their whiteness may exceed the snow,
> If thou thy mercy do extend,
> That I my sinful life may mend,
> Which mercy, thy blest word doth say,
> At any time obtain I may.

While the physician smiled, strange eyes twinkling, and clapped his hands, the minister looked appalled, and this left me pleased and frustrated. "Too idle for your tastes? Perhaps a fit, then? Will a fit amuse you?" I began shaking my head and hands and let my tongue loll. People sometimes traveled miles to watch a woman at her fits.

The minister began to look vexed, though Dr. Devlin held his gaze on me. "That will do," the doctor said, as if we'd planned this eccentric outburst together. Clasping one narrow black shoulder, he steered the minister toward the graves. "Go along now," he called over a shoulder, "lest you rouse the dead. I'll expect you at dusk, at the line. Yes?" He winked at me, and I drank in sweet complicity like a tonic. Such unaccountable tolerance (I was used to being scorned, even stoned, for my thespian efforts) brought a rash of heat to my ears, but Dr. Devlin's wink satisfied me in a way that nothing outside the forest had or could. Like Simon's favor, it seemed a miracle.

I might have lost interest then, my heart grown fat on the physician's sport, if not for the sneaking suspicion that they had—caught in their own drama—already forgotten me. My curiosity could scarce endure such a slight, and I slipped into the woods, creeping to the edge nearest them to kneel in shadow where the lady slippers bloomed. I listened with the babble of the distant stream at my back as they strolled, the doctor asking from time to time, without resolve, after the minister's health and welfare. Was he warm today? Had the pain returned to his chest? Were the visions still troubling him? Had the herbs eased his stomach at all? What was it that weighed so heavily on his mind? He was aware, no doubt, that the rigors of charity, of forgiveness, would exhaust even a stout spirit. And having opened his heart to many a penitent, having borne the weight of countless sorrows, how can the responsible man rest while wickedness prevails, while the very heat of Hell seems to bubble up through his floorboards at night? "What will you tell the sinner, sir? Turn back? And what if such path is closed to him? Damnation is a pity, but there are more pitiful things. You sense the truth in my words, don't you? It pains like a rotten tooth, Arthur. Extract it from me."

"It's difficult to know what is true," the minister cut in sternly. "It is a difficult truth—though silence leaves a bitter taste in my mouth—that God alone can craft right judgment."

"Would that He exists, then."

The minister seemed to stoop under these words and brought shaking fingers to his temples. "Why do you toy with those whose trust you have savaged? Were you not my friend once? Daniel? Were you not *her* friend?"

The doctor soothed his charge with sentiments too soft for me to hear and held the other's shoulder as if to steady him. "Death is friendship's fond reward," he called at length to the rocks and trees, to the pigeons and me, and sent one hand sweeping through the cemetery air. "And love's. For sinner and saint alike, Arthur. But now," he prescribed, steering the minister tenderly back toward the churchyard gate, "you must return to your rest."

"What do you want here?" droned my pastor. "What would you have from us?"

"I would have you instruct me," said the other firmly. "I crave spiritual guidance, which it is your civic duty to provide, is it not? As mine is to provide healing herbs and poultices."

"Then make a public statement, Daniel," he urged, anger flashing in his eyes. "Confess your crime. I have so counseled you—"

"But what do I gain by doing so without her consent, against her will? Shall I rob her more? Would you?"

"Would *I?*" The minister's vehemence frightened me.

"No," the doctor acquiesced. "Of course you wouldn't."

I knelt on a stick as they passed, and it snapped. The sound cut the air. The minister didn't turn back, but the doctor did. He walked to the edge of the clearing, cast his searching gaze into the dark where I crouched as one in prayer, and bade me in little more than a whisper go home where I belonged, before he saw fit to tan my hide.

*L*ater, in the garden, I told Mother of my strange encounter with the minister and his boarder, the new physician in town.

I had been weeding absently, watching plants sway in the garden Mother kept for physic, listening without care to the uproar of crows across the basin and imagining, with a sly and dreamy smile, that Simon was listening too.

No sooner were the words out of my mouth than Mother rose and rushed to me as to one in harm's way. Clutching my shoulders, she fairly roared, "What *are* you, child, that torments me so?"

This bewildered me, and I must have flinched, for her face softened, and her grip relaxed. "I have heard as much—that he is returned to

Boston—though our good minister would not have me know. As if our paths could fail to cross."

"He?"

"The doctor you speak of, Pearl, is no friend of ours. He is a devil."

Delighted, I tried to conjure his face and could not. "But the Miltons say—" I tried to twist away, but she held my shoulders fast and swiveled me round again. I knew better than to meet her eye, knew well how ferocious her resolve could be.

"Had I known that he stood in that good family's house before me, I should never have crossed the Milton threshold." Mother let go, exhaling hard, and walked away from me. "As for the minister, Pearl, has he not suffered enough for his sympathies? Why persist in going where you are not wanted?"

I knew enough not to pout but rubbed my shoulder for effect. "If I did not go *there,* Mother, I would go nowhere at all."

She ignored my wit. "I'll remind you. We have no use for doctors or surgeons. We have Goody Black, the midwife, for our ailments." Mother settled on her knees with a hard sigh, staring past me at the sea. "Obey me in this."

Her distraction humbled me more than admonishment could. In a feeble effort to recall her, I walked round and knelt before her. I reached out for the stark red "A" on her dress, which frayed artifact was, even in my earliest memories, like a ripe plum to my eye. Without a word, I placed my pale hand upon it, flat against her heart.

ONE SOUL THAT KNOWS YOU

I felt a hand on my shoulder and rolled awake in a blur of midnight black. Mother whispered, "Come, now. The governor is dying."

I groaned and tried to roll back toward the wall, where a patch of wattle showed through the mud plaster.

"Pearl, wake now."

"I don't care for him," I murmured. "He tried to keep you from me."

"Forgive him now, Pearl. We must forgive if we are to be forgiven. And besides, the messenger said it is Governor Winthrop who strives tonight for Heaven, not Governor Bellingham."

"No," I pouted, and resisted her efforts to roll me back toward her.

"Up, naughty girl, or I will leave you here alone in the dark for the Indians."

That got me, and I sat with a sigh and let her rattle me. My forehead against her warm neck, I went limp and breathed my mother's familiar scent. I felt the relief of her slowing heart. Languid as a little girl, I let her pull a dress on over my shift, tug and crimp and impatiently adjust me as if I were a piece of her embroidery. Entertaining a drowsy memory of my latest sampler, I remembered my promise to complete it before the Sabbath.

As she brushed my hair and pinned it back, I marveled at how my eyes adjusted to utter darkness. There seemed no moon tonight whatever, yet when Mother bent to wipe my face with her handkerchief I saw before me the scarlet letter that was my own birthmark, and floating above it Mother's pale moonlike face.

"Aren't you afraid?" I asked.

"No, Pearl."

"Will the witches be out flying? Will Mistress Tibbins in her headdress watch us from the trees?" Mother smiled a distant smile and took my hand. She lifted her small sewing basket and we set out into the night.

"Why do you bring the basket?"

"To take his measure for a robe."

I roamed ahead, though not far. It was the blackest night I had ever seen, with clouds thick above and fog ahead of me. I felt a strange thrill at the way the weather held the world in a damp embrace. How easily, I thought, the familiar might bleed into that other, olden faery world. Mother took back my hand as we moved through the sleeping streets, perhaps to calm herself. Though it was hard to see beyond the nearest dwelling or fencepost, I made Mother pause as we passed the scaffold, but she only yanked me forward.

"Tell me again—"

"No," she hissed, and we kept going. "No, Pearl. I am weary of sad stories. Ask me for a happy one."

I thought and thought about her command as we passed the residence of Governor Bellingham, who was not dying. His gabled house was dark and still, like most others, though for a moment I thought I saw a flicker of light beyond the casements. We spoke not another word as we traveled through fog and silence to Governor Winthrop's stately home, where a servant let us in and took our cloaks. Looking at me, she raised her forefinger to her lips and with stern gaze gestured to a high-backed chair by the door. Mother nodded and bowed her head, and I sat down.

Wide awake now, I could scarce keep still in the dark as they went upstairs with the lantern. I sat on that chair surrounded by the shadowy objects of a powerful magistrate. I sat on my hands, listening hard to myriad footfalls and murmuring above.

As it often did, my mind wandered to Simon, who would be asleep now under the gaze of his carved figures. I imagined those sentinels springing to life one by one, stretching their crooked little limbs and stooping to peer on his sleep. Movement on the creaking wooden stairs startled me out of my reverie, and the servant appeared again, guiding the venerable Reverend Mr. Wilson, who must have been watching with the others at the sick man's bed. While the girl went for the minister's cloak, he tipped his hat to me, a dim smile flickering on his grave old face with its white beard, which seemed to register too well my presence, and I struggled to keep my feet still under the chair. I hardly drew breath until the servant returned with the cloak and a second lighted lantern.

Then a terrible shriek cut the night, a strange half-human sound unlike any I had heard before, not wolf or even the din I imagined witches making deep in the forest where they danced for the prince's pleasure. It was far distant, but all three in the room stiffened, wild-eyed a moment, and looked to each other for assurance.

"Is it the fiend?" I asked sincerely, and the reverend with pinched lips squeezed my shoulder to silence me.

"Pray not, child." He ducked out the door, bowing his head, his monstrous shadow flickering with the moving lantern. The serving girl leaned full against the wood when he'd gone and met my eyes. We shared a nervous, fleeting smile, and then she disappeared into a far room.

And did not return. Nor did Mother, though I heard from time to time the grating of chair legs on the floor upstairs. At length I slid off my own chair and paced the hearth room. I paced and let fear tempt me to the door. I went through it, out into the cool mist, easing the door softly shut behind, padding off with pounding heart in the direction whence the noise had issued, not because I wasn't afraid but because I was and would know to whom the devil beckoned. I would see them sign his book, glimpse the bloody bread he would lay on tongues as black and bloated as eels. I would know who they were, which goodmen and women *all of whom reviled me* would answer his call, coming to him through the night, leaving behind their beds and Bibles.

Compelled onward by the horror of my thoughts, I became gradually conscious of the strange sensation of blindness. I even closed my eyes to block out the dim red-gray glow of the sky and to feel completely what Simon felt always. I let my ears guide me, fascinated by the story they and my other senses told me. My own heartbeat was louder than all else. I'd never pitied Simon and didn't now, but I knew perhaps for the first time why the pace of his world must be slower than my own.

As I neared the scaffold—I knew the sharp slant downhill into the clearing beyond Governor Bellingham's house—I heard the eerie, muffled sound of male laughter. It was furtive and cold and cut me out of my shallow blindness. I opened my eyes to a shock of red sky, to what I would later learn was the glow of a meteor. Freezing on my feet, I saw in the faint light a figure looming on the scaffold. It babbled and lurched, and soundless though I was, it turned and looked right at me.

"Pearl," it said in rapt surprise, "did you hear me calling in your thoughts?"

I neither spoke nor nodded but stared. *Had* I heard him in my thoughts? And what could such a summons mean? Shame fogged my vision.

How quick he was. Before I could commence blubbering, he was at my side and kneeling; his arm, the one that didn't have a bottle affixed to its end, had braced my slight shoulders. He smelled of spirits and tobacco and leathery male sweat, but also, faintly, lemon verbena or some other sweet herb. He hauled me close so I was smothered in his shirt, the same white linen, now soiled, he had worn on the day he gifted me with a feather in the field. "There, there, pip. Don't squeak so. You'll wake the town, and I'll be slapped in the stocks come Sabbath day with every unruly servant, wife beater, blasphemer, ballad singer, and hedge tearer from here to Salem Town."

"Sir," I gasped, "you're squeezing me."

He pushed me lightly away with his free palm and took a drink that dribbled down his collar. "What business have you here in the black of night—" He tipped gamely toward me but righted himself—"with the devil for company?"

My feet would back away, but I forbade them. "Are you the devil—truly?"

"I am one soul in the world that knows you."

"Are you the prince of Hell?" Persisting was a thing I did exceedingly well.

"Would that I knew the truth, Pearl, so that I could lie to you. No, not a prince—just a man."

"A drunkard?"

Little impressed with youthful insight, Dr. Devlin took another swig, and the lines deepened round his eyes. "Is your mother there, Pearl?" His black brow peaked. "Hidden in your palm or under your bonnet? Is she there?" He caught me again and tried to steal a look under my cap, but when I flinched and brushed his hand away, real concern dawned in his eyes. "Settle down. I don't bite. Why are you not in your bed, girl? What brings you out—here of all places?"

His doleful expression charmed a bit of charity from me. I smiled, and the smiling made me bold. "What brings *you* here?"

"Do you always favor a question with a question? I confess *you* bring me. She does. And the night air—and this scaffold. I've been studying the nail heads in the wood, Pearl. Know you that once, when herbs and bloodletting failed a patient of mine, one dear to me, I found my head empty of all wisdom imbibed at the Royal College." His words came racing now, and I could scarce keep up with them. "An old method for curing ague says to situate yourself at a crossroads at midnight, and that is precisely where I found myself. Turn three times—so the wisdom goes—whilst driving a fair-sized nail into the ground up to the head. Then walk backward from it before the clock completes the twelfth stroke, and *voila*, the fever is expelled, moving instead to whosoever next steps on the nail. And what of the hapless soul who earns the ague, you ask?" He caught his breath in a sigh. "What can it matter but that somebody does? All bindings are commodities, Pearl. All life is barter. This sturdy scaffold: you have stood upon it—you know it? Or rather, your mother has—with you in tow."

"For three long hours," I put in, perhaps too willingly. "Her arms quaked holding me. The governor and his men frowned down on us from the meeting-house gallery."

"Now, that's the sort of morsel I crave, Pearl, as I patiently haunt my side of the line. We had a bargain, after all, but you've not returned to honor it. Have you another morsel for me? I would know you, Pearl. I would watch your mother walk these muddy roadways year after vanished year. How has she suffered? Where might she pause at market? Who will ease her day's burden with a smile?"

"Spit on her hem, more like," I murmured, cross that his talk had turned from me to my parent, who had, in my opinion, earned no such trifle.

He settled on a creaking step of the scaffold to urge me on, oblivious. "I hear, for instance, that you own the prettiest dresses in Boston. And that your mother flits to the dying like a moth to flame."

"She tends the sick."

He nodded agreeably. "She has a healer's hands, but without hope to guide them."

"Tonight she watches at the governor's bedside. She'll help the servants and have his measure for a robe."

He looked up. "And how are you here by yourself? You should go at once before you're missed."

"You haven't paid me yet."

He surveyed me dully.

"All life is barter," I reminded him.

The doctor felt in his pockets, sighing as he searched, and his bottle made a soft *thunk* in the grass. Because he came up empty-handed time and again, and because it seemed to pain him, I saw fit to give him more chatter. I told in a soft voice of my mother's watch at the governor's deathbed, of how tonight I'd crept up the stairs (but once) and heard her speaking to the doomed worthy almost as she spoke to me, in a mother's voice. (Had

the presence of Death made him a puling baby, then?) I told of my unfinished sampler and her matchless embroidery (she would not make pretty
that savage emblem at her breast, though I begged her to decorate it and
spite them all), of Eden and the coiled serpent, of brushing Mother's long
hair in the coppery twilight. I told of her lilting voice and the ever-fresh
supply of impromptu lullabies that came like salmon from the rivers, slip-
pery gifts from another world. I withheld her early effort to drown and be
quit of me (this lives like a sore under my tongue, and I never air it), but I
did describe her sporadic witless days and nights. I told how her strength
seeped away and her neck seemed broken and how, at such times, I had to
rouse and dress her, though her glazed eyes were Hell's windows. I told of
things lately on my mind, mine alone, of Simon and his princely brother, of
stones hailing as I outran the resident holy pygmies, of the lure of the forest.

At last, slowly, he drew his pockets out and left them hanging linty for
me. He pressed three warm fingertips to my runaway mouth and bade me
stop, for he swore his heart was breaking, and it vexed him. "I have only a
bitter, small specimen, Pearl, but you will have it in pieces. Let me repay
you now, and we'll resume our game in a more fitting time and place." He
paused to consider. "I have neither feather nor coin to offer, but you've
heard of the great city of London?"

I nodded. Of course I had. What mooncalf hadn't?

"You know it's a vast stage, then, with all and sundry calling 'Show!'
night and day, even under the offended nose of Cromwell. This you
may know, but have your deprived ears heard of Bartholomew's Fair at
Smithfield?"

I sank to the night-moist grass in a willing heap, parked elbows on my
knees, and gazed up at him. He paced the scaffold as if it were a wooden
balcony from which a painted sign emblazoned with the words "Show!
Show! Show!" hung. "A fair, sir? I have heard of them. We have none in
Boston, though Election Day is nearly—"

"Of course you don't, which is why I propose this as your due. Imagine
a full fortnight of puppet-plays and hobbyhorses. Can you do that, Pearl?"

I nodded eagerly. He leaned close and I smelled the bottle on him, a heavy sweetness.

"As you step upon the grounds, you hear first the criers: 'What do you lack?' and 'What is it you buy?' And it unfurls at you like a great banner of brilliant color and sound and motion: wooden stalls adorned with ginger-bread and mousetraps, theatrical booths and toy shops, pantomime op-eras and masquerading beggars, street performers, human freaks—"

"Freaks, sir?"

"Such as the girl of sixteen years, born in Cheshire, no more than eigh-teen inches high though she can whistle like a seven-foot sailor. Or the Giant Man, or the man with one head and two bodies, or the Little Faery Woman. Or, best of all, the man who can put any bone or vertebrae in his body out of joint and back again. And the animals, Pearl! As freaks go, wit-ness the famed Horse and no Horse, whose tail stands where his head should do. Find puppies and ponies and whistling birds for sale, and join the swarming children who scour the ground for apple cores to feed the bears. For these bears dance, Pearl. What's more there are performing dogs, peep shows, acrobats, dwarves, conjurers, and waxworks. There are pick-pockets to spare, and mountebanks hawking rare and curious potions. There are canvas tents to dance and drink in, eating houses where you'll find the most succulent roast pork imaginable. There is a symphony of ballad cries, drums, rattles, and bagpipes, and not least a rope walker who dares the journey with a duck on his head and a wheelbarrow before him containing two droop-eyed children and an Irish wolfhound. In short, there is spectacle, Pearl, living and breathing—and apprentice, lord, and milkmaid enjoy it together. Now," he said wearily, for his bottle was drained, and with the dream of the fair receding he seemed as bereft as I knew I would be when he sent me away, which he promptly did, "go back where your mother set you down. Or rather," he added abruptly, "first— come up here a moment."

I stood my ground.

"You've been before," he explained solemnly, "you and your mother both, but your father was not with you. Come, and I will stand on his be-half, and we will step forth in spirit, all three together."

Daniel Devlin staggered up the scaffold steps. I felt, in the face of his evident lunacy, a throbbing in my chest and ears, and at length I understood that it was not lunacy but some bitter truth that plagued him. His face seemed distorted, and his eyes shone as he backtracked, fumbling for my free hand.

A voice that came from me but seemed not mine whispered, "Sir?"

He looked straight through me, and I shuddered. "Come, Pearl. I have tarried long with ghosts. Take my hand."

"Will you bring him? Will he stand with Mother and me tomorrow noontide?" I was riveted by the sight of a shadowy figure across the way that for a moment I mistook for the very fiend whose name was bandied about Boston like hayseed (he must be out here somewhere, my father), come to witness our vigil. But it was only the minister, out from the parsonage in his nightshirt, as pale and wasted in appearance as I'd seen him. "Pearl," he barked, "step down from there at once. Away from that man—"

"Why confound her more, Arthur?" came the doctor's slurred demand.

I might have guessed that the minister would brim with pity, and I tried to shut out his whispered rhetoric by focusing on the quiet of the surrounding night. Unlike the last time we three had stood together—near Mistress Weary's grave—it was the minister's tone that seethed with a malice of consolation. But I soon succeeded in not hearing him at all. I smiled outright at the astonishing pair the doctor and I made on the scaffold, in full view of the good but useless minister in his nightshirt. At length I began to giggle uncontrollably, even as the poor appalled man of God came stamping up the steps to clasp my wayward arm—and Daniel Devlin transcended his tippling to leap from the platform like a cougar, to vanish into the gracious dark, laughing also, like the terrible villain I would one day discover he was.

I wonder now, years later, what else he might have done, which action—*relent confess apologize grovel demur*—would not have seemed preposterous, or pointless, or false. Leaving is as close to grace as some of us will come.

*I*t was not many days later that Mother and I happened upon our minister on a secluded stretch of beach. So many strange things had happened, were happening, that I thought little of it when Mother shooed me (and due modesty) away and rushed to speak with him.

The night I stood with Dr. Devlin on the scaffold, the minister had at first remained a long, strange while across the way, as if we two were in fact players on a stage in the fog and not people he knew. At last he crossed to us, and his words, sharp at first, gradually soothed the doctor's ravings. He spoke of the dangers of a life of the mind, of a life lived in books, of a reality blurred with dreaming by day and tippling by night. He seemed to know well the doctor's plight. As the man of God paused for thought, the physician began to look cornered. The devil came into his eyes, and he leapt.

I had slept poorly many days since, with the doctor leaping and leaping through my thoughts: wicked and foolish he seemed, pitiable and dangerous. On this afternoon when Mother and I met the minister out walking at the shore, I wandered drowsily in the tide, digging a stick in the sandy pools and chattering to my reflection. I dragged my bare feet along the packed sand and amused myself by scrawling Simon's name in giant letters for the gulls to read. I had gone to him the day after the infamy on the scaffold but found only the empty garden. I had leaned against the beech and watched the new kitchen greens wave in a gentle breeze, feeling as bleak and hollow as I ever would.

Despite my efforts to conjure Simon now and hold him in view, it was the doctor's face that stayed as my mind churned over and over his strange words on the scaffold: *Did you hear me calling in your thoughts? I am one soul in the world that knows you.*

I watched with grim resignation as the tide washed my handiwork away.

S-I-M-O-N. I chanted the letters over and over, watching from the corner of my eye Mother's agitated stance. It was, of course, the physician they spoke of. The minister's earnest voice came like waves: *My finger, pointed at this man, would have hurled him into a dungeon once. . . . I thought to let him lodge with me that I might coax him toward a public confession . . . such splendor in a man lost. . . .* His words scattered like gulls on the wind. *I have offered and offer still to assist you . . . though it be too late to invoke the law it is not too late to clear your name. . . .* Away on the wind. Wind and tide, stink of fish . . . *magistrates . . . He would have you accuse him! He taunts me, knowing you will not. . . . Does he pity those who loved him once?*

Mother's proud hands gestured at the air, and they were two bodies drawn together in the ocean's roar, their words churned and muted. It was a strange, unsettling dance, for it reminded me again of how little I knew and how much the world kept from me. Mother held her back very straight. She blazed with purpose, and the beloved face, the lips that kissed me each night but now spoke coldly to our only friend and counsel—dull and ineffectual though he sometimes was—looked not familiar. *He has seen Pearl, you know. Do you know? Look at me, please. Hear me . . . he speaks of her . . . to her as to a familiar . . . he harps on your brand.* The minister cast down his eyes at mention of the careworn "A" at my mother's breast.

Mother glared out to sea, as if the sea itself had failed her.

Furtive as a cat but I think he does wish at last to wear the stain that is his alone to bear . . . and I can in conscience only give him leave to speak it if I might act on behalf of right . . . cannot it seems find courage to set right his soul nor forsake earthly fear. You can be just and publicly accuse him . . . for the child's sake if not your own. . . .

What will she gain, Mother countered, *seeing the old sore ripped open?* I tore across the beach holding my skirts high. *The child. The child.* A sickening word, really—*child*—helpless as a snail, but it set me spinning and whirling in the sun. I kicked at the water's white foam to send it flying. I played a lunatic in hopes of distracting them from their passionate debate, but they never once looked at me. *Is pity easier to bear than scorn, minister? I think not—for my child.* Mother shook her head. Her stern air dissolved in tears.

The child turned to other live creatures to assure herself that she was there at all. She poked at a horseshoe crab, collected starfish in a line, and even laid out a jellyfish to melt in the sun. *He will not go until he has what he came for. We must ask what that thing is . . . the simple if lamentable alternative is to go. Travel as you've dreamed to your mother's people in Leiden.*

At length, frustration throbbing in my ears, I gathered pebbles into my apron and took to pelting the rigid, hopping sandpipers, outside myself. I wasn't really trying to hit them, but I injured the wing of one little bird and felt a sinking dread as it bounded away. I spilled my stash of pebbles to the ground and stared at my hands but could not recognize them.

Watching Mother from this distance, I saw the dull letter at her breast. The sun made a mockery of it, and I was inspired to craft a lovelier version from eelgrass, and to plaster it on my own budding chest. I twirled and preened and vaguely heard Mother, closer now, calling me. I looked up in time to see the minister stride away, but I was too consumed by the artful "A" on my dress to pay him much mind. At length Mother came and exclaimed at my damp garb, and made as if to brush away my weedy costume. I darted out of her reach.

"Pearl," she said, almost gently, "that sign is not yours to bear."

I pursed my lips and let the words slip free. "'A' is for apple." I watched carefully to see what reception this pronouncement—this challenge— might find.

Her eyes for an instant's glimmer seemed to consider me in a new and more serious light, despite my sodden dress, but quickly grew distant again.

"'A' is for almond," I went on in the dull, unquestioning tone usually reserved for Dame Ashley. "Angel, alabaster, able—"

"Adultery," Mother sighed heavily. "As well you know. And to do with no heart save mine."

No heart, indeed. I wanted to lunge at her and knock her down. I wanted to weep and be comforted, to shriek and claw at her, but instead I stood barefoot in the sand, soothed by the vastness of the sea. Our lives could be small there, and I could take comfort in the whispering tide. I ripped the seaweed from my dress and wrung it like a cloth, watching what little water remained drizzle over my narrow wrists.

Brushing away tears she had been too rigid to touch, Mother turned and set off without a word. I followed with one last pensive look at the sea. Mastered by some dim need to torment her, I trailed and taunted all that evening as we walked, supped, and readied ourselves for sleep. *No heart save mine, no heart save mine, no heart save mine. "A" is for arse and ale and alchemy and anarchy and ashes to ashes and atheist and Anabaptist. . . . What, pray, is the name of my father?* To this last, she answered as she always did but with barely contained rage and anguish: "You share the same Father we all do."

By bedtime, she had threatened to shut me and my treacherous blasphemies in the closet.

Even after she had tucked me in and kissed my brow, thinking me asleep, I felt mischief surging and let my eyes spring open. My voice rose from my startled throat, and Mother fairly leapt out of her skin. "'A' is for absent—"

She placed her cool hand over my mouth, sternly, and shook her head. "Sleep now, Pearl."

MOON AND STARS AND SEA

*T*he next eve at twilight I went like a criminal to the line. Without so much as a "good day," I told Daniel Devlin—who stood alone in our meadow as he claimed to have done every sunset since first we'd met, smoking his pipe and listening to the unquiet sea—of Mother's anxious meeting with the minister. "Why do they speak so of you?" I demanded. "What are you?"

"How know you they spoke of me?" he asked with a dire shine in his eye. "And did they name my crime?"

I shivered, pulling my cloak close against the sea air. How bright and ominous it was, like an unused blade, to hear an adult speak in such open and teasing tones. I crouched in the soft spring grass, near the bird's nest I couldn't see. As we settled in unison—he on his side of the line and I on mine—I ripped and knotted the squeaking blades, my pulse and the sea wind deafening my ears, and he took up my hand to still it. I snatched it back, my voice shrill. "You mustn't cross over!"

The doctor drew his hand back. "Forgive me, Pearl." He went on quickly, as if his train of thought could little bear digression. "None will—name it. It's my luck and my curse. None speak my name at all. I might never have existed here, and this more than anything calls me back each night to this savage view." He motioned vaguely in the direction of my mother's cottage and the blinding ocean sunset. "You, at least, see me as I am."

I was tired of gibberish, and said so. "You will tell me my father's name," I announced. "That will be my payment."

He regarded me with interest. I understood in his ready gaze and the restless way his fingers wound a length of grass round and about like a woman's hair that he would, if not for our bargain, reach to me again. I felt for my part frail and willing and, as such, furious. "All life is barter," I reminded him grimly.

"Not tonight, Pearl." He shook his head. "Not yet."

My lip quivered and I bit down upon it. "*Why* not?" I asked, snared in the agony of almost.

"Because it will not please you to know."

"Nothing would please me more."

"It will not please your father, Pearl. Not yet." He reached into his basket. "And here," he said, drawing out something that moved, "is what I have instead. Little consolation, perhaps, but homeless now that some feline jester has carried it far from its mother's nest."

It was a just-fuzzed mouse, shining pink under its new fur—young, wiggling, and black with a tan spot on its rump—and as it slipped from his grasp to my less sure one it squirmed horribly, tiny claws raking my skin. I gasped, peering close with cross-eyed pleasure. After a time, it resigned itself and lay panting like a sick lamb. It would die soon. The pant told me so, but I would care for it until then.

We sat in comfortable silence on either side of our line until the sun hissed into the sea and shadow curled in the meadows to sleep, at which time he sighed, "You and Mouse must go to your chores. Keep him well, and well hidden. I fancy witches favor less wretched creatures as familiars, but the righteous folk of Boston mightn't see it so. They are ever alert for such signs in you and your mother, and free with their accusations."

"I don't care."

"I suggest you keep such careless thoughts to yourself." He smiled, almost tenderly. "Lest you wake a sleeping dragon."

. . .

*A*s fate unfurled in me like a sail, I waited for a day when Nehemiah would not hoard Simon, when I might spill Mouse into his watchful hands and share with him my strange new concerns. At last that day came. I found Simon, sans Liza, at his leisure on the chair in the garden, whittling his little figures. I hissed from the trees, though I remembered too late that he might startle and cut himself. But he did not; nor did his face light up as before. I sensed with terror that his brother had slandered me more. I had not seen Simon since the day after the churchyard, and I sensed that I must take the situation in hand. We were, both of us, ruled by the whims of adults, but there was power in our games, and I resolved to bring him back to me, whatever obstacles that other adult world might raise.

"Have you ever wet your feet in the bay, Simon?"

He seemed weary at the thought of it, or at the sound of my voice. "Go away, Pearl. I've no time for you."

"Yes," I said. "You look right busy to me."

A smile flickered on his mouth.

"Do you know where stars go when their light burns out?"

"I trust you will tell me."

"They fall in the water and hiss and become like flesh."

"That is of no concern to me."

I came to the fence, forgetting myself a moment. "Isn't it? You care not about the business of the moon and stars and sea?"

"I know more than you credit, but what I don't know is of no concern to me."

"Then you have no will to know?"

He raised his head sharply, and for perhaps the first time I really looked into his eyes. They were, when he bothered to open them, the palest ice blue—not a feature at all but an absence, and absence made them ugly—but he was beautiful.

"Pearl," he said, and the weariness in his voice did vex me truly, "my will is not mine. My will is blind."

"All the more reason to feed it with pictures and light. The stars," I began, "of which I speak stick themselves to the quayside and wiggle when you lift them. I've seen many colors in my day. There are plentiful wonders in the tide."

"Go to them, Pearl. I go with you in my mind."

"Is your flesh ill?"

"My eyes are dark."

"Is your mind dark too?" I persisted, pleased at the anger growing in him, at the tight mouth and white knuckles.

"I beg you, Pearl. Leave me."

"I won't."

We sat a long time with those words on the air, and I might never have known of the other presence had Simon not raised his startled head like a deer. I too looked up, and there was Nehemiah, barely visible in the window frame in the gloom of the room beyond. The casements were open and he had been standing, listening. The window emptied, and soon he was outdoors and before us. Simon shrank at his footfalls, and even I was too surprised to retreat.

"Come here, girl."

I stood my ground, scarcely able to look at him, so much a young gentleman in the fine attire of a merchant's son. Simon, it occurred to me, never wore such garb, but the simple stuff of farmers. Was he less loved by his father than this shining one?

"I won't bite." He snarled like a dog, and then winked with a nearly hearty laugh. A giggle bubbled up in my throat. But then, taking my cue from Simon, who seemed at best frozen in his chair, I cast my eyes to the ground.

"So it's the wretch from the rain. What do you want here?"

I pointed, bold as you please, to his brother. Simon sat deathly still in his chair.

"For what reason do you want him?"

"He wants for amusement."

"Few in the colony have time for amusement, Pearl. You are freer than some."

"My mother is generous," I conceded. "But he is not working now."

"And where would you escort him?"

"I would take him to the bay to seek stars."

"So you would."

"And I would make him a birch boat."

"I see."

Simon shifted uncomfortably on his chair but seemed reassured by his brother's change in tone. And his eyes, the elder's eyes. How to describe them? It was as if Nehemiah saw for two; his amber stare was that intent, and he did seem to note some gracious change in me. "Return him before early candlelight. Chores need doing and scriptures must be read."

"I will, sir." I bowed as low as I could and nearly tripped in my own exuberance.

"And Pearl—" He was not looking at me but rather at his brother, who seemed to sense the elder's gaze on him. "This is our solemn secret. My brother is in your care through no wish of mine. You must take pains that he is well and quiet in his travels. No mischief, or you will have my wrath and God's."

I nodded eagerly, still too afraid to move. He went to his brother and took the knife from his pale hand, and helping him dazed to his feet, led my charge to me. Nehemiah did not help Simon through the fenceposts, but rather took his hand and reached across for mine, and gave me his brother's like a gift. "Farewell, then."

I tried to thank him, but he shook his head and waved us away.

"Simon," I cried. "Simon!" And that was all. We ran, or I ran and he stumbled behind. As we went, arms swinging, I imagined Nehemiah, stern but smiling back in the window frame, and in my small, half-senseless mind, he seemed a lonely figure.

"Where shall we go first—" I felt resistance and looked back at Simon, startled to find that he had dug his heels into the earth. He wouldn't budge. "What is it?"

"You will leave me," he blurted in a pitiful voice.

"I wouldn't! On that other day I was at the end of my anger. I was revenging your cold words."

"And what if I have said other words that might damn me?"

I put my hands on my hips. "Well, you haven't. I should know."

"And what if I do? What if I don't mean to and do."

"I won't *leave* you, Simon. Not again. Not ever."

"On your honor?"

"On my honor."

His faced seemed to soften then, and he held out his hand. I held it in both of mine and studied it—pale and bony with dark crescent moons for nails—and even, on a violent impulse, kissed it. He made a noise like what comes from a horse's behind and yanked the hand away, but I snatched it up again, and we set off, laughing.

There were no starfish that day. I looked and looked and apprised Simon of all I saw on the way. I brought the world to his hands, and draped all with my words. We rested near shore not far from my and Mother's cabin and began our inventory. Simon liked the crab best of all, even better than Mouse—who rode in my apron pocket—and while I held the claws closed, he ran delicate fingers round every complaining curve. "It struggles."

"Wouldn't you?" I asked, watching his face. His expression changed with his hands' observations. He laughed, but only faintly—too intent on his task to devote himself to mirth. "Loose it, Pearl."

I set the crab down more gently than ordinarily I would have and led my friend into some rushes along the shore, where we stood with soaking shoes and listened to the blackbirds trill. I felt suddenly an awesome weight of responsibility, and said in a voice far more adult than I felt, "I must needs bring the world to you."

"Oh, I know the world well enough." Simon laughed his good-natured laugh. "I just can't see it."

He told of fishing once with Nehemiah in a place like this, and of how he had been too anxious touching and sniffing everything to concentrate on his end of the net. "I remember dipping my hand over and over into the water and tasting it. It seemed forever before I understood that it was salt." He told of his dim memory of coming over from Mother Europe on a ship, of the rock and sway and panic, the sound of rats scuffling in the night. "Nehemiah has been my eyes, and when he is at sea or consumed with study as he often is, I must needs depend on Liza."

"Is he patient?" I asked, feeling almost jealous of this now beneficent older brother.

Simon laughed. "Nehemiah? No. He is vigilant."

I led him back to the pebbled shore. "Vigilant?"

"He watches over me."

"But he let you from his sight today."

Simon's voice was puzzled. "Mayhap Liza convinced him after all. You must look fit to him now." His hand, which had been paddling in the tide, splashed water in my general direction. "I can't imagine where he learned that notion."

But I was too taken with the subject to jest. "When will he return to his work? Will your father go back to sea? Will you be alone with Liza?"

Simon hung his head and seemed distracted. His hand waved back and forth in the water.

"Simon," I threatened. "Tell me."

"My father is scripting our journey as we speak. It was Mother's wish to come live among the elect; Papa has no love for them. We'll return to London by way of Barbados." The color had drained from his face.

Stunned, I demanded, "You don't like to sail?"

"I don't like to leave you."

"You mustn't." I nearly choked on my words, desperation surging through me. "Election Day is coming. Your father mustn't leave before Election Day."

"It's not my wish, Pearl."

"Then your brother. Can't he do something?"

"What should he do?"

"Stay behind to care for you," I demanded. "How can your father leave her buried in the churchyard?"

Simon seemed offended by this idea. "Mother is not in the churchyard now. Her soul is well gone. It must be true what they say about you—that you are as wild as the faery folk in Old England. You know nothing of the Lord God, do you?"

"I know well enough, and I don't care." I spat out the words and then, as usual, regretted them. We sat in obstinate silence, my ready sin staining the air between us. Simon seemed almost frightened of me again, or of what I might draw out of the dark toward us. He was not pious as his mother had been—as his brother was, at his convenience, Liza claimed— but Simon was trained to fear as some were to penance. He owed a vast physical debt to others.

I ran to search for birch peel at the tree line. I called to him as I worked, and sang in my broken voice, and struggled with the desperation that over and over again blurred the beautiful world.

"Pearl!" Simon called when he had not heard my voice for a time.

"I'm here."

"Tell about your mother and the babe at the prison gate."

"You know already, Simon." I spoke dismissively but was secretly glad. It was my favorite story.

"Let me hear it again."

"My mother wears a scarlet 'A' at her breast for adultery. It has been there since my eyes first beheld the world, and it marks us both. We are alone." Though I confess, as I stole eager glances at Simon (forgetting that he couldn't see me) and remembered Daniel Devlin's hand winding the meadow grass round and round his strong fingers, I felt less alone than once I had.

"Is it because she's a harlot?"

This riveted me. I forgot my generous mood and ran at Simon like a bull and pushed him over in the sand. He lay there, stunned and still, and curled into a ball. Even in my fury, I imagined what it felt like, his black world wheeling, the sensation of falling without sight of the ground. I punched his arm without conviction, half sitting on him. "You asked me for my story, but you are like the others."

"Whoa, sorry! I'm sorry, Pearl." Slowly the ball of his body relaxed to resemble a shrimp, and he laughed hoarsely; the elegant hands I loved patted the ground, and he righted himself and sat up, brushing sand from his cheek. "Go on—"

"I grew inside Mother in the prison, and she raved long after the midwife had gone, and we came out, where she stood holding me on the scaffold. We stood hours in the summer heat, though Mother shielded me with swaddling, shouting up to the magistrates in the gallery that I should never have an earthly father more but just a heavenly one. And then we came home to our cottage and were jeered at and mocked ever after, and when I was a small child not long off the leading strings, Mother feared they would take me away, and begged the governor have pity on a poor mother, and the young minister intervened on our behalf." I was struck by the recent image of our earnest savior pacing among the graves in the churchyard; his words were a jumble now. *How have I kept this bitter secret thus long, only to find it lodged under my very roof?*

"I don't care for him," said Simon, "though he rides like an angel in others' affections."

"Why not?"

"I don't know. His shaking voice speaks not to our woes in this world. He's afraid of them, I think." Simon shrugged. "Perhaps he is false."

I was shocked—and delighted. For too long, the minister had been our only friend, but his friendship had ever smacked of bookish charity. "What secrets has a saint to hide?"

As I dug in the sand with my heel, Simon grinned sheepishly into space and swiveled his head as if to listen for footfalls. Criticizing even so much as a sermon could invite a public whipping or worse. "I don't know. It's not my concern."

"And neither is my mother your concern," I said. "Neither am I, by rights."

"But you are," he said, and seemed to shrink under a great gloom. "You will be my fondest memory."

"Will be?" I asked, appalled. "I *will be* wretched."

"The letter," said Simon, "the 'A' means that she loved another to spite God and his sacraments."

"I know," I complained, "but what love is it that spites God? Is not love God's gift to us?"

"There are laws, Pearl."

I hung my head. I knew about laws, and knew that I was not mindful of them. Mother tried to teach me scriptures and, on the path to the meetinghouse, talked often of society and its expectations for me. No whistling, no running, no laughing overloud. Keep clean, don't dally, sit straight, don't shuffle. Be meek, be humble, be prudent. Prize public spirit-edness and weanedness from the world. Strive, above all, to become a no-table housewife. Forsake the glamour of evil. But Mother was as apologetic in her presentation as she was insistent, so her words flew out of my frivo-lous head like flocks of wild birds. She knew and I knew the danger therein, but we had been fortunate in the wake of ill fortune. For years, we had been largely left alone.

Sometimes as we sat at our supper in the light of the reed lamp, I dipped my bread and searched her face for evidence of her wrongs. What I saw each day was a sad woman with the light gone out of her, except when she took her hair down and let me brush it, her long neck moving with the motion, her head swaying just slightly, enough for me to imagine her a dancer in the rain in some clearing in the wood without me, perhaps in the arms of the devil-prince we heard so much about. My mother was no witch, I knew, but there was a cool defiance in her, a corner of her soul kept at bay by daylight, that intrigued and terrified me. I felt that it did not, like that dark, sad majority, belong to me.

"Do you know this man lodged with our minister—Dr. Devlin?"

Simon nodded, drawn out of his own thoughts. "I do. He looked in on my mother once or twice. Why do you ask?"

"He meets me. He speaks to me."

"Meets you where? What business has he with a girl? Are you ill?"

"He would tell me something. He has . . . a secret."

"And you would hear it, no doubt." Simon laughed nervously and leaned forward. "Perhaps you would be wise, Pearl, not to meet with him more. Where would he see you? Perhaps he means you harm."

My stubborn silence displeased Simon, who commenced without delay to peck at the fellow like an old hen: "He seems every bit a gentleman, learned and charming, when he comes to converse with my father. But I've heard Father caution Nehemiah—"

"Simon—"

"—that many a gentleman has dirt on his hands and thorns in his heart—"

"Hush, Simon. Do you follow law always?"

"If I do," he admitted, "it's because the people who guard it have always been my eyes."

"And now you have me."

He began scratching in the sandy earth with a fragment of clamshell.

"And now," I accused, "you will leave me."

"Not I, Pearl. You promised you wouldn't leave me out here," he motioned to the great world, "and I make that same promise. But I have no means to keep it."

I sat very still for a moment, fighting off a surge of sniveling, then leapt to my feet and began to pace the shoreline, careless of my shoes, which soaked through, and the hem of my dress, which dragged. "Tell me of London."

"It's loud and smells of piss and the devil."

"But are there plays and markets and carriages racing round with beautiful people in them?"

"Beautiful, I don't know. But there are people, too many for my taste. One day you will go there," he assured me. "One day."

I felt the tears burn behind my eyes again. "Is Barbados very hot? Are there strange fruits there, and animals?"

"I don't know," Simon confessed. "I've never been. Father doesn't take me when he trades, but as we'll not be back to live, he must——"

I walked to him and covered his mouth with my hands. "Let's not speak of it. Don't say it. One day I'll come to find you by the turnips, and you won't be there. Let it be so."

Simon stood unsteadily, brushing sand from his breeches. "But now tell me more about your life. I'm fashioning a doll of you to carry in my mind."

"A doll," I scoffed. "Can a doll do this?" I cartwheeled in the sand and nearly collided with him.

"What did you do, fool?"

"Never mind." We sat a long, laughing moment, resplendent without words.

"If you wish, I will not visit the doctor," I offered at last.

He pondered this long and seriously. "I wish no harm to come to you. I cannot—and never could—stop what will come, and that is my curse."

"Forget curses now." I took his cool hand once more, tugged him upright, and we set off for the southern extreme of the peninsula, where the wide ocean lived and the pipers scurried. "Let us go to the waves."

*I*t took some time, this journey, and twice we had to sneak through the backs of farmsteads. We dodged some small craft too, fishermen returning or preparing for outings. I described it all as we went, and we spent a few moments at the edge of the wood, where a stream flows down to the sea, and listened to the knocking of a woodpecker.

"That's a bird, then?" Simon echoed with wonder. "I've heard it many times."

"They stab the dead wood with their beaks and pluck vermin to eat."

"It sounds like my teeth chattering," said Simon, "in the meetinghouse in winter."

We traveled thus until we reached the shore and sat with the waves rolling closer and closer until they covered our calves. Neither of us moved. I said that for all I cared, the sea could swallow us.

"It would anger God."

"Yes, but imagine the life under the sea. Imagine, Simon. We could be as merfolk."

"We have no tails."

"We could grow tails, and traverse the world, and the salt would heal your eyes."

He smiled weakly and hung his head, scratching in the sand. "Tell me, Pearl. Your mother is a godly woman?"

"A good woman, yes. Mother reads her scriptures. She tends the sick."

"But you are wild, Pearl."

"Do you blame my mother for it?" I laughed.

"I fear for you."

"Fear for yourself, Simon." The gentle waves were rolling to our waists now, and though I didn't think it strange at the time, that we should sit so quietly and let the tide own us, I wonder now what held us there. It was foolish to soak our clothes, and though I was no stranger to foolishness, Simon was quite the sanest boy I would ever meet. I remember leaning back on my hands and studying him from head to where he was swallowed by the sea, memorizing Simon at his ease, and it is for this reason that I well remember what happened next.

Daniel Devlin appeared at the corner of my eye like an apparition at the tree line, and I had the sudden uneasy feeling that he had been by all along. He was already halfway down the beach, striding hard behind his staff, when I realized he was real and not a figment. Simon started and shrank into himself at the sound, but I felt quietly fierce. Despite Simon's late warning, it was not the peculiar doctor—whose presence I had grown used to—I feared; it was Nehemiah.

"So, Pearl, you fancy yourself a craft? Are you heading off to sea? And who is your companion?" He didn't allow me to respond but, kneeling by us with a theatrical groan, answered his own question with unseemly satisfaction. "Caleb Milton's son. I tended your mother, did I not?"

"Yes, sir," said Simon, scrambling back on his hands like a crab. His wet legs plastered the sand to him.

"Simon knows all about you—"

"I know nothing, sir—"

Puling baby, I thought. "Coward—Simon!"

"The boy is blind, Pearl. Forgive him his caution. More caution would suit you well."

"Are you collecting today?" I demanded.

Dr. Devlin nodded, a gleam in his eyes as he shaded them against the glare from the sea. "I have grubbed up a few roots."

"Have you something for Simon's eyes?" I rifled in his basket, angry with him for disturbing what might well be one of my last days with Simon.

He only smiled his arch smile, amused by my impertinence. He regarded Simon at length as if considering his worth, reached a practiced hand to my friend's face, and ran a finger lightly over each closed eyelid. Simon flinched.

"Be still, boy, and let me look at them. I suspect you're well beyond germander and clary." He pulled one pale lid open as far as it would go, showing the red under the lower lashes.

"He is a worldly physician," I reminded Simon, who knew the man well enough but was shaking—whether from the cold water or fear I knew not.

"No," said the doctor, and pushed Simon's head lightly away as if it were a meal he was declining. "Only one man could heal the blind. Does your father know you are here drenched, partaking of a lady's charms?"

"No, sir." Simon began, almost imperceptibly, to rock. I hoped he would not mutter or weep.

"How old are you, boy?" The doctor reached a hand behind my head and roughly pulled it forward, as if to display me. I struggled, but he'd cupped my neck fast in his strong hand. "What would you see if you saw this girl? Would you think her lovely—even as the rose is lovely to fingers that would pluck it?" He loosed me and leaned in close to Simon's sallow face, his voice a menace of calm. "I will answer your questions so you do not pine. She is fair but no fairer than other maids, though her eyes are wilder mayhap and her hair of more gloss. She is too young to be plucked. You cannot see this, but you know it, I trust?"

Simon nodded with effort, blazing red in the mug now.

"So bid all boyish temptation adieu and be the friend she needs, or you will have me to answer to."

And what could Simon do but nod darkly and knit his brow? Can I describe the pleasure this exchange gave me? How I did, in my battered innocence, love them both that day for their absurd efforts to protect me one from the other. Who before, besides Mother and the minister (wed to their myriad duties), had ever squandered an instant's time on my welfare? I felt a very queen, and these my loyal squabbling lords, until the doctor turned talk back to mundane things and recalled for me Nehemiah's show of trust. "Does no one know you're here?" he asked.

"No one," I blurted. "It's my doing. I thought he wanted for amusement. He is kept like a mushroom in the shade of the yard."

"So he is," agreed the doctor. "Our world has little use for the frail."

"Then you see," I urged, "the worth of my deed."

He reached to stroke my dark curls, but this time I lurched away from his hand, which looked to my eyes large and overcapable in the glare of sunlight. He straightened, supporting himself with his staff, and his voice held a trace of laughter. "So I do, Pearl. Your mother would be pleased."

"You will tell her?"

"I should like very much to speak with her, but think you I shouldn't tell of this?"

Tired of looking up at him, and of Simon's trembling, I stood unsteadily and stamped the water from my shoes. "I think not." I pulled Simon up and bade him stand by me. "I think that if you do, I will be heartsick." I squeezed the water from my hem and roared at the bemused man like a lion of the jungle, half mad with worry for Simon, but it was only my friend and not the staid physician who jumped. Simon's face had lost all color. I had to giggle then. Our situation seemed quite hopeless.

"Pearl," said the strange fellow, not once but twice (dear Pearl), savoring the name like a sweetmeat. "That you may know me one day as forgiving, I bid you go home peacefully, children. I will guard your secret from all and sundry, saints and devils alike. But put yourselves not in jeopardy. Many a stern master would forbid you this pleasure." He gestured at the sea, the wind, the very air it seemed to me. But there was truth in what he said, and I was grateful, and pitied him. When he did not have the minister to minister to, or town business, this visitor to our shores seemed to me at best a melancholy wanderer. I was still troubled by the encounter that had taken place not far from here with my pastor and my mother, when I had played in the tide and overheard snatches of their strange, impassioned conversation.

I took Simon's cold hand and squeezed it. He had stopped shivering, warmed some by the sun and the man's near mournful voice, and now we three stood without discomfort, caught in the spell of the gentle ebb and flow of the waves.

"I do favor the sea," said Daniel Devlin. "You have a journey looming, do you, Master Simon? Your brother spoke of it when last I supped with him at the inn."

"I do, sir," he murmured.

"Barbados first, is it?"

"Yes."

"Bear tidings to London for me. I am loath to return there yet but have fond, deceitful memories to stay me."

I elbowed Simon, and he said softly, "I will, sir."

"Good day, then." The doctor spoke almost cheerfully, tipping a hat that wasn't there, and wandered off in search of catnip and pennyroyal, thoroughwort and wormwood. I clutched Simon's arm and watched the physician go. I felt the sorrowful weight of time to come and whispered in Simon's ear, "Remember me."

"Keep your promise," he hissed back, his forehead blindly bumping mine, his soft lips unwittingly grazing my cheek, "and stay clear of him."

His seed

I woke at home that night raving. Mother soaked my head with a damp, heavy scrap of linen and sang to me, and I slipped in and out of half dreams. In one, I stood again on the scaffold with Mother while screaming floodwater rose round us. In another, Simon swung from the gallows, his sightless eyes covered by a useless band of cloth, his beautiful hands limp and flapping at his sides. In still another, Daniel Devlin, in his playful singsong, whispered my name in the darkness.

Mother and I had gone to call at a sickbed that evening. As the hour was already late, I was allowed to rest on a trundle pulled from beneath the old grandmother's bed. The babe of the house had met the speckled monster yesteryear, she said, and the bed was all that remained of him. The gnarled woman spread a coarse blanket over me and sat by the hearth to take up her embroidery. For a while, I lay watching the steady motion of her right hand in the flickering firelight. As the fire dimmed, the dark crept into the folds in her dress and flesh, and before long she took to muttering. Her eyes darted to me from time to time, as if to assure herself that I was still there, and she rocked to and fro on her straight chair like a brat at Sunday meeting. Her restless gait, her dark wrinkles, and her acid muttering unnerved me, so I closed my eyes and feigned sleep.

Before long and to my drowsy dismay, I found her up and creeping round the trundle bed. I felt my muscles tighten under her shadow. I kept my eyes open just enough to follow her movements. She peered down at me, then paced to the edge of the hall, by the stairs, and listened there, whether for my mother's voice or the groaning of her fevered daughter I know not. Her words grew louder and more sensible, and I made out that some of her muttering was for us: "Like a thousand and a thousand others, our nurse hath signed Satan's book in blood . . . bears his mark on her . . . his seed sleepeth in my darling's trundle. . . ."

And then she was over me again, and I saw the shadow of a knife. I would have screamed, but when my eyes opened fully, it was not a murderous hag I saw but a tearful old woman. Perhaps it was her dead grandchild she saw, but the tenderness in her sticky-looking eyes was clear, and I closed my own eyes again—for once the dutiful maiden—and left my life in God's hands.

It was a lock of my hair she wanted, as a charm perhaps, but I felt her sawing gently at one of my black ringlets, weeping and muttering as she worked. She would sign a covenant, she said. She would surrender herself like Mistress Tibbins and *that one in there if only if only if only* he would *spare my child my last and only* and not steal the fevered one like those others—children, grandchildren—who had been sacrificed to this black and merciless land. "I would surrender myself to write my name in your book," she whispered.

Having secured her prize, she stood and hobbled back to slap the knife upon the table. The metal rang. She slipped the lock of my hair into her apron and took up her pacing again, and then I really did close my eyes and let sleep claim me.

It was an uneasy rest, to be sure, and when Mother woke me a short while later, and we entered again the airy world of moon and stars, I could not be sure that my encounter wasn't all dream, and so did not tell of it. Mother seemed preoccupied, and when I asked about her patient, she only took my hand and squeezed it.

We walked thus, and I felt a thousand questions leap to my throat. We had talked little of real matters since the afternoon on the beach with the minister. I had in the days that followed tormented her with lavish questions; I knew she wouldn't or couldn't answer them, but tonight, without the fever of mischief in me, I felt a mute sympathy.

Finally, as we reached the cottage, dark beyond the moon-glimmer of the sea, I mustered the courage to ask why she had quarreled with our good pastor.

Mother let me in under her arm, the lantern illuminating our cottage full of shadows, and set the light on the table.

"He has come back to see me at last to my grave," she said absently as I shut the door behind us.

"The minister?"

She shook her head but said no more, standing by the bed and gesturing for me to come to her. I slipped out of my dress while she took up the key to pull taut the ropes supporting our mattress. Then she held the edge of the blanket and I slipped under, wiggling and squirming for comfort. "Shall I brush your hair?" Drowsy again, I hoped that she would say no.

Mother shook her head. Instead of stoking the fire on this cool May night, she lit the reed lamp to save candle, blew out the lantern, and dragged her chair over to settle at my side. As she took up her embroidery and began to work—her face firm and determined—I let my eyes droop closed and thought how different was this lovely shade from the old woman's shadowy form back at the sick house.

But as I lay half awake watching the gentle motion of Mother's arm, I imagined that she who loved me *was* an old woman, tearful and wretched, while I lay dying in another room. I realized, in a fleeting moment, that time alters all, and that one day I would not be here in the safety of this cottage with Mother stitching at my side, but engaged in some other, unforeseen part of my destiny. This was so violent a revelation for my young mind that I cried out.

Mother reached across and stroked my ear, smoothing my wild, curling hair behind it. "A nightmare so soon?"

"I imagined we were old," I said. "You were like the dame in the chimney corner tonight."

She drew her hand away from me as if stung. "That day will come." Mother laid down her needlework with a sigh and blew out the reed lamp. She slipped fully clothed into bed beside me, gave my cheek an absent stroke, and rolled away.

I lay a long while in the dark, letting my eyes soak in what light there was. We were but days from a full milk moon, and I could see well enough the interior of the cottage and its stark contents.

The only ornament was a small collection of my samplers, with jagged lightning stitches and bright disarray, that Mother had pegged to the walls, perhaps to contrast with the single gorgeous cloth born of her own hands. Though it had been dulled by years of soot and dust, Mother's silken mural was my earliest experience of light and fancy. It showed Eden before the fall, a bright, incongruous world of paradise birds, elephants, and willow trees. But there was an apple tree, too, at its edge, and a coiled serpent whose scales of glimmering yellow-green silk seemed to glow where the other threads had dulled.

As a very small child I had stood with strained neck to stare at that image, my gaze flitting ever to the bright snake. By the time I was old enough to articulate them, I had learned to keep my questions to myself. And questions they remained: Why did God hate the apple so? Was it not what gave the Puritan fathers mind to cross the wide ocean to build their city on a hill? To craft the great ships and navigate the seas? Was it *wanting* that God deplored, or disobedience?

I tried to crowd these questions from my mind, listening instead to the still night. I knew that bats swooped through it, that raccoons and skunks grubbed and hoarded, shaking the rushes and moving with soft step through tangled thickets, and this soothed me. But I had also the old dame's words in mind now, and his name, and could not scrub them away with happier thoughts. I had heard many a time from the children at Goodwife Ashley's or in the street that I was "devil's spawn," but somehow it had never meant more than two words rattling together like stones. The old woman at the hearth, though, had wanted a piece of me to seal her covenant. She had called me his "seed." From seed came a baby.

I put my arm over Mother's trim frame, then sought gently for her mouth with my hand. I had the habit of checking to feel her warm breath on my skin, to ensure that she was living beside me, that I was not alone. *His seed.* Perhaps he was, as the teasing went, my true father—the dark prince himself. Did I need Daniel Devlin and his trinkets to confirm what had ever been there, in the downcast eyes of the pious, in the gossips' searing stares? His name was stitched into the fiber of Puritan Boston, and into the brand at Mother's breast.

Contemplating this long and tearfully, I determined to stay awake till daybreak, so that Mother could not go to him. At the same time, I imagined her dancing out there in a plowed field, a shade in her gray gown against the dark earth. Her hair spilled down her back and spun with her motion, and her face and hands glowed moon-silver.

At length, this fancy seemed too real to ignore. Had she left her body? I felt again for her breath, and came to doubt my own senses, for there seemed to be none there. I sat up and stiffened, looking wildly this way and that, my heart racing. I slipped from the blankets and strode to the door. I opened it and stepped outside, forgetful of heathens and of Mistress Tibbins and the other hags on their brooms, and was almost instantly calmed by the shimmer of water and the cool, sweet air. What evil could live out here?

I stole behind the cottage and up the hill to Goodman Baker's nearest field, startling a doe at its edge; I paused to watch her bound away and stood in the dewy cornfield in my shift slapping at mosquitoes. It was then I realized that it wasn't Mother I'd imagined out here at all, but some other, older version of myself.

"What if I am Satan's child?" I asked Simon the next day.

Once again, Nehemiah had entrusted him to me, but this time he had given me a list in a note for Liza, who had gone ahead to market. "I forgot a few things, and you'll needs catch up with her and give her this. We must make our adoption of you public, I fear."

When he smiled, I lost all will to be insulted. I caressed the smooth paper with my forefinger and smelled the just-dried ink.

"I shouldn't waste the paper," he said, "but I trust not your memory, and Simon's hopeless, of course."

"She can read?" I wondered aloud, more impressed than I meant to be.

"Yes, our mother taught Liza well. In a merchant's home, there is much movement of provisions. She would have taught you too were she still with us."

"I can read right well," I said imperiously, but it was hard to hold a frown when he fixed those knowing eyes on me. "You are merry today, Master Nehemiah."

"Yes, eager to be gone from the shadow of that dark wood." He looked thoughtful. "I should like to see a play if I can, or talk with better than a cooper and less than a Harvard bore at the tavern."

I expect his worldliness made me nervous, and I found myself grinning like an imp. "Aren't you a fine, haughty rooster then. " I had already learned that his airy moods were fleeting but intense, and that I might jest with him when the wind was favorable.

He made as if to lunge for me, and I nearly collided with Simon, who had stepped out of the house. I was sorry, for Nehemiah immediately became serious again. He lifted his black hat and smoothed the gold-brown hair from his brow. He replaced the hat, looking a moment longer at me than any man or boy had general cause to. He seemed to study me. "You are the picture of your mother," he said at last. "Except the eyes."

I had introduced Nehemiah to Mother before Sunday meeting last. Though she'd been on hand to nurse his ailing mother—and Liza and Simon would have credited her for it—Nehemiah and his father held no such thankful bond, as they had docked near to Mistress Weary's passing, when the business was all conclusion. Nehemiah no doubt saw outside the meeting hall that morning not a real woman, one to whom his grieving family was indebted, but a bloodless figure carved of infamy. And like many before him, he'd owned my mother with the gossip's smirk, his gaze slipping once or twice to caress her scarlet badge. It was slight and polite, his derision, but Mother and I were familiar with its shadings, and so my parent kept her head bowed all through that interview.

I wondered how, having thus reduced her to her humblest posture, he could know that our eyes varied.

"Your mother's are nearly black. Yours are the deep brown of soil."

Indignant, or unnerved, I looked away. "Come, Simon. Let us find some mischief." I went for the younger's hand and looked over my shoulder as we made for the gate. Nehemiah was still watching. I put a bounce in my walk and held my capless head high.

"*I*f you are the devil's," Simon replied, "then I am damned."

"It can't be so," I said. "You are too good."

"We're all born to sin."

They were not his words, I knew, though true enough if the ministers and magistrates knew best, and surely they did. I heard the shrill of children by the churchyard and, with my practiced instinct for evasion, steered Simon off our course.

"What is it?" he asked.

"I would avoid those cretins."

"What cretins?"

"You hear them, don't you?"

He stopped walking to listen a moment, his mouth twitching in concentration. "Yes. But who are they?"

"I don't know," I said. "I don't care. They're plaguing the market, I expect, jesting till the tithing-man catch up with them."

I took him on a shortcut past the budding, gnarled apple trees behind Governor Bellingham's mansion. As a child I had thought that grand house with its glistening, glass-pocked walls of patterned stucco and its rose bushes and curling pumpkin vines the most fanciful place on earth outside the forest; that the rich-hewn hag Mistress Tibbins sometimes poked her head out the lattice of a chamber window to startle passersby with dark nonsense made the place seem choicer still. As we journeyed down the hill toward market square, I saw the pillory and stopped short.

"What now?" quipped Simon. "Rampaging swine?"

"Have you been to the scaffold?"

He bowed his head. "I know that many have stood there."

"I have stood there."

"I know it."

"Not as a babe, but lately. Come thither, and I'll tell another strange tale about the doctor."

"I've heard enough about him, Pearl. We have market business." He tightened his grip on my hand as if to hold me back, but I tugged and propelled him along behind me. I stamped up the steps with Simon struggling for balance behind.

"Remember you said that you did not believe the minister?" I whispered, raising my face to the spring sunshine, heedless of the view of the market ahead—and of those who might well have a view of us.

Simon had wrenched his hand free to frantically search for my mouth. After patting and pushing at my shoulder and neck, he found the offending organ and pressed his hand tight against it. Leaning close, he whispered, "You promised."

I smelled the sweet dirt on his palm and felt the terror in its trembling, and saw suddenly where we were. "But the doctor lodges with the minister and swears he can tell me who he is, my father—"

"I don't want to know," Simon whispered. "Nor should you. I want to be down from here. Now, Pearl. Before we're flogged."

I took his hand and led him back to earth. We walked briskly, speechless. I didn't know if he was angry or simply cautious now. We were almost to market when Simon squeezed my arm. He had heard them first this time, and when they burst over the bushes shrieking like savages, I was ready.

How unsafe Simon must have felt with me! I wanted to care for him, and I would, I thought, but my methods must have seemed atrocious. I leaned on the long stick I'd secured as if it were an innocent staff.

The boys whooped and hollered, circling us with fluttering hands. The noise they made was worse than a flock of startled geese. I knew this lot, and feared only for Simon. On my own, I could outrun any one of the pasty snails, and there was always the wood, which stopped them as a beaver's dam stops fish.

A boy I knew as Jacob (I considered both he and his leering older brother, Gideon, chief among my enemies) did a heathen dance close to Simon. He stopped his yowling long enough to ask what was wrong with Simon's icy eyes. He stood still and leaned forward to peer at them. "He won't open them," he called over his shoulder. I threatened with my raised stick, and Jacob laughed. He waved his arms and jumped up and down. "Can you see me, boy?"

Simon shook his head. He must have been terrified, but seemed the picture of calm.

"What do you see?"

"He sees a wicked wretch." I stepped forward and between them. Jacob made a mock-astonished face and whooped again, turning to his friends for support. They answered in kind.

"Run home, infant, and let your mother rock you at her stained breast."

I glared but had not the usual bouquet of foul words. Simon's presence had shamed and disabled me, and the truth is, these boys and I were probably a bit bored with our routine by now. Simon was the only new part of it.

"Leave him," I said softly, aware that I was begging. "He is frail and wants mercy. Think what will happen if the magistrates find you've harmed him." I dropped my stick at Jacob's feet, an offering, and took Simon by the arm. None spoke as we walked away, and I marveled at the ease of it. We entered the market square, and I held my head high, even when Liza found us and rushed as she might to a spark that's leapt from the hearth. She seemed like a stranger, and I dropped Simon's hand and thrust Nehemiah's note at her.

She read her young master's spidery handwriting greedily, then brushed at Simon's sleeve as if to rid him of my touch. "You may go now, Pearl."

I felt her betrayal as if someone had slashed me with a blade, but Simon spoke up quickly. "Nehemiah's right with her now. He's sent us off together twice already."

Her brow furrowed, sheepish Liza looked me up and down. "I'm a servant, after all, not your mother. You've too much need. My young master said so soon's he came for the funeral, and I've too much work already—"

"Have you a mule?" I asked.

"You know I haven't," she said sharply.

"Then you'll need my back."

Liza rolled her eyes, and we went shopping.

"What does your father trade in?"

Liza answered for Simon, her voice flat and studied, as if she kept a mind full of such lists. "Fish and pipe-staves, masts, pitch, tar, wool, and pork. And goods from the islands."

"Is his ship very large?"

"Very large," Liza said impatiently, as if the subject bored her greatly. The basket on her plump arm swung with the rhythm of her motion. "Where hath such a little woman learned to question so large?"

"Does it offend you?"

Liza laughed outright, and Simon covered his mouth to trap his mirth. "When I'm not stone drunk, everything about you offends me," she conceded, "but I'll survive it."

We walked briskly. In the end, there was nothing for me to carry. Liza quickly discovered, muttering and knitting her brow, that many of the provisions Nehemiah had requested were unavailable. "Election Day is nigh," she said, "and tomorrow is baking day." Sometimes she spoke as if I wasn't there, but less often as the afternoon wore on. "I'll needs make conserve of wormwood soon," she told Simon.

"What use has that?" I asked.

"Prevents the seasickness." Liza heaved the basket higher on her arm. "So do clove-gillyflowers, burnt wine, stewed prunes, currants, Spanish rusk, and ginger. And juice of lemons well cures scurvy. You're striped at the capstan with a cat-o'-nine-tails if you filch the surgeon's lemons."

"Lemons?" I asked, wonder in my voice.

"That's a beginning." Liza slapped a mosquito flat on her wrist and flicked it off. "And we'll needs take bushels of meal besides, and pease and oatmeal."

"What more?" I urged.

"Methinks a gallon each of brandy and oil and two of vinegar. And then dried fish, cheese, bacon, sugar, pepper, and store for beasts."

I looked up at the tangled canopy of leaves above us, stopped in my tracks by the press of light there, then scurried to catch up. "Will the waves crash on shipboard? Are there serpents in the deep?"

"I'll not say more." Liza's voice was firm. "I have work to spare and more work waiting, and *where* is your mother, child? Haven't you chores of your own to do? Haven't you a plot to tend?"

I shook my head vigorously.

"Wool to card?"

I shrugged.

"Liar," said she, mouth twitching back a smile. "I've seen you have. You're your mother's curse, dearie."

Simon stood a moment between us, or the diverging sounds we made, but soon followed his father's servant away from me.

*S*imon's family continued to engage themselves in the business of leaving me. I came to stand under the beech only to find Nehemiah with his sleeves rolled up, nailing barrels closed. Used to seeing him in his gentleman's broadcloth and gloves, I couldn't help but stare. He was all his brother was not, and just now his strength appealed to me.

He sensed quickly that he was being watched and waved me from my shelter. "Stop loitering, girl. God hates an idle hand. Help with the work if you must haunt the shade."

I sauntered to the fence and climbed through, lingering a moment more to watch him work. I was fascinated by his arms, of course, as I rarely saw a man other than the blacksmith in his shirtsleeves, and certainly not a young and princely man without a frock. Nehemiah rolled the barrels to the wall and took to chopping wood, pausing from time to time to wipe the sweat from his brow with his hand.

I lifted the split pieces as they fell and, when I could hold no more, walked them to the woodpile. I felt anxious each time to be back by him, as if this bond of work held magic. We said very little but moved in harmony, and I felt a strange safety in that yard where the sun beat down, a familiarity that even my time with Simon had not inspired. Always, with Simon, I felt a responsibility to see for us both, but on this afternoon I let my eyes blur and my mind wander where it would. I sensed that Nehemiah would let no harm come to me.

"Where is Simon today?" I asked finally, a bit guilty perhaps.

"He is gone with our father to market. He has no seafaring garb." Nehemiah laughed. "He had once a hat, and left it in the rain."

"What will he do?" I felt a surge of panic. "In London?"

"He will do as he always has." Sensing that this answer wouldn't do, Nehemiah swatted my head lightly with his palm and smiled. "Liza cares for him."

"But who will tell him about London?"

"He has been, Pearl. And I was born there."

I let my voice carry the gravity of my words. "Then you will tell him?"

"Tell him what?"

I sighed. "What it looks like."

"You do him wrong to think he can't know what he doesn't see, Pearl. He sees much without his eyes."

"He needs me."

"I wager you need him."

I veered away with my wood then, and let it rain noisily down on the growing pile.

"You might arrange them more securely," he said.

When I saw he was in earnest, I made the face I made when someone scolded and continued on my sour way. He called after me once, and then I heard the singing ax.

.   .   .

"$\mathcal{W}$e will soon be gone from here." Mother was pacing our small cabin like a madwoman when I came in. "We should feast and sing." She picked up the big kitchen knife and stamped outdoors and round to the back pen where we kept our lonely piglet. The others, including the sow, had all been traded. I followed, and cried out when she cornered him. Her eyes were wild.

"But the leaves are not turned. He's but small!"

"He'll be our dinner tomorrow noontide." She stamped for balance in the straw and muck and, taking the squealing piglet's hinder parts between her legs and the snout in her left hand, she stuck him through the heart with her long knife. He twitched and fell limp.

I winced and went forward to help her hang it. I was not unused to slaughter, quite the contrary, but I was not used to it at my mother's white hand.

"You forgot your apron." I motioned to her smeared dress, more than a little frightened. Mother never slaughtered our animals herself but traded for this task with Goodwife Baker, who grumbled the while of Mother's tenderness and took a healthy share of beer or cider in exchange. Still holding the knife, Mother wiped her cheek with the back of her hand and left a streak of blood there as well. She seemed frozen to the spot, and I took the knife from her and led her by the hand to wash.

She sat very still as I wet the hem of my sleeve and used the underside to dab at her cheek.

"Will you cry?" I threatened. "Will you leave me again?"

"Leave you?" she asked, in a stranger's voice.

"Leave your wits, I mean, and be sad, like those times before?"

She smiled. It was so trusting and luminous a smile I half believed in it. Mother rarely smiled. I helped her out of her stained gown and into the other that resembled it. Unlike my wardrobe, which was as vast and colorful as my mother's private fancy and skill with embroidery, her own dresses were an identical, dour gray. She quite ably unclasped the red "A" from the fabric puddled on the floor, shifting it to the laundered gray at her breast.

"When the pork has bled," she instructed, adjusting the hair under her cap, "boil it if you please, Pearl. The rosin's there to strip the hair, and don't let me see you've thrown out the organs." She laughed lightly, like a maid. "Mayhap I speak too soon, as I won't trouble with them now."

I blinked as she opened the door and stood silhouetted in the light.

"Mother?"

"Let us prepare a leek soup and gooseberry cream as well. Let us be merry, Pearl. We will soon be quit of him. The minister has arranged all."

"What mean you?"

"I mean we are going."

"Going *where?*" Dumbfounded, I closed my eyes and rubbed my temples. What an idea—that we should be anywhere but here, as now, always.

But when I looked up, Mother was gone.

*I*t was the strangest sensation, waiting for her to return. In truth, I didn't know for certain that she *would* return. Never had I taken such focused care with my domestic duties. I sifted the wheat and rye for maslin and mixed the sponge. Imagining myself a lonely woman grown, I banked the fires and worked flour into the bread dough. I boiled the little pig in the iron pot and scrubbed the flesh with rosin, stripping off the spiny-soft hair. I split him and carefully, methodically, cleaned the intestines for links. Fleeing the heat and the flies, I gathered young leeks from the garden and retreated, relieved, to the woods behind the cottage to forage for gooseberries.

It was during this last task, as I stood under the trees with my head bent back, watching the patch of sky there, that I felt the pain of Mother's pledge. *I mean we are going. The minister has arranged all.* A hawk swooped soundlessly to a nest hidden among the leaves, and I wondered, Would I never see this place again, these woods, the shoreline where a million of my vanished footprints were layered under the sand and tide? How large the world seemed suddenly, and how gentle the sturdy trunks, the leafy monotony of dappled light.

At least I would not be the one left behind.

I imagined Simon in his new hat, facing the touch of spray aboard the deck of the *Marietta*, his father's merchant craft. I thought of Liza working into the night, mixing conserve; Nehemiah nailing barrels closed. Now, at least, my mind could number my own chores among theirs.

Going where? *Where?* Did I dare hope . . . England?

*M*other did return, much calmed and almost secretive in her merriment, surprised by the advances I had made toward tomorrow's meal. "Tell me," I commanded—and again when she did not rally—but was soon silenced by something fragile in her expression, some shadow stowed beyond the mask of confidence.

"Come with me to the forest, Pearl. I know you love it there."

Dazed and jumpy, I let her lead me. I stumbled at her heels. I did not resume my badgering all that long walk, though there was much I ached to know. Perhaps we too were bound for bold, noisy London, where I might live by Simon always?

At length we came to the wood, and Mother shrank into its shadows, timid here where few immigrants found welcome. When I saw that she was content for my sake—if wed to her silence—I let that refuge lure me fast. I flowed in under trees that had long been the shelter of my childhood. I fashioned a haphazard crown, knitting leaves and petals into a length of vine, and then, settling the crown on my head, knelt by a pool of stale rainwater. The dark sheen that wore my face rippled and was still. The wind made a mournful quaking in the trees. Leaning to match my lips to the lips of my double in a panicked farewell, I was startled by Mother's call, and my crown dropped into the pool. *A sorry queen this is*, I thought, poking the wet mess and rising, *that will not rule her own mind.*

I tried memorizing the slant of light through the trees but was overcome when I sighted her through a gap. Flooded with sunshine, Mother might have been a forlorn figure from a faery tale, and perhaps because I knew that faery stories were not kind I ignored her pleadings—ill disguised as idle comfort. We would go now. Away to Holland. *Holland!* We would begin new, blameless lives.

Holland.

How alone we were. Alone, it seemed, we would always be. And now I would have neither Simon nor the doctor nor even the forest to soothe the monotony of my outrage.

I bounded off again, resolved to erase her from view, and tripped on a tree root. My landing startled a fox from her sleep under a thicket, and our gaze met. I lay supported by my hurt hands and looked into her eyes, and felt for an instant that my limbs were her limbs, that we shared space and size, and that her heartbeat was my heartbeat. She stood over her bed of leaves and stretched cautiously, nose twitching to take me in, and I felt my own nose twitch. We crouched thus, or I crouched and she stood firm, until the cry of a crow broke the spell and my sleepy fox fled from me in a flash of cinnamon.

Can I tell you what I remember now, so many years later, of this afternoon at the edge of wilderness? Perhaps I was no child of prophecy, but I seemed to know on that day more than I should. Seeing my mother there, out of place in my realm, I understood that even this familiar world that I knew with a wild knowledge would go on without me. Could go on. I lay listening to the pigeons' soft lullaby, the juice of partridge berries staining my lips, and heard that were I taken from this place forever, it would heal over the lack of me like a wound. There would be no trace.

It might not have mattered, such knowledge, before Simon. Before the doctor stroked my brow on the scaffold and begged forgiveness for I knew not what.

I felt the desperate weight of change on my back, and I blamed those who had left me in debt. I lay in the damp leaves among the beetles and longed to trot after the fox, out of reach. But I felt the trodden path nearby and as like smelled my own blood there in the pairing of my mother and the wild—the stain of my history, red like the "A" at Mother's breast.

*A*nd it was because I lay elbow-deep in leaves, dreaming like a fox, and did not credit her nagging, that my mother found some remnant of her old self in the forest. When silence drew me back to the clearing, I found her seated on a mossy stump. At her ease! Very much at liberty in her thoughts. Her abundant hair, lank for want of washing, spilled to her waist in the friendly sunlight, and I stood mute as the stones in the blabbering brook.

"Pearl," she said cheerfully, "you look as if you've seen a ghost."

How still she was, but her strange, laughing eyes followed me as I leapt from rock to rock, biding my time. "*Why* will you take me away?" I accused.

"Why?" she said easily. "Because I can and should. You have always been at home here, Pearl, but to me this howling wilderness is where Death lives, leering from behind every trunk. It's tiresome to dwell on it, but before I lost my good parents, before he touched me and I withered—" She sighed, and her eyes shone with bitter things unspoken. "I did not dwell much on death. And so perhaps it *is* a ghost you see before you, the faintest glimmer of that other girl who is gone now."

"*What* girl?" My voice roared as fire will through a closed barn. "*What* man made her wither?"

Mother brought a finger to her lips, and I saw the girl-ghost shimmer, uncertain. "I was reminded lately in a dream of my aunt's plump face and good voice, of the kindness of my mother's people, who dwell in a town called Leiden. It is the very town from which many of the southern pilgrims hailed. But my aunt's family stayed behind in English Alley when their fellows sailed, even as Dutch tolerance strained and war with Spain threatened anew. Mother lamented that her sister would not forsake 'the good and civilized shadow of the Pieterskerk.' My aunt's letters stopped coming after my parents passed, but I absolve her, for I had no will to reply—to explain how shame held me here."

My mother's words seemed measured enough. At another time, her nostalgia might have soothed me. But today my eyes saw a shade truly, blighting the wood. It was not her luminance or loose hair that vexed me but some offending absence.

"Come, Pearl," said she, stepping forward—more her old, resigned self again. "Let us go home now." She straightened when I gestured to the bare gray fabric of her dress. I watched the image of me in the brook likewise raise a stern finger. We stood in judgment, she and I, as I had seen many a powerful magistrate do. The woods, it seemed, the trees, were reeling.

"What is it, Pearl?" One of Mother's hands took in the front of her dress in a sensible caress. "Don't you know me, girl?" She gestured to the bank. "It's there. Look down at your feet—across the brook."

I saw the dull red lying in sunlight, and it seemed to harmonize with the silvery water. "Take it up," I threatened with a child's wrath. Surely I was holding fast to the child who would no more haunt these dappled paths. Tears seared my sight, and when I would not give them leave, the good world blurred. "It's law."

Mother stooped to retrieve her cloth brand from the bank. "I'll bear its torture a few days longer," she granted wearily. "Perhaps the forest cannot hide it, but the ocean is large enough."

Swiping fast at fugitive tears, I knew the forest could hide anything, heal over it like a wound, though it wouldn't do to say so.

With a courteous nod, Mother fastened the threadbare "A" to her dress. Next she gathered up her hair and pinned it roughly under her cap. She looked at me with dull eyes; I shall never forget the way she looked at me. "Do you know your mother now?"

*O*ur noontide meal the next day was cloaked in anxiety. Mother's foot hopped under the table like a hare, her heel tapping. Her hands shook as they passed the food we had so carefully prepared to and fro. We ate and drank of the same cup and trencher. Any splendor that might

have marked this celebratory feast was lost, for Mother's nervous de-
meanor infected me fast. I could scarce stay in my chair. The cottage,
which was dark on even the brightest days, was on this dim noon nearly
black and stank of cellar. Mother would not waste tallow, and there were
no reeds handy.

"Are we merry because tomorrow is Election Day?" I pressed, circling
the table slowly at first, then nearly skipping in my urgency to engage her.

Mother spoke not at all. A smile twitched on her lips. In the dim light,
I saw that her eyes shone with a mild, private madness. It was not the first
time I had glimpsed it there, but it was now paired to coming action.

"Be still, Pearl. Stop that dizzying."

"Will the minister walk in the procession?" I was afraid to ask more,
but the words came unbidden. "Will our Dutch relative remember your
face? Will there be forests across the sea, and foxes?"

Mother supported herself with a palm on the table. Then she stood
and began shifting objects on its surface in a mockery of tidying.

"I'll take them." I cleared it while she strode to the window. She did not
remain long, gazing with melancholy eyes at the sea as was her habit, but
broke away to orbit the room as I had the table.

"God forgive me," she said, almost hissing, "that I care so little." She
crossed to the door and let it swing shut after her, leaving me home alone
again for only the second time in my life. Eerie it was—abandonment—
even for one so used to solitude as I, who cherished it on my own terms.
But outdoors. Not here.

Our dank cottage by the shore, like many homes far from town, had
little to commend it to comfort. My ragged-stitched samplers, the stained
tapestry of Eden, and the buzz of flies seemed to mock motherless me, and
I felt a sudden panic as if the prince of Hell himself had entered the cottage
unseen or sent his demons to swirl about the musty air. The dark crackled
now with menace. I felt suddenly the clay of the packed earth beneath my
bare feet and fancied the room a grave, and that the chorus of swirling
demons I couldn't see conspired to haul me fast below.

.　.　.

*N*ehemiah was in the yard when I came crashing through the brush in unbuckled shoes, my face stained with tears. He let me fly into his arms and held me hard, as from habit. He muttered and cleared his throat and stood back, stunned. You'd think he'd been kicked in the skull by a horse. He glanced first at the ground and then, sheepishly, at me. "Merciful Heaven." He looked more boy than man in that moment, though his firm embrace, so fleeting, had soothed the sobs from me. "What plagues you, Pearl?"

But I couldn't speak. How could I explain?

Simon's face appeared in the window. "What is it?"

"Pearl is afflicted," Nehemiah answered.

In a moment, Simon appeared at his brother's side. They stood there and studied me with their separate methods as if I would shoot sparks or grate out a shrill song like the blacksmith's anvil.

Cross now, I smeared a hand through the last of my tears. "I was only frightened." When the wretches kept at their vigil, I began to squirm with warmth, doubting that I knew them at all. I felt my too-loud voice at my throat before I could stop it. "Is it a *sin,* then?"

They exchanged a wordless look, though Simon, of course saw nothing. Crickets roared in the fields.

I stamped my foot. "Then damn me to Hell."

Simon hushed me and sought again for my mouth. He was always silencing me because his world was much too loud, I think, like thunder, and mine was too much my own.

Nehemiah laughed lightly and took my hand and Simon's in his other, and Simon let my mouth be and groped for my free hand, and we stood thus linked and wordless in the warm sun. It was only for an instant, but that instant has been my candle in the darkest moments of my life.

Remember me

*M*other dressed me like a doll the morning of our grandest public holiday. She combed my curls and produced a ribbon from her sleeve like a minstrel from Elizabeth's day. She babied me, holding open my scarlet Sabbath dress so that I might step in without deflowering my hair, and I let her do it. My clean shift smelled of lavender and the sun.

As she leaned close to dab at my face with her handkerchief, I heard a faint tune in her throat, a ballad lighter than a lullaby, with less intent. It disturbed rather than soothed my mood, which was already stirred by last evening's anguished wait. Restored to confidence now, I wiggled to be free of her, but first Mother kissed my forehead and laughed the airy, unfamiliar laugh that so troubled my wits in those, our last days together on New World soil.

Simon and Nehemiah would watch the procession, I knew, and of course attend the meeting where our pastor was to give the Election Day sermon. Even before we arrived at the market square, I heard the merry murmur of voices, the grunt of wrestlers, the squeal and clatter of horns and jostled beasts and fowl. Two men stood on the platform of the pillory exhibiting with broadsword and buckler as we hurried past, Mother gripping too hard my arm. The crowd mocked and encouraged, and the beadle hollered at the sportsmen to make haste and come down. None glanced at us as we passed this infamous site, for Mother was as shadowy as ever in gray—even her lone red ornament seemed a shadow this morning—and there was in the square a bright blur of new arrivals from every side. There were the dark-clad townsfolk I saw regularly, but also hearty frontiersmen in buckskin, and solemn painted heathens in groups of two or three. Mistress Tibbins, Governor Bellingham's sister, stood in velvet finery gossiping with a wide-eyed servant; the girl dared not walk away as would the gentlefolk who knew their neighbor to be a witch.

But most colorful of all were the mariners, especially the commander of a vessel from the Spanish Main—possibly the very ship on which we would sail away to Holland—with his gold trim and ribbons and sword scar. Mother kept hold of my arm, looking hawkishly here and there. When the novelty of color wore off, I too cast into the crowd for Simon and Nehemiah. When I found them—Nehemiah with his arm woven tight through his brother's—I could not convince Mother to let me go. Her distraction was such, and the noise of the square so great, that to pull her ear to my lips at all took violence. I nearly ripped her sleeve. "Simon is there!" I cried, pointing eagerly. "Let me go to him."

"Not now, Pearl. Stay close at hand."

I realized with sadness that my anxious parent knew and cared not for whom I pined. His name was of no account to her. "I'll go to him—" I broke free and scarce heard her complaints if there were any. I nearly knocked Simon over with my haste, but was stopped short by his father, whom I recognized from the funeral proceedings for Mistress Weary of this World.

A big, sun-dark man with gray-black hair combed carefully under his beaver hat, Caleb Milton surveyed my intrusion with such open curiosity that Nehemiah stepped forward, pulling Simon with him to explain me. "This is Pearl," he offered apologetically, "the sprite who's presumed to air Simon out of doors."

"Well, then." He took up my hand in his fine glove and kissed it, smiling at the warmth in my face. "I greet you with all due gratitude, Pearl. Our Simon is treasure to few, but shines all the greater in our affections for it." One glance at Nehemiah's mock gravity and Simon's sheepishness had me choking back mirth.

Caleb Milton thumped me lightly on the back and tipped his hat. "Go on then, Pearl. Laugh. It's a day for laughter." He craned his neck and became again a man of worth and worldly concern. "Nehemiah, I see there our ill-tempered customs officer. Let us converse with him."

Simon blushed, and his father lifted his younger son's chin. "Go with your faery friend, Simon. We will fetch you by and by, before the sermon."

I bounced on my heels before finding composure and accepting, once more, Simon's hand. But it was his father's gift this time, for Nehemiah seemed almost unwilling to let Simon go. He looked back over his shoulder as he walked away with his father, and it was, I understood later, the pitiable look of the boy inside the man.

*W*e spied, choosing one and then another from the multitude to follow, and I apprised Simon of each subject's every move. There was the wench who let a man mutter and moan into her neck in the rear of the churchyard until our giggles stopped them short and he stamped off, leaving her with a crooked cap. We were perplexed by the plaintive shape of Dr. Devlin, who stood like a statue some distance from the meeting-house, where people were already beginning to throng. "He doesn't move a muscle," I told Simon, who begged me to describe the Indians instead. "Perhaps his heart has stopped."

"Do the heathens wear bright feathers, Pearl? Have they hatchets?"

"There are pirates too!" I half forgot the doctor, who at that very moment perhaps had fixed his gaze on Mother in the crowd—a lamb in a lightning field. "Desperadoes from the high seas, Simon, with palm-leaf hats and gold on their belts. Their beards are shaggy and they smoke tobacco to spite the beadle."

Simon sighed with pleasure. "Do you see my father?"

"Forget them a while," I sighed, looking on the dark visage of the doctor. "We have but little time left before we both sail away and apart forever."

"Both?"

"Mother would deliver us to her old Dutch aunt."

"You will come to the Old World?"

I shrugged without thinking. "I see Witch Tibbins circling my mother on her broom."

Simon jerked my arm forward. "They're coming! I hear the drum and clarion."

Soon enough I heard the military music approaching, but I was too much interested in the witch to relent. "The procession will take its time." I tugged Simon along to the shadow of the pillory. A small, scarcely discernable emptiness of space had formed round my mother and Mistress Tibbins, and I kept us to the border of that crowd. Replete in her elegant triple ruff and velvet gown, Governor Bellingham's sister carried a gold-headed cane, and her hand shook in balance, the knuckles white with leaning.

"Simon," I hissed, "the witch has hold of Mother's arm." Simon was caught up in the approaching music, and I saw that he would stamp his feet and march had shyness not its grip on him.

The procession entered the square then, and the music seemed instantly close and loud, as if it had been let through a doorway. The crowd murmured and cheered as a magnificent column of soldiers and magistrates strode past. It was impossible not to revere them in their steel and embroidery, shoulders squared, high white heads crowned with plumed morions or steepled hats. I stood transfixed a long moment, and small. I knew not what shamed me but that I was, despite my scarlet dress, a common brown bird in a jungle bright. Mother too, with her begging gaze, seemed reduced in the wake of this glittering snake that flowed into the meetinghouse.

I can only imagine, even as a woman grown, how her heart must have shriveled at first sight of the minister. He seemed insanely grand and simple among all those fine old men, lit behind his eyes with an ardor neither love nor pity could penetrate. He walked between and past us like a splendid stranger, no longer the good and accessible counselor who had sworn assistance by the seashore but a holy man at Heaven's brink. Perhaps Mother's woes had hurried him there, but hers were crowded among many, and he was gone from all now.

"Simon—" I shook his arm. "The minister knows me not."

Simon's face questioned, but he did not speak. When the tail of the snake vanished through the meetinghouse doors and the assembled began to filter after, I crossed into the emptiness around Mother. Mistress Tibbins had let my parent—caught in a dream between the pillory and the procession—drift some distance, and I let fall Simon's hand to go to her.

"Mother," I said as softly as the din around us would allow, "has the minister forsaken us? Will he yet escort us aboard and speak for us?"

Mother held a finger to her lips, and her eyes seemed to me blanker than Simon's.

As if beckoned, Mistress Tibbins returned to nurse on our woe. "This minister!" she chimed. "You know him, mistress, the same man who waters your secret with his cleric's tears?"

Mother took a step back, though I was lulled by the woman's voice, which seemed not the cracked pealing of a hag but the voice of an altogether younger woman. "Madam," my mother said, "I speak not lightly of a learned and pious minister—"

"No, indeed. Nor would he or any man speak for you in your time of need. Your own mother's ghost came to me in a dream. She looked on in shame as he took you."

The old woman turned from Mother's colorless face with a faint smile and leaned close as if to kiss me. Backing away, I heard through her strange and barbarous laughter the minister's voice—as if for the first time—spilling from the meetinghouse. I made out not its words but only the muffled music of them, the rise and fall of a mood that seemed to transcend time and place. I felt that voice snuff out all else around me until Simon came swimming into my mind's eye. I realized then that I had left him behind in the crowd. "Simon?" I rasped.

I whirled about, looking. I searched the faces, each tuned to that voice—now rising, now falling. I began to elbow and shove and cry out Simon's name, but the bodies stood like trees in a dense wood, unmoving. The minister had captured the crowd, and me with it.

"Simon, here I am—"

I panicked to think of him alone and dark among these captive souls, with only that unearthly voice for comfort. I ran as far as the crowd would allow, turning and turning and shouting. I would have left my body then if I could. That was what the dying minister's wordless sermon told me to do. Fly above, apart, away. But I would leave my body puddled on the market square and soar above the other sinners not to free my soul, but to keep my promise to Simon.

*N*ehemiah found him first. When I at last thought to steer my search to the rear of the chapel, they were there against the shaded wall. Simon's face was pale and tear-tracked. Had I imagined before that day that blind eyes couldn't shed them? "Please," I said, and it was all I could bring myself to say.

Simon stepped away from the safety of the wall and chafed both wet cheeks with his palms. He winced, and his long fingers fairly tore through his hair in his anguish to smooth it back and compose himself. He held out his arm, and instinctively Nehemiah reached for it, and I knew that neither of them, now, would reach for me. My eyes implored Nehemiah, but his were pitiless.

"Leave my sight, Pearl."

I tried to bar their way, but Nehemiah thrust his palm at me and shook his head gravely. I backed away.

"Simon—" I said, but a great murmur sounded beyond in the crowd, as if the sermon had struck a particularly lofty note. "Please look at me."

Simon straightened as if to speak, but Nehemiah spoke for him. "He *doesn't* see, Pearl. Why in God's name can't you remember that?"

I watched, stunned, as the crowd swallowed them. So many events troubled my mind and eye and ear that day that I could scarce comprehend my part in any of them. *Remember me,* a voice roared inside my head, deafening my wits. I found Mother with a press of strange gossips from Newtown or Roxbury or some other outlying settlement all around her. She turned from their quiet venom again and again, but they quickly reassembled to have her red letter in view. Even the seamen and Indians were drawn anew into the old drama of Mother's infamy, loitering nearby with raised eyebrows while the gossips hissed. And through it all, my pain at watching Mother stripped of privacy, the memory of Simon, whom I had betrayed, and of his brother's scorn, wove the eerie rise and fall of the minister's voice. Why did he sound so? I think now that he was already gone (and counting it a mercy) and that we, his flock, heard in his Election Day voice the coming silence.

Nervous affliction soon had me racing round the square like an unbroken horse. I danced and leapt and gravitated toward the bright, scarred shipmaster, who laughed a hearty laugh and tried to seize and tease me. When he couldn't, he tossed me the gold chain from his hat to play with. I wound it round my neck and my waist, hovering near his strength and size as if I might, by charming him, invest in his defense. For the first time I was aware of using charm that way, a woman's way, to exact protection.

"Your mother is yonder woman with the red letter. . . ." Coaxing me forward with a smile, he snatched the chain back, unraveled it from me as if I were a golden bobbin. "Will you bring a message for me?"

"If the message pleases me, I will."

The revoked chain settled with a soft *chink* in his waistcoat pocket. "Tell her I have just conferred with Dr. Devlin. The gentleman says he will— should an escort prove required—meet you both aboard ship this evening, after he's cleared his lodgings. We sail for Holland at sundown."

*M*other only stared past me when I brought this news, then met my eye long enough to slap me for wandering. The press of gawking strangers had gradually eased her back almost to the pillory, but they seemed of little account now that she wore again her familiar veil of resignation. Her plans, whatever they were, had unraveled. The plaintive voice that had so moved the crowd now ceased, and a great silence followed. For a moment the hush in the square was so profound it frightened me. Then an uproar ensued as people began to spill out of the church exclaiming over the minister's sermon.

Mother pulled me close and squeezed my shoulders when the music resumed and the procession began to snake its way outdoors. In an instant, a great chanting welled up. The stamp and roar of applause followed the priests and soldiers and civic fathers on their stately path, but it was the saintly minister for whom the people cheered. He who had burst shining into the square seemed in full daylight drained of color and weight—a bloodless, wavering creature of the air. He looked, as well, a little fierce. And for the first time in my life, I trusted him.

Once Reverend Wilson stepped back to assist him, but the young minister waved a hand and grimaced. The man who had once plucked my infant form like treasure from the sea was very near now. When the crowd, stamping and clapping, parted to let him pass, I almost broke from Mother and ran to him, consumed by a pity I had never before experienced, not even earlier behind the chapel for Simon, for myself. I could see as well as anyone where the minister's hallowed footfalls carried him. He walked on, and we watched him go. All of Boston watched him go, and he did not come back.

Word filtered out in fits and starts that he had collapsed inside the parsonage. And when at length this news reached Mother, like a rank apple passed from hand to hand, she buckled at the knees. She knelt among the Election Day crowd in Market Square, her body drained of all resolution, and I found myself in sympathy not with my unhappy parent but with a confused and changeful public. Thwarted in their merriment, the promise of a day's release and enjoyment broken, their hunger unmet, they came to chaos. There was weeping and sighing aplenty, expressions of abject disbelief, but my mother was an easy object of contempt, and contempt is easier to bear than disappointment. When the constable came to force a harlot overcome with emotion to her feet—cursing at what looked to be her stubbornness—the crowd turned evil. Had she dashed out the brains of a sucking infant, their displeasure could not have been greater, their insults more harsh. "The Lord shall deal bitterly with you!" one among them cried repeatedly. I felt a soft weight on my shoulders as the marshals parted that sea of louts, lifted my mother bodily, and carried her away.

THE VOICE OF THE WORLD

*H*ere *I am.*

Here, I mused as the new day dawned, *is the truth my senses tell me. I am small. My curves rhyme with the sky.* Always there has been a voice that flows through me as a current races under an opposing tide. It's the voice of the world, all things at once, and I hear it when I strain to: hawks slicing air, the ferns unfurling, fishes breathing black, circling the depths, the serpent curling through crisp leaves. This voice soothes me in the worst of times.

Thus, even with Mother nearby in the stocks, the gray fabric of her back streaked with spit and rotten peel, I felt no fear that morning when her quickened breath joined the earth's chorus, when he came as from nowhere, stepping from a dark place in my vision.

The night before, the marshals had shooed me back into a jeering crowd while they fastened Mother in. Liza took me in hand amid shouts and jostling, but no sooner were we home in the little cottage by the bay—Liza snoring like a tempest in Mother's featherbed—than I fled out to the starry dark again. How else abide the thought of my parent slumped all night in a blanket of filth and mosquitoes? Too weary to lift her head when I bounded back into the now abandoned clearing, Mother only hissed, "Hide yourself." So I was well concealed by hedges when he came with the blue of first light. Sore awake and cold in my bed of leaves, I blinked and rubbed my eyes.

He is the devil, I decided anew. For he came to her with such purpose, his hair wild and black as a wet pelt. His walk was unpredictable, measured and lurching, and he wore neither a gentleman's sad-colored garments and ruff nor a farmer's garb but plain wool breeches, a white linen shirt that glowed in the early light, and no hat. He seemed serene one moment and dizzying—flickering, unsteady as an apparition—the next. His voice was jagged like his gait, a deep singsong that would not let the listener rest.

"Good morning!" the doctor called in a merry tone, and I saw Mother crouch and stiffen at his approach. She tried to draw her ankles from the holes in the wood, but the stocks held her fast, and her head swung away, draping to one side like a flag battered by wind.

"Yes, the rumors are truth." With his back to me, I inched closer along the hedgerow, parting the leaves. "I am returned to find you more or less where I left you and worse for wear . . . if such thing be possible." He dabbed at the wood of the stocks with his knuckles. "I've been to call on all my old fellows now and have even encountered our imp, Pearl." I strained forward at mention of my name, and he knelt. "Did she tell you?"

He reached out gingerly as if the touch might singe him, with first a faint brush of fingertips and then more roughly, turning her chin to him. When Mother would not meet his eyes, he rose, proceeding to pace like a man well satisfied with the direction of his thoughts. It was clear he didn't value but squandered his words, for they tumbled out in a reckless way, as if they too were like to burn him.

"You should have heard the worthies at the inn, devising your punishment. 'To the scaffold!' they cried. 'There to lament dragging the pastor's name rudely to earth even as that cherished soul made his ascent.' Righteous mouths dropped open when I reminded them that such measure was, in this case, mere repetition. That your first public shaming—indeed, the ever-glowering red letter at your breast—has done little to snuff your pride. That humility is, these many years later, still a stranger to your heart.

"Imagine the abundant grave murmuring, the mighty bobbing of wigged heads. 'Why not,' I humbly submitted, 'bring her low instead of elevating her once more on the scaffold, where those of baser nature might mistake her for a martyr? Are not the stocks appropriate censure for a woman who sinks to her knees before the multitudes . . . who weeps for a man who was in every way her better and a comet for the Lord? Why not,' I went on, well pleased with my innovation, 'leave her outdoors to face alone what will skulk from the wilderness? Let her privately and earnestly reflect, with due assistance from the night, on her black nature, and the infinite and fearful loneliness that awaits the sinner hereafter.'"

Some sudden movement made Mother flinch. "And lo, here you are. I guess I schemed that I should come to you here. Did it frighten you, the night? Do I frighten you? Was the weather kind? Will you have my pity?"

He resumed pacing, his theme shifting direction with his stride. "Would that I had killed him, past friendship notwithstanding, but I wager it was too much maniacal flailing, paired with an excess of melancholic black bile. Too many holy words hurled like bricks from the pulpit. It was bound to happen to one so frail. There are even absurd rumors—so I learned when I floated your name among the greedy minnows of this town—that he was the father of your bastard. Hence your shameful display of emotion yesterday. Hence the righteous alarm of our town fathers."

He paced before her, hands held primly behind his back. "'*Was*'? You ache to ask. I see it in your eyes." Again his face darkened, as if two moods were at war in him. "You would beg of the Lord God or the universe or even a mere physician: Can there be no hope for his recovery? I'm afraid 'was' is the word. I examined him myself."

I knew I should look at my mother, study how this dire news fashioned her face so that I might do my best to soothe away the lines and pain there later, but it was him I couldn't look away from. "I regret to report," he went on, "that he was marble cold, if flawless as an infant. Speaking of infants, where is our live specimen? Perhaps I'll take her with me when I leave these shores. She is mine, after all, as much as yours."

Mother's head began to sway, buffeted it seemed by invisible slaps. How mute and deflated she was. Had he bewitched her? Did a specter have her in thrall? I felt fury rear in me that she would not find strength to fight his onslaught, spit on him at least. I felt too, again, a fascination beyond recall. I could not unpeel my gaze from his angled jaw, his tireless mouth. Was it true? Was he my own one?

Mother smacked lips bloated with thirst. I thought to run and fetch cider for her but was, even without stocks to hold me, as much a captive audience as she. Mother tried to speak but failed even to hold up her head, so he lifted it with a fist under her chin.

"Did you love our late minister?"

"He listened." Her voice issued like a rusty hinge. "He gave me comfort. You begrudge me that?"

"You would not have wanted for comfort in my care."

Mother's laughter rang out hideous through the square. I feared it would wake the dead that dawn, never mind those whose sleeping shops and dwellings formed the edge of Market Square.

"I would have righted all, in time, were we wed."

"I'll have no husband now."

He leaned forward, tracing her mouth with the flat of his thumb. The hoarse tenderness in his voice made my cheeks burn. "I *am* sorry."

"Good, Daniel." She closed her eyes as if to blot him from her sight. "God retrieve you, then."

"God is dead to me." He seemed astonished by this, his own blasphemy. "He died when you did not."

"Then you're beyond saving."

For an instant more his face loomed, and he looked to breathe her in. "And so, it seems, are you. Your ship has sailed to Leiden. Yes, earnest Arthur at his end would shelter no more secrets. What will you do? And of more interest, am I so rank that you flee *now*—when the wrath of Puritan Boston year after year did not unsettle you?"

Standing, he swerved away with a roar that for all its beastly urgency lacked conviction, as if he'd long since worn the feeling behind it thin. "I would rage or plead my case further, but you may as well know: I have a wife and infant back in England, and these I will cherish as I should have cherished you and the child had you allowed it, had you forgiven—" he waved his arms—" as you would have this merciless place forgive you."

His pacing brought him so near my hedgerow veil that I heard the leaves stir. "When the boy was born, sliding into my hands, I thought of little else but you, bearing yours alone those long years ago on prison straw. I cooled my wife's hot brow, saw that her milk had come, installed her quarrelsome sister, and set out at once for the shipyards."

"Why will you not go to them?"

"Credit me this—" His voice broke, and she winced. "That you would have had me once. That I might have courted and won you if not for my grievous error. Don't look so, mistress. It will pain me more to know it might have been thus—and revenge you better."

He tried and tried to lift her chin more, but she labored to keep her eyes from him.

"I'm sworn to heal and yet again my hands wish to harm you for your power over me—"

"Your kindness has harmed me most of all."

"I saved your life."

Mother looked up for the first time of her own accord, full in his startled face. "And then soiled it."

I felt such pity for him, though I must have understood now that he was beyond pity's reach.

"As a young man in London," he went on, "I oft lurked in playhouses, a frustrated scribbler. That instinct has lately returned, and so I am writing your story, our story, from which I am surgically removed for your sake. How will I tell it? Shall I give you a nobler lover?"

He ranted about the minister—*a* minister, not our lately pastor any more than a sparrow is a hawk—and a crippled sorcerer, as bitter in aspect as the potions he brewed. He invoked demons and strangers and stageworthy lives as if these could be of use to us now. "Will you not take passion over loathing? Cannot life become art," he roared at the end of it, "to save itself? I confess, the quill falters in my hand in a way the scalpel does not, but history, at least, should revenge you."

"Spare me more words," came Mother's weary whisper.

"But how then shall I be *punished*?" The doctor's hollow eyes did not jest, but I could scarce unravel mockery from mourning in his voice. He paused a long while, as if he too was concentrating on the voice of the world, and then he turned on his heel. "Pray," he called back, "remember me . . . who looks out from your child's eyes."

A GOOD DEATH

We would not see the minister buried. Though Mother was released well before his interment, a messenger came to our cottage at sunup bearing a letter sealed by the governor or good Reverend Wilson or another town father. Mother would not say which one. I expect that the simple words she read aloud were meant to relegate us to shame and retrieve their young saint from ill association.

Pity his memory.

No one came to the cottage to tell of the eulogy or inquire after us, and Mother did not budge from the mattress. As I ordered and reordered the room, needlessly shifting linen and ladles and baskets about—craving, above all, a purpose—I saw Mother in a corner of my vision, her arm flung ominously over a side of the bed

When the sun began to set that day, and when I had lifted her limp wrist and let it drop, whispered and pleaded, dabbed her head with a dripping cloth, and tried to roll her toward me, I panicked and began to blubber. I sat on the floor and screamed, covering my ears against the noise of my voice, but no one came. Mother lay curled like a shrimp, breathing but no more living than was the minister. Crows shrieked back in the trees outside, the ocean slept, and at length I understood that the demons would come for us both if I did not move. I left the cottage, half believing I would find the doctor out waiting in our field of rye, but that field was bare, and I fled to my old familiar path through the woods to the beech tree.

"Simon!" I braved the open sunlight by the fence, waiting until the shake left my voice. "Simon, come out—"

Nehemiah appeared briefly in the window and folded the casements closed.

"You will come out to me, Simon!" I had never heard that voice before, the one that escaped my hoarse throat—shrill and commanding but laced with a desperate compassion only lately learned.

He did come out, but with Liza bustling behind. She yanked the fugitive back, and I heard Simon protest and the side door slam. Then Liza returned, arms crossed and lips set in a stern line. She was still angry no doubt that I had eluded her to go sit by Mother in the stocks, and had surely heard of my misadventure with Simon. I must have looked a fright because her rock face collapsed into softness, and she came to me at once and let me cry against her scratchy forearm. I couldn't speak, and she brushed the matted hair from my face. "What new tragedy is this, child?"

I hiccuped and licked the salt from my lips but still could not speak, so she eased me against her bosom, which smelled faintly of vinegar, and held me until I stopped. When I'd exhausted myself, she leaned back to look at my raw face, touched a forefinger to her lips, and brought it to my lips; this simple gesture gave me the strength to tell her that Mother wouldn't budge.

*L*iza and I spoke little on the narrow path back to the cottage. It took longer than usual as Liza puffed and grew red in the face and cross at the brambles I let snap back and hit her. Our boots crackled sticks and startled a quail from her hidden nest. The air felt and smelled of rain and my heart raced, but I wasn't weeping now, and when we came at last to the clearing—where a dark cloud mass huddled over the sea—and to and through the cottage door, nothing had changed. Mother was still limp but breathing, still absent.

"Cold water." Liza knelt by the bed. "Run for a bucket of the sea to slap her to her senses." With one rough heave, she rolled Mother toward us, gasping to see her waxy stare. My beautiful mother, dark hair loose from its pins and spread under her like a bloodstain, was neither asleep nor awake, like one enchanted. I flew for our pitcher and ran down to the shoreline, breathing deep of salt and fish and freedom. I stood perhaps a moment longer than I should, listening to the rush of the tide, and then I did something I rarely did unless chided. I prayed.

But God must have fancied it a selfish prayer, for He spat my words back at me in the form of rain, and once it started, it didn't stop. The water in my pitcher when I returned was part earth, part air, and woke Mother soundly. Liza tried everything else first. She begged and cajoled and threatened. "I'll hate to leave you sleeping in a soaking bed this night, miss. You and Pearl will catch your deaths. But see if I won't. See if I won't empty this bucket full in your face."

So she did. Mother's eyes widened like flowers at the sun's touch, and she sat up spitting and shrieking, and then whimpered like a babe for us to leave her alone.

"We'll do no such thing." Liza fished out Mother's hairpins one by one from the tangle of dripping chestnut hair and pulled Mother to her feet to undress her. The first thing she did was slowly, almost reverently, to unfasten the worn cloth "A" on Mother's chest, but Mother groped weakly to get it back.

"You won't be needing that now, miss, in the privacy of your home."

Mother glowered at us and her voice cracked. "You have no earthly idea what I need."

"Haven't I, then?"

Mother licked her dry lips and considered the older woman a moment; I feared she might bend low and bite Liza's hand. "I'll have it back, please."

Liza handed the badge to me. "So be it. But out of that soiled dress first." Liza tapped Mother's side. "Lift those arms."

Mother lifted them but seemed too feeble to hold them up. Her weakness and black-shadowed eyes frightened me, but Liza was my champion now, and I watched her work—tugging and crimping and buttoning—as one watches her own triumphs in a dream.

When Mother was fully dressed, and I had pinned the scarlet letter back by her heart, and she was seated stiff as a doll in her rocker with embroidery idle in her lap, Liza pulled me aside, kneeling, and whispered close to my face. I did not recoil at the sight of her black back teeth or at her breath, sweetened with mint but far from sweet.

"I'll bring Master Milton now," she whispered. "He's busy, with the voyage upon us, but he'll know what to do. Mistress had her share of afflictions." Then she turned and barked out my mother's name.

Mother started but didn't look up from her lap.

"Rise now!" Liza said.

At last, Mother raised her head.

"What you *need,* I'll have you know, is to care for this child." Liza stood and brushed her dress smooth with one authoritative hand. She nodded once at me and walked to the door. "There is no sin more foul than despair."

*W*hile we waited, I shook the rain out of my hair and brushed Mother's. The rain had stopped as quickly as it had begun, and now, with Liza gone, the world was hushed and solemn. I hummed the lullaby I remembered best, and absently Mother began to hum it with me. She never could resist a tune. Her head, though, did not sit firm against the tug of the brush as it normally would but listed here and there, and her hand hung over the chair edge. I steadied her head as I worked, as if she were my puppet.

"Won't you finish Dame Ashley's gorget now, Mother? I won't learn a thing if you don't ply her." I moved the limp hand up to rest on the embroidery in her lap.

Mother didn't smile. She seemed not to hear my voice at all. Alone with her, I felt again the hot breath of fear at my neck, but soon there was murmuring and a crunch of footfalls on the shell fragments of the garden path. They came in through the back, first Master Caleb with Liza and then, to my astonished relief, Daniel Devlin.

Mother assumed once more her stance from the stocks, pulling back in aversion with downcast eyes and flared nostrils. When he approached and caught her wrist to arrest her movement, she yanked it from his grasp.

"You will," he commanded, "look to me now for the help that should have reached you before."

He tried, kneeling before her, to take her cheeks in his hands and turn her face, but wily Mother only closed her eyes. *How like a child she is,* I thought, and it was a funny, searing thought because it explained so well my recent terrors.

"I'll take nothing from you," she murmured.

The doctor seemed to despair of her words and cast a helpless, almost apologetic look at Master Milton.

The other man, clearly bewildered, leaned alongside the pair. "Good woman," he said, "what are your plans?"

She opened her eyes to look at him, and I could tell that the presence of Simon's father in the room unnerved or embarrassed her, but still she kept mum.

"Please say," he repeated, "what plans you have on behalf of your child, Pearl?"

"Pearl," Mother said, in a scant whisper, "is an orphan."

Her words chilled me, but it was Liza who roared: "How dare you!" She edged in next to the men and took Mother's shoulders fiercely, rocking her forward. "An orphan's life is no life at all. Get up and do what God gave you to do. Bear what He gave you to bear."

Mother glowered at her, but when Caleb Milton spoke again—in a deep voice that reminded me of Simon—she retreated into her sightless stare. "He died a good death."

"Few have died better," put in the doctor, shaking his head as if to ward off sarcasm or some other, darker inflection, "or more revered."

"Ah, but her pastor died," scolded Liza. "And herself can think of little but herself."

"You know me not!" Mother croaked, her eyes cornered and half mad, and I saw a baffled Caleb Milton quit the room.

"I know you," the kneeling doctor said, laying his forehead on her arm. She leaned away from his weight and nearness. *"Do I not?"* the doctor went on, the dark pulse of his voice muffled in her sleeve, his black hair snaking in her lap. He raised his head tentatively, like a contrite child awaiting a slap. "And should your strength fail you so late—"

Liza didn't gasp exactly, but her surprise drew from Mother a great raging sob that forced the doctor's retreat. Restored to himself, he paced apart as Mother shook and roared. None now went to her. Who could? Caleb Milton, who had perhaps held a gentleman's vigil outside the door, returned to the fray, his tone paternal and businesslike. "The doctor tells me you were to sail to Leiden?" When Mother did not reply, he went on, "Good woman, I have a corner for you and your child aboard the *Marietta.* We are bound in the end for London, and from there you can easily find passage to Leiden. The people here will tend the minister's memory. He belongs to them now. You and your child are an impediment."

Mother's stare briefly blackened Daniel Devlin, resting almost imperceptibly on his stricken face. I saw them together in that moment *for* a moment as my parents; they were an unwholesome match at best, but in that moment I was whole. This unlikely notion eclipsed even the idea of the minister lying hard and still under the earth, even my anguish for Simon and Nehemiah, even rats aboard the *Marietta* and sea serpents in the deep, even the thrill and stench of London. But it was a moment only, for Mother could not keep the hatred long from her eyes.

"We will stay," she said firmly. "Our home is here."

"It will be less homely than ever it has been," said my father, "even with me gone. The minister has always acted on your behalf, interceding where need be, but no more—and now you have waked a sleeping dragon. Pearl will suffer."

"Pearl knows no other life."

"But why?" asked Caleb Milton kindly. "Must she suffer? She knows no sin."

"She is naught *but* sin." Mother turned wearily from the men to Liza, her voice desperate, rising. "They sat me in the stocks because they suspect me. They don't know it yet, but they do. They'll wake and say I sank to my knees to cut him down. Perhaps, at length, they'll claim I killed our minister with black arts and brand us witch or worse if we flee."

"Mayhap." Liza stepped forward and touched her arm lightly. "And they may do so if you stay."

"They were affronted by your arrogance, not black arts," the pacing doctor announced. "I will remain behind and account for you." I watched his fingers trail along the wall and linger on Mother's embroidered panel of Eden, as if to trace the serpent's coils. "I'll describe your repentance in a wilderness settlement south of here and assure them that Pearl's education is well in hand. Calmer heads will prevail," he said assuredly. "Public memory is short if robbed of fodder."

"But *why* will you, sir?"

He whirled on Mother and his voice echoed through the dim cottage like a pistol shot. "I *will,* and my will must be understood."

Mother looked down at her hands, resting on the embroidery. They seemed to seek the needle and thread as solace, but she laid them flat. "I'll not thank you." Her gaze darted from one face to the next, settling on the doctor, who could not meet her fierce eye. "I'll never thank you."

"Nor forgive. I know it, and I relinquish you. Let me do what little I can here, and then—"

Everyone waited in stunned silence, it seemed, for some finality to pass his lips. He only trailed off: "But allow me this."

Caleb Milton, who was either at a complete loss or too offended to delay, strode to the door. "I'll send my son with a wagon. You'll be ready at sunup?"

"We will, sir," I blurted, but Liza embraced me from behind, hush-hushing and absently smoothing curls behind my ears.

Mother lifted her head in a faint nod, and Mr. Milton waited firmly but discreetly with a hand on the knob for the doctor. And a long, aggrieved moment it was; my father clearly longed for some closure, some offering or farewell that she would not grant, and he consumed us both with greedy, gold-flecked eyes. At length, he came and kissed me fast on my forehead, his hot palms hard at my jaw.

Liza regarded his passing with a darker shade of her master's confused disapproval, then bent and whispered to me on her own way out, "Don't let her from your sight."

J removed the samplers and Mother's panel from the wall, yanked the damp linen from the bed, and stuffed all into the trunk. We slept covered by our cloaks on the bare, wet mattress that night, and when once my cold feet woke me—or the thought of Nehemiah coming with the sunrise—I slipped outdoors. Keeping the cottage door open and my ears alert, I surveyed the sea and the wood line across the basin, the hollyhock stalks swaying in the garden breeze. I breathed in cedar and salt marsh, rank and fresh at once, and listened for the owl, the snuffling and rooting of wild pigs, the harmonizing of crickets back in Goodman Baker's fields. I looked often toward the meadow, but each time I did, it was empty. Was Daniel Devlin out there somewhere now, roaming with his staff as before? Haunted by my mother, he would now haunt me, it seemed. I understood that I would not see him more; he would not come again to the line to barter. I had found and lost him in a single season, my last of childhood.

What I had taken from his startling interview with my mother by the stocks was that I was not part elfin, nor any portion otherworldly, demon or pixie, as all Boston would have had me believe. I was only human. The voice of the world told me so, but I had—will ever henceforth have— only human words to answer with.

Inside I fed the embers but felt confined by the hearth and sought again the damp, black air with a mug of cider to quell my thirst. There was little moon that night, but I shivered and studied the faint pattern of stars till my neck ached. I recalled stories of those who lived among them, the hunter and bear, the crab and bull; unlikely though it was, I seemed to re- member a man's voice telling those stories to me as a small child. What man? The minister? Perhaps I had been a colicky babe, and Master Brack-ett, the jailer, had regaled me. I know it was not my father.

Who was Cassiopeia, whose name echoed like a spell? Why did I re-member only names and fragments, and why didn't I see what others saw? To me there were a million pictures in the stars, but I saw no hunter, no bull. I could identify the great ladle in the sky, and that was all. I thought of Simon, who saw nothing others saw, and it was only when I looked down at my cold hands and found a tear on my wrist that I realized I was crying again.

Mother's voice from the threshold startled me, and when she came and sat and pulled me shivering beneath her cloak like a great black bird taking me under its wing, I let myself sob openly. I blubbered on about the stars until Mother kissed my brow.

"They are the same stars in England, Pearl."

Words.

She rocked me beside her and her hair spilled over me like water, and she whispered the words over and over because she could not know they were a lie. "The same stars everywhere."

I was asleep in Mother's chair by the hearth when Nehemiah arrived, stony-faced, to retrieve us. I saw in his eyes that a question or two would not permit him to be quit of me. We loaded the wagon without a word. Mother, whose face wore no expression at all, helped little, but our awkward labor was brief. How pitiful, I thought, that a lifetime could be reduced to a trunk and a few sacks. I stood a while in the dank and cheer-less cottage after Nehemiah had carried out the last of it, yet felt nothing for the dirt room without its contents.

It was the waking world outside that I mourned as we passed, bumping along on the wagon. The birds were at their morning roar, and new pink sunlight smeared its pale paint over the pebbled shore, the pine and cedar and birch across the basin, the wash of fields that pointed west to town. I breathed the sea and watched the marsh grass glimmer until I could see it no more and felt my breath catch in my panicked throat.

Now and then we saw a husbandman with his hoe, but there were few souls afoot this early morning. We did not return to the Milton house, as I had hoped and imagined we would, but made directly for the harbor.

"My father thinks it prudent to avoid the marketplace," Nehemiah explained, "though you will want provisions. Dr. Devlin has arranged for purchases in Barbados. But we have plenty to stay you."

He looked only at Mother as he spoke, and his voice sank to her as to a child, but I cared not. My ears and heart had been seized by such an uproar I took little notice of my sullen companions. It was as if the ground screamed to me, and the quaking leaves; as we neared the harbor, rattling and bouncing, the wheeling gulls cried, *Wait!* I stiffened on the lumpy sack and hugged myself, shivering, for the sea wind here had more space to play with speed, and though I marveled at the harbor full of ships, I could not imagine boarding one.

Mother looked up only once, when the wagon stopped. Nehemiah secured the reins and leaped down, offering his hand to her. When he did the same for me, I sat, unyielding. "Tell me, Nehemiah—you're so right and wise—what use is running away?"

"Pray, Pearl," he snapped, and with a great lunge, snatched me down by the waist. On the ground, I fancied he encircled me an instant longer than he had to, his low voice stern but not unfeeling. "Say your fond goodbyes. Do you want a fresh scandal to set sail with?"

It grieved me when he let go. I little saw what difference scandal made. Prison straw. The scaffold. Holland. Gulls squawked and circled overhead, and I saw now, at the foot of the gravel path beyond a stand of reeds, a great ship docked. "Was it your mother's name?" I ventured. *"Marietta?"*

If I'd thought to lure back his sympathies, my query had the opposite effect. Nehemiah now studied me as one does an opponent, with hard eyes, and spat on the ground. "No," he said. "It was not."

He went for the heavy trunk while Mother heaved sacks and I hung back, stroking the nag who'd hauled us here. All was brisk and silent. No one called me idle, and I stared at the gravelly cart road leading west toward the woods and imagined myself there, the back of me, receding. Suspended between worlds, I dreamed of the deep, needled shade of a secret clearing in the forest, of my body shaped to earth like candle wax—and Simon beside me, sleeping sweetly. I buried my mouth in the nag's mane, murmuring to soothe us both, and dozed on in my parting daydream with a smile on my face.

*W*hat a desolation of waiting that day was. With Nehemiah behind dragging and kicking our belongings up the path to the harbor, Mother and I gaped. How unready it all seemed! All around were disordered heaps of unstowed goods—boxes, timbers, barrels. Great skeins and coils of rope surrounded the wooden ship, and tangles of rope hung with mysterious complexity from it. Everywhere milled crewmen and passengers, customs officials and searchers. Nehemiah left us and returned to see to the wagon, and Mother—a grave figure with a basket of embroidery stiff at her elbow—stood mumbling like one in prayer. Perhaps she *was* praying. I see now that I knew little of what she lived through in those days. I was living through them too, and all that morning felt hollow and red-eyed and jumpy until the wind at last caught us up, and I let the sea have me.

When all were aboard and the contents of the ship had been heaved and shifted and settled, there was still more waiting. Infants wailed, and people paced and rearranged themselves and their worldly goods. Clearance was forthcoming, a crewman called down to the crowd, and the ship owner, Caleb Milton, had yet to arrive and instruct his captain. I wondered if Simon and Nehemiah and Liza would live and sleep in the lower deck with me and Mother and the masses, or in the great cabin with their father and master. I determined that I must know, and clambered above decks to look for Nehemiah. I did not consider how I might approach him, or that he might with a single stern glance repel my approach. He did exactly that, and turned to speak to one of the crewmen. But I was patient. I found an out-of-the-way trunk to kneel behind and rested my elbows on it, chin in hands. Thus situated, I watched him, and he felt me watching, and colored and scowled. I focused on his creased brow and despite unease waited until he slapped the crewman on the arm and laughed with false heartiness as the other man began unraveling rope.

He came at me so abruptly and with an expression so fierce that I cringed behind the trunk. But he reached over and plucked my arm, hauling me up like a rag doll.

"I have a question!" I begged, shielding myself from the blow I half believed was coming.

"Say your piece, Pearl, and then learn the virtue of silence. Men at sea have little time to tarry with infants."

I wanted to shout that I was not an infant, nor was he a man; he might seem so to a world that claimed boys quickly, but I knew better. I wanted to say these things—*any* thing that might draw him to me, whether in sympathy or anger—but instead I demanded, "Where will Simon live on board?"

"He will live away from you, Pearl. Ever away, if I have anything to say about it."

"But I never meant to leave him alone . . . and dark. . . . I never would. He loves me," I murmured, conscious that I had lost any real audience I may have had with Nehemiah. *Remember me.*

He leaned close, and for one bewildering moment, I felt his breath on my face. He hesitated and licked his lips as if he might swallow the bitter words before they passed there, his eyes puzzled, almost tender. I wanted to touch those lips—chapped and full, red from wind—but it was only a girl's impulse.

"You are lucky to be loved at all, Pearl, and for that you have your luckless mother." He backed away and surveyed me with the same puzzled eyes as before. "Go to her. I won't look on you again."

And for many, many years, he didn't.

ENGLAND

DORCHESTER

*M*other and I spent seven dreary years in Dorchester, arriving with a letter of introduction from Caleb Milton at the home of his spinster sister and her servants, whose ranks—in exchange for room and board—we joined.

Mary Milton was woman's supervisor at a charitable hospital. I heard Simon's father tell Mother at sea that the institution was really a workhouse for poor children, who spun and carded and made bone lace for the local merchants. Its overseers meant well, he said, and the hospital did train and later find apprenticeships for many young men and taught girls womanly arts that would serve them well.

"It is a dangerous time to be masterless," Caleb Milton had warned.

His sister was soon impressed by Mother's talent with a needle and kept her busy apart from me. I longed to hear my mother's soft voice and feel her hands in my hair, to breathe a restless energy that was in some way like my own, but for years, though we ate and slept together, she was absent from me.

On shipboard, I had been her shadow truly. Nehemiah had once claimed my mother's eyes were black (and why correct him when it was *my* eyes that craved his notice?), but they are in fact as changeable as the sea: pale gray or slate, softness or storm. Watching her eye the waves with tenderness, I feared for us and kept always by her on deck, clutching her cool hand or humming to her. But in the drafty house at Dorchester, she occupied a chair in the dimmest corner—stitching, stitching, her eyes fixed on the carefully controlled patterns, the fitful colors.

At first, our exile felt in every way like death. Here the Puritan fathers were nearly as stern as in the New World, and I felt I mustn't falter. Mother had shut away her scarlet letter, and I could little risk reminding her. I spent hollow days doing Mary Milton's bidding or avoiding her when I could. Often I stole away to pace the circles at Maumbury Rings or roam about Dorset on the old Roman road that sliced straight through that country. I carried my shoes down land over springy turf. I jostled and conversed with sheep. Sometimes I listened for the voice of the world and heard instead, dimly, the minister's voice—the voice of his parting sermon—or the doctor owning my name or Simon whistling sweetly while he carved, but these could not linger in that stern, open landscape. They went on the wind, and I was anxious always, for the sky was everywhere here, pressing, and there was nowhere to hide when some godly soul came wondering what you were about and why you were not carding or spinning.

In my thirteenth or fourteenth year, the local authorities at last tallied the occasional mild complaints of farm wives, and Mary Milton was instructed to make more use of "that odd wanderer" from her household. I was put to work among her charges at the hospital.

Still I managed to slip away from time to time. Returning to the home that was not my home after these outings, I stood where the road ran near the edge of the plateau and surveyed the valley. I stared at reapers in the cornfields around Compton Valence or the vast earthwork of Maiden Castle peeping through haze and felt amazed that somewhere below—where the church towers and little thatched houses and the Georges Inn and the hospital huddled—was my life. There Mother sat fevered at her needle, unmindful that I was a ghost in my own body. Each time I paused again on that road we had come in on, I felt like a stranger at the gates of some mundane stop in a larger journey.

We had not been in Dorset a year when word came via London and Caleb Milton that Daniel Devlin had arranged a modest and fluid trust for me, with a property in London and land rights in the New World. In a letter contained with the official documents, which did not include a return address or claim me as his heir so much as obfuscate, he urged me to think on him "with some small measure of tenderness" and see to Mother's needs. Rather than exploit our unexpected good fortune, Mother arranged with Caleb Milton, the executor of the trust, to let the London property, and we lived on in Dorchester in unmitigated boredom. When I pleaded, Mother said only (and with little-disguised contempt for its source): "Your wealth will not perish, and London is full of intrigue." What I didn't know then was that we were bonded to Mistress Milton. Mother, who seemed to scorn social ambition, might have plundered my funds to dissolve our contract, but why? And where would we go? Mother's aunt in Leiden, her stepson had informed us some time before by post, was long since dead.

In fact, Mother allowed Caleb Milton, as English executor, to invest some of that wealth in his shipping concerns, and so it was that we received frequent letters sealed with wax. I sat at Mother's feet as she read them aloud, and they made my eyes glaze except for the occasional description of the merchant's life at sea—a life I had briefly taken to, despite the seasickness that had plagued me half the journey and the fact that I was sick at heart for the loss of Simon. Nehemiah was true to his promise; we crossed the wide Atlantic and I glimpsed Simon not once.

I sat at Mother's feet as she replied to these letters, dipping her pen so like a lady that it was hard for me to accept that her beautiful hands toiled all day—not for our welfare and pleasure but for Mistress Milton. Since I could scarce write myself, I claimed the postscripts for my own, dictating to Mother my effusions for Simon. I suspect now, years later, that she never wrote them down, at least not all, but rather scrawled a polite greeting on my behalf. I even accused her so on more than one occasion, as her hand did not match my exuberance and she never let me gaze long on her fine penmanship, but she would only smile and lay down the feather.

The ink trail on those postscripts grew ever longer and more elaborate after I began my tenure at the hospital among companions. In my early teens, at Mother's insistence, I learned to write to satisfy the plague of words that were my heart's blood. Remember, Simon, when we found the turtle by the Charles and held it wrong way and its stumpy legs flailed? Remember how you laughed? Does London still talk of the King's execution? How I wish I could walk with you there. Were you mazy and lightheaded on ship? No dose of wormwood could soothe me. Oh, but the biscuits were rank with maggots. Remember the heat as we neared Barbados? How wretched hot it was! Did you tarry on the deck for air? I looked for you and Liza. I looked everywhere, every day. Did Nehemiah help the men when the timbers shrank and the pitch between them melted? Did he help them spear that porpoise? Did he carry your hand to its smooth skin? And did he tell you its insides looked for all the world like a swine's? Did you hear the bawdy crew singing in the night? How scandalized was I when one with scarce a beard told me the Turks would come. He showed me his stash of lemons too, and bade me guard them with my life. You would have liked him, Simon. He wore great Spanish leather boots fit for his father. He spat snuff and bragged of skewering privateers. Do you love me? Will you remember? I remain your humble servant. I have no other friend but you.

This was not strictly true, of course. I made friends in Dorchester, where none knew my sordid history and the worst they had to hold against me was my accent. They were poor hospital children, servants (I never thought of myself so, any more than Mother did, but rather as one exiled among them) and orphans, different in every way from the cretins back in Boston—those pygmies with their holy scorn.

These English children, peasants and orphans among the Dorchester Puritans, had light in them, despite the dark monotony of their days. I carded wool beside them for years, and we laughed at trifles, our voices echoing under the high ceilings. I taunted the boys when I was allowed in their presence, and they in turn taunted me, and my breasts budded and intrigued me—and them, I dare say—and I half delighted in my ordinariness. The other half of me, in me, slept.

The truth is, I held even my favorite of these friends, a slightly younger girl named Truegrace, at a pleasant remove. One thing I had learned from

Mother in those years, and from the spinster Milton too, was this remove. Women without men were solemn and watchful in public. Girls without women were more so.

At night I dreamed of wilderness, cool and close—of a fox's stare and the beetle- brown earth riddled with the roots of trees. I dreamed of dew-heavy leaves laced together like fingers to cup the sun. It was when these dreams were beginning to fade, and I to grieve for them as well as for Simon, that Mother announced one day in 1656 that our contract with Mistress Milton was ended. We would go from here to a new home, a better life. "I have thought little of life, Pearl, these years past. But you deserve more than what I've promised myself."

"A life where?"

I had complained for seven long years of the monotony of Dorchester, where despite the teeming markets they still turned itinerant puppeteers away and sniffed out Papists, while many villages had brought back the maypole to spite the Protectorate—but this place was now more real to me than the world I kept alive in my postscripts to Mother's letters. It was more real than my dreams. I could touch it. I could huddle with True-grace in the hedges and fling pebbles at passing lads, and wish for and expect little. "To London?" This alone would quell me.

"No, Pearl. Your New World property will stand, but I've petitioned for sale of the London building and release of funds for a house in the country. I await Master Milton's reply."

*H*er reply came riding into town one Saturday and nearly took my breath. Truegrace and I were traversing the Roman road, whispering forbidden thoughts. She brazenly looked up at him while I, focusing on the *clomp* of hooves on gravel, caught only a glimpse of profile and smelled the horse's sweat. I felt his presence though, and with it—as the back of him receded—a clenching in my stomach. Truegrace of course prized from the moment the glamour of a faery story. When I blurted out his name, a question, she hissed, "You *know* him? How like a lord he is, Pearl!"

He had tipped his hat, but he hadn't seen us, not really. He was on business. He was all business, for that was his realm now. Like his father, he was a man of the world.

What silly girls we were, and how little I knew myself then or the dark in my own heart, and in the heart of the world. I had forgotten more than I'd learned in seven uneventful years, careening to womanhood with hardly a second thought. I was about eighteen years old, comely like my mother—though I probably didn't know it, or knew in the shallow way that I knew other wiles I thought I could control—and I was a fool to race to the tavern with Truegrace behind, begging. I was stupid to step panting, still a girl, into that brown world of men without so much as pausing to pat the horse out front.

When I opened the door, the pipe smoke seemed to hang suspended in the air, as did the clamor of voices. I think I have never felt so exposed in my life, and clumsy Truegrace grinding at my heels didn't help. Truly she had as much grace as a gourd, but every man in the tavern turned to us. It took some time to locate him among the glaze of faces. Nehemiah had settled near the back and was just then pulling off his gloves.

I marched to him, a child again, demanding, "How is your health?"

His eyes were bright and expectant when they found me. "I am well, Pearl."

"You look well."

I heard a man behind us whoop. Nehemiah quieted him with a look, though I thought I saw prideful laughter twitch at his lips. He stood with a little bow and motioned for us to sit. Truegrace obeyed, but I kept behind her, settling my hands on her shoulders. "This is Truegrace," I said. "She is fourteen."

Truegrace nodded and nodded, as if I had said something controversial that required support. Nehemiah cast a forgetful smile at her and turned to me. "You won't sit?"

"No, I mustn't. Mother is anxious to speak with you."

"And have you no time for me?"

Without meaning to, I must have clenched Truegrace's bony shoulders, for she writhed and finally slapped one hand away. "Pearl! Vile creature! That *hurts.*"

Nehemiah laughed, and with a shrug I joined in and pulled a bench close to the table to sit upon.

The others in the tavern seemed to have forgotten us, and a good thing too, for how quickly those seasoned men at their pints would have seen through my calm. A great need had been ripped open in me like a scab, and it must have shown in my face. Why else would Nehemiah study me with such dire bemusement? "You read my letters," I accused.

"I read your mother's letters."

"But mine too. They were mine also. And you never answered. None did."

"They gave their words over to me like apples into a basket, Pearl. Blame me for their silence."

I swiped a stray curl from my face. "Liza is well?"

"As can be expected, at her age."

Truegrace, all this time, sat stiff and ready, with a kind of beatific grin on her face.

"Your companion thinks us ungainly rude, Pearl."

"Oh, no." She shook her head with vigor and sipped at the watery brew that had been set before her. "I think no such thing, sir."

I half expected her to go, but for Truegrace this shining stranger was a diversion and our talk merely sportive. If he were strange to me, I might feel the same and welcome the chance to bask in him. *If you were strange to me.* "Do you ever miss New England?" I demanded.

He sipped his ale and shook his head. "Almost never. Though I dare say I miss your childish visits. They were never dull when all else there was."

Truegrace nodded with satisfaction, and I nearly slapped her. Was I as silly a wench as she? "You might have encouraged them more."

His round eyes, golden brown and liquid like the ale he drew from, evaded me. He set down his glass but kept his head bowed. "You'll want to know about Simon."

"Of course."

"He is still blind." Nehemiah looked up, and those great eyes with their dark brows startled me.

Truegrace must have found the silence between us a puzzle, but she sat dutifully through it, smiling her vacant smile.

At length, Nehemiah finished his ale and took in the dim interior of the tavern. "I see the men play at dice, but have they no amusements here? No shuffleboard? Billiards?"

"Did you read even one of my letters to him?"

"They were not my letters to read. They were Father's."

"Your father shared them, surely."

"He did, and perhaps read some aloud to Simon when the spirit moved him. He is a busy man."

Truegrace nodded, but her expression had lost its willingness. Perhaps she was bored.

"I'll show you to your aunt." I stood and pulled stubborn Truegrace to her feet. "But don't tarry," I cautioned. "I am busy."

I listened from Mary Milton's chamber, which could be accessed from the servants' quarters, as she met with Nehemiah and Mother. Transformed by doting, Mary did most of the talking, and I winced through her banter, waiting with my cheek pressed to the door to hear his voice again. Mary Milton had never been unkind to me, but in seven years she had made little impression on my heart.

Her nephew gave a jolly report of the family, by turns boyish and authoritative. Though I longed for news of his brother, Nehemiah's talk turned to politics, the commonwealth and strict moral laws. London theaters had been closed for years but were furtively reopening, though wrestling matches and bear baiting were yet prohibited. Music was frowned upon, except hymns, and Wednesday was a fast day. Non-Puritans complied in public, but in private they gibed and sniggered.

"Here they are more true. But you are one of the elect, nephew, are you not?" teased Mary Milton. "Like your mother. Surely *you* don't wear two faces like your father."

"I am a Seeker," he said, and I did not hear more, only Mother's conspicuous silence. I wondered when she might speak, but I knew it would not be until she was spoken to.

Before long, Nehemiah seemed to weary of their conversation and began a brisk if complicated explanation of our financial affairs. The property in London had been sold to a merchant who had led the Miltons, in turn, to land here in Hampshire, in New Forest, with a middling-sized cottage and remote surrounds.

"And Dr. Devlin has approved these transactions?" Mother asked, and I heard in her tone that it pained her to speak of him. I had tried and failed to engage the topic so many times that I no longer asked, and perhaps, as a consequence, I was not averse to forgetting him. He had never—quite— seemed wholly real to begin with.

"The doctor has granted my father full rights to manage these affairs and to act on Pearl's behalf." Nehemiah's voice dropped, and I imagined from my place behind the door that his eyes had too. "In strictest confidence, of course." He went on briskly. "If you accept the Hampshire offer and settle there, you've rights to cut peat, and to collect firewood and mast, but the laws there are old and complex from William's day, so we must confer with the verderers in Lyndhurst to learn them."

"It will do very well, Nehemiah," said Mother. "Thank you, and please extend our gratitude to your father. He has been a good friend and wise counsel."

There was an instant's silence before Mary Milton began to chatter on about supper—a celebratory feast, she called it, for our honored guest.

How bloated his head must be, I thought, and it occurred to me that the sound of his given name on Mother's lips had made me jealous. How had they such intimacy as that?

Our hero would scarce meet my eyes at supper but afterward surprised us all and scandalized the servants—who had never warmed to Mother or me and were of late more in tune than indifferent to our household stature—by asking Mother if he might walk with me in the yard before sundown.

"I must give Pearl news of my brother, Simon."

Mary Milton lost interest immediately, as if Simon were of no account. But Mother saw my urgency and consented with a prim nod.

Frequent shadows, whether Mother's or Mary's or the servants' I don't know, appeared at the casements as we paced back and forth round the front garden boxes. From time to time, I pulled a weed, trying to feign indifference, for I could not forget their eyes on me long enough to display my mood. It was a tangled mood, to be sure, and when I came near him, I went by as quickly as I could.

"I have stung you, Pearl."

I cleared the gravel from my throat and said, "Would it suit you to think so?"

"Lay aside your armor and consider that I alone have been Simon's eyes. For most of his lifetime, I've cared for him. I have loved him."

"As have I. As has Liza and your father. Your mother too, no doubt."

"You speak as if you know it."

"I assume it."

"Well, don't." He came close, and I could see that he wanted to lay a hand on me, stop my pacing, grasp my arm. Something. But he dared not.

"What does it matter who loves him," I said, "but that we do."

"You have never heard him howl should you forget and move one small item in his chamber. You've never watched him huddle in a ship's corner to rant at the storm he can't see. You've never truly studied his fingers while he carves, have you? The precision of it, the concentration. It's terror that rules him. You have no idea how it was for him when you saw fit to leave him there."

I scoffed, slapping at the brown-edged mint. "*You* have cloaked him in terror. And I do know. I curse myself every day. I avoid regret for the waste that it is, but I regret that error. I was thoughtless—" I began, but the words wilted on my tongue. I licked my lips. The salty meat had made me thirsty. "The light is fading," I said.

"I know it."

"Then forgive me."

He walked to the other end of the garden. With his back turned, he said, "Your mother has lost something of her radiance. But you draw from her as from a well."

I looked up, pink and astonished. "Well, I'll have no credit for that, will I?"

"No," he teased, "nor blame, I hope."

"*Why* won't you forgive?"

"I will, Pearl." He turned back. "But I won't know what to do with you instead."

So there it was.

I crossed my arms. "There is nothing to *be* done."

Nehemiah turned to me with a smile ghosting on his lips. "A wise man knows it."

He then brought what must have been a dozen letters from a pocket in his coat. Tied with a faded ribbon, they were wrinkled and warped, stained with salt. All bore the address of Mary Milton in Dorchester. "Now it's your turn," he said. "Forgive me?" He tried to hand them, but I fumbled and the packet fell. He knelt and held a hand up, as once he had behind the church in Boston to ward me from Simon. This time he would not let me stoop. He placed the letters in my palm and, standing, folded my fingers over, then turned my hand aright and covered it with his own. I stared with shock at it—large and sun-dark, strong-veined, so unlike the memory of Simon's milky, boyish one. I could as much as hear the servants gasp.

"You were a good friend to Simon," he said. "I thank you for it— too late."

I freed my hand, and the letters. "I am still. I was your friend too, and will be again if you'll have me."

His eyes roamed over me in the fugitive light, and he shook his head as if to clear it, standing tall and lordly once more. "Would that I took a child's pleasure in friendship."

I knelt by the carrots and, though they were nowhere near ready to pull, began to blindly tear, enjoying the wiry tension of the greens. I knew that I was coy, like the light, and that for the first time there was something at stake in that coyness. This was no village boy trailing the hem of my dress. Inside I was shaking. I felt a dangerous, sinful bliss. I had forgotten everything, even my father's briefly reanimated face, even the letters lying by me in the dirt.

He kept many paces from me but knelt to mimic my gardening stance. Though he craned, he spoke almost too softly for me to hear, and with a peculiar begging in his eyes. "Remember me?"

Near dizzy from minding those eyes, I turned from him back to the gentle earth, and nodded my defeat.

DEARE NEHEMIAH

*T*he letters were unreadable. Some crumbled as I opened them while others were so smeared by salt water, I made out only scattered words: porpoise . . . yours . . . ship . . . hands . . . Liza . . . stern . . . London . . . touch . . . touch . . . true . . . King . . . devotion. I knew that spidery handwriting, and that Nehemiah had spent patient hours collecting Simon's words as Mother had collected mine, *like apples into a basket,* only to hoard and keep them from me. His choice to do so vexed me truly, but I could spare no wrath for him who consumed my every thought. My stupidity apart from Nehemiah was matched only later by my stupidity in his presence, but those letters, Simon's letters—so longed for—were a puzzle I would lose the will to solve.

New Forest was no forest in the sense that I knew one, but there Mother was my only master, and our cottage was remote, and I had my will. For her part, Mother softened and flourished, and even left her embroidery chair to venture out into the far-flung villages and surrounds. Her good works were more specific here. Only rarely—now that we had access to modest wealth—did she embroider gloves or burial shrouds for the gentry to bring a shilling to our cup. Instead, she befriended Sarah Atkinson, a local midwife, and eventually traveled with her to the homes of ordinary women. While quiet Sarah mashed herbs and boiled water, Mother was their gentle champion, soothing them in their birthing agony, laughing lightly with them over their mistakes at love, reading from the scriptures to prepare them for a good death. She had scant mind for herbs, though she used them when she could, but Sarah taught her much in those months—including a gift for listening—that would stay her well, and that she would one day bring back with her to New England.

"Love" was not a banished word in New Forest, for love required at least the illusion of freedom, and there among the roaming ponies, the fog, and the heather we were free—or freer—in our relative isolation. Perhaps, as Dr. Devlin had suggested the morning my mother slumped in the stocks in Boston, it was the minister she had loved, if dutifully, from a seemly distance. Once I watched from the doorway as she consulted a looking glass, her fingertips roaming tenderly among the tiny lines round her eyes as if the eyes were a stranger's. I did not think she felt my shadow when suddenly she sat up straight and announced, "He would be beyond middling age now." I nodded at the question in her voice and left her alone with the unnamed ghost.

But it was here in New Forest, too, that Mother freely spoke the name of my father, acknowledging me as the fortunate result of their unfortunate and shameful union. Her aversion to the mention of him fascinated and unnerved me, but I was no longer a child who blurted demands and raged at silence. I measured out my questions like a woman, and some few of them Mother answered.

Though she had heard me dictate my heart to them in our letters, it was only here in New Forest, months after Nehemiah's Dorchester visit, that she asked about his brother and my history with them. Faced with her own neglect, she shook her head with a mother's rue and kissed my forehead. "He fancies you," she announced that day, "Nehemiah."

I scoffed.

"He surely does, and he'll be back after winter. You'll see."

She knew something I didn't, perhaps.

In New Forest, I received his letters—and penned replies with a concentration cultivated during my patient years at Dorchester; I heard for the first time Simon's manly voice in my head as Nehemiah brought me late those words that were my due.

One such letter came in a parcel with mother's heirloom watch. Thinking to wear it and look the lady, I'd lapsed and let it fall into the well while Nehemiah was with us in Dorset, and he had fished it forth with a hook on a horsewhip. He had taken the watch back to London, to a watchmaker he knew, and his letter was devoted to its return:

Mistress,

The artificer having never before met a drowned watch, like an ignorant physician has been long about the cure. But I present the Watch at last and envy the felicity of it, that it should be so near your side, and so often enjoy your Eye, and be a party to how your Time will pass. But take care, for I put such a spell into it that every beating of the balance will tell you this: the pulse of my heart labors as much to serve you, and more truly. For the watch, having received so bold a soaking, may sometimes fail (I despair it should ever be a true servant to you more). But as for me, you may rest knowing I remain your most affectionate, humble servant,

Neh. Milton

After these formal charms came Simon's simple call to seize and ride one of the famed wild ponies of New Forest to London. "I'll take time out from my busy and populous days and be waiting," he told his brother's pen, "by the window."

Somehow, to imagine Nehemiah transcribing Simon's words—and perhaps thinking them childish, even hesitating under the shadow of censure—robbed me of the sweet blush the elder's musings brought.

I woke some nights after reading that letter to the low pulse of rain on the roof. Slipping from the bed, I felt all the old urgency of childhood. My furtive feet, remembering, led me to the door and through it into the damp. Mist rolled over the earth, and when my eyes adjusted to the bright curtain that draped the dark, I made out at some distance the silhouette of a deer or pony. Did that pony bewitch me? Perhaps I heard Simon in mind and was transfixed by the peculiar image of him waiting by a window in London. Waiting for what? What he could not see beyond the glass?

I half believed as I minced along the wet grass—confirming that it was a pony, not one of the deer whose ancestors were beloved by William the Norman—and absently clutching the watch, that I would mount and ride that creature. In truth I had never scaled a horse in my life despite a passing acquaintance with many. But I felt a naive certainty that the animal would let me near enough to subdue it, that I would scramble on its back and gallop through the stark of night at my ease. I would ride not to Simon, I thought, not to London at least, but just away and back to myself—to the part of myself I had left behind in the wilds of New England—and Simon would be waiting. Would he know me now?

As my vigil dragged on I felt the nearness of others. Our cottage was well outside the closest village, but there were land holds peppered all around the Forest. The people we had met here were kind, but we had no proper neighbors and trusted not the phantom ways of distant community. We only slipped in among the villagers to haunt the shops, or Mother went like a charitable shadow with Sarah. When I approached, the pony bared its yellow teeth and shook its wet mane as much as to say, "I don't know *you*," and I was subdued.

Clutching myself in the cold, I felt a writhing in me and longed to be held by other arms than my own, and felt Nehemiah's hands and golden eyes traversing me. I had felt lust before, random and blithe and framed later in conspiring laughter with Truegrace, but never this sudden rash of it that left me caught and afraid in the night with my sin. The still trees sagged with rain, and the quiet was cut only by the distant barking of a dog. Perhaps it was but the faint ticking of Mother's watch, but here in New Forest I was reminded of my old, wild home across the ocean—and of the events that had forced me from it. Craving I knew not what from the present, I felt instead the weight of past and future. *They will meet one day,* I mused vaguely, clucking to the pony to hear my own voice.

The dumb animal went on grazing, lifting its heavy head. Its slow jaw worked and worked. "I knew your language once," I scolded, but when I stepped forward with outstretched hand, the pony stiffened and raised its head. Light was rising beyond the fog, and I stood barefoot on the cool grass, smiling at my own idiocy. I walked inside then and lit a candle, content in the glow of our cottage. Mother slept on our new feather bed under a comfort and the coverlet she had embroidered end to end with indigo vines and flowers. I knew the drowsy warmth of her embrace, though I stood apart from it, as outdoors I had known Nehemiah's hands on me (though they had never *really* been, I reminded myself, and bade the devil go). It was this knowing, this richness in absence, that finally calmed me.

Day had burned through the fog. I sat and rubbed my hands warm and wrote to Simon of the naughty pony that wouldn't let me ride it. For his brother, I spared only, "Deare Nehemiah. How cool-green and quiet it is here in the morning, after rain. Yours in remembrance. Pearl."

*H*e came with the spring as Mother had promised, and alone. I saw him riding from some distance, and had time to compose myself though my mind cast about for protection, as Mother was off cutting peat for the fire.

"Are the others well?" I demanded before he had even dismounted, stroking absently his horse's foaming neck. "Why have you come?"

"Why not?"

"They're well, then?"

He jumped down from the horse and caught my shoulder. His weight was more than I would expect, or my strength was less. "Well enough, Pearl. And you are fine—" he looked askance at the modest cottage—" here? You favor your home in the New Forest?"

"It's not much of a forest."

"It's not a wilderness. I might expect you to be grateful for that."

"You might, but you would be wrong." I don't know what ruled me. I had tempted this moment to come, and now it had, and I was as welcoming as an adder. "In fact, I find it very pleasant here." I took the reins from him so that he might loosen his pack from the saddle. "Very."

"As well you might." He nodded overlong and slung the pack onto his shoulder. I followed to the door of the cottage, where we both stopped. He waited for me to speak, and I almost felt too ablaze in the face to say it.

"Mother's not there. She's out gathering peat."

He cleared his throat and set the pack on the ground. I noticed his garb was plainer than before, more Puritan than Cavalier, though thankfully he had not followed the Roundheads and cut short the hair that fell thick to his shoulders. "Let's walk, then." He raised his arm, and I gave him mine, aware of the elastic bulk of it twining.

Eager for the first word, I asked, "What meant you before in Dorset, that you are a Seeker?" His phrase had puzzled me since my afternoon of eavesdropping behind Mary Milton's chamber door. I steered us toward a stand of oak where a path led out to a meadow. I don't know whether it was shady refuge I craved or the bright glare of safety beyond. He shook his head and stopped me under budding trees with their peeling trunks. "To whom did I pledge this?"

"To your aunt."

"I remember it not."

"She asked if you were of the elect, and you answered that you were a Seeker."

His smile was mild and flickering. "The Lord Protector spoke or penned once words that moved me: 'To be a Seeker is to be of the best sect after a Finder, and such a one shall every humble Seeker be in the end.'"

"Then you seek fine words?"

He took back his arm and stopped where the tree line met the windy field. "I remember once my mother took me on her lap to tell of an Indian raid soon after we arrived on New World soil. I was a babe when they came, and Simon not yet born. She swore as they swept the village that she would rather die were it God's will or never see me more in this world than that I should be sold to a Jesuit. Mother's passion was such that when a French courier slipped me a biscuit at market years later, I ran and cast it into the smith's well. What an error! For it dawned on me that my foe must surely have worked some spell into the treat, some poison, and I lived in dread for weeks. The smith and his wife and brat were sure to sprout wings at Sunday meeting, or a goat's beard, or else choke to death in their sleeps.

"Mother spoke often of Papists torturing the Protestants so that I hated the sight of a Jesuit. And now—" he paused and looked out over the blank fields—" under the Protectorate we hang priests and brand Quakers. We bore hot holes into blasphemous tongues. A law is nigh that wills all landowners over sixteen to disavow Catholicism or forfeit two-thirds of their property. I should cheer—I know it—yet I pray for guidance. The God I seek—"

I hushed him with a finger at his lips, and he seemed to see me again. He caught the finger in his fist as once I had seen a stealthy savage catch a fish. With a sly grin, he bent my arm behind my back and mashed me in a ridiculous kiss that stunned us both and tasted of pewter. When he let me have my breath back, we bowed our heads and kicked at acorns, and spoke no more of God.

J refused to let him stand behind and haunt me with his hands by the hearth but sent him out to Mother. No gifted cook, I tried that night truly, and baked my secrets into bread. Nehemiah had set a bench and chair outside the cottage door for them. Their voices lulled me as I worked at the sieve or kettle, and though I heard not the words, I knew with some resentment that I was on their lips and that my fate belonged to them.

As the cottage filled with the smell of stewed meat and spices (Nehemiah had fished from his pack dainty parcels of cloves, mace, aniseed, and allspice), I felt a choking warmth and longed to be out in the evening air. I was appalled, perhaps for the first time, by my coddled state. Mother had kept me well and completely, and yet I would be consummate with these labors one day, wedded to a house that was my house, to a husband's name. I blamed Mother for sparing me, and railed against Nehemiah and wished him gone, and burned my hand on the iron pot, and let fall the ladle in a fit of clattering.

"Pearl!" Mother found her way in to me and caught my shoulders from behind. "What violence is this?"

"He'll have me for my puny fortune," I whined. "My father's puny fortune."

Mother winced but soon buried her face in the nape of my neck. I felt her sigh, or laugh, or otherwise remonstrate. "Hush now, strange girl."

He was at the threshold, I knew, and I cared little. "I'm not ready."

"You have yet no cause to be," she cautioned lightly. "But mayhap you are afraid."

"I am not afraid!" I made as if to bolt, and she circled my waist and held me close.

"You are willful," she whispered into my hair. "You have always been so."

"You would be rid of me."

She said nothing, but it was true. I knew it. I jerked around to face her. "But we have a home now finally. We are home now."

"My home is not here."

"Then where is it?"

"It's by the scaffold." Her eyes left me. "On my knees."

"Thou shall worship not false idols!" I stepped back and spat on the floor between us, then felt Nehemiah's hands on my shoulders and began to shriek, rail, thrash—until he pulled me with him to a pine chair by the wall and sat with me on his lap like a child. "Pearl," he said, and kissed the edge of my ear lightly, so lightly. "Be still, Pearl."

I felt that they had trapped me in a fierce heat, in my raw skin, that I would be caught and peeled and dead now beyond saving, and I craved Simon's cool and willing hand in mine, the open air. But I went limp on his brother's lap.

Mother stood across the room and smiled at us as at two small strangers, and said in a bemused voice that she knew of an old country custom; without an inn nearby and with no spare couch on which a visitor might sleep, she would allow us to bundle. "I see no reason to keep the fire tonight or waste candles." I felt the brush of Nehemiah's chin as he nodded behind me.

"I heard once of a parish with a quaint innovation," she added. "And while I doubt not your piety, my own experience leads me to prize virtue perhaps too well." Her eyes dropped to me. "Pearl, don't look so. You know not the ways of the world. You'll keep your full dress." She looked up again. "And after we sup, Nehemiah, you'll cut a log to place between. Something heavy enough."

I nearly laughed at her lunacy but felt drained and limp with him behind, holding my wrists and breathing into my hair.

"You should know with some certainty he with whom you'll lie, Pearl. Sleep beside him."

We lay under the covers in the last flickering candlelight, and Mother's slender arms heaved a trimmed sapling between us. I felt it draw the cloth tighter over me like a shroud. I felt no more the bruising nearness of him. "Mother?" I squeaked, but she only blew out the candle.

"Sleep, Pearl, or hear of his intent and speak of yours. There is no harm in it."

No harm in it?

But as she settled into bed on the other side of me, I could feel him there, and if I turned my face in the dim night, I would find his face, but how could I? I was never so seized with stiffness, and I imagined the face of old Reverend Wilson traveling in the dark, settling like a wasp on my skin, then floating back into view, his mouth moving in reproach. I felt that I was stung with wasps on every trace of skin. What skin kissed the air— collarbone, wrist—tormented me, and I wiggled to burrow deeper under cover, and my head roared. When at length Mother began to snore, I listened to the silence on my other side and stole a look at him. The log came just to his chin, and I felt it move as he shifted and rolled to his side. He was struggling against the blankets even as I wished to be consumed by them. He did not struggle free, but only enough to raise himself slightly, to bring his face near my cheek, to breathe on me and make me shudder.

"Pearl?"

"Yes," I whispered.

"Turn to me."

"No."

"Marry me?"

"No."

"You care for someone else?"

I shook my head, though he probably couldn't see so much as feel me do it.

"Then turn to me."

"No."

"Your mother wills it so."

"She would be rid of me."

"She would return to New England but wishes it not for you—that wilderness."

I gasped softly, and turned to him. "When?"

"As soon as you'll be my wife."

His mouth found my chin. I could feel him straining up against the log, the tidal pull of blankets, and would have laughed at the absurdity of our nearness were I not so cross with lust. "Nehemiah?"

"Say it again," he whispered, and his teeth made for my lower lip and dragged across it. "I like the taste of my name on your lips."

"Nehemiah."

"Again." He plucked at my lip with his teeth. I could see the liquid shimmer of his eyes but little else.

"Nehemiah."

He mouthed yes and went on teasing with his teeth, his tongue.

"Where will we live?"

"We will live wherever you like, Pearl. We will live in our bed."

I stifled my laugh and felt his hand snaking in my hair. He would not plow back the blankets to free us for embrace, but crooked his arm at an ungainly angle over his head. He twined my hair round his fingers and the pain made me wince and lick my lips—already dry without his care. And so we passed the night, writhing and stilling when Mother shifted or changed her breaths; writhing and tasting, and at some point I fell asleep in a hot tangle of sin averted—not, I knew, by me. He kept the log between us like a promise.

$\mathcal{W}$e were wed without banns in a rather clandestine ceremony the next afternoon by Minister Lacey of Lyndhurst, with Mother our sole witness. I knew neither a betrothal in any proper sense nor what my portion might be, and before his reading the kindly if doddering old reverend—with whom Nehemiah or Mother had presumed to confer apart from me—mumbled of my youth and complained without conviction that we had not had an espousal ceremony to instruct and prepare us. He said I would "reverence, fear, and obey" Nehemiah, which tempted my smile though never drew it forth. Both Mother and my groom stood as solemn as death, it seemed, and I could find no pleasure in their faces.

"Know," said the old man, addressing me with the Bible trembling in his hand and spittle in a corner of his dry lips, "that the God that graciously placed thy good husband here will be here with thee and comfort thee if you submit and trust to him."

His words seemed to me so tangled that I wanted to stop the good man short: Which would I submit to, my husband or my God? But I knew the answer well enough.

Mother and Nehemiah nodded and smiled, and I confess that I trusted them enough to nod and smile too and speak my vows when the time came. I wondered, Did Mother imagine how those words might have tasted once on her own lips? I felt a rash of pain for the young woman she had been once . . . trusting . . . in what? Why had my father left her alone? What had his strange words by the stocks meant, by turns tender and taunting, tortured and accusing? She had never said. She would never say.

We had a good supper with good beer. Sarah Atkinson brought sweetmeats and a gift of Banbury bride cake, though she could not stay—with twins due in Ashurst. We played cards, and laughed a little, though Nehemiah spoke hardly at all. Before the minister left, he took my hand in his two raw red and trembling ones and nodded, speechless himself a moment, before saying with hoarse warmth, "Good day to you, Nehemiah Milton his wife." His Wife, when the minister went away whistling with his staff, let her Liege lead her out to the stand of oaks, where she, little afraid in daylight, kissed him till they reeled and the ground called to them.

"What a perfect maze I'm in." My husband sank to his knees, encircling me as if I were the trunk of a tree that would stay him in a flood, speaking his wet words into the fabric of dress between my thighs. "My heart is too much devoted to creature objects."

Words. I groped to cover his mouth with my hand, and might have willed him bed me right there were it not for Mother, all in gray, whom he glimpsed below the rise walking with her basket toward the moor—perhaps to aid Sarah in Ashurst. I let him lead me back by the hand, though the smell of earth, the damp air, pleased me.

And because I was not a Seeker but, at not yet twenty years old, an opportunist, I did not then notice how close and hot it was inside the cottage, how dim, and that she had already packed our trunks, our every object, that none but the bedcovers remained.

YOUR HUMBLE SERVANT

*H*ow far was London? Countless muddy miles away, it seemed, and Mother so silent as the wagon bounced. Even our forays at strange inns, the smoky swirl of faces, the thought of standing at long last outside Simon's dark window, could not distract me from her silences.

Caleb Milton would sail from London this summer or sooner, to Boston on the way to Virginia—Nehemiah too, perhaps—and Mother would again be his passenger. She would go home to her cursed scaffold, and I would remain.

I imagined her rattling the rust from the keyhole of our old cottage, the cold iron key in her palm, the open door and bleed of sunlight on the dirt floor. I heard the sea and smelled the marsh. Above all, I saw the dappled mouth of the pine and beech wood and felt the velvet dark beckon. It would be nearly autumn when she arrived, and I imagined the stain of berries on my fingers, lichen and cool stone, the sag of grapes and, in the meadows, the bobbing husks of milkweed; these I gathered as a child for their down—from which, when I didn't send the faery tufts flying on the wind, we wove candle wicks. I heard the complaint of chipmunks as I entered again the remote clearing where once I'd found a deer's antler on a bed of moss. I prowled in mind the churchyard that now housed the minister's bones, the plateau overlooking the ocean where my father had addressed me in a meadow.

New Forest had not been without like pleasures. I mourned as we went from it to yet another unknown, though Nehemiah assured me the property was mine to return to. But there was no eclipsing that other world, a child's world, in my heart. And it was sharp memories of that place, as the horse clopped along and Mother and Nehemiah talked of the *Marietta* and storms, of how best we might correspond between shores, that brought Simon back to me. Because I realized, as we stopped by yet another tavern on the way to London, that I had forgotten what he looked like. Unlike Nehemiah, who was flesh to me, it was Simon's essence I'd clung to all these years, not more. His face now swam into view as a drowned face bobs to the underside of ice, and I shuddered at this, my latest betrayal. As we climbed down from the wagon, I went straight to the inn's outhouse and sat in the spidery dark to cry for the boy Simon who was no more.

A short while later I found my husband in the stable, where in the closed dusk he would not see my eyes. I stood quiet as a dormouse and watched his strong arm brush the mare. He hummed to her and seemed in a trance of sorts, recalling the remote and self-possessed boy I had known long ago. When I spoke his name, he started.

"Mother has gone in alone?"

"It's a godly crowd here," he assured me. "No gaming. A goodwife came for her cloak."

I leaned against a wall. "You will sail straightaway with your father— when we reach London?"

"He's your father now too."

I nodded and felt my brow crease with its burden. "He knows his first-born has wed a sprite born of a strumpet?"

Nehemiah looked up sharply. "What, Pearl?" His arm stopped its rhythmic work, and the horse stamped and snorted.

In the quiet I heard the soft bump of other horses shifting in their stalls, the steaming splat of dung, the scrape of shod hooves on flagstones. "Have you forgotten?"

"Some things are best forgotten," he said.

"*My* father, for instance?"

Nehemiah, who was still generous then, stood and pulled me to him, tried to embrace and contain me, but I felt the devil stiffen in my skin.

"Will I spend our lives correcting you, Pearl?" His voice was level and hoarse in my ear. "Your sentence has ended now."

"Where is he, husband? You know him. Why have I no letters bearing *his* script?"

"I cannot say, Pearl. My father and I were enlisted to act in your interests and shelter you, but——"

"Where?"

He sighed. "London somewhere, I expect. I don't know exactly."

I reached out for him, my hand brushing his cheek in the dark. "You've taken your duty to brash extremes, husband. Nowhere in such contract——" Before I could offend him more with my bastard status, we heard footfalls coming toward the stable. He set me back and turned again to the mare, who shook her mane disdainfully. "Go in and warm yourself. The mud was frozen on the wagon wheels. April is waylaid."

A man entered and tipped his hat to us. A gust blew the stable door closed behind him, which sealed in the dark. He was, from the sound and smell of him, plainly drunk, and just as plainly trying to conceal it, and he nearly fell over from the effort. "My good sir and lady. The wind has grown frightful since my first pint. I think I won't venture up on that beast lest the tempest blow me off." He motioned to a shadowy horse down the row and hiccuped.

"You look thin enough for it," teased Nehemiah. "How far is it, sir, to London?"

"A day's journey more. You've not been this way? Then you don't know our fair proprietress—a widow fresh, and my heart's delight."

"May your delight meet its match—as mine has."

I looked, seething with apology, for Nehemiah's shadowy form.

"Step out into the light with me, friends."

I felt my husband grope for my hand. It was almost completely black inside the stable, with no lantern and daylight gone from the cracks in the wood. Perhaps this drunk was one of the thieving butchers that ruled the

London streets at night in legend. I was afraid of him, his merriment. Nehemiah steered me with a hand on my back, and I groped for the iron door handle. The cold of it cut me, and I felt the relief of having mastered the unknown. With my blindness returned my grief for Simon. *He is a man now.*

The lamp blazing by the tavern's sign soothed us all three, I think, for when I finally saw him, our visitor seemed a small, nervous creature, dainty and red-faced, all in silk. A gentleman by law. He shook Nehemiah's hand and sandwiched one of mine warmly between his palms. "Zeb Hall's my name. You're a bride?" he said, and his birdlike head bobbed with knowing.

"How—?" began Nehemiah.

"There is no blush rests on a maid's cheek like matrimony." He bobbed and bobbed with pinched lips, and sputtered with laughter, and before we knew it, we were laughing too. He clapped his hands, blew on them, and rubbed them in the cold. "I'm no seer, lady. It was your good mother who told me. I came out at once to seek your advice. What said he that made you relent and love him?"

Nehemiah laughed and made as if to swoon.

"We were children together," I confessed, feeling as disappointed in this answer as my audience looked to be.

"There is no trick to it, then?" asked Master Hall, and I saw his cloud of icy breath. "No charm? Any good neighbor might achieve the hand of so fine and modest a one?"

I bowed my head to keep from braying. "Pray, ask him. The winner knows his wiles better than I do."

Our friend nearly toppled Nehemiah with a hand on his shoulder. "Confess, good sir, your methods."

Nehemiah balanced for both of them, but his smile weakened. A gaggle of gentlemen had exited the tavern, and their sure steps and gruff voices seemed to drain the humor from his face. "I don't know," he begrudged us. "I don't know how I mastered her—though I'm grateful for it. I feel certain your widow will prize your offer, sir, but now we should return to our patient mother."

The men nodded at one another as if they had forgotten me, and Nehemiah steered me in.

We never saw Master Hall again, but long did I wonder how the widow had met his advances. I looked for her in the crowd that night as we supped, imagining one as fair as a princess, but she was doubtless no less ordinary a widow than I was a bride and did not distinguish herself among so many.

In every life there is a moment or sum of moments when we openly resign the visions of youth, and I know that I did so that night. My mother and my lover, though a hand's reach away, seemed far from me as they dined and readied for sleep in strange quarters. There were things I would fault Mother for, pleas I would voice, that I could not in front of the husband who had mastered me. Simon was a blind man alone by a window in London, and I was a fatherless woman grown fine and modest in a strange land, nothing more.

When the wagon stopped many weary hours later, I let the veil of urban bedazzlement fall from my eyes and looked up at once to a high window. I knew, because Simon had told me in his portion of our letters, that the hearth room faced out over the street. He heard the wheels, he said, the cries, the ring of footfalls on cobble, as in a ditch, and he could not easily master the disorienting curved staircase, which had no rail. There was no figure in the window, as I had imagined, but I leapt from the wagon without Nehemiah's hand, forgetting that so indecorous a feat might vex him.

I raced to the entryway of what seemed to me a very fine, tall house, but before I could touch the shiny handle, the door swung open and Liza caught me in a suffocating embrace. The very smell of her brought tears to my eyes, but I laughed into the coarse fabric of her dress—a finer one than ever I'd seen her wear in Boston, though not so fine as to invite the contempt of the law. She backed me up and shook her head.

"Pearl!"

"Pearl Milton, I'll have you know," Nehemiah called from the cobbles. He had unloaded most of our goods to the filthy curb.

"Why, yes, I'd heard as much, but who'd believe our good fortune? Come in and warm yourselves," she called, and reached out for Mother's hand.

Mother took it easily, and let herself be led inside the fine building and up to their apartments. There was no one at all by the great hearth when we entered, though the room glowed with expectation. There was a plate of figs and sweetmeats with a bottle of wine on a table covered by a clean red rug. "Where is Father?" asked Nehemiah, dropping two sacks on the floor. "He might help with the trunk."

"He's stepped out to see to his spring cargo. We expected you earlier."

"And Simon?" I ventured. "Where is he?"

"He's just behind you, Pearl."

I whirled about and nearly collided with him, a tall man in a soiled white shirt, a hairy man.

"What a beard!" Instinctively I reached for it, though I knew better than to take his hand or crowd him in embrace. He winced at my touch, and his dark hair fell past his shoulders into his face.

"Simon. Do you know me?"

"I know you."

"I confess, your fur frightens me a little." I laughed to show I was jesting, but he didn't smile. He smiled not once that day.

"With my brother gone, there are none I trust with the blade," he explained in a hoarse whisper. He smoothed the hair behind his ears with long fingers. "Liza's hands quake like aspen."

Liza laughed and slapped at him with her apron front. I cast back in memory for an hour Simon and I had spent once on our backs under the tree whose round, thin leaves shiver and trill in wind. The wind that day had seized the yellow leaves and scattered them to the low sunlight. I had named that sound, that tree for Simon.

Nehemiah shifted and sorted our belongings. "You might ask Father," he spoke over a shoulder. His voice seemed cross, and wearied me. "You needn't wait for an invitation."

"Father is consumed with work."

"You get what you ask for, brother. No more in this world." He cleared his throat, and I moved away, escaping to see again two familiar paintings. They were the same family portraits that had graced the dark hall of the Milton house in Boston. I was amazed at how awkward these images now seemed, how foreign. The child Simon looked a young fiend with his hooded eyes exaggerated by the brush.

As if to separate me from their likenesses, Nehemiah firmly took my shoulders, his voice rising in false cheer. "Have you nothing welcoming to say to your new mother- and sister-in-law, Simon? They've waited well to bask in your presence."

"I remain your humble servant." It was so polite and cornered a speech that I couldn't bear it. I wanted to kick him or leap on his back like a wildcat, shred his ill-kempt frame to pieces.

"What *is it,* Simon, that incites you to melancholy—today of all days?"

The muffled anger in my husband's voice united the room. Liza sailed to him and took his arm. "Let's do our best with the trunk, young master. I feel quite able on this happy day."

Mother offered her help as well, and the three of them went out, though Nehemiah cast me a grim look. When I heard his steps retreat, I turned to Simon. "What has become of you?"

I meant the two of them, of course, though I don't know that Simon took it so. His chest heaved like a trapped animal's. Without a word, he lurched away and left me in the sitting room of my new home, where the children on the wall accused me.

"*H*e has lost his mirth of late," said Liza as we worked in the kitchen that evening. "Little in this city will have him—little that's safe—and he spends the better part of his days alone."

"He *chooses* to," warned Nehemiah, who had come in for glasses. "I have offered and offered, until the offer wilts on my tongue. Simon has nothing. He wants nothing."

"No one *wants* nothing," I said, and saw the knife in Liza's hand stop chopping.

Nehemiah stood behind me, his voice low and dark, though he slyly kissed the nape of my neck. "The world is large, Pearl, and there are many people in it that you will not fathom. Some are thieves, murderers, some godless. Others, like Simon, are flesh waiting to die."

I turned in time to see his shadow cross the threshold. Liza had covered her mouth with her hand.

"What—?" I stammered.

"It's my great sorrow," she replied, "and their father's too." She brushed the loose hair from my eyes. "And yours now."

"But I don't want it." I paced the room while Liza watched. "I don't want—"

"You had other plans?"

"Yes, of course I did. Of course."

"Well, so did I."

I looked at her in surprise.

"*But, dear Liza,* my lady is thinking, *you are a servant.*" She smiled warmly and took up her chopping again. "And so I am."

*Y*ou can't imagine how I tried to draw Simon back to me—to himself, I believed. Nehemiah would explain, with strained patience, that Simon *was* himself. He was every bit himself. It was my picture of him that had warped and buckled with the weather of years, with absence. "He's a man without god or purpose," Nehemiah pronounced, "and God has well repaid him."

When he wasn't damning Simon, my husband endeavored to saturate me in his London society so that I might be well supported and entertained during his absence at sea. It was an honorable end and brought a whole wardrobe with it, but I little wished that for myself. What I wanted was not a new dress with peaked bodice for the Red Bull, another tortoiseshell fan or flowered satin mantle lined with sarsenet, a bird's-eye yellow hood to wear on Whit Sunday, but to be still. To stare up at the sky. To hear the rush of wind in leaves and my own voice in my head, not the voices of others, so many others, strangers, that flowed through my urban days and nights. And to know that Dr. Devlin lived, ate, slept, labored somewhere in this vast city, that my father walked these same narrow, congested streets with no will to call on me, to meet me again at the bartering line, was an agony made more vivid still because I was forced to imagine anew his forgotten face and his voice, rinsed faint by years. Who was to say I hadn't passed this now mythical figure on the cobbles already, that we hadn't bumped shoulders in our separate errands?

Mother, for her part, was like water when I went to her. My hand moved through her. She was already gone in mind to kneel by the good minister's grave, I think, her scarlet "A" pinned fast to her breast.

One evening, as Nehemiah was to take me to a turtle frolic, I rifled through Mother's trunk—our trunk; I had always thought of it so— until I found the infamous badge wrapped in a scrap of linen. I knew instinctively what the flat parcel, so neatly folded, was and plucked it open one corner at a time, as if I were depetaling a flower. Mother slept in Mr. Milton's chamber while he was away, and so I went to his looking glass with the red letter pinned to me, but the sight of it on my new dress, a gentlewoman's dress, repelled me, and I slapped the stain off and left it on the floor. I remembered then my own youthful model of seaweed, and the smell and swell of the ocean I had played beside.

The turtle frolic was held in a tavern by the Thames, where the smell and sound of the sea seemed at least nearly possible. A sociable captain Nehemiah knew had caught the two-hundred-pound sea turtle and towed it back alive from the Caribbean. There was rum and punch while a West Indian ship's mate cooked the beast with great ceremony, telling Jumbie stories all the while, and at first Nehemiah kept me close by him, as there were few women on hand this night, and few of those were respectable.

He offered to see me home, but I saw that he was eager to remain and shook my head demurely. How inexplicably demure I was in those first days of wedlock! There never was so good and modest a wife, who kept her eyes trained to the floor.

How quickly too did the worst in that room seek me out. I felt their looks like cats clawing at my dress, and when Nehemiah lapsed into society and drink, they each found a wall to pin me to.

I smiled and nodded at these ribald men and women, sipped until the punch unhinged me, until a man came to stand by me whom I could not deter and uttered my maiden name with grim delight. He circled and studied me, his face familiar, and my eye cast about for my husband.

"No longer." I let my brow rise in the manner of affronted ladies.

"No, you are wed now, I know. To Nehemiah Milton. We are fellows, you see. I knew him in New England."

He was saying, of course, that he had known *me* in New England, though I could place him not on my mind's map.

"I warned him about you," he teased. "But he would hear none of it."

"He knows me."

"Not as I do," he cautioned, "as a baby witch with a branch in her hand."

He hushed as Nehemiah came striding. He smiled a weasel's smile and shook my husband's hand. They seemed awkward together, though it may have been my own horror that ruled the moment. "You've met Gideon Metcalf, Pearl? He says he knows you."

"He mistakes me." I felt the rum coursing in me, and a mean lightness. The group of men by the cooking pot had launched a round of song.

Nehemiah leaned close and whispered into the din, "Gideon was a clerk to Governor Bellingham. He knows the old tale well enough."

"And tells it, no doubt." What I saw in Gideon Metcalf's eyes was my own small self shrieking, brandishing a stick, tearing my dress on the sharp brush. The noise and smoke of the tavern made me reel. "But I forgive him for it. Now you'll forgive me," I said, "if I step out to take the air."

The weasel Gideon bowed as Nehemiah guided me past and out where the air kissed me. He led me along the quay, where he made a sloppy try at it himself, but he was drunk and he knew it, and knew enough yet to take public care with sobriety and decency, and we walked in silence a while, our heels clomping on the wood.

"Are you sorry, Pearl?"

I stopped by the rail and looked at the cold, floating moon. "No." I was not coy that night, with the rum in me, and knew what brand of sorry he meant.

"He hears me not—Simon."

"I know. Nor will he hear me."

"Then you've tried?"

I looked up at him, uncertain. "In my way. He's my kin now."

"But no matter—you *would* try. You will again—while I'm gone?"

He would seem, to another listener, to be requesting it. But I knew that he wasn't. "No. I shan't have time. I'll needs help Liza run the house, poor thing. She is old. Simon will do as he will—or won't."

"We'll see to another servant or two when I return. We'll need help with *our* household." He nodded overlong and touched my lips to silence me. "Father needs Liza."

I felt my youth in that moment, and my mother's going, and spent a tear or two that he wiped tenderly away. I loved him but knew also that I must now, and when he put his forehead to mine to ask of our unborn children, I nodded more, and blushed at my feet.

No child settled in me, at least not in the two moons before Nehemiah went to sea, though Mother whispered what she had learned from Sarah Atkinson, and Liza plied me with broth of stewed Lady's Mantle and mugwort, Devil's Oatmeal, and other plants that whispered of heat. She tucked hawthorn and violets into my drawstring pocket or my hair. She fed me market figs to increase my seed, and cooked with more spice than before.

None of this did Liza muster in a way that would seem unusual to saint or stranger, but I knew what she wished for me. I knew how happy it would have made my wayward mother too, had I conceived before she braved her journey. But when Nehemiah embraced me at shipside, I felt—mixed with my fear and grief at Mother's going—my young body's complaint that my husband should be taken from me when I was still barren. The journey would take months, as many as four, depending on the mood of the sea. And when I thought again, as Mother held me, of her homeward walk through that dappled forest that I knew so well in my dreams, I felt the chill of my fate. Liza pulled me to her side as the others boarded and said we should go; the ship might linger for hours, and with it my distraction. "Let them go," she said.

Back in our hollow rooms, Simon sat as usual by the window. He seemed to me to live at that window, in that chair, though for all practical purposes we had vanished to one another since my arrival in London. I knew not what to make of him. My eye avoided him, and because he spoke little, my ear did too.

In that time I had learned to dress like a lady—with four new gowns, none made by my hands or Mother's—an army of silk that made me stand taller. I had learned, more or less, to sound like a lady. At first I deemed it play until Nehemiah scolded me. "Your station has changed, Pearl. You must needs be a model for our children, and a light for the servants. Their educations will rest with you."

With me?

I saw Mother cover her smile that evening with her yawn. Perhaps she could imagine it no better than I could. She did not give my husband his due.

Once Caleb Milton had completed his local business and returned to us, the house had bustled. Liza and I were once again set loose upon the markets, but this time to prepare for a journey we would not make. Caleb Milton was a jolly man (who urged me to call him Father, though I couldn't master it in that short time). He took my hand often and smiled, but his smile slid as quickly away, like sea foam, on other errands. I never knew whether he approved of me or not. Perhaps his approval was too easily won and meant little, but those few days before the *Marietta* departed would be my last days of trying.

I noticed that he alone acknowledged Simon when he went. Caleb Milton knelt by his blind son's chair and lifted the bearded chin in one broad hand. "Don't haunt Liza round the house or frighten Pearl. Be merry in my thoughts."

My father-in-law did not kiss his son, or pull him into his bear's embrace, but held the chin long and sternly as one holds a child's. I complained in mind that Simon was not a child, but I was moved just the same by their affection. Simon's lip did not quiver. His hands did not float from his lap, but his angled head told me that he was breathing his father in, memorizing his smell and the sound of his voice. "Good-bye, then, Papa."

Would that my parting words for Mother had been so gentle. Just the night before, she'd found her dusty scarlet letter on the floor while she bundled up the last of her belongings. She cornered me and seized my hand, leading me without a word from the room where the household was gathered over pear cider and cards.

"What means this to you, that you can leave it lying?" She held it pinched between her fingers like some wet relic from the sea.

"Your shame," I said, "which is your habit." I looked her in the eye, and for the first time since the eve of my marriage, she looked back.

"Say what you will, Pearl, but I understand my duty."

"Call it what you will."

"My first duty, the minister taught me, was to you. Now that you are delivered—"

She laid the badge aside and took my hands. One slipped to my stomach, as if my womb were planted. "I won't forget you. But you must promise to tend well your babes. Do not go from them."

"Why would I? So that I might sail away and shrivel inside? Adopt the dying—and give my future to graves?"

Mother ignored my accusations. "Because you are a wild girl, and the hearth doesn't soothe you. But there's no other place for mothers."

"I'll serve God's will."

"It's *your* will that concerns me." Mother smiled and dropped my hand. She tucked her festering letter into her pocket, and on the morrow she was gone.

*A*fter Liza led me home from the harbor, I leapt two steps at a time up to our flat. I marched to his chair and stood abandoned and trembling. "I will shave your fur now, Simon. Make ready."

His face bobbed away from me. He had known I was there, but my direct address had startled him.

"You look a fright," I pronounced. "And it seems none will call the barber for you."

"My beard offends you?"

"You offend me."

He swiveled on his chair, and the legs dragged and squeaked on the floor. "I won't let you near me with a blade, Pearl."

I laughed a most impudent laugh and knew that Liza would be listening with relish. I leaned close to Simon's ear. He smelled rank and sweet, like October woods when the wet ground is choked with leaves. "They have gone, and you will grant me my chance, Simon. You owe me that."

"I owe you nothing."

"You soon will, then. I plan to pull you back from your precipice."

He snorted. "It's a pity the Theatre won't have you on stage."

I went to root through Caleb Milton's chamber but saw at once that Liza had left the blade and bowl of water standing.

*H*e had a fine, manly jaw under all the fur, and clenched it the while. When I moved under his chin, I raised a rash of gooseflesh on his neck. His Adam's apple traveled in his throat as I scraped at the tender space below his nose. Little by little, the dull hair dropped in his lap.

"You were never afraid of me before."

He made a low noise in his throat. It might have been laughter. "Wasn't I?"

I put down the blade on the bowl edge, dabbed at him with the rag, and squeezed one of his lean-muscled forearms. "You are bony as ever, Simon. Don't you wish to take your health outdoors?"

"I go out when it suits me. Speeding carts lack mercy."

"I've not seen you go once since I've been here."

"You've seen very little, Pearl, since you've been here."

"What mean you?"

He swayed, knowing he was trapped by me in his chair. "Nothing."

"Say it," I threatened.

"I've nothing to say."

"Aye, and no right to say it either, brother."

"Brother." He spat the word on the floor and turned full away from me.

I would have touched his long, curved back in its soiled shirt, but I knew that to do so would unseat him. "Anger won't soften him any more than petulance will. Nehemiah wants to see you live."

He spoke only to the window, placing his hands on the cool panes, but I thought his fresh face must look as white and expressionless as a winter moon. "He wants to see me dead—and off his conscience."

"Then, Simon," I measured. " Make him regret it."

WONDERS

Simon drew away from me that day, and I could not follow. Perhaps it was not in him to incite regret or other woe. For a time, I spoke to him as one speaks to an old dog in a corner of the floor, because that was how he acted.

Liza dressed me well morn and eve, and set my ringlets, and I went among the lesser of the merchant class to the drolls at the Red Bull, to watch rope-dancers and fire-eaters, to eat well and be merry. I saw Italian dancing puppets in a booth at Charing Cross, and graced tables at inns and eating houses with my neighbor Bess and other righteous married ladies, growing just-plump on tarts and cracknels.

One day as I was passing one of the new coffee houses in Fleet Street, I thought I saw my father enter. The building had a windowless front, and such smoky lairs were the realms of men, so I could not be certain, but after that I found myself—regularly and at random—roaming the narrow streets in my New Forest clothes (not to muddy the new with old habits) and delighting in the overbuilt timber rooms that shadowed the cobbles like great, drooping bosoms, in creaking carts and the clomp of hooves on crooked stones, in the jostling rows and husky cries: "Twelvepence a peck of oysters," or "Hot baked warden pears and pippins!" I took pains always to watch for pickpockets and the dangers any woman alone on the dim London streets must watch for—not least the possibility that some lordly thug or pair of louts might take a fancy to my face and drag me away kicking to their pleasure. But I was quick, and I could not resist going out to see the maidens balancing fresh cream and cheese on their heads or extending trays of hot pudding and pies, though I knew it would displease my husband. Peddlers had brushes to sell, or hats and caps, or knives, combs, and inkhorns. Now and then a liveried carriage bearing gentry rolled past, flinging rank water, and I glimpsed the fine ones within. Perhaps I was looking for him, after all, though I would not have confessed to doing so.

One excursion in particular brought the doctor forward in my thoughts. Bess came rapping one night to say I must make haste to join her downstairs. Her cousin had hired a coach, and a friend of said cousin knew a manservant in a fine house, one Sebastian Busby, who would for a nominal fee ("A kiss!" she roared into the echoing hallway, and a muffled bout of giggling ensued) admit them in strictest secrecy to view his master's hall of wonders. "Come down, Pearl!" she called through the closed door, and Liza looked up from her mending with a tight-lipped nod to where I stood struggling into my best petticoat and stuff gown. Simon, as usual, was where I was not.

"Coming!" I hoped my voice carried, and it must have done, for as I went out I found him in the dim chamber off the dining room, standing quite still as if caught between tasks—lurking, more like, without a whit of courage or conversation to tempt me home where I belonged. I paused once, thinking to bewilder him with a sisterly kiss, knock him off his guard, but that I should fret and hesitate only grieved me.

What had become of us? How still he was! As if, like some marked prey, arrested motion would save him.

*O*ur destination was a world away, and a perilous ride it was in that creaking hackney hell-cart. The cousin, George, was a mawkish youth, a near illiterate prentice bookbinder, and Bess spent the whole trip exposing his slovenly ways before excusing them. George consoled himself with wine from his flask, which it took great, pinching pains for Bess to relieve him of now and again, though neither of them needed more drink.

"This Sebastian Busby"—the reality of our outing was beginning to dawn on me as we rattled west over stones and cobbles—"who is he? I don't fancy George here will be much protection, come to that."

"He's a decent sort," said George.

"With a big fine house all to himself," crooned Bess with a wave of the flask, as if this well resolved it.

"And where is your William tonight?" I ventured.

"He's like to be where your Nehemiah is," Bess scolded. "Other than where he belongs."

I sat back humbled as the coach skidded on a muddy turn, and begged the Lord for mercy.

*W*ith its arched windows and graceful pillars, the stone house had probably been a monastery once, or part of one, but as pock-faced Sebastian Busby shushed us in through a servant's entrance, I saw that its interior was hardly austere. There were, it seemed, a thousand flickering candles on wall branches well out of reach of rats, and this profusion plagued our host, who lamented the night long that we'd been much delayed and his candles laid to waste, and whatever would his master say when the household returned?

But in the extravagant shadow-glow I saw a great quantity of damask and gilt leather adorned with painted fruits and flora; there were elaborate borders and tassels, and positioned here and there alongside or atop the heavy furniture were lacquered cabinets, celestial and terrestrial globes, barometers, and musical instruments. The ceilings were high and likewise ornate, and as we entered the gentleman's study I felt criminal and duly frightened.

We came to a tall door at the rear, our timid footfalls sounding hollow on the stone, and Sebastian stopped us with a scabby palm. "Here it is," he whispered. "Behind this door." His hooked thumb cast a garish shadow.

"The hall of wonders." He leered at Bess, no longer furtive now, all business. "George told you my price."

"If that's all," Bess brayed, winding her arm through George's and then unwinding it, betraying her nerves. "No wonder's so wondrous as *that,* Mr. Busby."

"I'm a simple man," he said primly, and when Bess leaned forward with a shrug to peck him on one scarred cheek, his ruined face was transformed, as if pride had touched it for the first time, or a woman had, and with a flourish he let her through. He then pried a coin from George's hand, cautioning, "Paw the treasures lightly! Or I'll put the dogs on you." Another profusion of candles beckoned through the cracked door, and George vanished therein.

Sebastian now regarded me, his aspect expectant. "Imagine it, won't you," he said, "the entire cosmos arranged in a single room. All the world's funds of *naturalia,* its marvels and miracles, at arm's reach that you might contemplate in miniature the most excellent abundance of God."

I crossed my arms and grimaced, but it seemed a small enough price to pay for such a promise, so I kissed the wretch without rancor, though his strong tongue parted my lips and slithered through like an eel. I then walked with the fiercest, haughtiest carriage I could into that long gallery with its pillars and flickering candlelight.

There were, indeed, too many curiosities for the eye to behold, artfully positioned on shelves and in countless narrow drawers aligned shoulder-high and labeled with melodious—and, to me, meaningless—words: *conchilia, mariana, succi, fructus, semina, ligna, cortices, radices, sulpura.* Trailing me all through that shadow-chamber was Sebastian Busby's voice, dull and too mannered for its station, the voice of an ambitious servant who has swallowed if not digested his master's speech: *repository of incomparable rarities . . . coral is of special interest to the curious . . . the accumulated skeletons of tiny ocean creatures . . . deposits form shapes that resemble plant growth . . . combining in one form the animal, vegetable, and mineral . . .*

I drew my fingers, electrified, over countless perfect shells arranged in a dizzying spiral. Petrified crabs, starfish, dried chameleons, pressed plants, skeletons so dainty they might have been knit together by a spider. There were a flawless scale-clad armadillo, glinting minerals and delicate fossils, insects entombed in amber. There were a pallid crocodile embryo in a tall jar; clay figurines appropriated, said our host, from Egyptian tombs; petrified wood in all manner of tortured poses; a stuffed orange jungle hen and sundry other fowl. There were as well an artful pincushion of beetles in every garish color of the rainbow and, suspended from the ceiling, the birch canoe of a New World Indian and a dozen or so monstrous turtle shells.

His flask emptied, young George occupied himself with the word "ammonite," which he spoke like a mantra until Bess cuffed him. "These!" she called out, pausing agape before row upon row of small creatures preserved in jars. "He's a necromancer, your master? Will these walk again? Sebastian? Answer me!"

"Let me into your bodice," he murmured, "and I'll show you his notebooks." Our host, who now watched Bess unflinchingly, was nearly doubled over under the delicious pains of commerce.

"When hens make holy water," she retorted, flicking at the glass of the unborn crocodile with contempt. "Foul old relics."

Sebastian Busby grew prim again. He invoked the Royal Society, to which his master (and my father) belonged, whose members witnessed firsthand the painstaking experiments of leading scientists. "He vows they take the blood of one dog and drain it off into another. . . ."

"A bumblebee in a cow patty thinks himself a king," murmured Bess, who grew ever less patient as she drew open drawer after drawer and forced each closed again with scarcely a glance at its contents. She next skipped up and down the gallery, her satin *swish* and merry shadow wreaking havoc on Sebastian's concentration. She was unfettered and empty-headed, I thought with envy, wishing to empty my own head—for it writhed now with horror. Wonder, indeed, but horror too, that the universe should be so dryly distilled, encased for the drunken pleasure of two frivolous cousins and a licentious servant. Learned men would not stop, perhaps, until they'd drained the pulse from every living mystery or seen it stopped up in a preserving bottle. I closed my eyes and traced the curves of a conch as Simon might, with hungry fingertips, and the sea surged in my ears and behind my lids.

"It's time we went." I set down the conch and steered Bess veering toward the locked gallery door. Obstinate Sebastian stood his ground, so I showed a bit of stocking to speed him along. George guffawed and flashed his own clad calf, and Sebastian Busby—his prospects, scholarly or otherwise, dashed to pieces—led us unceremoniously out to the cool night and our waiting coach.

J hardly saw Simon the next day—he made sure of that—but after supper, I stood by him at the window and we listened, if not as one, for the watchman's cry: "Look well to your lock, your fire, and your light. And God give you good-night." He refused my own humble "good-night," however, so I could little report on the hall of wonders or anything else. Eventually he strayed further still into sleep, and I summoned Liza, accosting her with, "Oh, but he is stubborn. I inly burn at what he won't say, and he *snores.*"

She smoothed my hair and fetched a blanket for Simon. "You exhaust him, I've no doubt, Pearl. Give leave for his frailty."

"He's no more frail than I am, and a good deal more cruel."

Liza smiled, and I went to my cold bed cursing husband, mother, and brother through my dreams.

But I soon saw fit to try again.

After we'd supped one eve in near silence, I trailed him soundlessly into the hearth room and there sat picking currants from my palm to pelt him one by one, tasting one or two between, enjoying the warmth of the embers. He brushed the treats away like flies but could not hold stern. "Give it to me," I commanded, "your laughter. I will own it yet."

"You're a most excellent fool, Pearl." He leaned forward on his hard chair, hands hanging as if he were stirring something in the space between his knees. "I think I remember when I stopped smiling," he said. "Freely, I mean. They say our memories reach not so far back, but I know this much."

His white hands moved to his face now, and grasped mouth and chin as if he were trying to conceal part of himself. His voice came muffled. "I was five year or so when my eyes went. Everything changed as it would, but I fancy what knocked me about most was not being smiled *at.* I knew I was a frowning brat, but not why—until it hit me that I wasn't seeing *them* smile: Liza, Papa, my brother, the baker, everyone. I had to strain for my smiles, fish them from the dark, for no picture invited them, no face did.

"But you knew me straight away, Pearl. Your every felt gesture was a smile, a tease, a pleasure. You spoke my language."

"Speak it with me now."

"I can't."

"Why not?"

"I'll not survive it."

"Are you surviving now?" I accused. "In this chair, under this same roof?"

"In my way."

"Your way is folly. I won't let you have it, beginning tomorrow at sunup. Do you feel the warm sun rise, Simon? Or do you sleep through till our footfalls wake you?"

He shook his head to stop me, but I wouldn't stop. "Do you hear the mice before you scoop the oatmeal, or must they bite you first? Do you trust not your instinct to thrive, Simon?"

"It pleases you to judge me?"

"I find I can't help it." I raised my head, imperious, and was struck again by the reality of his blindness. He had never once seen what I saw in the looking glass when I cared to look—my figure, my curls, my furor.

"Where will you take me this time, Pearl? Where will you lose sight of me? In a theater, perhaps? An eating house? And what next, a brothel? Where will I thrive when you pity me?"

"Simon—"

"I need none of what you can describe beyond these rooms."

"What else can I give you?"

He suffered a grim nod. "I've been saying as much, I think. So it's best you leave off trying."

"I can make you trust me."

"You can do anything, feel sure. But I'll pay for it. I think you have never understood that."

"I wish you could see me, Simon. I'm smiling." I reached for his hand, but it slid away like ice.

"I have no face for you. I've none for myself. I imagine it—that once or twice I saw my small one in a puddle or the horse's trough, like a moon shining—but I might be wrong about that face. It's been a goodly long time."

I shuddered to think of the day my mother and I had tarried in the forest near Boston, of my own pale face bending to kiss its double in rainwater. What if that dim, wild girl were all I had now? "And your parents?" I demanded. "Nehemiah? Liza?"

He shook his head. "I recollect only that Nehemiah was fleet, always blurring."

"Might we try, Simon, just slowly? I shan't forget again."

His brow creased, and he sighed the words: "I'll do what pleases you."

It pleased me to bring him everywhere, though he tired quickly. Our arms linked, we walked along the Thames, where the gulls shrieked and sailed on broad currents. This came to be his favorite walk because, he said, he felt the weather there. "To one with eyes," he said, "a fair sky and warmth make the day fine. For me, wind and rain are best, and thunder better still. I hear the whole shape of the world then."

But the narrow, crowded ways taxed him, and after an hour of weaving and my reckless descriptions, he would slow and fade. His beautiful hands flitted often to his face, as if to hide his own features, revenge himself on the diverse ones he could not see. Once he asked me to find him a remote place—an alley or a nook behind a scrap of tree—where he might relieve himself, and it struck me that his privacy depended so completely on others. He might, after all, mistake any quiet moment for solitude.

Only my arm or my voice told him I was there, so I chattered and hummed. When clattering carts came fast upon us, or a maid emptied a bucket from above, he groped for a wall or brought me off balance. Once a mongrel leapt snarling from a doorway, and I saw later that Simon had left bruises on my arm.

He might too, as we walked or sat within the London din, request some small object to hold. I would pluck a bit of herb from a garden box or buy him an apple from a cart, saying the words aloud, *red, round,* as once I had the letters of the hornbook for Dame Ashley. One morning I asked why he no longer carved with wood.

Simon was bewildered at first, and then pursed his lips in what might have been a smile. "We don't cut our own wood here, so scraps are scarce. And I'll tell you true, I lost my knife."

"Then why did you not ask your father for another?"

"I did, once or twice. He forgets."

"Did Nehemiah forget also?" I gnawed at my thumbnail.

"No. He forgets nothing."

"But you have no knife."

"No," Simon said lightly. "I have no knife."

We were breakfasting in Black Horse Alley after a walk one morning when the inn's proprietress circulated with prints advertising "A Most Extraordinarily Sagacious Pig." While Simon nibbled his cheese and toast he'd softened in a mug of ale, I read the print aloud: "'This porcine philosopher, returned from a grand tour of Scarborough, York, Banbury, Oxford, and Bath, is pleased to be returned to his educated London pa-trons and will perform feats of wondrous intelligence for your amusement at the courtyard of the Beef and Barley four Saturdays running.'"

"My brother-in-law is the conjurer," our hostess explained conspirato-rially, whisking away the crusts near my elbow. "The hog reads, writes, and casts accounts. I'll swear to it. They'll be here on the hour." She passed to the next room, and I read the remaining print aloud to Simon, who smiled somewhat sadly.

"Shall we stay?" I asked, flicking him under the chin.

He sipped his ale and assumed the concentrated look he wore when he was listening. The many smoky tavern rooms hummed with muffled conversation, not least that of a party behind a screened partition, from which also issued a raucous, rasping cough, waves of shrill laughter, and the clinking of glass. It had already been a long morning for him, I knew, but Simon had so little delight in his life; I resolved that he should have this. "Come now, brother. You must endure for my sake. It's pointless for me to go on living, having never yet seen a pig cast accounts."

He smiled again, so sorrowfully this time that I took his hand. Red in the mug, he felt around for the trencher of cheese I had carelessly moved, and he looked so relieved when he found it on the table that I ached for him.

*L*ondon spectators had their pick, to be sure, and animal acts were commonplace. During my brief residence, I'd seen wind-tossed prints and pasted bills announcing Russian flea circuses, dancing turkeys, drumming hares, and vaulting apes. There were renowned Chinese starlings trained to play cards and a "Wonderful Dog That Will Play Any Gentleman at Dominoes That Will Play Him." But I confess, when the innkeeper's brother-in-law entered the courtyard in a petite cart pulled by a vast black hog in a red waistcoat, I thrilled like a child. "The man's dress is sober," I told Simon, "but the pig sports a red waistcoat! It's a big black boar pig, I think, and his master in the cart looks grave as a ditch digger."

More chairs and benches were fetched, and the patrons shifted here and there round the performance area to suit themselves. I slid my own chair close behind Simon, who had a front-facing bench, and absently combed his hair with my fingers as we waited, toying as I watched the cart enter the courtyard. To my surprise, his head gave with the work my hands were doing, and I felt him relax into them and into the jovial crowd.

"Here, ladies and gentlemen, you have a race unjustly maligned," said the showman, and his animal paused dutifully, snortling and sniffing the air.

"I hear it," Simon whispered, bringing his head back. I went on stroking and smoothing his tangled hair, though an old gossip down the row sneered at my posture. He turned again to the conjurer's voice, and lest he lean away from me, I draped my arms lazily over his shoulders from behind. "He's loosening the harness. . . ." I whispered in his ear.

A small boy with knee patches dashed out and wheeled the little cart away. "Can brute creation reason?" boomed the showman. "The classicists among you will recall and henceforth consider the young man turned by the enchantress Circe into a hog. When his chance came, did the gent take his right form again? No, he did not, friends. He remained a sapient swine, preferring this to the state of Man and, what's more, calling it a *favor.*"

The man walked to the center of the courtyard whilst the child who had removed the cart now returned, beating a steady backdrop rhythm on a tabor. The pig trotted obligingly after his trainer. "Some among you would survey Tuck here and envision only cracklings or, worse yet, spot a foul, smelly brute, but I am come to acquaint you with a most marvelous and unrivaled beast, an Extraordinary and Sagacious Pig. Dublin-born, he is well traveled and, thanks to a precocious beginning wherein his dear mama wandered into a great man's library and supped on volumes of Plutarch and Aristotle, learned beyond compare. What the bookish sow did not do to prepare her unborn youngster, I, friends, have undertaken since. In our travels, Tuck has studied with a noted Chinese philosopher, mastered Greek and Latin, and is enabled with assistance to hold discourse upon French cuisine, Flemish art, and Danish antiquities. But enough said. Let us now proceed with our demonstration."

I smiled into Simon's neck, absently breathing him in. "He just slipped the pig a piece of apple," I whispered, "and now he's opened the lid of a box."

"Herein lie several marbles." The showman shook the contents and walked to Simon in the front row, holding out the box. "Young sir, assist me please in recording the number." He nudged Simon with the box, and my brother shook his head, panicked, but I reached forward and plunged his hand in. "Feel them," I murmured. "Don't run."

"Have you a count?" the man asked kindly, noting now Simon's blank eyes. "When you have, speak not aloud!"

Simon nodded and blushed, and the man smiled at me, turning gravely back to Tuck. The crowd murmured.

"Tell me, Tuck," said the showman, laying a number of typographical cards on the ground before the animal. "How many marbles are in the red box?"

The pig snuffled and, though it seemed to take an excruciatingly long time, tapped his right hoof on one of the cards. The man held it high for the crowd's approval. "Nine!" he called.

I whispered, "Is that right?" and Simon nodded eagerly. The man repeated my question for the public. "Tuck has selected the number nine. Sir, does this match your calculations?"

"Yes," Simon whispered, and when I thumped playfully on his chest with my palms, he called out, "Yes! It does."

"Well done, Tuck! Now then, I will lay down a quantity of cards and would ask Tuck to demonstrate his unrivaled knowledge of English letters. What words will best challenge this rational beast?" The man paused for effect. "*Leviathan? Extraneous?* I have on these many cards three of every entry in our alphabet." The crowd was inspired to shout out all the uniquely torturous words it could think of, and it took some while for the showman to pluck one from the maelstrom. Twice his boy had to lay down the tabor to sweep away orange rind and other debris that had rained onto the courtyard stage and distracted Tuck.

A dour-looking old man in the rearmost row, meanwhile, cried, "Black magic!" as the clever hog tapped out "s-a-r-t-o-r-i-a-l," the letters of which the conjurer held up in queue. Though no one heeded the heckler, his chins trembled.

Tuck proceeded to beat his master at cards, answer questions using the four principles of arithmetic, tell the hour and minute by reading an audience member's watch, guess the ages of diverse people in the courtyard, and bow graciously when the heckler pronounced, "The devil inherited a herd of swine!" or "Diabolical black magic!" into every lull.

"In fact, it's simpler than that, good sir," the showman countered at last. "Tuck is justly proud of his red waistcoat. Never in the many years of his extensive education have I beaten him." I saw the man slip his charge another bit of apple, then snap his fingers. Tuck lay on his broad stomach and cut a pitiful figure by placing front hooves alongside his eyes as if to cringe.

"When my student displays obstinacy, I merely threaten to render him uncivilized once more and burn the waistcoat in my hearth fire." The man deftly and discreetly signaled with his hand, and Tuck rolled over like a dog, poking his porker's legs skyward and wriggling them in alarm, which hilarity I described to Simon in detail. "Whoa, Tuck!" the man called. "Whoa, sir!"

The crowd, all but the heckler, who'd gone, pitched and roared with laughter. I felt Simon shudder with mirth under my arms and felt too the fiercest affection to see him so content outside his thoughts. I gave the pale of his neck above the linen collar—I'd earlier twined the crow-black hair and set it to one side—a quick kiss, and rather than flinch, he turned his face easily and grinned back at me. I folded my arms more soundly about him, laid a cheek on his shoulder blade, and forgot the crowd and even the Extraordinary Sagacious Pig, for my brother was glad.

MEMENTO MORI

*W*hen did London wilt for me, despite my reunion with Simon, brown and shrivel like the stripped stalks of Goodman Baker's autumn cornfields? I know not exactly, except that it must have been when Liza first grew sick with the cancer and Mother's first letter arrived.

I think of the two events as one; it may be that Liza brought that letter as a kind of offering or exchange, but before I opened it shut the door. With searching eyes, she brought my hand to her left breast, wincing. What I found there was a hard knob no bigger than a pea.

It increased in very little time, and sometimes looked red. She took the advice of the surgeons I summoned, had oils, sear cloths, plates of lead, and so on, but by September the knob had grown like an anthill and spread across her breast. For many weeks, I applied poultices to it. Eventually they broke the skin, and a watery thin stuff came stinking to the surface, though it did not flow forth. It hurt her so much as winter threatened that I came racing out of my bed several times a night to dress and change the plasters. She would now permit no surgeon to dress it but only me, and often Simon came to the room and sat silently by, unseen and unseeing, as I soothed and clucked and wrapped her.

When Nehemiah returned in December, finally and alone, she was at the end. With Liza too weak to argue, my husband (after entertaining and abandoning aloud the idea of bringing my own reputable father to call on her) brought back the first surgeon we had consulted, and the staid man cut away the breast—every sinew and nerve—by degrees with scissors. In a fortnight or little more, it appeared mere flesh, all raw so that she could scarce endure any unguent to be applied. A great cleft appeared through it like a scar after lightning.

Gasping apology, Liza had me read to her from the Psalms, and I took a hard joy in them, though it wearied me that with Nehemiah home, Simon would no longer come to the room and sit with us (nor walk out with me when I could breathe the hard air inside no longer). Sometimes I must shout over Liza's pained cries. *Thou hast beset me behind and before, and laid thine hand upon me. . . . Whither shall I go from thy spirit? or whither shall I flee from thy presence? If I ascend up into heaven thou art there: if I make my bed in hell, behold, thou art there. . . . If I say, Surely the darkness shall cover me; even the night shall be light about me. . . . Yea, the darkness hideth not from thee; but the night shineth as the day; the darkness and the light are both alike to thee.* Poor dear clutched my hand so tight my bones lamented, and then one day in midprayer, she did die.

Marvellous are thy works; and that *my soul knoweth right well.*

*D*eath was our companion that year. No sooner had we brushed the dirt of Liza's grave from our hands than a letter arrived from the ship's priest with news of Master Milton's demise. Caleb had died of consumption on shipboard with numberless others, and slept now cradled by the sea.

"But he was like a great tree!" I lamented. "There was no felling such a one."

"There was and ever is," said my husband with vacant eyes. "*Memento mori.* I have learned as much, and take it to heart—as we all must."

These words apparently gave Simon no comfort, for after we had picked at cold herring pie a long, agonizing while, he pushed his chair back so hard that the legs scraped a song on the boards. He groped his way out without a word, and we soon heard the clamor of objects in his chamber, things falling or things flung. But when I made to go to him, Nehemiah held my wrist. "Let him be."

"Be what?" I implored. "Alone?"

Nehemiah closed the letter in his other fist. "It's Simon's way."

I believe it was on that day or soon after that my husband's sleeping piety bloomed like a great thorned flower. He would sooner pray than speak. He would urge Simon and me to do the same. I have prayed my life long, but sporadically, when it moved me to do so, when the voice that sang praise was clear in mind and not a muddle. Now we had prescribed prayer or readings morn and eve and sometimes between. One dim afternoon, as Nehemiah made ready to go and interview the brother and sister that Gideon Metcalf would let go from his service while in Italy, I went to Simon's chamber and found Nehemiah pacing behind the younger's prayers. I saw him kick his brother lightly in the bony backside. "Why must you mutter, Simon? Why do you begrudge God at every turn?"

Simon, on his knees, did not budge, nor did he reply.

"I might have known I would wear the yoke of you always." Nehemiah went out and past me without a word, and the landing door slammed like a musket shot.

I took my brother's hand and, though he could well find his own way—perhaps I craved the warmth of him—led him out and across the hollow hearth room to his chair by the window. I dragged a straight chair near and reopened Mother's last letter. I had been carrying it folded in my pocket, meaning for some time to share it with Simon, who listened intently, without blinking, as I read aloud. The letter held word of the garden, the look of the little bay that kept our cottage like a pistil at its scented heart, the kindness of my former neighbors now, with time's passage; they had prayed over her and blessed her, and the women especially did know Mother now as one among them. The work of the Apostle Eliot had made more traffic with the Indians, and the town had spread like moss over rock.

"'You would not know Boston now,'" I read, "'so much more brisk and industrious is the mood of it. But the woods beyond still yawn, and the stars shine as before. I remember now our last night here and wonder yet if these are the same stars you see in England. Perhaps I misled you that night, as these lights seem devoted to this place alone, and wink on the good minister's stone, which I will sometimes chance to visit before Mistress Tibbins and her lot claim the night. I step as silent as a cat that the sexton in his lodgings won't rise from his pipe and find me there. Your child form is still much felt in this place, too. I sometimes think I see her running in the fields or chasing chipmunks along the stonewalls. I am not lonely with so many ghosts (you may laugh, not weep, when I say it) and the charity of new friends and neighbors to stay me. How does Nehemiah? My needles are busy with sweet things for the baby.'"

My hand fell to my flat stomach. Since his return, and with grief to greet him, Nehemiah had watered me with his prayerful tears as he lay over me, but his seed would not favor me. My solemn, almost secretive husband was not for me to own in those days. He spoke of little but his work, which consumed him much since his father's death, and his mind roamed over plans for me but rarely rested in the moment where I lived.

When he returned with Gideon Metcalf's former servants—now our own—I wondered had he inquired as to why they had been discharged? Margaret was a pretty girl, creamy pink and strong of shoulder, but would not meet my eye to rue the devil. Her gangly brother had a shifty look that well reminded me of his former master, the weasel Gideon. But perhaps my view of them was stained by this history.

"They were discharged because Gideon will long be in Italy."

"It's not the custom for servants to travel with their masters?"

"Yes, if their term be not up and they have a mind to. These would keep to England. The boy, William, has much to learn before he can be his own master."

"I wish Liza were here."

He took up my hand and, quickly, laid a kiss in my palm. "But she is not, and these will do—and you will work less and worry less."

"I rarely worry," I teased, and then thought to make better use of my husband's attentions. "But for Simon—a little."

Nehemiah sighed and rolled his eyes. "Mag will see to him now. You will run the household. I can't forget that Liza managed this feat for my mother in her helplessness, and you, thus abandoned, have much to learn about housewifery."

"I know my excuse. Not so long ago, I was a servant myself," I said coldly, "and thoughtless. But how did your mother fail you?"

He walked me back against the wall and touched his fingers to my hair, though he seemed sick to look at me. "You are full of hard, musical words like your father. You should hear him at the coffee houses, spewing his science among gentlemen, quoting licentious poetry, carrying on before God of dissections and body-snatching—"

How freely he spoke of the doctor, as if he had seen him but yesterday! I fought to conceal my surprise as my husband, languid with desire or just weary, rested his forehead on one of his arms, now propped on the boards. His voice came muffled in linen. "You'll not persist in reminding me of your ungodly origins, Pearl. I require you to please me now, as my wife." I slipped like water between him and the wall, felt him harden against my hip, and vowed that I would.

*B*ut I could not please him. I believed I would and did try, for a while. I pored over Liza's calendars and accounts, went to see each of her people in the markets. I set Mag to what tasks suited her, though Nehemiah doubted always my choices. "Get her up to launder at four," he said, "and you'll not have to bake the bread."

When he saw me heaving a cask of beer down the cellar, he barked for William and shook his head at me. Mag, for her part, studied carefully the current between us. Before long, she could predict better than I what would or would not suit him. "Master will not like to see you scouring, lady," she would say, and, "That is more befitting my station than yours, Mistress Pearl." I don't recall what year it was, but when a periwig he'd ordered made after the fashion came full of nits, I found a grim satisfaction in pinching them one by one between my fingers, and he, finding me so, slapped the wig from my hands.

Perhaps I was but a servant in my heart.

One evening when Nehemiah was at the tavern, Simon said, "He will not be content, Pearl."

"He?"

"My brother."

"My husband, you mean?"

"He is that, yes. And no more content for it."

"You fault me?"

Simon shut tight his expressionless eyes as if they smarted. "I would be the last to do it."

"Then why do you speak so?"

"I hate to see you scorned by him in my place."

"You don't *see* me at all." The words stung even my own lips, and I immediately begged his pardon.

"'*Sorry*,'" he said, "'is a fool's gift.' A wise child once told me that."

"Wise she never was, Simon. Tell me, why does he hate us? Why won't he let you out walking? Why does he scowl when I read scripture?"

"Can you honor your father, the doctor, Pearl? Though you knew him not?"

"I know him."

"You know nothing. Not even where he lives. You know less than anyone, and yet he made you and has sheltered you."

I shrugged.

"And you honor God?"

"I honor God," I mimicked.

"And you know Him?"

"I do."

"You do not wholly. Yet He made you."

"What is your purpose, Simon? May the devil speed you to it."

"Nehemiah is our master. Like the father on earth and the maker in

Heaven, he acts for us. We must not ask to see his accounts——" His murmured words seemed to vex him, and he frowned. "I mean only that we must love and trust even what we can't see."

"Where then *does* my father live, Simon? You know. Everyone in this household knows. Tell me."

He shook his head gravely. "It will lead to nothing."

"Then so be it. Make haste——"

"Nay."

"Simon——"

He whispered something, and I had to kneel before him, my hands clasping his rigid knees.

"I would know." He refused to raise his head or credit my nearness. "I am not afraid to look on those who master me."

"I've heard mention of lodgings above an apothecary in Camomile Street and Bucklersbury," he hissed into his lap, "at the sign of the dragon."

I leaned back to give Simon rest, but he raised his face and pronounced, almost desperately, "He is more than we know. And he knows best for us."

Of which "he" did Simon speak now? His brother? The Lord God? Perhaps, to him, there was scant difference. I heard Mag come to the hearth to feed the fire, and with no just cause I inched closer on my knees and leaned in again, whispering, "And should he prove to be less?"

For the first time, the adult Simon reached for me——not to balance himself or be guided. His palm found and cradled my cheek, then slipped away. He sat back as far as he could go in his chair. "What's the good in supposing it?"

I felt a rash of heat on my leg. Mag had banked the fire beyond blazing. "Goodness, girl," I snapped, "are you trying to burn the house down?"

"I should wonder as much myself." It took me a moment to understand, but I straightened up and looked at her with all the Hell I had in me. "Say it again and I'll cut your tongue out."

"Forgive me, Mistress." She bowed with a coy smirk, more court minstrel than maidservant.

I left them and escaped to the clamorous streets.

. . .

*O*n Sabbath after meeting, I asked Nehemiah to walk with me by the river. He relented only, I think, because we were surrounded by neighbors who nodded their approval when I murmured, "You are more like to find God there than in your account books."

Nehemiah waited for the pinch-lipped crowd to melt away before he warned into my ear, "The world need not know that I labor on the Lord's day, Pearl."

I was silent in apology, silent until we reached the river. He pulled my cloak tighter around me when we stopped to watch the barges and wherries crossing their windy paths. "I have always cherished the sight of water," he said low into the wind. "The pull of a journey gives such purpose, I want not to step to earth again, except to return to you. The deck of a ship suits me." He looked at me intently, his golden-brown eyes as liquid as his voice. "But now I think of Father sleeping in the sea. The ship's priest said he committed the body to the deep to be turned to corruption, and I wonder ever since if the crabs visit him. And do cruel storms reach him there, or does he rock gently with the tide like grass? And on the day when the body is resurrected, and the sea shall give up her dead, will his smile be a mouthful of coral—"

"He is above now, not below."

Nehemiah sighed bitterly. "Do you believe in the celestial shore, Pearl? Is it as real to you even as your wretched wilderness across the Atlantic?"

"I thought the idea might please you."

"But does it please *you?*"

"It does."

"Then you strive for grace?"

"I have a sore history, husband."

"Do you embrace your history, Pearl, or do you embrace God?"

I turned to the wind. I listened for the shriek of gulls as they flew like arrows pointing toward the sea. I imagined pinching the tiny boats, toy boats, between my fingers as they tossed on the windy Thames. I concentrated on this, all this, but could not rinse the panic from my blood. "Tell me what you want me to embrace, Nehemiah, and I will embrace it. I am sworn to you."

I could see that it was not enough. He kept his gaze on the bobbing craft. "I'll not command you. What use is there?"

"Why do you blame Simon? What has he done that makes you rage at him?"

"He has done nothing. I rage at *nothing*."

"And when he tries to do or be other than nothing, you begrudge him. He would stand here now and listen, and feel for a moment's time at home in the world. But you bind him to his chair."

"And what should I do instead, Pearl? Bind him further to you?"

"What mean you?"

He took my chin and lifted my gaze back to him. "His comfort costs me either way. I mean that you are your mother's daughter."

Her face swam into my mind with a surge of longing. "My mother," I repeated dully. "Would you offend me by saying it? Think hard on your answer."

He said nothing but began to collect small stones and hurl them into the water. "I don't know, Pearl."

"You must know."

"I don't. Nor do you. The truth, it seems, will die with her."

"They called me once the devil's seed. Do we know that they are wrong about that? Can we know?"

"I know."

"You said you didn't. You cried dumb just a moment before——"

"Hush, now. The ferrymen will all row closer to hear you."

"Perhaps I am also a witch. Perhaps I've bewitched you, and the spell is thin now, and you are fearful?"

"Stop, Pearl."

"Why does no one speak of *him?*" This last word felt more liberated than spoken, and the windy Thames seized it with glee.

"Him?"

"My father."

"Because he is at his best a gentleman, and wills it so," my husband said sternly.

"A gentleman." I laughed. "Indeed. A prince. Perhaps his royal black blood will boil like pitch in our children's veins—"

Nehemiah did not slap me hard, but hard enough that I bit my lip. My mouth filled with warm blood. I liked the taste of it. I liked it.

"I am silenced," I said in the flattest voice I could muster, and spat a wet, pink mouthful into the river.

If he mistook my resignation for triumph, I'll not be blamed.

A CRIME AGAINST MY MEMORY

*F*or days I kept Simon's words like a stolen gem under my tongue. I walked toward Camomile Street and turned back. I came countless times to the sign of the dragon, felt my chest tighten, and crept away again. Once I came as far as the casements and peered down through smoky glass into a shop set below street level, a typical apothecary lined with glass jars and waxy wooden drawers packed no doubt with herbs and powders, pills, treacles, and dentifrices, pomades and love-charms. Bloodletting bowls dangled from the ceiling to advertise an affiliate surgeon, who in this case was surely Dr. Devlin himself. Here was no scholar's cabinet of wonder, but needy souls came begging for a bit of Thames water turned *aqua cinnamoni*, no doubt, for moss and smoked horse testicles, may dew and henbane. Such shops invariably featured dusty light falling at a slant while some black-clad figure with eyes too big for his head sidled out to paw the skull his ilk displayed along with folios in ancient tongues.

There was a squat little woman in this shop also. Finely but soberly dressed, she gripped hard the hand of a pasty, ill-behaved boy who tugged and leaned away as if to topple her. I knew at once they were my father's wife and brat, those he had dared speak of while my own mother had slumped in the stocks in Boston. I watched the pair chatter with the apothecary until my sour insides threatened to come up, and then I fled that spot, tainted.

Before long, curiosity drove me back. I stood one afternoon under an awning across the road and watched the shadowy comings and goings till he came striding into the jostle of midday, eyes fixed on a wrinkled broadsheet as he neared his entryway.

"Sir," I cried out, striding across crooked cobbles to my father's evident horror, "I have an ailment." Strangers flowed past and between us as he stood dumbstruck, waiting for me to light under his nose like an apparition. I stopped an arm's length away. Sad and gray and shrunken was he who seized my arm and led me into the facing alley, where none could trample us. "I am stricken," I assured my escort, who set me against the soiled wall and stepped back to look on me, astonished.

I was little surprised that my presence displeased him, but his disappointment—that fate should so intrude upon him wearing my face—was tangible, and disappointment meant that something had been expected of me and I had failed to deliver it. His tongue lay, evidently, under a lead weight.

"You said when first we met in that field in New England, Doctor, that my care with words pleased you. Do I please you now?" I forced a shaky smile and felt the heat in my face. "Where is your faith in words now?"

He clasped my arm and startled me with his strength, which seemed unlikely in one so wan. Plainly vexed, he asked where I had come from, and how, and to what end?

"To satisfy myself only."

"There will be no satisfaction here, Pearl, for any of us." He looked at me with such glazed eyes that I wondered whether he, like Simon, was blind now. But he rallied quickly. "I have done my best for you. I have endeavored to support you inasmuch as I could. Is it money you lack?"

"I hadn't thought of that," I replied grimly. "Nor to find you so sallow and shrunken, with your doughy child and dusty shop."

"I have labored my life long to disappoint you." A glimmer of the old play creased round his eyes. "And here at last I have succeeded."

"I confess, I liked you better when you were the devil—may none hear me say it—but I will not grant you idle chatter. All life is barter," I commanded, searching hard those haunted eyes. "And if I am to accept, go on accepting, the gifts for which you will not be accountable, your worldly allowance and your unworldly penance; if I am to soothe your conscience, you will return the favor. You will, sir."

"Did I claim a conscience once?" he mused, but his look was stealthy. He worried, I understood, that he might be caught in the light with this secret so long kept; I stood in the face of the sun, and nothing would grow while I did. "I might be said to be impoverished in this regard," he admitted wearily. Gray and ordinary he was. A crime against my memory.

No prince but a man.

"Scorn me now," I said with no such intent, "and the other plump fruit of your loins shall suffer as I do. I'll see to it."

"Pearl," he chided, "why?"

"Does he amuse you?" I asked. "Your brat? Is he clever?"

"He is anything but. Sweet and dull as new cream on the tongue. And as innocent."

"You have no obligation, of course, to endure my curiosity, but innocent of *what* exactly?"

"His father's failings."

"Meaning me, of course, and my mother, whom you seduced and slandered."

"I would take credit for the former if I could." Agitation flickered in his aspect, but he rallied again, asking had I lately enjoyed the theater. "The playwright Wycherley's words," he teased, "bode well for you:

> When parents are slaves
> Their brats cannot be any other.
> Great wits and great braves
> Have always a whore to their mother."

I reared forward with all my might and shoved him back, and though he winced in surprise, he barely contained his smile. I *did* amuse him, it would seem. Worse, I was aware of amusing him. Worse still, I enjoyed it, though it came hard at my mother's expense.

"Did you never care for her at all? You returned to seek us out. Why, then?"

"Won't she speak," he entreated, "and do me the service of ending your unwholesome fascination with me?"

"I don't count silence a friend."

He looked round and for a moment seemed less the gray and craven gentleman with an untidy secret than the bright devil of my youth. He spoke in a dangerous whisper, crowding me back against the timber. "I returned because I had never left those shores in mind or spirit and wished to, for my son's sake."

"And was your wish granted?"

"I may as well tell you—" I saw his fearful resolve, saw the light of patience and affection leave his eyes; reflected there instead, as in pools of rainwater, was my own small form, pale and wild and forsaken. "I took her without her will. I used her and left her alone with her shame, and you are but flesh and proof of it."

I felt wither in me with the nearness of his tobacco breath whatever trust I had wrongly assumed. Recalling Simon's reluctance, Nehemiah's chastening of me by the Thames, I knew now my own foolishness, my womanish lack of wit. What had I wished to learn? If my father had misled me, he was, Nehemiah might argue, entitled. To give and retract, create and disown.

I fought to get past him, my lips pinched in an agony of fear. He held me, and I struggled. My heel hit a slick of rank kitchen peel, and his strong hold righted me. "Let me tell where I've come from just now." He held a palm flat against my collarbone as if to staunch it. "Have you seen a gangrenous wound? I had one on my rounds this morning. Know you how I heal in such cases?"

I shook my head, weakened by bitterness.

"Maggots are the filth of the earth," he explained, "but they're avid. They feast on dead and damaged flesh and, by so doing, clean the wound. The truth is just this pretty, Pearl, but it will serve."

"Why did you return for us?"

Perhaps I needed to hear him say that his New World endearments and lately aid were another form of dalliance, a violent thoughtlessness—as mere as my mother's virtue—but he brought a finger to his lips to shush me.

"I would heal my wrongs," he said, "but how then spare you the cure?"

For a moment I let the urgency of those eyes flecked through with gold and sorrow (beguiling they were, as the serpent) hold me fast. But I soon began to drift, hearing as through gauze, for he seemed to be addressing no one.

"I'm roused some days, often with scalpel in hand in the anatomical theater at Warwick Lane, to discover myself an imposter. I've come through life falsely. Grateful I am then to be a physician, for the shock of blood on my hands recalls me." He displayed the hands, turning them like meat on a spit. "*I am alive,* these steady friends assure, and worthy of life. It may not be what Dryden knows when the ink flows freely, but it's something.

"And so I am allowed to dream on, glad as any dog to rest by my hearth of an evening, to gnaw a mutton bone while the boy I sired plays marbles in firelight. *That* man lives here—" he motioned toward the mouth of the alley—" on this street, and looks on you now, his clever daughter from another life, from another, darker land, only to wish you were never born."

Consumed by pity for himself, perhaps, he stepped into the shadow of the far wall. I sidled out into a streaming crowd and, because he did not call, I did not look back.

PLEASE YOURSELF

*I*t was not only Liza and Father Milton who died in those days, but the Lord Protector himself. Oliver Cromwell stormed Heaven in fall of 1658, and his son Richard shrank in his shadow. Just two years later, Parliament ordered the King's birthday in May to be kept as a day of thanksgiving for our redemption from tyranny and the King's return to his government. The cannons boomed, the bells rang, the bonfires flared. The Royalists came out of the woodwork. Nehemiah was among the throng for the King's coronation, saw the grand procession from the Tower to Whitehall, and said Lord Monk rode after the King with a spare horse, and that the King, in a rich embroidered suit and cloak, looked noble indeed.

Nehemiah did not sail that spring but went to Charing Cross in October to see Major General Harrison hanged, drawn, and quartered—the first blood shed in revenge of the old King. "He looked as good in spirit as a man with that fate can," Nehemiah told us, "though the happy roar drowned out his words." The general was unceremoniously cut down and his head and heart displayed to the crowd, which whooped more with pleasure.

When I wrote to Mother of these and other events, I felt strangely aloof from them. I felt my gossip spill onto the page but little understood what use she might find in it. Such matters were for men and courtiers. "I am still without child," I wrote in closing, "so rest your needles."

Now it was Mag who circled and fed me all manner of folk wisdom: Do not let Master hug you too hard. Eat no late suppers. Bid him drink mum and sugar or, better yet, juice of sage, and wear cool drawers. Keep stomach warm and back cool. Lie with your head where your heels do lie, or at least make the bed high at feet and low at head.

While Nehemiah would have no whimsy, he listened for all such methods and did report a few himself—offerings from the wives of citizens in his circle.

But it was understood that I would fail him in this most sacred duty. He spoke often and mournfully of his father, though the business thrived twofold without the elder man's easy ways to hinder it. Sometimes I felt that Nehemiah would crush me into the mattress, his fever for a son was such, but he was gentle often enough to redeem us. Even when his disappointments chilled, he did touch me, and I threatened to fly apart. Sometimes, inexplicably, I heard the reverend's last sermon—or the wordless swell of it—in some far part of my mind as my husband loved me, and I half believed it was this grateful sensation of splintering to pieces in my bed that kept our child away. I was no round and waiting ball of dough in which an infant might grow, but a storm of glass.

What I longed for most in those days was Liza's calm. Her heavy hand on the small of my back, leading me through the market or guiding my hand in the kitchen. Her hoarse consolations as she tucked a blanket round Simon in his chair. Instead, I had strange Mag, who seemed to plot my ruin at least as often as she loved me. She did nothing wrong; she cooked and baked and cleaned as well as I could wish and better, but she defied me too. She never opened our strife to scrutiny, but I knew that she knew me, and in knowing disapproved, and she had no right. Her favorite ploy was to beg, in Nehemiah's presence, that I read to her from scripture. "I do so love to hear it, Mistress."

Mag couldn't read or write her own name (and a blessing it was, or I'd have no cause to sit by Simon now), and I was charged with her education. I had no mind for teaching, and less patience, and so much Bible reading did keep my heart on the edge of Hell always, for I could but fail in such a holy-vaulted place. I let my voice echo through the rooms, though. I let my husband hear it. I chose well the Lord's words for Simon, and did send them like spies to sit by him in the dark: *Yea, the darkness hideth not from thee; but the night shineth as the day.*

Above all, I tried to banish thoughts of the doctor. I would will away that dough-faced boy tugging at his mother's hand, those happy marbles clapping in the firelight, but he and they ghosted through my dreams. I remember standing one morning riveted at Simon's window as a red-tailed hawk hunted above the facing rooftops. How gorgeous was that frantic, whirling mass of pigeons, which dipped and dropped and rose again in the spired light like smoke. The hawk, for his part, lay cradled on air before tipping time and again into assault, but even as I savored this spectacle, my parent's words began to gnaw . . . *to wish that you were never born.* The aerial drama fled my sight as if jerked offstage by strings, and it seemed to me that my own distraction was to blame. I never saw if that hawk had his meal or hungered on while his massed quarry whirled through space. And even this small loss now bore Daniel Devlin's stamp.

"*I* would go to New Forest when you sail," I petitioned Nehemiah that spring. "London tires me without you."

Flattered, perhaps, he gave in easily. Perhaps too easily, I think now, though what use is yesterthought I know not.

Mag and I saw to the household as Nehemiah and William readied to sail to Barbados and Virginia. Mag cursed me and cried to leave her suitor, a young wheelwright, though I promised that he was welcome to visit a corner of the floor in Hampshire. "It is not much of a cottage," I warned, "even for the three of us. But there are miles and splendid miles for wandering."

"I have no joy in wandering."

"Then learn some," I said.

Between psalms, I whispered in Simon's ear of the moors, the stream-beds, the deer and ponies, the vast tracts of enclosed forest from which the navy drew its timber. I laughed, recalling for him Liza's evening tale by firelight when Nehemiah first brought me home to the Milton house in London.

"Oh, New Forest!" Liza had clapped her red hands soundly. "Know you, Pearl, that the glades are haunted there?" She spoke low to the assembled—in a voice made for children. "That ruthless William Rufus dreamed one night of a river of blood, they say, streaming from his own breast. The Red King ignored the omen and his lords' entreaties and joined the hunt next evening." Liza paused for effect, shadows flickering on her old face. "Was his fellow, Sir Walter Tyrell, blinded by twilight? Did the arrow truly glance off the great oak? We'll not know except that some say Ocknell Pond runs red . . . where Tyrell kneeled to rinse his hands on the way to Normandy."

She surveyed her audience with a vast sigh: "The royal cadaver was carted to Winchester, where not a single bell tolled. No prayer was whispered. For every subject knew him to be bound for damnation, baptized or not. Did you never see his ghost, Pearl?"

"Never," I'd confessed before the fire, shamefaced. "And how do you know such tales, Liza? Did you dwell once in Hampshire?"

"No, I've a trunk full of tavern castoffs, and a trick memory that keeps what it will."

I remember warm, bitter ale on my tongue that night, her storyteller's look of satisfaction as she slurped an oyster, the sweet smell of cedar smoke—and that I, a bride, wished to know again what a child had known smothered at her vinegar-rank bosom. How sorry I now was to think that she would not be here to soothe nor scare wits out of *my* children when they came. It occurred to me that I didn't even know if she'd borne any of her own ever, or lost them.

"It will be as before, Simon," I went on absently, though I little believed it. "I will paint your face with dew."

He spoke not one word but turned toward the window. Perhaps Liza's shade had touched him too.

"Why do you face always the window," I demanded, "when you can't see it?"

"I hear the world is there, and I'm here—safe from it. It's a happy arrangement."

"You would not go to New Forest?"

"I can choose?"

"You'd not balk if Liza were here. I didn't think to consult you because—"

"You have no obligation to consult—"

"Simon—"

"Mistress?"

"Simon!" The knowledge that I was shrieking came like sudden blood on my hands. Nehemiah and William came running.

"What is it?" demanded my husband. They both stood panting by the hearth. "What's wrong?"

"He angers me."

Nehemiah laughed and slapped Simon on the back. "It takes no great talent, brother."

William lurched away and back to his tasks in the cellar. I stood with my hands on my hips, courting their ridicule.

"What has he done?"

"He would not go to New Forest."

"He will go, but why don't you wish to, Simon?" Nehemiah's voice was surprisingly gentle.

Simon shrugged and blinked hard. "I have no wishes either way."

Nehemiah again put a hand on his brother's shoulder and reached for me with his free one. "I have here two ends of a candle. One that would burn too well, while the other burns not at all." He then called in a jarring voice for Mag.

She came in wiping her hands on her apron front. "Yes?"

"You will assure Simon that my wife will not abuse him in New Forest and leave him to fend for himself in a faery ring."

She slapped a hand over her mouth, her green eyes bright with her master's mischief. I saw not the humor in it and said so.

"Pearl. My brother hates change. His world is so much smaller than

yours, and you persist in enlarging it, to his horror. Leave him to his corner with that new knife you bought him. He'll carve the Forest clean before my return. But don't presume to know him better than I do."

I bristled at this, but it was Simon's blank expression that cut me most
because it argued not at all.

"We follow your whims because we fear your petulance," Nehemiah
continued. "But does that mean we're owned by them?"

It took all the courage I had to shrug, to hold my tongue and go from
there with Mag at my heels yelping.

"Get away," I hissed at her in my chamber, and she went, gladly, I
expect.

*N*ehemiah hired an enclosed carriage for the journey this time, so we
did not bounce ourselves silly on the wagon, and a good thing too,
for it never stopped raining, and there were no Zeb Halls to liven our stays
at inns. I watched Simon, who sat across from me, without seeming to for
many hours at a time. The rain sealed the four of us into a kind of drum,
and the listening sat well on his features, and he was quiet and thoughtful.
Mag chattered in the evenings, usually as we approached an inn, but was
dull and thick with resignation during the day. Nehemiah reviewed his
account books and instructed Mag in the running of the cottage. "If a
thing needs doing that a man will do, ask Reverend Lacey in Lyndhurst to
direct you. I've written to him and had his reply. He says that for what it's
worth, the kitchen garden is well sown by one of his boys. The agister or
keeper must know of any land questions to affect the commoners' ponies
and cattle, or the deer. The beasts will eat all if you don't mind the fence."

Mag nodded, and her dimpled chin bobbed with importance.

"And the donkeys will mate before your eyes while you wring the
washing," I added.

After a silence, both Simon and my husband snorted with laughter.
"Pearl knows the country well," said Nehemiah. A blushing Simon lowered his head. "But she'll need reminding," Nehemiah went on, "what to

fence in and what to fence out. She thinks to talk to the beasts and know them."

Mag laughed now too, and a smile flickered on Simon's lips.

"I have tamed many in my time," I teased back, and my husband smiled so warmly that I took his broad hand and brought it to my lips. He was never so kind as when he was going.

It rained and rained, and I slept against his shoulder.

Long before I was set loose among the trees, the green air filled my lungs like a sail, and even before we unpacked the carriage I was hungry to feel the earth in my fingernails, the clay suck of mud between my toes. New Forest was still not—and could never be—the uncivilized realm of my youth, with its endless promise. Many of the great oaks and beeches had been felled for timber, but the land was crossed with brooks and bogs, neat ornamental woods and tangled little patches of fir and holly that on that day called to me like Heaven.

In the evening, as Mag and I bustled about making beds and stewing the venison we'd bought in Lyndhurst, I could hardly keep from the window. The orange-soaked oaks with their great patches of lichen, the smear of sunset on the rise leading to the heath that would be golden in spring with the blaze of furze. How had I forgotten?

"I'm craving hash. I'll find a rabbit," called Nehemiah, who had just helped Simon order his things and settle in his chair. He had been kind to his brother of late, inexplicably kind; perhaps he knew the new surroundings would tax Simon.

I came racing out with my apron in a tangle round my hands. "Let me come with you."

Nehemiah shook his head, but I followed soundlessly. He knew I was there but didn't speak or stay me. He found a rabbit almost at once on the heath and took it with a single shot as I stood motionless and grateful among the dragonflies.

"Don't go back yet." I knelt in the coarse growth. The shadows were long and sweet on the world. "Say your good-byes here, where I'll hear them."

My husband smiled, but it was his father's smile and slipped as quickly away, back toward the cottage and his duties. He held out his hand for me, and I took it while the bound rabbit stiffened and swung from the rifle in his other.

I skinned the animal with great ceremony, though Nehemiah would rather Mag did it while I sat with him and Simon by the hearth. I meticulously scraped muscle from bone, piled the stringy meat onto a trencher, and draped the skin outside on the rack to air.

The cottage smelled rich now that the door had been left open to the night and the spiced stew bubbled on the hearth. I asked Simon did the smell of spring and supper please him, and he said it did, "very much."

Nehemiah sipped his cider and smiled often. He was as content as I had seen him in a year, though not with us, I fear, so much as with his renewed purpose. Mag asked about the journey, how long he and William would be at sea, what they would see and eat and trade, where they would dock.

"Are the women pretty in America?" she demanded after we'd eaten, adding quickly, "I mean to keep my brother honest."

"I have robbed them of their greatest resource," he said. "My wife's the only true native I know—born on that soil."

"Simon was born there too," I corrected.

"It's full of rocks," a sullen Mag pronounced. "So I've heard."

"It was," Nehemiah said, "and still is in the north, I wager, and with sand in the south—but the plows have tamed it some in Massachusetts, and well in Connecticut."

"I'll never go there. I've no wish," said Mag.

"You've no wit."

Mag found no fun in my remark, but turned to me seriously and asked, "So you *would* return one day, Mistress?"

I looked in desperation to Simon, but of course he did not look back.

Of all my failings, this unnerved me most. There could be no language in our looks, no exchange without word or touch. But he would know me for a liar. "I've no cause to return. My mother will to England before I'll go back there."

"Your mother?"

"It's a black innocence, yours. I've no doubt your former master spoke my mother's name a time or two, Mag. So leave the art from your inquisition."

Nehemiah laughed wearily and set his tankard on the floor. "I think I'll to bed now, with so long a journey to a journey before me."

Mag nodded with satisfaction, and I gave Simon my elbow. "Did he walk you round your chamber?"

Simon nodded but let me lead him to the dark little room at the back of the cottage that the minister's son had fitted with a straw cot and a shelf. He stood perfectly still while I chattered and took his hand. "I'll put a basin for you here, on the corner of the shelf nearest the bed, and your clothes will stay in the trunk. Your knife is by you?"

"Yes, in my coat pocket."

"Tomorrow I'll bring some wood scraps and show you the lay of the hall. It's no great space to master. I'll sleep with Mag in the only other room, beyond the hearth. The outhouse might be in the Orient, but tonight you'll do fine to feel your way outside and stay by the wall. There are no neighbors near enough to see you."

He sat carefully on the bed with his hands at his sides, flat on the mattress as if for balance.

"You might be on a ship with that posture."

"I'll like it not when Nehemiah goes."

"He'll go at sunrise."

Simon looked to want my pity.

"How long will you lament?" I urged. "Until he returns?"

His jaw clenched, but he said nothing.

"Sheepish wretch," I tried, and flicked my apron at him. Simon hardly flinched, not knowing more than the breezy whir of the cloth in the air. I leaned over him and kissed his nose lightly, but he seemed less grateful for my contrition than mortified.

"I'll try to smother the wicked mood you've made here and say you'll survive, Simon, you will. I swear it."

Simon turned to my voice, blinked, and thoughtfully traced his lower lip with his teeth. "I have already pledged to do what pleases you."

"Then please yourself for once." I stamped off sighing to my husband's bed, and nearly tripped over grunting Mag on her mat by the hearth.

*T*hat night, he woke us all with his shrieking. We groped through the dark and found Simon on the floor, tangled and thrashing in his bedclothes. Nehemiah took his shoulders, loosened the blankets, and tried to sway his brother awake. Awake or asleep, Simon rocked forward. His pale face glistened and seemed to me to swivel on his neck like an owl's. Mag brought a candle and cooed to him in so gentle and maternal and alarming a voice that I marveled he did not find his way to it as through a great fog.

What is it? What afflicts him? The words never left my throat. My toes curled on the cold floor. I hugged myself and couldn't speak. I couldn't look at him—shrouded in his blindness. His hands flailed but found not the voices he sought. Were they other voices than ours? My own would mean as little to him now as Mag's sure soothing, I saw, or Nehemiah's hoarse assurances; I think I hated this knowledge even more than I hated to see Simon suffer.

"This," cautioned Nehemiah over a shoulder, "is the terror I've told you of."

I nodded my head, astonished.

"It's but a child's witless night fears. They visit most when we move him from a place he knows. It was very bad on board ship and in London, too, at first. It will pass in a night or two."

"It will pass," I murmured. I stood apart like a tree sealed in ice. "Is he cold?"

"Fetch more blankets if you like. Mag, go to your bed. It's no great drama."

I went out with Mag and returned to find the candle extinguished and Nehemiah stretched beside Simon on the narrow cot. They lay crowded together like pups, perfectly still, Nehemiah's strong arm draped easily over his brother. I covered them, listening a while to the steady discourse of their breathing, and went quietly out again.

Dark where I am

I walked a while behind the carriage at dawn, but it soon left my view, for the mist was thick on the ground. The morning was overcast but warm, and there was not a soul on the heath that I could see, not even a pony, though warblers spliced the air. When I crossed to the far side, which took some time, and entered the water wood, lazily tracing Nehemiah's last kiss on my lips with my tongue, I was struck by the beginnings of the moss that would blaze green in summer, and heard at once the brook, and saw the milling forms of cattle lapping at the fogged water further in where the oak roots clutched the banks. I sat on a felled log, rubbing petals of wild violet between my fingers. Spiky leaves of butcher's broom arched over their tiny, star-white flowers and stood mixed with the yellow heads of spurge. I closed my eyes to this shadow-striped world at my feet, to the canopy above.

I closed my eyes and listened to the brook, to water dividing against the rocks, to better imagine this place as Simon would know it, and my anger returned. I was blind enough, and what was not to wish for? It was more desolate, to be sure, and less varied—his sense of it—but it was no less rewarding in its way. I moved here and there along the brook, flailing for tree trunks. I saw on my outer eyelid flickering shadow as the sun cut through the canopy. Did Simon see this?

Was it because he had no background for this landscape, no memory of what he missed—of what made the smooth of petals or the complaint of the red squirrel rhyme with leaf and sky—no sense of the wholeness, that he would not let himself hope for us here?

For to me this place was blessed, as the woods in New England were, though I would never have named them "blessed" any more than I would call my childhood days with Simon "holy." But here in the quiet (which would be to Simon a roar, I expect) I found my own voice unnecessary, the inner one that screeched and howled and clamored day and night—thoughts vying for attention. Here I could be hollow and calm in belonging. In London, my body was leaden, always flushed or sweating, stumbling or offending with its burden among so many. Here I could as easily layer my body with details of sense as forget it.

I lay flat before the brook and skimmed its cold surface with my hand, and felt that the ground would absorb me, and knew a patient and famil-iar loneliness.

*T*he night terrors did not return, but Simon took his time about all things and for a time did make me wonder if he would take to this place. Regular chores pleased him, so I gave him the sow and piglets to tend. The minister's son, at Nehemiah's prompting, had branded and transported them, and Mag and I had mended their enclosure. In the fall they would be set loose to forage for acorns and chestnuts, but for now they required care and feeding, which Simon was pleased to do.

"We never kept pigs before. I like the way they surround me with their snuffling when I come with the bucket." He laughed. "After our friend the Sagacious Pig, I'll hate to eat them now."

I smiled at the memory.

*S*ometimes he worked beside me in the garden, for after I introduced his hands to the new growth, he was deft at weeding round it. We said little while we labored but studied our own silences, though sometimes our paths crossed, and when I found him so close, working the earth in the raised beds, I wondered at his thoughts.

One day, I found the nerve to ask him to walk out with me. "It's a bit swampy in places, but the day is windy and fine."

He laughed. "You remembered I like wind."

"I remember most things you tell me."

"Will you remember this?"

"Yes?" I said solemnly.

"You must hold my arm unless I say not."

I nodded and nodded before realizing my error. "I will—as I did in London."

"We're not children now. I'll not be made to cry and plead."

"I know."

"It's dark where I am, Pearl."

I took his arm in mine and checked to see that he did not wear his good boots. "Mag!" I called. "Fire the bread, will you? We'll go gather salad greens."

"We've greens here," she said, poking her head round the door.

"But no violets. I know where there are violets."

She gave us her shrewd stare. "We'll want violets every day, then, won't we?"

I yanked Simon away.

"'Bye, then, Mag," he called in his deep, forlorn voice.

"Tell me," he said on the heath, the level sweep of which seemed to soothe his step. "You're bursting to."

"Well, the sky's flat gray, with the sun a dull glow behind. The birds dip and struggle with the wind. These flowers here, the furze, look a dull gold in this light, and there are ribbons of grass that way—" I lifted his hand and pointed—"along the stream. Marsh bedstraw, I think, and purslane in the muddy pools. It's the wood I would take you to. You'll hear the difference when we enter it. The cattle come to drink there, and in the evening the deer."

"What do the deer look like? I've no mind for them now."

"They're a tawny red, the color of the wild fall meadows in New England—do you remember that color?—and they're strong like horses, but a daintier shape. The males have great velvet antlers with many spikes. They crack heads and war over the wenches, like we do. They rub their horns raw against the trees and cough like Liza coughed before she died—"

"Is this the wood?"

"Yes. Mind you, step solid. The wet ground by the brook sucks your feet fast in, though not far. Did you feel the shadow from the trees?"

"I heard the wind had stopped."

"Shall we rest a while?"

"Yes."

I led him to the bank of the brook, where we settled beside the roots of a great old pollard, and he unraveled his hand from mine. "There are no others here?" he asked.

"None."

He kept his head down. His beautiful hands lighted on the new moss, floating and falling. "Do you wonder about Liza now?"

"Wonder?"

"Is she with God?"

"Of course she is."

"I mean, what is that like—what is Heaven? I can't imagine it, my father and mother there." I thought briefly of my own father, of the doughy boy in the dusty light of the apothecary, but again I did not speak of these to Simon. What could he have said but that he'd tried? That blindness was, at times, its own reward.

"I know what scriptures say," I offered.

"What do *you* say?"

"I say I don't know. I think," I said in a sunny voice, "that when I die I will fly into the veins of a leaf to live. Or a dragonfly's wing. I won't sit on the celestial shore fanned by spiteful angels."

"You're still a child, are you? Or a pixie——"

"Satan was an angel."

He shifted forward where he sat, winced, and smoothed his long, hanging hair behind his ears. "Were you true, Pearl, when you said that I should do what pleases me? To please you, I mean?"

I laughed uneasily. "In good faith, yes."

"May I touch you, then?"

I heard Nehemiah's voice in the carriage, punctuated by the rain. *If a thing needs doing that a man will do*—"Will you behave?"

His face lapsed into melancholy, but he laughed out loud in a mockery of it. "No. I think not."

"Have you never been with a woman, Simon?"

"Oh, every night. At least one."

"Tell me," I said softly.

"One, yes. A great mooning cow of a girl that helped Liza when we first made house in London."

"And you seduced her?"

He laughed. "She seduced me with one hand, I dare say. She pitied me."

"And that's all?"

"She was curious to know did I work the way the others did."

Now it was my turn to laugh, and I would have were I not so startled. "Of course you do."

"The next night she rode me like a horse. And many more nights too. I thought she'd crush me."

Now I did snort with laughter and let his hand wander where my mouth was; he plucked at my lower lip and circled my chin with his thumb. "Simon——"

"I know," he said. "I'll stop."

"I wish you would. I *don't* pity you."

"Not a little?"

"Not at all. It bewilders me to have you so bawdy."

His hand dropped to the new moss and roved a while there, and found its way to the clear water. "It's not that only. It's you. I would know you all

ways." He splashed and cooled his face with long fingers, and asked fool-
ishly if there were fish here.

"Well, *that's* pretty nonsense." I dabbed at his sharp cheekbone with my
knuckle. "'All ways,' is it?" I felt the brush of his dark lashes on my fingers
and knew that I'd meant to reach for him before, countless times; I had
some memory of it that was not mine. "Will we go to Hell, then?"

And Simon, as if he'd been corrupting matrons all his life, took my
raised hand and pressed the palm soundly to his lips. "I think yes." My
stomach pitched, but when he let the hand slip loose as if to release me, I
felt worse than sick. I felt forsaken. I too clumsily removed my dress and
unlaced my stays while Simon listened, astonished. He walked closer on
his knees. He bowed his head and kept it bowed while two white hands
reached to trace my woman's shape, breasts and belly and hips, with such
agonizing slowness that I more than once had to barter pleasure for reason to soothe the panic. Liza's voice crossed the years to me, chiming,
Come, you—and let's crown the King of May. His hair hung like black willow
boughs, and because I could not lift that bowed head, could not make him
look at what he touched, I sent myself running in mind across the heath,
falling and flying and falling like an injured bird. *Do you see me now?* Perhaps
his hands read the question on my skin, for Simon groped along the
ground for my cloak and eased me up, draping it over my shoulders. He
kissed me hard, deft forefingers tracing every curve and hollow in my
face, and even before the seal of our lips was broken, he turned those too-
intelligent hands to his own garb.

The shock of his paleness, his long waist, the flat moon of his stomach,
his sex, will never leave me. If a tree one day opened a mouth to speak my
name in the wood, I could not have been more surprised. There was no
delight in it, no fever, only wonder. Lucky we were that a forest keeper or
some goodwife out pulling onions didn't cross us in that glade, or I would
wear my mother's scarlet curse after all. Of course I ever did, and do, in
my blood. *And you'll be his bride.*

His long hair fell over me as he stood behind, and my cloak went at last
the way of my skirt and stays in a heap, and he crossed his veined wrists

over my eyes from behind, sinking his face into the crook of my shoulder as into water. Though I'd shaved his mug but two days before, his stubble grated. I wanted to cry out in complaint that he should walk round and be before me, not behind like a beast in the hay, but how could it matter to him? Our eyes wouldn't meet—*No, I should not like to look in those ice-pale eyes now*—and so I let Simon blind me with cool hands on my lids and felt the tender press of him, his hard warmth in the damp air, and his silent sobs. He was no longer behind or inside me but everywhere, breathing his life's sorrow. I was at the heart of a weeping world, in darkness, and that is where she came from.

"A" IS FOR ABIGAIL

*W*e were together but once more before Nehemiah returned. Simon and I were not sheepish after that day in the wood, nor scarred with regret. We laughed and talked as before. We were not the fools we might have been, nor ruled by the pangs of lust. The devil had won me, but I felt no greed in going.

The other and last time I lay with him was a night Mag went to her wheelwright, who had come passing through Hampshire. She would sup with him at the inn in Lyndhurst. Sup she did, and sleep, it seems, for she never came home till the light did, riding high on our mare like a conquered queen. I knew it would be so.

I lay awake listening that night, hearing only Simon's shifting in the room beyond. He heard mine too, I know, because he heard everything. I waited for him to come to me—perhaps it would not be my fault then, that he slept in his brother's bed—and when he did, and fit curving behind like a fiddlehead to touch and trace me in his slow and stately way, I forgot myself. I forgot myself and my duty but that I was content and slept with sweetness all surrounded. He did not blind me that night with his hands, for the dark managed it well enough. He was not unduly grateful, nor did I struggle like a weak bird to fly. Perhaps we had death on our heads even then, but there was no hurry in us. I know now, surely, that it could not have been on this good night that she was conceived.

.   .   .

I would name her Peregrine, like the wind in a bird's wing. But it was Abigail she came to be. It was Sarah Atkinson's choice, and Sarah was godmother, and so it was. The name meant "father's joy," she said as the household prepared to desert me (a green mother might not step out after childbirth until she was churched one month later) to ride to Lynd-hurst for the baptism. So saying, Sarah took Nehemiah's hands in her two capable ones and smiled her guileless smile. "Your joy."

It had seemed a long, dreamy pregnancy, perhaps because it was so wished for, and though she never dared say so before her master, Mag—who missed not a crumb on the floor—must have suffered doubts about the birth date. "So Master's seed sleeps no more," she pronounced with raised eyebrows when we were alone one day after my quickening. Her look made me laugh out loud, it was so befuddled. When could we deceive her? She was not above suspecting, but she must have believed she was too watchful for such intrigue. What's more she was too saintly in principal (if not practice) to imagine Simon and me fornicating in the open forest like mules, with woodsmen about.

I did as any good wife would and blamed myself for my own and my husband's childless months and years. Nehemiah scorned all talk of blame, and bade us all kneel to pray for the safe passage of the child into this world. "Lord, stand by your servant in her present condition now great with child," he led. "Give her a gracious delivery and the strength to bring forth life; preserve her through the pains of labor and travail, for many have lately died in childbed. Lord, give the child right shape and form, and make him an instrument of thy glory and a vessel of mercy. Lord, build up and continue our family still."

For all her untold knowledge, Mag cared for me through it as well as I could have wished. She alone kept order when the parish gossips came for my lying in and surrounded me in that dark, moist, warm room that was like a womb in its own right, with Sarah's calm voice leading them when they would stop laughing and chattering long enough to follow. They called me the "little woman on the straw" and tweaked my chin, and tied the skin of a wild ox to my thigh. They strung nested eagles' stones round my neck, poured sage broth down my gullet, covered the windows to trap the draft, and strutted about with their unmindful stories of pain and travail in the bloody path of Eve. They made Nehemiah roam all day to shoot enough partridges to feed us all.

From the moment my glad husband returned and found that my courses had not come, there was no more time for Simon and me in our lapsed innocence to roam the moors and glades. We were crowded in that cottage, and there was work always with Nehemiah and his expectations to feed, and it seemed he or Mag and later Sarah were always near. I took. it as a good omen though that Nehemiah agreed to let the birth take place in New Forest, not London; for all my fears that I would not survive delivery, I knew my chances improved here in the clean air.

Simon ate and prayed with us, but I saw him almost never, for he stayed well away from where Nehemiah sat with his quills and ink and books spread before him on the table, and Mag wouldn't have him underfoot, so he slowly weeded the same plot over and over, and he dragged his chair to the yard or set it among the pigs and carved again the little crooked figures of his youth.

Abigail's collection began with an apple. "'A' is for apple," he told me as I passed with my great belly to the lavender hedge where I spread the wash. "'B' is for bird."

"Do you remember the letters?"

"Not their looks, but I recall Mother chanting them for my brother. I remember her voice floating up and down. It was the only time there was music in it, for even her prayers sat dull on her tongue. 'C' is for cat."

"Will you carve one for every letter?"

"Those I can see a picture for in my mind I will. And why not?" He laughed a hollow laugh, and I wanted so much to stand by his chair and smooth the lank hair from his face. But I didn't. I wouldn't.

There was but one fleeting hour when I was alone in the cottage with

him before my setting in. Nehemiah was all day at Lyndhurst, but Mag
had only gone to gather mushrooms. I came quickly to Simon's chamber,
and the slam of the door made him jump. He stiffened and winced when
I brought his hands to my big belly, but for an instant his empty eyes glistened and he seemed to support it from beneath as if it were a great soap
bubble.

Sadness I might have stood—paired with mine—but I could little endure when he let his hands fall idle to his sides and settled in his vague-
ness. I saw that he felt not the least entitled to that thing in me. It did not
belong to him.

"You will go out now, Pearl," he said. "Please."

"I will, but first I have words for your keeping."

"What use has that?"

"Take them."

He extended a hand, and I kissed his lean wrist and spoke into his palm.
"Remember me?"

Did he nod, or wisely, politely recall his fist, whispering words I could
not hear? I don't know. But he did not let me touch him again.

*I*f I had left him alone, if I had lived with Simon but away from him,
by him but far from him, if I had kept that baby to myself and let Nehemiah have what was his, would it have changed me so terribly? I like to
think I would do anything. There are countless variations in a life, endless
leaf-strewn paths we might walk to our end, but what we choose is what
we endure, and there is no end to my endurance. Am I too proud of it?

*T*he moment I hit the air again, left that dim, moist room to ride to
my churching, I felt returned to myself, and fearful. Sarah had come
and gone with her groaning stool and salves and caudles, her cyclamen,
sowbread, and columbine, her rude and loving multitude of parish gossips.
Nehemiah had paced before the hearth as I shrieked and raged behind the

bed curtains at the pangs of labor. I had ripped and then healed. I had lain in the dark and nursed Abigail, who smacked her lips and clutched my thumb as if to pull it off. I lay in the dark and nibbled her tiny ear, and held her tiny toes in my deflated fingers, and kissed and breathed her milky, muscled form. She had come the thin blue of skimmed milk and bloody into the world, but with a lusty cry, and an appetite. How could I ever think to satisfy such an appetite?

I dressed well on the morning of my thanksgiving, and rode through the burning cold of the open air, and knelt whispering into my veil before the pulpit while Mag held my bundled baby and stood by my husband, and Simon and Sarah coughed with winter colds, and the priest said unto me, "Forasmuch as it hath pleased Almighty God of his goodness to give you safe deliverance, and hath preserved you in the great danger of child-birth: you shall therefore give hearty thanks unto God, and say, I am well pleased that the Lord hath heard the voice of my prayer; that he hath inclined his ear unto me: therefore I will call upon him as long as I live."

I think now that I have lived too long.

"The snares of death compassed me round about: and the pains of Hell gat hold upon me."

Simon's silence was unbearable.

"I found trouble and heaviness, and I called upon the name of the Lord: O Lord, I beseech thee, deliver my soul."

To whom was he delivered?

"And why? Thou hast delivered my soul from death: mine eyes from tears, and my feet from falling."

I will live too long.

"I will walk before the Lord: in the land of the living."

THREE

$\mathcal{J}$f it had not been winter at sea as well as in my heart, perhaps Mother would have received our letters sooner. Perhaps if the sea had not swelled and cracked with ice, my mother would have come. I might have had her wisdom. She might have stopped me. I knew well enough what my insistence would earn, but I insisted, and it was over in moments. Abigail was not a year old when I brought her to his hands. "Simon," I whispered, "hold her."

Because I cared for my husband, I spoke softly, though I believed he was outdoors. Nor would Nehemiah have thought twice to see the three of us together, except that I was kneeling by Simon's chair, and my brother wouldn't touch her. Simon would not touch Abigail but cowered as from a leper. "Pray, take her, Pearl." *Go home.* "Please." *To your fallen mother.*

When I looked back and found my husband behind in the doorway, I knew no lie could heal it. Nehemiah cast on me such a black and hollow stare that I froze under it. His eyes devoured the baby. I stood up, holding Abigail close to my chest, but he turned and shut himself in our bed-chamber. I listened for his motion, and Simon surveyed my silence.

"Was Nehemiah there?" he said dully.

"He was."

"And he heard you?"

"No, but he saw me. He saw me as I am."

"Go to him."

"No."

"Pearl—"

"No."

"For my sake, then."

I began to shake uncontrollably. I thought the baby would drop from my arms like an acorn from a tree, but Mag came in from the pantry with some task and her thoughtless chatter, and I thrust the kicking bundle at her. "Walk out with Abigail," I said.

"But I'm elbow-deep in dough—"

"Please, Mag."

She regarded me as Liza had once regarded me in the Milton yard in Boston—or the child who was me, sagging with rain. "What have you done now? Why are you trembling?"

Nehemiah appeared behind and, taking Mag's shoulders, steered her toward the front door. His voice had fury under it. "Take the child and walk, Mag."

"Well, then," she huffed in bewilderment. "I will."

The three of us listened to her going. Simon stiffened on his chair.

I thought the hard look of Nehemiah alone would kill me. I watched him take but one step, and then he was on Simon like a hawk on a mouse. He tipped him over in his chair. Simon howled and scrambled to right himself on the floor, and Nehemiah put his boot on his brother's stomach and stamped. I leapt to hold him back, but with one hand Nehemiah flung me dazed against the wall.

Simon was too breathless to debate as his brother stalked and kicked him scuttling round the room until at last Simon found a wall to support him to his feet. I begged behind all this while in a voice only half human, I think. "It's my sin, husband, mine. Look at me. Look at me—"

He would not. Nehemiah put his hands on the wall by Simon's head and crushed him with his shadow, and barked into his terrified face, "I knew I would wear the yoke of you always, and you've well repaid me, haven't you?"

"I can't see you," Simon wailed. "I can't see you—"

Nehemiah knocked his brother's head back neatly against the wall with one hand and held the other palm out to keep me back. "It's not your eyes that have you in this muddle, Simon, is it?"

"No."

"And to spite me the rest of you works just fine, doesn't it?"

Simon shook his dazed head in despair.

"Nehemiah," I threatened, "you will let him go."

"I will do no such thing until I hear from him—from *him*."

"What would you hear?"

"I would hear him confess that he has stolen from me since his birth. He has robbed me every day—"

"I have done it," I cried. "I have robbed you."

"And you will answer to your God. He will answer to me." Nehemiah grabbed a handful of Simon's hair and, pulling it, knocked Simon's head against the wall so hard this time that it lolled afterward, and I sank to my knees and groaned.

"You have a baby," I cried, half sensible.

For a moment, Nehemiah turned and saw me. "So it was for my sake that you mated with my brother like a cur?"

"A baby, Nehemiah—"

"I might have played the cuckold for a son," he said, and I could see that the pain in him was terrible. I tried to reach up for him. He checked me with a savage look and, stepping away, left Simon slumped and shaking against the wall. For a moment, we three were suspended in that drafty room. The fire in the hearth was gray. I saw Simon inching along the wall, but in the way that you see the leaves bud and swell and turn and fall, only half seeing, half recognizing. Nehemiah turned his anger to the table. He swept the inky pages of his work from it and kicked its legs, kicked the chairs until they tangled. It might almost have been ridiculous in the way that such violence can seem after it has played its course. He wearied. He was all sound and storm now. He would resign himself. It might have been ridiculous and grave, and no more, had Simon not been swallowed in that storm of noise. Simon had vanished. He was not there by the wall, yet the cottage door had not opened. He was gone but not gone.

I crept to the little hall that led back to the pantry. I looked and found the cellar door yawning.

*I*n the old tales, there are always three drops of blood. Blessings and curses begin with so little, and at first, that was what I saw. That was all I saw. When I came creeping down the narrow steps into the stench of radishes, I found him pale and twisted at the base on the dirt, and there were but three splashed drops on his right temple. His narrowed eyes were the same eyes really, empty now as before, but his graceful hands were still and his chest did not heave when I laid my cheek against it. I cooed to him as if he were my child. I stroked the hair from his face. I shook him and kissed his cold lips and owned him for the world to see, but he was dead.

And when I understood it, and closed the waxy lids and put my arms under his stiff back to lift his face to me, I found the blood beneath him, a small puddle—too small, it seemed, to be the source of all the years I would know without him.

I heard Nehemiah and Mag bickering above. I heard him bark at her to fetch the constable. I had not heard him descend halfway to the bottom of the steps and then retreat, though I understood that he had. It occurred to me that he might kill the baby while Mag was gone. He might lay her tiny body on the floor and strangle her with his hands. I wished he would do as much to me. I wished the world would end.

Perhaps it was the dark, cold cellar, the scarce weight of his head against my thighs, or the blood matted in his hair that my fingers could not comb through that set me snarling like a beast. The noise began low in my throat and seemed well reasonable to my ears. I think I also bit a meddling hand that tried to later pry me from him. Believe that if I could have been there to stop his soul and trap it for my own, I would have done it. I would have closed it in a bottle. I would have kept that bottle corked, even if it meant that he was cursed eternally. I would have ripped grace from Simon's fists because I could not stop myself from expecting and demanding too much of him. Even Nehemiah's dazed tenderness (my good and solid husband, responsible for us—all three—even then) could little retrieve me from my ravings. What a silly, broken, fiendish girl I was—still but a girl. *I might have played the cuckold for a boy.* And the mother of a girl.

How I did hate you on that day, Abigail.

WHAT WAS A
DAUGHTER'S TO KNOW

A swirl of voices plagued me in those days after the inquest called
an open verdict. The household was innocent, of course: Simon
was an invalid; Simon had stumbled and fallen in his darkness.
The magistrates repeated it over and over, reassuring, congratulating. Nehemiah was one among them. What other way could it end? It was not my
husband, after all, who was beyond his rights. For what would I punish
him? Nehemiah might have left me to some version of my mother's fate,
but he swore a simple tale was true; he protected me, and I did not digress.
Simon was blind. Simon stumbled. Simon fell.

When Nehemiah looked for me after that, he could not find me. We
could resolve nothing among so many voices. I heard my own cry out, "O
Lord, thou hast searched me, and known *me*," and Liza's, scolding, "What
you *need*, I'll have you know, is to care for this child." For a while I heard
even the baby's terrible cries, but my milk had dried up like a puddle after
rain. I half understood that Sarah had taken Abigail away to be weaned by
a wetnurse. I heard too my former minister's Election Day voice, a wordless sermon rising to thunder, and I heard Nehemiah's mutterings as he
paced the cottage, and I felt every day that the world should end, and
every day it didn't.

I was not permitted to lay out Simon's body. Mag did, and I came like
a moth to his pale candle. I watched from a modest distance while she

washed and straightened him and crossed his hands. I had laced the winding sheet with flowers and sweet herbs and sprinkled it with rose water,
and when she swaddled him in it, I had to leave the cottage for fear the
sexton might come for him or that Nehemiah, who had stepped out to
see to the pigs, would return and find me snotty-nosed. I ran to the water
wood, and because I would not kneel, I took off my old shoes and tore my
stockings as I climbed and settled in the fork of an oak to look down at the
moving brook. I heard through my sobs our old minister's clear voice in
my head.

Ever before it was his preacher's voice I remembered, but now I heard
his pensive words from the churchyard. He said: *Why do you hide among the
dead, Pearl?*

"Traitor," cried my child-voice.

Haven't you a friend to sport with?

"You wouldn't save us, and I hate you."

Don't lurk among the graves. It pains me to think of it.

"You wouldn't stay."

But he had no answer. One by one the voices chimed and faded—the
minister, Caleb Milton, Liza. Dead, all. My own parents might just as well
have been dead. And Simon spoke not a word.

*N*ehemiah would not cast me out but made no decisions for us in
those early weeks. He coaxed me from Simon's cot each morning
after the burial—for I might have stayed all day in that narrow bed, glassy-
eyed with loss as my mother had been in Boston. Nehemiah hauled me
upright and brushed my tangled hair as I had brushed my mother's and
begged me to my senses. He fed and blamed me, and cursed me with his
patience.

"What will you do, Nehemiah?" I roused myself to ask one day. "You
can't remain here."

"I'll remain where I must."

"You have your spring cargo to see to, your work. You must go to it."

"Go where?" He seemed sincerely perplexed and I would hold him but couldn't steel myself, and he wouldn't have stood it. Unless he was shifting me about like a puppet, we touched not at all. Even at Simon's interment, we had remained apart except once when we were going and I stumbled, and Mag could not support me while holding Abigail. In public, as a rule, I was brave for Nehemiah's sake and held myself tall and was stern with myself. It was here at home that I collapsed into my own weight.

"Will you to London? I've written your mother again. I hope she'll see her way across."

"I'll stay here."

"Why? To keep vigil by the bloody stain? To sap his memory of every goodness?"

"I'll keep to the open air."

"And the baby?"

"Your baby."

"I'll not hear it again."

"I'll not have her," I said, frightened by my words.

Nehemiah smiled pitifully. "Then who will?"

"Mag will keep her for you. Take Mag to London and tell her nothing. I'll see my way there when I'm able."

"You'll see your way?"

"I will," I lied.

"And who will help you?"

"I'll keep, with Sarah's care."

He knelt by my chair but did not take my hand. He knelt and said not one word; like a tree in a cruel wind he strained against words.

"You have always known what to say," I urged. My hands were fists under the chair.

He swallowed, and his amber eyes filled with water from the sea. My husband shook his head, and he left me.

. . .

As my mother's daughter, I was not strange to a life with ghosts, or to the toil of loneliness. But as a child I had known to stray from that toil and slip across the lines to faery. Before we came to England, my imagination was sleek as a weasel. I skipped and sang in the forest and dared the dawn to hold me. I was only half human, knowing naught but the promise of loss—weight like storm clouds, prophetic shadows. Now I carried that weight, those shadows, under my skin.

Simon's silence invaded the cottage, wrapped round me like a rope or a lover's hands and cut my breath. I clung to familiar tasks. I filled the bloody basement with turnips and potatoes and poorly salted pork, and prayed for winter. I let the berries wilt on their branches and felt my young back stoop when I carried water. The moon waned. I walked with him and through him, and he looked straight at me with eyes the icy blue of a winter stream; yes, at last he seemed to see me, but now he wouldn't speak.

I devised one day that his ghost wore Mother's eyes. Hers were a changeable darkness, not blue, but they had like depths. I think it was this gaze alone that pinned me to life. Why did she not come? I wondered when, but I never doubted that she would. Instead, in the spring, Sarah returned from her travels and cried to see me so thin, and at once set about bathing me and scouring the cottage. "You fooled me well when last I was here. I thought you fit."

"I am fit."

"Aye. For the grave."

I didn't answer, and she didn't ask. It took her three days to tell me her news, three days during which she scrubbed and tidied and administered mutton broth like a mother. "Eat," she said over and over, as broth dribbled down my chin.

"Now you will have another woe to keep you," she sighed at last.

I laughed like a demon. My eyes narrowed to slits. I watched her thin lips move as through a fog; I knew it was death they harbored. "Is it Nehemiah?"

"No, Pearl. He's well in London. Abigail is well. They're fine, but he writes they fear plague."

"Plague?"

"It's your mother, sweet. Word came to London that she was lost to smallpox in Boston more than a year ago." Sarah touched my hand as if to assure herself that I was still there. "A fellow or executor wrote last spring, but the letter never reached Nehemiah in London. Her estate was modest, Pearl. The second notice took its time coming."

"Would it never did," I said in a hollow voice.

"I've brought some of her things. They came with Nehemiah's letters through a Bristol captain I know. He was much delayed by my travels."

"Leave them, then."

"I won't be going, Pearl. Not till your husband comes. His letter says it will be soon."

I think that I must have sneered at her, or otherwise fashioned a face not mine. "I've left you too long, Pearl. I'd no idea when I went for my sister's confinement that you were so bad again." She looked startled. "Sit there—"

"Leave me."

"Let me keep you."

I rose from the chair and tried to go. "I'll not be touched."

"Oh, why in Satan's fire not?" Sarah seized and fairly smothered me, and I, pathetic wretch, slumped against her and marveled that such a tiny wheat-haired woman could be so strong. She held me stiffly and still. The reedy, muscled arms and red hands that caught babies on their way into the world, that had caught my own child—when? One year ago? Two?— were not soft, but they were mine while I needed them.

There is no measure for that need. Those hands chased the voices away. They made the garden grow, though I had thought to keep none of last summer's seeds. They mended the fence and chased the donkeys from the kitchen garden. They sifted the ravaged grain that was little more than shells and droppings now. They emptied the cellar of withered onions, laundered the linen, and aired the stinking cottage.

There is no cure like competence. Sarah and her sure hands saw to me as to an orphaned pup, and when my husband's household came the next summer, fleeing the plague that savaged London, I was plump and sleek enough again to look him in the eye, to kiss my child's upturned nose, though she rightly flinched from me as from a stranger, to embrace Mag and welcome her with her shifty brother, despite her servant's caution and ill knowledge.

With Sarah to stay me, I let Simon with his grateful new eyes go from that dark cellar and into the world, where he had never let himself belong before. I learned to see him not in the faded stain or above in the soon-to-be steamy, crowded rooms of the cottage, but out on the moors and in the glades, in the bee-loud air, where my heart has always lived.

*I*t was a fortnight at least before I could bring myself to look in Mother's bundle. I knew the badge of our ignominy would be chief among its contents, but worse than knowing (or believing I knew) was *not* knowing what else might be. I imagined her preparing the package laboriously, illness stooped like a harpy on her back, and I saw her sitting straight by candlelight to pen her careful letter. It was her dignity that struck me in these musings, and the fact that she had bought that dignity at so high a cost. Like me—whom she called in the shaky script of that brief good-bye her "pearl of great price"—Mother's grace and solemn carriage were a curse well decorated.

Her talents, and there were many, were most evident in her beautiful embroidery, and in contrast to the foul brand, the stark "A" she never would embellish, there were other relics in my bundle to stay me. First, the stained scene of Eden, which I dared not ponder long but folded again and set aside. There were elegant fawn-colored leather gloves stitched with silver and gold thread for Nehemiah; for me, there was a densely embroidered coif with a rich crimson hood for out-of-doors; and finally, for the baby, there was a tiny cap not unlike my coif, framed with the most delicate flowers and vines but ringed round too with the letters from the horn book. Sadly, it looked too small to fit the child Abigail was now. It occurred to me strangely that Simon too had crafted an alphabet, perhaps at the same time. I determined now that I would find his blocks for Abigail, together with his knife in the chamber that had changed so little since his death; he'd owned so little.

Why had she not taken her badge with her, I wondered, enraged with imagining, worn it fastened under her shroud? I circled the cottage until Sarah came home laden with goods from Lyndhurst to check my muttering. "For Heaven's sake, sit and say what ails you."

"Tyranny?" I complained, aware of myself pacing a stage I could not exit. "Goodness? Shame? How can I know what to make of her?"

"Who?"

I cornered Sarah and took her wrist. "You knew her. Tell me what she cherished."

Sarah shrugged with impatience. "You. She cherished you."

"But above all things." I resumed my circling. "What stayed her in her darkest hours? What kept the sodden flame of her spirit alive?"

"Your words are hollow."

"I speak too late, but I knew her not."

"You knew what was a daughter's to know."

"A shell."

"Think you to damn her for what she endured on your behalf?"

"Mine? Would I *choose* to inhabit a wretched world?"

Sarah's sun-carved face creased more in a scowl, and she made as if to spit. "God made the world. You thank Him with petulance."

"Now you sound like my husband."

"Your husband hasn't time for such base lessons."

I winced and took a shallow, grudging breath, my hands spread wide in presentation. My creased old satin dress whispered with my movement. "I expect you mean that he deserves more than a copemate like this one."

"I mean what I say, Pearl. I govern my tongue."

"Then speak. I invite you."

She steered me into a chair, holding a hand on my head as if in benediction, then let the hand slide abruptly away. "I knew your mother only a short while, Pearl, and she spoke little, but I never doubted that love and penance were her meat and drink. I'm sorry she fed the latter to you."

"I've no regret."

"You think to forget that you aren't far from childhood. You will."

"You think to *brand* me child—"

"More to it, I think that in Nehemiah you have a man worth having. I never saw but few better, and you refuse him. Do you refuse life?"

I laughed a hollow laugh and shook my head in disbelief. "I can little choose what life will withhold from me."

"Simon?"

"Begin there," I said dully.

"Mayhap you claimed what was not yours to have, nor anyone's. Is that not a sin in itself?"

"But *why* not?" I asked sincerely, and sought her eyes. "What put him beyond me? That he was blind? Is blindness not punishment enough?"

She looked away from me. "It's God's will, and you were sworn to honor his brother."

"And I did."

Sarah shook her head and looked for me again. "Then you ask too much, and your greed has stung you."

"I ask naught but what I'm willing to give in return."

"And think," she snapped, "what it's cost you."

I leaned back against the wall in part to muffle my hands, which would crave some violence. Almost at once, though, Sarah's low voice mastered my anger. "Of more concern to me now, Pearl, is what it has and will cost others. You are not the sole life of this family."

"Family?"

"It *can* be. Let me read you something."

She brought a wrinkled piece of paper with Nehemiah's spidery hand-writing from her drawstring pocket, and her eyes roved over it a moment before she spoke:

Good Sarah, did my last letter find you? Would that my gentle flesh had warned my wife of her latest sorrow, and not those pages, but I had no heart to keep her mother's death from her longer, so long having passed.

All London is afeared. The heat here is terrible this season, and the bills of mortality swell with names familiar and not. Many a house is shut up and some with the red cross and 'Lord have mercy on us' writ upon them. My wife will find me longing for the clean air as never before, and intent even to endure the rigors and constraints, and cruel boredom of New Forest now for Abigail's sake. Maggie keeps her well, and she is a prim and godly child with tiny hands. She looks little like her mother, but I find I love her no less for it. My time at sea has taught me to value re-turning *to* someone, lest I sail forever with my soul before me, fleeting.

We'll come when we can master London no longer. The heat will make it soon, for this devil's plague grows mighty while we wilt, and the roads out are clogged with panic. It will take a fierce frost to tame it.

Yours in good will,
Neh. Milton

My eyes stung as she finished, not for any one dark sentiment above the others but for the sound of his voice, so evident at his quill. His voice inhabited that room from which the others had been banished, and it was no ghost's whisper but a living voice. I stared at my empty hands and thought I would split like a seedpod, bursting with words and prayers for his safety. But God had no ear for such trifles, I knew, at a time when the roar and clatter of sinners' prayers would try His mercy. His plan had long been beyond my contemplation.

Sarah tossed the folded letter on the table as a tavern-sitter scatters coins, and went to her work.

I said that I learned again to see Simon in nature, but did I say how strange that good world was at first? Until Sarah came, I went out only to work the garden (and poorly that). The moors and streambeds and windy passes, the morning fog and hissing leaves had seemed too much haunted and seemed to ring with hard laughter—whose, I don't know. (I thought Satan's, but more like it was angels I feared, pointing from their lofty place to my breast without its brand.) The light outside, too, was ever bright and harsh.

What's more, my secrets were not mine. Until long after Sarah arrived, I wouldn't brave village scorn even for the taste of an egg, which I craved exceedingly, but lived only on what food I could grow or forage. After all, the constable had come that day. He had pried me from Simon while I snarled, and a fine story that must have made over his evening's pint. The minister and magistrates too knew of some grief in our lives that had not passed our lips at the inquest, though they had begged for it. We were a curiosity—a wife who seemed to live alone, apart from her child and servants; an absent husband. I have no fear of gossip and skill in enduring it, but I was too weak to stand before scorn in those two-plus years, doubting too much myself.

Nehemiah, who favored the world and its politics better than I, must have taken frequent pains to write to the minister and other important men in the parish to illumine and obscure our circumstances, nip gossip in its bud. Sarah encountered no intrigue, she said, when she braved Lyndhurst with our list each week. By all appearances, Reverend Lacey had joyfully received word of Nehemiah's coming, and prayed for their safe passage from the pestilence, though others, I suspect, were not so generous. London refugees found a frosty welcome in those days.

Little by little, fed by Sarah's goodness, my strength grew. Missing Simon, I found my way back where I belonged. I roamed out all morning some days or, if work or conscience called me back to Sarah, stole an hour to lie by him on the mossy bank of the brook in the water wood. I lay with my palms flat on the springy ground, floating on an emerald sea while turtles fixed me in their cloudy stare. The silver undersides of leaves and sunbeams dazzled my sight. Damp stained my worn wool dresses, every one, and I was drunk daily with serenity and weather. I had long since stopped yammering to him. He didn't answer, except at night in dreams, and I came to understand that while Simon wouldn't speak again, neither would he desert me.

THE GOODNESS OF MY DUTY

*I*t was with the sweetest apprehension that I awaited Nehemiah at New Forest. His letter to Sarah had given me hope, however meek, that we might one day be more than wary strangers— if not repaired, then requited in our anguish to be. What I didn't expect was that he would arrive almost merry, laden with diversions from the bookstalls round Saint Paul's—broadsheets, almanacs, gazettes, new ballads for my amusement and Sarah's—even together with word that the bells tolled almost constantly now in London. The dead numbered in the thousands, he said. The King and his court had fled the plague by water. Our baker and his hearty family, our vintner, our very physician had been carried off by God's wrath. "Imagine, Pearl—" Nehemiah blithely scooped up the child I could not bring myself to look at— "strolling all of Fleet Street and meeting not twenty people. Before, the burial carts squeaked past only at night; now night is not enough, and they ride among us by day with clanging bells, crying, 'Bring out your dead.'"

I shook my head, my lips set hard, but he went on stroking and teasing the little girl with the upturned nose who preened under his eye. "The bell tolls for fashion too," he continued, "for even the Francophiles won't don a periwig now for fear the hairs come from the fresh dead. It's a pitiful place, London."

"Have others been borne away? Our friends?"

He looked at me strangely, pausing a long while before he spoke, and when he did his words came too quickly, as if rehearsed. "With none to guide or board her, Gideon Metcalf's young wife was taken with sores while he was at sea. I and others learned of her shutting in too late to help her. The guards will let none in or out of such houses, and those who try land in Newgate or worse. He is a grave man."

I would rather have died than pity the weasel Gideon, but on that day I did, and all those who suffered. I knelt by Nehemiah and the solemn (in my presence, at least) child I little knew, and whispered her name. "Abigail," I said, "do you know me?"

She brought her dimpled chin as high in the air as it would go. "I know you."

"And will you kiss my cheek?"

I had not expected her to speak so well, like one much older than four. Her voice was so like a tiny woman's, I frowned to check my smile. "I'll thank you, no," she said matter-of-factly. "But if it pleases you, I will your hand."

"Very well, then." I gave it, but she only poked at my knuckles as if they were a side of rotten meat; she tilted her head as Simon used to do when he was intent upon a voice or a smell and wrinkled her little nose. "There, then. I've broken my promise."

"So you have."

Abigail went skipping away calling for Mag while Nehemiah shrugged, and I laughed, alone.

Mag was herself peculiar now, cagey and nervous. While she cooked, her spoon clattered to the floor. When she washed, she burned her hand. She was forever blurting curses and blowing on her knobby thumbs.

I ignored her shameless mood. It would take her time, I knew, to submit to a mistress again after making do so long and so well without one. "What schooling has she had?" I asked again, gently now.

"She's had prayer, and Master has shown her some reckoning on the abacus. That's enough, ain't it? At her age."

"She speaks like a dainty."

"There's no other woman there, Mistress, if that's your question."

"I've no such question, Mag."

"Good, then."

I watched her stamp back and forth shaking a singed hand in the air until it bored me to look at her, and then I left.

*N*ehemiah looked up from his books and smiled politely when I came in with the gloves the next day.

"From Mother."

He considered them at length. "She had a hand for pretty stitches."

"It kept samp on our table when I was a child."

He nodded and slipped on the gloves, holding them forth to model them, and then he did something strange. He stood up and, as if leading us in a dance, walked me back to the wall and brought his leather hands slowly to my neck in jest. He was gentle, smiling, but he ringed his broad hands round as if to strangle me, and his eyes never left my eyes. "I dreamed such a pose on ship that first spring. Every night for a fortnight, I dreamed it."

I did nothing to deter him, nor could I have, but I noted that we were alone in the cottage. Sarah had returned to her physic garden and her rounds. Mag had taken Abigail with her to market. "It's your right, husband."

One leather thumb stroked beneath my chin, but he neither tightened nor loosened his grip. "I woke up cold," he said, "planks and rats squeaking, waves sloshing, and I thanked God that you did not lie beside me."

Faint with effort, I kept my eyes trained on his mouth.

"You're not afraid of such feelings?"

"I've purchased them. I will own them."

He blinked hard and let the hands slide to his sides. "Be not so willing, Pearl. For once be less than willing. It's my great curse to have a wife so opposed to prudence and modesty."

"I'll yet learn those gifts for your sake. For Abigail's."

He blew air through his nose and sat down again, flipping blindly through his pages. "For Abigail's? And will the teacher learn *before* she imparts her lessons?"

"Nehemiah, don't."

"Don't what? Would you rather I sat like a pudding in my chair and said nothing while you ruled me, as he sat—"

"He?"

"How shy is your memory, wife?"

"How shy would you like it?"

He stood up again, so abruptly that the chair rocked and nearly tipped behind him. He leaned and pointed a finger in my face, and though I dared not touch him, I consumed even the angry nearness of him greedily. "Don't take me for a toy, Pearl. I'll not have it again."

I spiraled into a foolish defense. "How could one so old as I am hope to play with toys?"

He turned away to the sideboard and began to lift unwashed tankards, plates, and spoons. He slammed each down on the ringing wood. "If you play not with toys, then why is your work never done? And should I pity you your few gray hairs? You would have me pity you?"

"I wouldn't, husband."

"Let me tell you a tale, Pearl, about Simon."

I nodded.

"Once when we were boys, I let the ocean have him. Did he tell you that while you lay together in my bed?"

My lip twitched, but I did not answer.

"He was six or so, playing near shore while I cast my net, and he walked into the waves, having lost what wretched body compass he had. I saw him swept up lightly like a gull's feather from sand. I saw his little white hand break the foam, and I stood and wondered what it would cost me to be quit of him. I stepped outside myself and looked, and studied my willing face while I pondered it, and then I stepped back in, and it was as if water had filled my own mouth. I dove to him, yanked him sputtering from the sea, and held him cold against me while gulls shrieked over. And relieved though I was, I thought, 'May I never be so needy.'"

I saw in my own mind Simon at twelve and me some bit younger, leaning back on our hands while the waves eased over us, and Daniel Devlin watching from the wood line. *Quite the sanest boy I ever knew.*

"And look at me now," said my husband with contempt.

"It is I who need you." I tried to touch his face, but it was Simon's face I saw, and in any case Nehemiah pushed my hand away. "He fell on his own," I added softly.

Nehemiah shook his head with a mournful sound in his throat.

"If you crave a culprit, I'm the one that might have pushed him." Though my words were urgent, my mind was numb. Who was the boy who lay in the mud in New Forest that he had survived the waves, and his brother's grudging duty—as I had Mother's—only to perish in *my* care. Was duty, then, more sure than love? "Not you."

"But you soothed him first. You gave him that much."

"And took it from you."

His face went blank. "Lest you think *I* was true then or ever, wife, think again. Merchants and sailors—too many men—take their vows lightly, sworn to a whore that will sooner drown than cherish them. I have sinned too."

Though it smarted, I shook my head to cast it away. "You cared for Simon. He knew it."

"How does it matter now?"

"It matters to me."

"Take it, then."

"I'll not take from you more. You'll tell me what we need now, and I'll see to that."

He walked close but kept a suffocating film of air between us. I thought if he withheld himself from me longer, I would shriek and stamp, but he went on teasing me with his nearness, and I could little challenge it without seeming immodest.

"Perhaps I'm more like my brother than I thought," he said. "I can't reach you unless you walk me to my prize?"

Because I could not let him wound me beyond repair if we were to salvage this and survive Simon, I lifted his hanging hands and steered them lightly to my shoulders. But they sat like dumb paws there, for it was not wiles he would have from me.

Nehemiah recalled the hands with a solemn smile. "I will, for my own sake, learn to see you better before I close my eyes to you again."

Watch he did, while I kept house with humble heart, speaking softly to jumpy Mag and with stately prudence to William, who was ever out-of-doors anyway, delivering letters for his master. Nehemiah watched while I read scripture to Abigail in the heat, while I huddled indoors at the spinning wheel instead of roaming out where it rained and the cool wind blew across the moors. He watched me fawn and ache to win the fancy of a child who hated me with enough passion for both of us.

How I followed that little girl and courted her, knowing perhaps that to win her was to win the father; for Nehemiah was that now, in every sense. Strange and cold though she was to me, Abigail was his great joy, and he doted on her. So much power in so small a one was unnatural, I thought, little remembering my own childish tyrannies, and what feeling I could muster for my seed usually bubbled up to my fingertips in some vague wish to strangle her. Children had never endeared themselves to me, even when I *was* a child, except Simon. Almost to a one, they were cruel.

Never were a parent and child so mismatched—Abigail with her icy primness, I with my scalding impatience. I might have made a very poor mother indeed were it not for my debt to my husband. I might have beaten the child senseless had I freedom to do it, but I learned quickly how little freedom I had. No rules were announced, no proclamations made, but at long last I understood that society and all its many cogs and wheels are greased with longing. Every time he passed me, or I breathed some breath of him in a room deserted—ink, pipe smoke, oiled boots, the sweat in a tunic draped over a chair—I knew again the goodness of my duty. Is it not in order to be loved that we first learn to be good?

He watched my transformation well and with satisfaction, and meanwhile nervous Mag fed my child sweetmeats when I forbade them and, though I knew it not then, whispered in her tiny ear of the legions of demons that knew her mother's bed at night, the incubi that came to fuck me while I lay alone in Simon's little cot, of a grandmother's brand and the evils of a wilderness far away, of the bloody name that gleamed there in a forest in a demon book: mine.

Mag was also watching, and I can pity her now because I know that she too suffered pangs wrought of ink and pipe smoke and oiled boots. What lies he told her I'll never know, but he was my husband, and I was home now.

*I*t was on the same day that I found Simon's unfinished alphabet under the mattress—a pageant of intricately deformed block figures that stood for letters he couldn't shape: apple, ball, cat, dog, elephant— that Nehemiah invited me back to his bed. He as well as announced it at supper, and it was the first time I saw Mag look at him with more than a servant's eyes. They were perplexed, round, and wounded, those eyes.

"Pearl, you'll give your chamber over to William tonight, to make more room on the hearth floor for Mag and Abigail and the trundle Will's gone for. They've slept on straw long enough. It will do till we make for London."

Ruled by cleverness

*I*t was two more seasons before word came that the plague had subsided enough for us to return to London—though many, including the King, had done so sooner—and I tried all that desperate time to wend my way into Abigail's graces. When Nehemiah rode to the village on business, I walked out with her on the moor, but always the damnable child went stamping her pointy boots and whining, and complained of the damp in her soles, the sting of insects, the endless walking. She whimpered and fussed with her dress, and bade me carry her, and when I wanted badly enough to achieve a destination such as the water wood (which I usually if not always avoided, for Nehemiah's sake), I would do it. The proud face she wore in my arms even as she wrapped her legs easily round my waist was amusing, and I let her arguments blow over me in a storm of monotony. "Must we go there? I hate the trees," she whined. "And the beady-eyed birds too. And you walk exceedingly fast."

When I felt not urgency enough to carry her, I sat on the ground gnawing a ribbon of grass. I felt the wind on my face and breathed the sweet green of manure while she railed.

"You had an uncle once," I told her on one such occasion as she crossed her spindly arms and sniveled at the clouds. "You have his hands."

"I have my own hands, Mistress."

"Will you call me something more one day? For your father's sake?"

She shook her head. "My uncle was too blind to find his toes."

"Was he, then?"

"He was, and he's dead in the mud."

"He is," I said absently, "and my heart with him."

"Is that why you keep your hand there o'er it?"

I caught my breath and crept to her on damp hands and knees through the heather. It waved round us in a fury. I pinched her dimpled chin, hard. "Who told you that?"

"None told me." She sniffed. "I see it plainly for myself."

I sat back. "And what else do you see?"

"I see a witch."

"And?"

"The old gray cat that comes round the garden shed is her familiar. That cat scratched me."

"You're a brave girl, then, to speak so haughty to a witch."

"Papa will beat you if you prick me."

"Papa has never beaten me."

She lifted her nose in the air. "I've never asked him to."

"You're a clever beast. But do you know, Abigail, that love is better than cleverness? Many fine feelings will desert you if you're ruled by cleverness." Even as I spoke the words, half forgetful of their source, I heard again my father's sonorous voice and allowed myself to wonder, for the first time, if he had survived the plague.

"Where does my uncle live now?"

I had to look away from her then, toward the far side of the moor, where the dark trees soothed me. "With our Lord in Heaven."

The singsong of Abigail's voice jarred me. "Says my lady, 'Many fine feelings will desert you if you're ruled by cleverness.' Can he *see* the angels, or do they mock his blind eyes?"

"Mock him?"

"He was wicked. They will mock him."

"There's no room in paradise for such sport."

Again her singsong, as she rose to her feet and began to preen and smooth her velvet dress. "My lady says, 'There is no room in paradise for such sport.' But is there room there for the wicked?"

I made as if to chase her, but she ran with her cap flapping and gold hair bouncing loose from the bun Mag made of it each morning. I stumbled over a rabbit hole and fell on my hands with a bruising thud. Lying there ridiculous, I wished that Simon's pale arms would break through the cool crust and draw me down to him. I sank against the earth, his body, my heart, and then as quickly roared and pushed myself up on my palms, and laughed at her murderous audacity. She was my child, truly.

*M*y greatest worry in those quiet months was that I might talk in my sleep and savage our reconciliation. Dreams are a strange business. I slept now circled in my husband's strong arms. But even that safety, paid for with my mindful manners, could not wring the loneliness from me; it was a habit of two-plus years' time, during which I'd lived a pinched and solitary life, and when I was lonely, it was Simon I went to. I dreamed of him constantly, and because it was the only time he spoke to me now, I listened well, and told him who knows what.

On rare nights my dreams woke me; I groped through the fog of them and lay listening to the stark silence of the cottage, wondering with increasing urgency: Had Dr. Devlin survived the plague? Had that physician, already an avowed coward, fled London like so many of the others? I could not bring myself to beg Nehemiah for word, though. Admitting curiosity on this point seemed another brand of betrayal, since he had already sworn off my origins; I would not add insult to injury now. I lay awake, imagining Mag tossing and turning in the room beyond, and wondered what had come to pass in London between my ruined husband and our maidservant; something surely had in the years when I was absent, though Nehemiah would never trouble himself to acknowledge it. What man would?

I didn't wonder too much for fear it would overpower us all, but at night when I dreamed of the child Simon on the seashore, waving and beckoning as if he could see me, when I endured again the naked shock of him running, lean and pale, between the dark New England trees, I woke dismayed that he had slipped away again; shivering, I propped myself up on my elbow and peered at my sleeping husband while his eyes raced under their lids, and I wondered at *his* secrets, at a world in which hearts, all hearts, must keep them.

One Saturday morning after such musings, I stood by to help Mag with the baking. "Mag?" I spoke gently, but not so as to incite her. "What became of your wheelwright, Stephen?"

She cast a sour look at me but kept kneading. "He married in London."

"When was that?"

"While we were here, the time before Master Simon died."

"I'm sorry for you."

"Don't be, Mistress. A right scold she is and deserves him. I have my duty to Abigail now."

"A toad is like to bring more comfort."

"She has her ways." Mag looked up over her work. "Mother feeling don't come natural to some."

"You must have been a great help to my husband during our hardship, Mag, and a godsend for Abigail."

She had beaten the dough almost to death now. She pursed her lips and didn't say a word.

"I know you were, Mag. I'm sure of it."

"He said so?"

"He'll never say. Why should he?"

I saw that her hands were shaking. "You'll put me out?"

"I've no cause to put you out now. Do I?"

"None." She sniffed and swiped at her eye and patted the tear into the dough where I wouldn't see it.

I walked behind and took her stooped shoulders. I whispered, "But give them back to me now." When I drew my hands away, there were flour marks on her wine-dark dress. "The term of my generosity has ended."

I was nearly out of the pantry when I heard her mutter in a choked voice, "Neglect, more like."

"What?"

She kept her back to me. "The term of your neglect."

"Be that as it may, Mag. You'll see to it."

"How can I see to anything?"

"See yourself clear."

Staring down at the dough, she stood with her hands idle.

J had no stomach for bread that night, or much else, for I was too busy wedging spoonfuls of soup between Abigail's pinched lips only to have her spit them out. I didn't ask for Mag's help—this was her work, all things being right—nor did she offer it. Nehemiah seemed to find my maternal struggles entertaining until the mess and the noise grew too great, and he brought his palm down on the table. "She's old enough to feed herself. If she won't, she'll sleep hungry."

That night, I heard a bereft Abigail cry and cry, coughing and sputtering and cursing on the new trundle bed for Mag to turn over and hold her, but when I made as if to get up and fetch her, a drowsy Nehemiah caught my wrist and pulled me back to bed.

*S*he was a terror in her loneliness. Abigail's sense of entitlement was such that none could soothe her when the object of her earliest and strongest affection was withheld. It was not trinkets or the forbidden sweetmeats she craved, but what she understood to be her due—kisses and wicked secrets whispered, a warm embrace at night, stories and the hard rub of a rag round a sticky mouth—all of which had come from Mag and the flow of which was now dammed up.

No words were spoken to that end. Mag said nothing to alert Abigail that she was finished. But Abby knew, and I, a poor substitute for Mag, knew.

Nehemiah was aware of some disturbance in the house and of Abigail's increasing bad behavior, but he was little interested in its source, only in checking it. One word from him would silence her. She went from roaring savage to pouting infant in a moment's time.

"Why won't she love me now?" Abigail begged in Mag's presence—not of me, I understood, but of the powers that be. Stolid Mag only threaded her needle or set another log on the fire and walked on.

"She loves you."

"Then why does she run from me?"

"We all run from you when you're cross." I tried to lean and kiss her, but she sneered.

"*You* can't kiss me. You have kissed a donkey's backside."

"Abby." I shook my head sadly. "When will you learn that no love comes to lips that sting?"

"You have loved me when it was easy to do it."

"Did she tell you that?"

"She told me you know the devil."

I looked for Mag, but she had gone out to the garden. "I knew him once." I leaned forward and saw my daughter's belligerent little heart pounding under its threadbare shift like an animal's. "Can we craft a deal, Abby? I won't kiss you if you'll know it isn't *you* Mag is angry with. It's me. She'll love you again in time, but for now let me be your friend."

"I'll not call you 'Mother.'"

"I know it."

"I'll not love you."

"I'll not love you yet either. There is no easy love, Abby."

Her eyes told me that she had already forgotten her borrowed accusation.

HEAVEN

*W*e stood together once more under the oaks at New Forest, but Nehemiah did not kiss me. In an odd way, it felt shameful to be outdoors with him. We rarely went out together now, but did so separately, and returned together to the cottage at evening like furtive beggars. I wondered now, a day before we returned to London, how our reunion would fare in the brown light of the city, among so many pairs of eyes. I wondered who there might know of my evildoings, but convinced myself that to save his own face, Nehemiah would not have aired them. Even Mag and William seemed blank and forgetful on the subject of the past, but then, they would not talk of it with the mistress by.

"You're quite sure?" my husband asked me now, looking out to the moor. "I'll not rush you."

"I could stay on here. If you're ashamed of me—"

He considered the question a long while, and kept his gaze fixed on the browning moor. "Not ashamed, Pearl. I'm unsettled by you. I have always been. But I must needs see to work now. I have built new friendships, and old ones have blossomed, and I will expect to keep as good as a lady for a wife now."

I glanced at my plain wool dress, the one I worked in; I had stained many like it in my play. "Dress me for it, and I'll fill the part."

"I've no trouble dressing you, Pearl, or undressing you for that matter." He walked close and took my chin, lifting my face with effort. "But Nell Gwyn you are not."

Like most Londoners, I had heard of the King's mistress, a celebrated actress on a modern stage that featured women players. "I won't compromise you again, husband. I'll reward your forgiveness."

"And Abigail?"

"She's our child, and my heart's mission."

"She is not our child, lest we forget. She's yours, and in another way, she is mine. Never ours. But she wants for keeping, and for teaching Mag can't provide."

"Won't provide."

His eyes held mine for a moment but did not inquire. "Yes, well. Much needs doing, and we will do it. But what of this, Pearl?" He waved his hands like a sorcerer, and the whole browning summer world fixed in my focus. "*Can* you leave it? I'll see this place shut up. I'll not return here without another Black Death to drive me."

"Not at all?"

"Not ever. Haven't you noticed how I keep to the village? It's not boredom only that calls me there. He shouts me away."

"You hear him?" I saw the dismay in my husband's face, and realized there was hope in my voice, and resentment.

"I hear his silence."

"Let me show you a place he loved, Nehemiah. Walk out with me today."

"What my brother loved is not mine to know," he said severely, and strode back toward the cottage, which stood dappled and quiet in sunlight below the rise.

$\mathcal{W}$ould that we could memorize all facets of a place, or a face, and carry them in the trap of our hearts. It's but few and paltry pieces that time lets slip through that choke, and I know I have forgotten the best of them. I walked alone to the water wood when Nehemiah left me that day under the oaks. I went a last time and sat without weeping on the bank of the brook, and smelled the decay of too much ripeness, and wondered what, beyond extremes of weather, Simon *had* loved. Did I know any better than his brother what had moved him?

Was it a season's promised chill and the sweet crack of frost on the grass underfoot? Was it birdsong that he loved, the explosion of a fig on the tongue, my hands in his hair—or were these my guesses merely? Perhaps he loved as simply as he lived, and it was the squeak and bustle of mice under the hearth floor that pleased him, the smell of wood smoke, the steel of his knife and the sweet slide of shaved cedar, footfalls moving toward or away from him.

"*Did* you care for me?" I demanded plaintively. He had never said so, and said nothing now. Try as I might to see him again as my confident lover here in the wood, it was his last moments of fear that my imagination, in defiance, seized on now that I was leaving this place.

All the way to London I rode with a kind of dread. I felt New Forest being peeled from me like a skin. Abigail chattered and kicked under my bench in the coach, but I couldn't steady my voice to scold her. I closed my eyes and replayed over and over Simon's inching along the wall, in terror, away from us. I felt his hand grasp the well wall of the cellar door but only an instant after his bewildered feet had turned the threshold. I felt, above all, the bruising fall, the reeling dark, the final *thwack* of bone against stone. *Us.* The word shone like a candle in a room full of the howling damned. I would blow it out if I could, but how? It was we, both of us, that Simon had meant to elude, not his raging brother only. The last thing I had done for Simon was to drive him away from all care and goodness, and into the darkest solitude imaginable.

"Pearl?" My husband spoke softly while Mag and tiny Abigail slept slouched in the coach. "Stop now."

I nodded with more eagerness than I felt and swiped at a stubborn tap of tears, cross with myself for shedding them before him. "I will."

"You must. Let London be a line we cross."

"It will be."

I felt his breath in my ear and his nearness, though my traitorous eyes were closed. He said, "It must be."

T he streets were still quiet with the pall of plague, though thankfully there was no telltale sign of its ravages that I could see. There were no death carts or groans, no bloated, blackened bodies heaped now at road-sides, no guards posted outside infected houses, no physicians walking alone along the crooked cobbles with colored staffs. Gideon Metcalf and his servants were in the flat when we arrived, with a fire blazing. Mag's waxy face lit up at the sight of him, and she went to him as to a brother, and he embraced her and whispered in her ear with his wet, pink lips, and they laughed, I believed, at my expense. Nehemiah watched their reunion with aloof bemusement. So he was not jealous, I thought, for his whore's sake. I saw Mag look once for my husband's eyes, but he deprived her. Her brother, who came in behind us with the big trunk, did not look pleased to see Mag with Metcalf, but then William rarely looked anything but dour.

"My boys have beaten back the dust," said Gideon, "and aired your rooms a bit. But food we haven't, so let us step out tonight. Your return calls for cakes and ale. I know of a lady who's pledged to host some waits and a dancing master. I know too the fellow on the cittern, and they're a merry bunch. You'll come along, Mag, so I can smell your neck again." He buried his face in it, and lost his hat in the squealing scuffle, and I smiled in spite of myself at their antics after so long and solemn a ride.

Nehemiah lifted the hat from the floor and held it forth while Gideon blushed. "You'll want more wine from my cellar, friend. We'll be a mo-ment refreshing ourselves."

"I wager more than a moment, man." He waved a hand before his nose, and his beady eyes twinkled. "The very posies shrink from you. Country living has its charms, but—"

"Abigail!" barked Nehemiah. "You'll not walk on the chairs."

We all turned to find her pouting, and a shadow crossed Gideon's face at the sight of her, and I remembered suddenly that he had lost his new bride to the plague. I determined to soften my opinion of him, at least for one night, but the way he pawed at Mag made it work. Though she seemed on the surface to enjoy his attentions, I could see as the evening wore on that it was for Nehemiah's sake Mag made herself merry. But my good husband gave her nothing, not so much as a frown—not, at least, while he was sober.

*G*ideon was true about one thing. They were a merry crowd that welcomed us back to London. They were substantial lodgings the lady kept, and her maids served baked apples and a whole venison pasty, cold, with gallons of ale, wine, claret, and sack while the waits played.

When you have been away from music for a long time, it comes as a kind of miracle to your ears, and I felt my body rise to it through the sweet warmth of the wine. Many times I tried to meet my husband's eye, but for a while that night he was no more kind to me than he was to Mag. We had lost the habit of society in New Forest—I especially—and when at last he led me out to the floor to dance the shepherd's holyday, I was full of pity for myself, and felt perhaps too much gratitude as he touched his palms to my palms and let me into his golden-brown eyes. I swam in those eyes, and stepped lightly, and each time he came close and his palms met mine again, I felt again the shock of belonging to him. We were a handsome couple, I knew, and his eyes never left me after that, though I began to see toward the end of that night the workings of his strange new habit, which was to drink too much and follow from some distant place in the room my every move with an absent, puzzled, and slightly ferocious stare. But I was lulled by his nearness and the wine, the recorder and flute, the murmured laughter and sequenced clomp of heavy jackboots and Louis heels on the wood floor. It was a fine, perhaps false, way to be reacquainted with London, and I was so grateful for our good mood that at one point, while Nehemiah was down helping to haul a cask from the cellar, I took pains to thank Gideon for his trouble in inviting us.

When I came to their corner, he pulled away from gnawing at Mag's collarbone (it looked so!) as if it were a side of beef and he a mongrel. Her bodice was crooked, and his foggy eyes took stock of me standing without my husband. When he spoke to me, licking raw lips, I felt stained. "Mistress. Welcome to our corner of iniquity."

"I came only to thank you for your invitation, sir."

"'Sir,' is it?"

I rolled my eyes, already weary of him.

"I should like to jest with you a moment, ladies." He cleared his throat, all ceremony, and straightened his cravat, which had cloth enough in it to make a sail for a barge. He wore too a monstrous large periwig that made his lean body seem slighter still. I was, for my part, relieved that my husband had scorned that fashion once and for all in favor of his own locks. Mag tried hard not to smile while Gideon spoke, though his eyes were on me, and once she slapped his hand when it crept to her backside.

"A merchant had wooed an abundance of girls and did lie with them," he began loftily, "upon which he refused to marry them. One girl he did solicit very much, but all his charms would not do. Then he married her and told her on the marriage night that if she had let him do as the others did, he would never have had her. 'By my troth, I thought so,' she said, 'for I was so served by half a dozen before.'"

I laughed politely and glared at Mag, who was having difficulty fending off his advances. "You might try more modesty here," I bent and whispered to her, "for your master's sake if not mine. Perhaps the girls here could use some help."

She curtsied coldly but made no move to go. "I'll see to it, Mistress."

I didn't bother to nod or acknowledge her, but as I was going, I heard Gideon say, "Ah, but she would heal us all like her father, the physician, who did little to heal my Jenna, nor his own brat, for that matter. The other, legitimate one, that is."

I walked back and stood with my head cocked, eyes narrowed. There was wine in my head and murder in my hands, but they were small, those hands. They were weak. "I am gravely sorry for your loss, Master Metcalf, but truly: Has your wife been long enough at her sleep that you can play so wicked with your hands and words? Healer I'm not, but my heart is in what I do."

"Your heart only?" He grinned his challenge, and I knew my earnest logic seemed pathetic in this setting. "A pity that's all," he said. "I've heard you have no heart. Just like your father. No sooner were his wife and babe shoveled over than he fled like gentry, leaving London to fester in her sores."

"What you've heard I have no salve for," I said, "but it's best not to strain the bounds of friendship. My husband, I know, values yours. I understand the Royal Navy is courting your favors now?"

He tilted his head, obviously delighting in a little blood sport. "So it is, and so your husband wills it."

"I thought as much."

Mag coughed and pulled away from him. She shook her head in bewildered disgust and staggered off to look for more sack. It was well past time we got her home, I saw, and I wondered yet again how much she knew of her lady's history, when I myself seemed to know so little. But I had unfinished business. "He lives, then, the doctor?"

But disclosure was the last thing on Gideon's feeble mind. He stepped close and blew his reeking breath on me. "I know you," the Weasel said, his good humor gone. "And don't forget I do."

I stared back at him.

"Do you remember winter in New England, Pearl? You must recall sitting wrapped to the chin with our feet on coals in the meetinghouse? Oh, but wait. You and your mother could be spared no seat. But I liked to watch you from afar even then. You left your little body hunched against that far wall—didn't you?—and traveled away to some mischief. Even your mother couldn't stop you, though she was as much his as you were."

"His?"

"You know him. The devil." He spat the name with foolish relish, as if invoking a bugaboo to scare a child, and I could have laughed to hear him say it, but instead the old furies and indignities of Boston bloomed anew in my mind like carrion flowers. I thought too of my father heading away, alone—always away and always alone—from stricken London as once he had sailed from the New World. I saw him from behind, a miragelike figure with a bundle, growing smaller, shedding substance. But had he survived the leaving this time? Or had the divine Shepherd at last lost patience with this stray?

"I used to imagine riding her," Gideon whispered, jarring me and clutching his groin a furtive instant, "your mother. And I suffered *hard* in public." His voice rose gaily. "I liked to watch you both in the meeting-house." The weasel motioned to my silk dress, creamy yellow with black embroidery and a black velvet topknot at the bodice. "A little yellow bird with a black heart. I like to watch you still, Pearl."

I gestured lightly. "Tell it to my husband."

Gideon whirled like an actor on stage and caught striding Nehemiah in a great embrace. Their hearty laughter rose above the pipes and timbrels. I heard now the words of the ballad that seemed, in my present confusion, obscenely cheerful:

> In praise of a dairy I purpose to sing,
> But all things in order; first God save the King!
> And the Queen I may say; that ev'ry Mayday,
> Has many fair dairy-maids all fine and gay;
> Assist me fair damsels, to finish my theme,
> Inspiring my fancy with strawberry cream.

THEIR EYES

*T*hat night, after noisome Gideon and his servants—including the unfortunate new girl, a plain wench named Anne, whom Gideon had enlisted to stay with Abigail—had gone, and I'd lain some while with Abby, I heard Nehemiah, his drunk step, steal up to the garret. I was not surprised that my soused husband retreated to Mag, nor even especially angry. I had no right to anger, nor fire for it, but my loneliness was fierce that first night back in London. Here I was, and here I had nothing. Not Sarah, not the moors and ponies and the water wood, not even Simon's bloodstain in the cellar. At one point, I slipped from bed and went out to the great chamber. The fire in the hearth was dead, and I lit a tallow and saw myself move like a ghost in the diamond-shaped panes of the window.

I still thought of that corner as Simon's, and it took some moments before I could settle there on his chair. I closed my eyes, and listened to the unquiet street below, and to the soft scrape of the bedpost on the old wood above. William had Simon's old room now, while Mag had his bed; it was narrow, but it was no pallet. I felt a killing calm as I pondered how pretty was fate's wit, to have them tumbled on the same lonely mattress where Simon had dreamed away his quiet years.

You must promise to tend well your babes, Mother had cautioned. *Do not go from them.*

Go where? I wondered. What would I do? Where did I belong if not here?

If it be your will, I thought, *give me strength for Abigail.* Was it God I beseeched, or Mother?

I clamped closed my eyes and felt the whole swirl of that great city in my ears. The highway robbers hunkered at its borders, the lunatics shrieking at Bedlam, the pits where plague victims—my own half-brother, fat little cherub, among them, it would seem—lay piled one atop another with but a thin layer of dirt between them, the still mounded churchyards and teeming alehouses, the King and his court—restored at Whitehall since February—gathered in their late-night finery round the spinet or virginal, the typhoid groan of prisoners at Newcastle, where men were piled quartered in the closets till their kin retrieved them, the birds of paradise preening, the great serpent shifting in the dark of its enclosures at India House, the rotting heads of criminals, set on spikes to look out over the Thames from London Bridge even as ballad-singers intoned nearby, the bakers breathing yeast, elbow deep in chalky dough. Silence, tumult, silence, layer after layer of it, and no harmony between them.

I fought not to picture my husband's dark hand against the cream of Mag's plump breast, the way those strong fingers would press and knead upward over chest and collarbone, cup round the neck and slide under the dimpled chin, or the bruised look her lips would have when we gathered at the table to break our fast. Would she sit Abigail in her lap? The thought left me hollow. It was those sounds, that city alone that filled me, and promised to suffocate me if I stepped out into it.

He woke me in the chair hours later, and I was stiff and dazed by the sight of him from whom I had unraveled myself in dreams.

"Wake, Pearl, and go to your bed now."

"My bed?" My voice was flat and hoarse, and I would not meet his eyes, though he tried to draw my face up to him. I jerked away from his hand for fear I might smell her there. My tongue sat heavy and furred from wine.

His weary voice had a smile in it. "Surely you don't sit in judgment of me?"

"No," I said vaguely. "I judge my fate as just. And you never beat me. What more can a wife ask?"

"You mock me for not? I'll see you change your mind." His threat had no heart in it; he was sober now, and ashamed.

"I mock myself."

"And well you might—for a hypocrite."

"Shall I own her apron and scrub the floor for her too?"

He laughed uneasily and knelt by the chair. "You are mistress of this house. It was the drink only, and an old habit of consolation."

"We'll be wanting drink every night, then, won't we?"

I remembered with astonishment that it was Mag's phrase—from the day I had told her I would take Simon to hunt for violets. The day Abigail was conceived. I felt the sudden warmth of Simon's hand in mine as we crossed the windy moor. How sour that playful arrangement of words tasted on my tongue now, when it had seemed sweet to my ears in New Forest. Was I so innocent as that—then?

"Mayhap with his wife in the dirt, Gideon will have her back now, if she's not used up, or make an honest woman of her, one or the other."

Nehemiah looked out at me through puzzled, patient eyes.

"I'll not have her curl my hair. Before I know it, she'll be grating root of wolfsbane into my ale. This is poison, husband. This life. *Our* life."

He studied me long and thoughtfully. Even as my tongue prepared to seal my fate and set the pace for a long life of punishment and drudgery, the path of a scold, he did me the service of silencing my thoughts; he laid his head in my lap like a great contrite hound and we sat quietly thus while the light broke the line that lay out on the fields and moors beyond our brown and rancid city. The sunrise caught the gold in his hair, and I stroked his head. After a long while, he lifted it, and said hoarsely, "She'll go, then."

I did not make him tell her. I did so myself, for I could not hate Mag, nor even blame her for trying to retrieve what I had, in my guilt and grief, so long cast aside. I had selfish reasons for bearing the news, too. She wouldn't cry for my sake as she would for him; I would not grant them that interview.

"They're kind people," I explained, "and they have a bed for you at once. Your situation will be identical to this one, but you'll have no tops and puppets underfoot, for the couple is childless. William will stay on here as apprentice, unless he prefers not."

She betrayed no feeling as she curtsied and turned to gather her things, but her disappointment was tangible.

"Mag?" I called, and she turned to me a face blotched with effort and last night's excesses.

"Yes?"

"I don't blame you for it," I said. "I'm no great lady. I've no airs to put on. But a body can't have two hearts, and a house—"

"I know it well enough. It was you that didn't."

"I do now."

"I see, Mistress. It's good you do. Thank you for your mercy here today." She curtsied again, and it was my misfortune that Abigail woke then and came tumbling out of bed and toward our voices in the larder with a squeak of surprise to see us crowded together in it.

"Well, then, Abby, I guess your mum won't mind if I give you a kiss now, will you, Mistress?"

I shook my head, and winced to see her kneel and embrace the suspicious tot. Abigail squirmed in ecstatic alarm, following without so much as a glance at me when Mag invited her to "come along and say the catechism while I bundle my things. Let me hear how well you do it."

"My duty," the child began with a bouncing sigh—for she was happy, I knew, to think her Mag did care for her once more—"to love, honor, and succor my father and mother; to submit myself to all my governors, teachers, spiritual pastors, and masters; to order myself lowly and reverently to all my betters—" Her little voice carried round the house like an echo in a cavernous place, and when I could bear it, and their familiar laughter, no longer, I left our lodgings and walked down the great curved staircase to the street.

I looked up and down it, trying to think of a place where Abigail and I might be happy, though I was not fool enough to expect miracles. I stood like a common punk in a strange doorway and waited for Mag to go, lugging her sacks, and when she did, and I heard her steps ring hollow on the cobbles, I cried.

*N*ehemiah was still shut in his study when I came in again, and Abby was in Simon's chair, surveying the street with panicked eyes. "Where is she going?" she accused.

"You'll see her again," I lied.

"When will I?"

"When it suits her to come."

"You sent her away. She said so!"

"I did. Yes."

She glared at me with unmitigated hatred, and crossed her scrawny arms, and I think it was in that moment when she loved me least that I saw Simon in her most keenly, and longed most for her approbation. Though her hair was as light as his had been dark (a full head of the gold that streaked Nehemiah's), now that the layers of baby were receding, I could see that she would have her father's noble jaw and high cheeks. And she had Simon's long, graceful hands, to be sure. "Abby? Come here."

She shook her little head fiercely.

I resorted to bribery. "I'll take you to the Tower to see the lions."

She looked me over, lips white with pinching, her prim little nose pointing heavenward. "No."

"The lions have teeth like daggers, and I know one, named Crowly, very well. He is my own pet."

"I don't believe you," she accused, her dirty face streaked clean with tears.

"Come here, urchin." I snatched her arm, pulled her to me, and fairly smothered her until she quit struggling, and felt an old memory of Mother's gentle gray-clothed arms containing me this way while the northeast wind raged outside our cottage, shattering waves like glass on the frosty sand in the bay, and I felt too an even dimmer memory, a surge like milk in my full breasts, and then set my child back docile and wiped her snot with my apron edge. It did no good, but smeared what was already there. "Cry, cry," I said. "It's hard to think the tears will stop, but they will." I lifted her, amazed at her lightness, and carried her limp frame to our chamber; I drew the bed curtains, and that was where Nehemiah found us later—curled together in the big bed, sleeping with a house full of chores left undone. I watched drowsily through the cloth gap as he removed his waistcoat, then walked round, and felt the mattress sag as he twined behind, and we three slept the suspended morning away in a sweaty tangle.

*B*ut whose eyes were they—Abby's? I wondered as we rode later in the hackney to the Tower. Nehemiah, for Abigail's sake—for all, perhaps—had decided to lay aside the afternoon's work and accompany us to view the Royal Menagerie. In truth, I had never seen it—nor once been to visit the great fortress that was this nation's symbol—though I'd heard the menagerie spoken of in our social circles. I was intrigued by the tales of wild beasts caught and circling at the gates to the stone heart of a teeming city.

If the Tower, which had housed kings and queens and murdered princes as well as criminals in its myriad rooms and towers, was not the heart of London, it was—prominently placed at its southeast corner, guarding the approach to the city up the Thames—its stern brow. I liked not the sight of it, and could not help but think of the stubborn, harmless Quakers starving in manacles alongside more notorious lawbreakers because they would not sign the King's oath of allegiance. When we stepped out of the hackney and began our trudge up Tower Hill, I could not have imagined that just weeks from now this hill would swarm with homeless, burned, and wailing multitudes. Today the hill was quiet. We were the only public at the Lion Gate, and once we'd crossed the stone causeway over the moat and the drawbridge, and paid our fee to a sleepy guard, we turned right inside the semicircular tower toward a door painted with a lion. Nehemiah opened it and waved us in, and we were met with waves of stench and noise—musk and shit, the restless, shifting grunt of bodies circling wooden cages. The barely audible scrape of claw on cold stone.

It was dim inside, despite the torches burning, and Nehemiah and Abigail went at once to find the lion gallery. I heard their echoing voices as I walked from enclosure to dank enclosure, peering in at a cringing porcupine (though they could not bring him moonglow nor green needles to nose among, the creature lacked even a log to cower behind, I noted with sadness) and a bickering pair of bird giants called ostriches, one of which pecked unmercifully at its partner. But it was the trio of emaciated wolves tearing at a rat's carcass that stopped me cold. One looked up at me where I stood peering in; heartsick with fascination, I courted the indifference in its yellow eyes. When it turned a bloody snout back to its task, I felt impatient to have those eyes back on me. I felt a glutton's wrath, for my memory was reeling.

It was no one moment I remembered, but rather the springy damp of sodden leaves under my small feet, the roar of New England weather in my ears, the dark snap of a stick in the pathless snow as wolves brushed my frozen play at some distance, padding heavily from tree to tree. I was a poor choice for a meal, and at last came the whisper of consent when they moved on as one, and the relief of wind filled my ears again. I was, I realized with a funny gratitude, remembering the feeling of being hunted.

Though these sorry beasts had little use for the hunt now, I knew they must recall it if even my inferior senses could summon a green place long and far away, the lock of my limbs, the keening wind. I slumped against their wooden bars and mourned for them until Abby's excited voice called me back.

When I found her with her father in the gallery, Abigail was leaning perilously over the rail roaring down at a pair of mangy lions. Her mockery little fazed them. The male slept by his water cistern without once lifting his great, maned head. The female circled and circled, and never stopped circling while we stood transfixed like the fops who flattered the King while he played at tennis. Nehemiah's hand shot out to steady Abby when need be, but his good reflexes did little to soothe me. "Down, down," I said, and set her upright.

"Papa says my lord King James brought his mastiffs into the pit and let them battle over scraps of meat."

I shuddered to think of it, absently watching the shoulder muscles of the she-lion as she paced below.

"Who would win?" Abby's earnest voice echoed through the tower.

"Next you'll take to cockfights," I chided. "The lions." I little believed it myself. They were strangers here, without advantage.

Nehemiah stepped close. "I wager the dogs." He spoke into my neck and, though his easy arms round my middle were warm, his voice chilled me somehow. "They're relentless."

Abby sighed her miniature Mag sigh and raced out to gawk at some other poor soul while Nehemiah breathed into the nape of my neck. My shoulders tensed, but I felt the unwelcome swell of lust. I had almost determined to turn to him and let him kiss me full in this wretched hot prison that reeked of piss-soaked hay when he said something that stayed me.

"I read him your letters."

I relaxed my shoulders to encourage his words, but he pulled away and began to pace the gallery like the she-lion below.

"It was a kind of sport, I think. I'd rattle the page till he begged to 'hear from Pearl,' and then his strange hands would start their little drama, smoothing his thighs like so—remember?—and that black tangle of hair. His hands were ever busy, you'll recall, but rarely, when his mood was stirred, they were near frantic. He had so little, you see, and you were most of it."

"You said——"

"I said not, but I did. I read him every one, at my leisure. It was a strange science, the way it transformed him. It took some while once your mother's letters started coming for me to recall you in my mind. My memory of New England was poor once we left it. I purposed it so. But when he dictated his words back, I was given to understand that you, a child merely, had been somewhere none of us, even Liza, *could* be——inside his darkness. It made me wonder. In the end I guess it made me want you for myself. I'm dark in my way, too." He laughed bleakly. "Simon's was a fortress, and I was too impatient to scale its walls. I was no hero or light to him, surely."

"You were."

"I was cold, like our mother. It will be recalled to me at the Judgment, and I won't deny it. His loneliness was ever like a weight round my neck, and I quailed at it. At seventeen I was quick to give him to you, and glad to see him go. But your grief is tedious now——"

"You cared for him. With your father at sea and your mother's distraction, he might have ended in a place like Bedlam with howling in his ears."

"You don't hear me, Pearl." He acted stung when his fingertip grazed my cheek. "Wife. Your grief is *tedious.*"

A great, shocking din sounded beyond from the cages. Our looks grazed each other, and we raced to the outer holding room to find that Abigail had climbed the wooden grate of the wolves' cage. The animals, affronted by her intrusion or merely squabbling over rat's bones, had formed a loose circle like revelers round a bonfire. They minced a dance and threw back their heads. Their varied sounds were the logs they heaped on that blaze of sound——a riveting whimper here, a peal to Heaven there——and their anguished sport had incited many of the other beasts in the tower to frenzy. Nehemiah snatched Abby down and scolded her while I, drawn as if by the siren singers of old tales, drifted back to the grate.

"The lads and I used to track them all evening. Twopence a head," my husband called over the fading din, "back in New England."

A beefeater arrived, and he and Nehemiah chatted gamely about the habits here, the history of the beasts, the legendary white bear that swam once from his keeper's chain in the Thames. But I stood under a blazing torch clamped to dank stone and could not tear my eyes from those mangy wolves—quiet and shifty now—and felt again that frozen terror in the snow, and my youthful fascination with the hunt. I saw a wilderness, far off, reflected in their yellow eyes.

Any cure will do

*Y*our grief is tedious. His phrase floated through my busy days—
for my husband was loath to sponsor a new maidservant and
scant help now that his tippling involved him more than his
household did. After Mag's departure, he spent night after night at the
alehouses with Gideon. At home, when he was home, we were a bitter
pair, with Simon's ghost between us and no other to distract from it. My
grief was tedious indeed, even to its owner (though it was no longer grief,
exactly, but something else) and before I knew how to name my mood—
abandonment? betrayal?—I was begging Simon to go from me. I might
have traded every memory of him that dry August for the warmth of one
touch.

One Wednesday when Gideon and Nehemiah emerged from the study
to take refreshment, I suggested an outing. Gideon seized on the idea, and
said that we must all to Whitehall to watch the King eat.

Abby clapped her hands and bounced, and even a grave Nehemiah,
who had a mind to business that day, had to smile at the absurd interrup-
tion. "To the river, then. I can't see ending up in a gutter on that account."

Nehemiah paid the ferryman, and we took our seats together with a
lady and her waiting woman, both finely dressed for mourning and
bound, like us, for the palace. Gideon, of course, took the opportunity to
charm them, or try.

"I bless the moment that gives me an opportunity to enjoy your company." The Weasel bowed his big French hat, steadying himself with a hand on the edge of the boat. "That's a reckless bit of rowing, sir," he complained, turning. "I'll have you know you carry the very sun and moon aboard. You might go gentle with them."

I winced and shook my head, enjoying the lazy hiss of the boat's motion through the stinking current, and when I looked up and saw the humor in her cultured face, I smiled—though it was not my place to do so—to have the lady know that Gideon was harmless. He wasn't quite, of course, but she needed no discouragement. She suffered a disdainful nod, and when Gideon moved on to test her handmaid's graces, the lady winked at me. She was not a young woman exactly—or her red-gold hair and fair, flecked skin had aged her beyond her years—but she was young enough that I did not cower in her sight, and she was beautiful in that way that only wealth can make one beautiful. I liked her, and was surprised when we disembarked and she took my arm in an easy manner to ask why she had never seen me at court. Nehemiah hung back, keeping Gideon at bay; he walked with the maid and with Abby tugging on the ribbons of his waistcoat sleeve. "Where's the King?" Abigail commanded. "The King, Papa! And the Queen?"

"I've not been to court," I replied.

"So you haven't." She sighed. "She'll not find the Queen here. Is she your little one?"

I nodded, and the gentlewoman paused abruptly and caught both my hands in hers. "I would give anything for a girl," she whispered. "I've bred a half-dozen boys who died before they could be blessed. And now the Dutch have slain my good husband three months ago, and I'll not another child bear."

I did not tell her I was sorry, though I was. She was so urgent, so easy with me, that I felt she must be melancholy with grief, but her station was such that I could not draw away without rudeness. She let go of my hands and leaned close to whisper playfully, "He will bring you ruin."

"He?" I said in a dazed voice.

"That man is your husband?"

"Gideon? Oh, no!"

She made a sour face, then smiled like a patient teacher. "I mean the other."

"The other?" I shook the fog from my head. "Yes. He is Nehemiah Milton, a merchant, and I am Pearl. Our daughter is Abigail."

"He trades at the Exchange?"

"Yes. With the Port Essex Company."

She kissed my cheek as if gifting me with a farthing for some service, then turned where the path divided to pause for her waiting woman. When the other caught up, my companion stepped forward and leaned slightly in her heavily boned mourning finery to stroke Abby's cheek. I prayed my daughter would not blurt out some evil, but Mag had taught her well, for Abby only sank into a mincing curtsy.

That rare bird only nodded at Gideon, dismissing him, but she stood a long while before Nehemiah, and he, unsure how to thank her for her attentions, did as the etiquette books demanded; he bowed, kissed his own hand, and then kissed the edge of her fine black silk hood. She smiled radiantly at him, and walked on.

We took a facing path, toward the public garden, but our frivolous outing seemed to sag now under her shadow. I wondered if the others felt as I did. We three were largely children of the New World (and Nehemiah with a Puritan parent) and not, like many English, reared to view the gentry as divine—yet even I could not banish my impression of her as otherworldly and the sense that by merest virtue of our proximity, I had somehow been made small.

If I was not reduced by her on that day, I soon would be, for a week later I found a letter in my husband's waistcoat addressed to him at the Royal Exchange. The snapped wax seal was unreadable now, but the ink inside was plain enough:

Sir,

    Mrs. High, widow of Commander High of the Royal Navy, greatly desires your company at her lodgings right of the sign of the elephant in Holborn below Gray's Inn, on 18 August 1666, noontide.

When my husband had not come home for a week after that date, my father the doctor came, rapping drunkenly one night. Abigail was asleep, and William had been gone these many days too; I had no servant to answer, so I went myself. When I saw him I pulled the door to me and peered through a crack, astounded, and could little bear the relief. He was alive, and I was glad of it, and now I could resume the satisfying task of wishing him dead. I tried to force the door closed, but he slipped a foot in. "Have you no kind scraps for me, Pearl—no pity for a famished man?"

"My husband is not in," I said, as if this well settled it.

"Obviously I've not come to see him," he replied with a wooden laugh. "He is, I happen to know, with his expensive new whore. She'll clean you out of house and home with her habits. He'll not afford her."

"What do you want?"

"I want entry. I've words for you."

"My interest in hearing them has long since waned."

"Naughty child." He gave the door a light shove that took my balance, and I fell back against the stairs. He slipped in and shut the door. The hall went dim but for the flicker of the streetlamp visible in the narrow panes above the entry. "We can talk here if you will, or up by the hearth where you can see me."

"I like not what I'll see."

"Your lack of favor pains me truly, but I'll not be deterred."

"How do you think Nehemiah would look on such a rude show?"

"He's looking on something else right now, Mistress, and he'll not wish to see either of us for what we are, will he?"

I saw his hand waver in the dark like a pale crab. With a dull throb in my head, I took it. He helped me up but followed at a safe distance, alert perhaps that I might haul off like a mule and kick his drunken frame down the stairs had I leverage.

I walked to the hearth, and the doctor followed. My heart was thudding in its cage, but the room with its red-gold glow seemed unnaturally quiet, bereft almost, and my image in the candlelit lead of the windows ghostly. "What do you want?"

"I would know what you did to him, to make him forget so well his mother's Puritan teachings. How did you make him so free? He never was before."

"What matter is it of yours?"

"None at all, except that I wonder, and wondering is my entertainment for tonight."

"I've done nothing."

"That's not what Gideon Metcalf would say, or your former housemaid, for that matter."

"I care not what they say."

"Thanks to Margaret, in fact, I've something to exchange with you." He rummaged in his waistcoat and came out with a tiny parcel, tied with makeshift ribbon. He let it lie heavy on his palm. "Haven't you cause to wonder?"

I did wonder, in spite of myself, how others—even Mag, even the Weasel Gideon—would characterize what had passed in New Forest. How grave was my sin? I think I had no moral center now; I no longer understood what was right and wrong in simplest terms, as the ministers in New England would have me understand, and surely it was to some degree this man's fault, this faulty father. How now would such a one instruct me? I longed to know what penance would heal my wrongs but trusted no earthly adviser to tell me. Our own minister was a distracted Scotsman with a lazy eye that seemed to look always past me; his sermons were no better than rote mutterings, and who dared challenge him? Who was like to bother? For others this pastor was, the world was, ever what it should be. *Judge me, then,* I thought vaguely, and knelt on the wood floor to grasp the little parcel. I untied the twine slowly, forgetting my father's mournful eyes on me.

My gift was a crooked apple carved of wood, Simon's first utterance for Abigail, the "A" that was my birthright.

*W*hen the doctor removed his wig, I saw that his once-black hair, now clipped close, had mellowed to ivory. He sat facing me for a time, then fed the fire whilst I composed myself, rolling the carved block between my palms. Mag must have found it under the mattress.

"What saw you in that blind bean of a lad?" I held my tongue, but the doctor poured me sack to loosen it and, at length, shamed a smile from me. I shook my head, all indolence, but in my heart I went to my father as a Papist goes to the priest's booth. "We were children together," I begrudged him.

The doctor rolled his eyes. "You and Metcalf were children together, and I don't see you weeping on his account."

"Simon had no touch of the world on him," I tried, "but he was of the world, like a river or a tree."

My parent blew impatience through pursed lips. "That won't do for an answer, I'm afraid. If you ask what I saw in my plump wife, lowly though she was, I'll say it plainly: she had good firm breasts and a thoughtless laugh that amused me. She let me make her laugh, and that was her goodness."

"You miss her?"

"I miss her. I miss the boy. But they've gone. Have you seen plague sores? Though it may mortify you to hear it, I saw that sweet groin (which I knew with the greatest affection) made black and swollen, lanced with pus, and my child ringed with vile roses. Your brother sleeps now."

"Brother," I echoed disdainfully.

"One wonders what your blind boy had that *his* able and agreeable brother has not."

It wasn't every day I was invited to talk of Simon, yet no perfect answer came to my tongue, and I despaired of it. "He accepted all I gave him," I tried, "expecting none of it."

"Well, what lackwit wouldn't?"

"He was like the sun," I protested, leveling the heedless man in my gaze, "and I reached for him and grew taller. But the sun has no sympathy for those it warms."

"Girlish swill. He was dark inside and out. He left you in the gutter, and his brother too."

"He didn't," I complained, but my eyes blurred again, and when the doctor sat and draped a pungent arm round my shoulder, I seemed for a moment to feel Mother there too, her gray arms rocking me in my tedium. "He just left."

The doctor set his chin atop my head a moment, then commenced to stand and pace as if waked from a dream. "Nehemiah will come creeping back in a month or so. I know her name, and she was a whore even before the Dutch skewered the commander. She'll cast him off."

"And another will take him up."

"You will."

"I have tried."

He relaxed on a facing bench and draped an arm over its back, toppling a nest of embroidered cushions. "Try harder."

"With what art?"

He retrieved one pillow from the floor and, aiming, flung it at me. "Serve him better than the others do."

"Oh, you're a fine adviser." I snatched the cushion up and bounced it back, hitting him square in the gut. "Fine and shallow as a plague grave."

He dabbed spilled beer from his breeches and went with a grim laugh into the larder for more, calling, "School yourself, woman! We're not so complicated. A good tumble cures the hardest male memory."

"Is your memory cured?" I yelled back. "Will it take so little as a whore to banish the ghost of your wife's laughter?"

When he settled again, holding forth the contents of his mug, he confessed, "Any cure will do."

"And what of my mother? You know she sleeps in the clay in Boston?"

"I know it," he said, "but I have done my turn for her. Now I have but you left to ruin."

Our eyes locked in expectation, and I smoothed my skirts. "Go ahead, then."

"After some trouble with the new rule in London," he began in the lofty tone of a bard, which bluster did little to conceal his apprehension, "I came among saints and Quakers to the New World. I docked in Boston as a newly skilled physician but a young man, too, restless of nature with a mind to seek out more tolerant parts, Rhode Island, Virginia even, to encounter Indians and adventure, to move as the wind—"

"Your oratory is diverting, sir, but I would have you forsake theater this once and tell the tale plainly."

Shifting on the bench, he raised a forefinger, undeterred. "But friends introduced me to other friends, a young Harvard seminary student, your one-day pastor, among them, and I found a city wracked with smallpox and influenza; everyone that cold autumn, it seemed, was taken with fever or flux. I found myself drawn in as the aimless are and was soon employed alongside your worthy and charitable grandmother, a very font of community service and homely medical sense. Her daughter too soothed the sick of Trimountain."

I caught my breath to think of Mother a daughter, younger than I was now.

"She had a quiet, intense nature that gave me sweetest pause. 'And what, Dr. Devlin, do you call this instrument?' she would whisper, knowing me to be less than stern. 'Why do his eyes cloud so?' And 'What herb is that?' Curiosity, like much else, is held to be a curse in women, but I would see it nourished in any willing breast. 'Daniel,' I corrected under my breath, courting her black eyes. 'Call me Daniel. Please.'"

Embarrassed, I crossed my arms before me, less to bar his tenderness than to contain my creeping unease.

"This industrious idyll would not last," he said as if reading my thoughts. "Illness is an opportunist. Within weeks, your grandmother sickened. Your mother and I nursed the good woman and, soon after, her gentle husband. But both were taken. No sooner were they shoveled over than your mother took ill. I sent charity's gossips from that house and kept vigil by her narrow bed, a girl's bed. My tasks as nurse completed, I recall just sitting, hour after hour, rocking violently in the old pine chair so it screeched on the boards.

"That she seemed half in the world and half out made her more, not less, desirable. I sat that first nightfall weeping like a child—inexplicably, I believed, and ridiculously (I was scarce more than a boy, you see)—into a pillow. How base the world seemed, and how frigid my God, with whom my relations had ever been uneasy at best. Mayhap I suffered a kind of madness, paused outside time, forsaking meat and mead. The old gossips came and went with rags and water, rapping with their knotted knuckles. Unseemly it appeared to them that I should be so long alone with my charge. They were right, of course—old women often are, though who will hear them? 'I'll go at dusk,' I assured, for it was the dark that offended them. But night came, and a new day, and I held fast. One crone rapped and rapped; went and came rapping again until at length I drew open the casements and brought a grave forefinger to my lips; she read danger in my looks, no doubt, and stalked away.

"On the third night your mother suffered abundant chills. I banked the fire and, inexplicably resolved, lay beside her. But once there I couldn't bear her pallor and shivering or my own confusion of feeling—for while I would do anything to soothe and protect her, I understood, dimly, that she required protection *from me*. Thus, restless and afflicted, I up and barred the door.

"I have heard midwives urge a mother to hold her newborn (blue with cold) to her bare flesh; here is warmth that cannot otherwise be had, and so, with due ceremony, I undressed her. This act, as you can imagine (you must try, for this was no physician's mood) left a mind starved by silence and dread, and a body that toiled without sustenance, in an anguished snarl. We were neither of us sweet-smelling nor wholesome in aspect, but when I let myself relax against her—" the doctor drew a harsh breath— "Have you held a fevered body? Can you fathom such an embrace? It is the softest belonging, your boundaries obliterated by heat. We lay thus, and she made soft noises in her throat. Perhaps they were the complaints of an offended maid, but I did not heed them. My base nature was coursing now, and greed will ever savage love." He sucked in breath and raised his palm as if to stop a blow. "Sit back and hear me *plainly*. You *will* hear me. On what ceremony would I stand with Death in that room, courting her in my stead? Perhaps it *was* only lust, but I felt—resolving to be once with her while the blood ran warm—that I would stop time. I would hold water in my hands." His hands fell still in his lap. "And so it was."

So it was. I could only stare at the man who had uttered these words. He seemed to sense that I was slipping away, that it could not be helped, and his voice hurried. He padded across on all fours like a beast and lifted my chin. He smoothed the salt from my cheeks, and though I would have liked to stop up his mouth, to rant and kick and bite like the child I never had been for him, I was a woman now and duly modest. I curled inward like a flower and let him speak into my hair. His woe rained over me.

"Your parent was a good deal heartier than her own had been, I need not tell you, and survived both her illness and my malfeasance with little memory of either, though she seemed vacant and puzzled and would scarce meet my eye or anyone's after."

The doctor got up and leaned at the hearth wall. "What had I done? Whatsoever it was, I would let her forget. Was it not better so?" He stared into the flames. "I removed myself. I stood patiently and invisibly by while she filled her baskets at market. I glimpsed her on her way to the church-yard where her parents slept, or in the meeting hall surrounded by the pity of goodwives and gentlewomen who would, in due course, revile her." He looked up and back at me, a remembered terror in his eyes.

"But when she came with the spring to say that she was sick and con-fused, that she could not hold down her food, could not look on food some days, where would I retreat? I confessed, puling like a woman. I asked for her hand and her forgiveness. She was roused, to be sure, and I can never forget that she damned me with her waking. *And you a physician?* she accused. *Sworn to heal?*"

He returned to the bench, sat, and drank greedily from his tankard. Our eyes met over it, and when he spoke again his voice was dull and quit of urgency. "Days passed, and the magistrates did not come for me. Arthur rapped once, merrily flaunting some philosophical question he would see dissected, but there I sat, mutely growing whiskers in a closed room. When I could, I steeled myself and went to her servants' entrance, though she barred the door. Believe it, I tried every trick *I am a man, after all, and take what I will,* every temptation *I invite you. Who would not see their enemy flayed before them with blame?* but she stood at the window unmoved. Her eyes looked out like featureless coal, and I understood that I was to her no more.

"When she began to swell, I sailed for England. She would say nothing rather than debase herself with the truth, and those charged with her moral education would not likely have credited such truth. To Boston's elders, she was one more wayward, masterless young woman, afflicted with Eve's curse. Until her parents' estate could be untangled and plundered, they gave her prison straw with the brand to wear at her breast, and she had no solace in the world, I know, but the pity of your young minister. I'll grant she cherished Arthur for placing his flesh second to his soul and because he would not, even when he knew, have her loathe me." He laid his head against the bench back, closing his eyes. "Though she managed it. I doubt not she would have cut my throat if she could."

"She loathed me more," I offered, though he seemed at rest, seemed to have forgotten me. "Mother tried to drown me once."

"*Once,* Pearl——" His laugh was hollow, and he sat up with pinched brow, startling me now with those strange eyes—"was long ago."

A NIGHT AS BRIGHT
AS THE DAY

I woke to the sound of my father staggering round the dim room in search of his wig and gloves. The sun was just cresting the city. It flowed into my chamber and spilled over the heavy bed curtains. It would be another hot, dry day. His tale ended, he'd helped me to the mattress, tucking the bedclothes round me and drawing the panels closed before settling himself nearby on the floor. I lifted one pale hand now to draw back the curtain, but let it fall again to my pillow. I had neither will nor courage to face him, to look on him and think of my mother. Perhaps his candor had been only a maudlin product of the ale, but I knew this at once for a lie. How sick and sorry it made me to look at him, to be *of* him. And yet I was, and we were only this—two forsaken people at sunrise.

I lay silent until my visitor, having banked the fire and milled about the hearth for some while, could stand his own idleness no longer and went from my house, my husband's house, leaving behind a sheaf of thin leather notebooks. Filled with spidery script, the notebooks recorded bits and pieces of a troubled dream, distorted fragments of a drama that mimicked life, his own and that we shared, but little resembled the professed (and confessed) truth. There were scraps of truth drawn no doubt from history my father had witnessed or heard reported; I recognized in his cast some semblance of the child me (a wilder shade thereof), of Mother (the drama's passionate heroine), of the minister (its lofty and tormented hero), and of the author himself (here a wronged and gnarled old demon, a physician but otherwise unrecognizable).

I lay heavy-limbed as I read, impatient, and presently flung the notebooks aside, weary of fiction. Waiting for Abby to wake and tumble down the stairs from her new bed (Mag's, once Simon's) in the garret, full of oblivious demands for the day, I made a list in mind of chores that needed doing, market errands, mending—and then it struck me that I was thinking of life in ordinary terms when life had ceased, long since, to be ordinary. Life was a dismal cloak of failure and discontent on that morning—and now that I could acknowledge having failed, was it justice or folly to let that cloak be my shroud, to let my body suspire and take its tasks while the rest of me withered?

Before dark that evening, I arranged for my neighbor Bess to keep Abby overnight. I set our lodgings in good order, filled my pocket with coin, and secured the drawstring pocket inside my plain wool dress. I walked several blocks to the Royal Exchange. The crowd in the courtyard was thinning, so I waited across the street, watching the twilight paint uneven cobbles, smelling the drains and the stench of various trades along the roadways leading down to the river and the wharves, all belching smoke and fumes. One by one, the well-dressed men in that vast courtyard dispersed. I don't know how I imagined I would find him among so many—or why I did not walk up to the galleries to confront him—but I stood fast.

As it grew dark, the watch went by armed with a rusty halberd. He half nodded and half winked at me, and I lowered my head. A drowsing drayman passed too, letting his horse lead him home.

When the majority of men had gone from that watched courtyard, watching me as they went, I sighed with despair. Unless he had spent all day trading at the coffee houses or had taken another exit, Nehemiah had forsaken even his work for her, and I would not have him back this night.

Though I knew I risked my honor and my coin there, for surely I would be taken for a prostitute, I took refuge in the closed well of a tradesman's doorway, dumb with disbelief. I sat on a crate for I know not how many bleak hours. My limbs would take no direction. But what if he didn't come with the sunrise? What then?

As the night wore on, though I could scarce lift my head, I noticed a strange new mood in the streets and heard a faint murmur as of voices far away. The men passing through that lane were not solitary rakes straggling home from the Boar's Head and other alehouses but came trotting in pairs or threes and went past without so much as lifting an eyebrow at a woman alone at this hour. My own eyes stung for some reason, and when I saw the watch appear again at the corner I ran to him, fighting back dread at the confusion in his face. There was an acrid, half-familiar tang in the air. A squealing horse took the corner, wild-eyed, with its cart jerking along behind.

"Why is the street so?" I demanded. "What has happened?"

"All of Pudding and Botolph's on fire, Miss, and the wind tempts it here. It's ripe for the bridge! Go preserve your goods if your home's nearby." He pointed with his halberd.

It was all clear then, and the selfish glaze of stupidity left me. I began to run uphill toward a plane of smoke and sparks that were like a million stars riding the moonlit sky above a labyrinth of timber.

"Jesus," I said flatly, and slapped a hand to my mouth.

Many feared the devil on that night and the nights that followed. Had the Dutch, with whom we struggled at sea, landed to wreak their revenge on Monk's victories? Were the French and Papists hurling fireballs? Or had we angered God beyond all repair? In light of my father's confession, I felt like the very sick source of sin, as soiled as any alive under Heaven, and I agonized. Had Mother hated me as she had him? Had she loved some part of my father that lived in me? It was this last that troubled me most somehow as I waited with my own small daughter in my arms at

Simon's window. For Abby, it was a great stage—that Sodom burning beyond the glass. It would not touch us. Perhaps many felt so at first, as none
seemed to be fighting the fiend; rather, I'd noticed on my frantic journey
home through panicked lanes, they scrambled to secure carts, lugging sacks
of goods down to the glowing river, hurling furniture into the Thames.
There were screams and prayers, to be sure, but did the fire grow bold so
quickly because we did not believe in it? With the plague so soon behind,
had our great city no strength for new calamity? The faces I saw were all
clouded with disbelief. Not one reflected even a tenth of that great flame.

Bess came early Tuesday morning with the rumor that even our Lord
Mayor had not suffered himself to lose sleep over it, and now the fire was
pitifully out of control. The dry east wind blew and blew and did not stop
blowing till Wednesday. The fire would burn for more than three days and
take the better part of the city with it.

Bess urged us to pack a sack or two and make ready. The fire was moving swiftly west, though the King and his brother, the Duke of York, had
been roused to action—with soldiers and trained bands in the streets
armed with squirts and leather buckets. They were pulling down houses
and hoped to stop the blaze at the Fleet River. "But Pearl," she said, "Cheap-
side will not be spared."

"Saint Paul's?" I asked dumbly, for the great cathedral was just west
of us.

"I fear for it. I fear for all of us." Bess bowed her head when Abigail
came bouncing into the room. "Make ready, Pearl. Tempt your husband
out of the garden and bid him get you to Moorfields or Tower Hill, or Is-
lington if you've kin to shelter you."

"The garden?"

"He's out digging a grave for the gold and plate he can't carry, like
mine own." She was scarcely able to stand still now, her agitation was
such. "I like gold as well as the next, but I'll give that hound a good kick
before I'll let him go on digging. The cellar will do—"

I did not hear what more Bess said. Some time later, I found myself
staring at the floor, where my neighbor stood no longer. I broke free

of that spot and hurriedly dressed Abby and myself in layers, cloaks and all, though it was warm enough to melt under them. I filled a basket with food and another with small tokens: my sewing kit, letters and documents, Mother's watch and the baby coif she'd stitched for Abigail, the carved apple that was Abby's father's. I stuffed our finer clothes into sacks and, at the last moment, tucked in Daniel Devlin's unread notebooks. As I worked, I realized for the first time that morning, with dumb astonishment, that Nehemiah had already rifled soundlessly through these rooms while we slept. He had removed what remained of his personal wardrobe and most anything of value, except the furnishings and bedclothes.

Panting, I herded Abby downstairs, sat her on the staircase, and made her promise to remain there. "You mustn't move, or the fire will have you. I'll be around back in the garden with your papa."

"But *where* is Papa?" she begged again, her chant of late. "Why can't I see him too?"

"You will see him, but now I must speak with him alone. I'll be back, and we'll go away."

"But the fire is come. Look at the smoke, Mother—"

Mother. It was the first time she had so named me, and I could little pause to enjoy it. I kissed her forehead, trying not to think of the yellow-gray smoke that billowed in sheets over our street and the great, crackling roar that I knew preceded it. "Sit here for just a moment. Promise?"

She nodded firmly, though I could see that she was frightened.

"Guard the baskets and open this door for no one. Many are running in the streets. Thieving too, I fear."

Nehemiah seemed not to see me, even when I spoke his name. His face was tracked black with soot and sweat, and his back stooped from shoveling. "Husband?"

I went forth and touched his soiled sleeve, but he only jerked the arm away. "This is not time to air our grievances," I pleaded. There were kegs of wine piled beside him with several burlap sacks alongside. He kept digging. "Do you mean to see all this buried before the fire comes? Bess tells me Lombard and Cannon are already alight."

"I've watched my masts go up in flames with the warehouses. There's a river of bubbling lead in the streets. The spices I brought last spring from the islands scent the wharves and sting the eyes." As he ranted, he sent dirt winging blindly over his shoulder. "The fire shot through the galleries of the Exchange in minutes, it seems. The very kings tumbled from their lookouts in the eaves. I have little left," he rasped, "but what you see, and what exists on paper. What new torments will God think to tax me with?"

The unholy silence that followed did more to unsettle me than his words. I began to shake, and focused my gaze on the great clods of earth he'd moved, soil clutching a tangle of roots, browning lavender and rosemary. Smoke swirled overhead, and the crackling roar of the distant fire was too near to ignore. "That will not be undone, husband. But what will you do for your child? Will you leave her on the steps to burn?"

He thrust the shovel at the earth and turned to me with such savage eyes that I thought I would wither. It was a cruel, cold man that looked at me then, and no man I knew. "If I had let him drown all those years ago," he said, "I would have none of this to account for."

"What mean you?" My voice cracked. "Nehemiah? 'This'?"

But I knew. How long had I known? A long while. "I'll take him from you," I offered, only half believing I could do it. "And his child too. We'll go."

He gaped at me, and the white of his eyes in that soot-smeared face, the wet shine and good, deep brown of that stare, were familiar again. He buckled under my words, and his knees struck soil. Though I tried to aid him, he would not have it but lurched away on his knees and retched. I pray that one day I'll forget the sight of him there heaving with his mane full of ashes, rocking over his shovel like a crazed supplicant.

"Leave the wine, husband, and let this grave stand for Simon."

The air was dizzy and sweet with cooked brandy. I heard a splintered roar of crashing timber. London was Hell, and she was wailing. Presently, he grew mindful again. I half expected Nehemiah to stammer and lift my hand to his lips like a gallant; it was that tangible, the effects of my gift upon him. Using the shovel to support himself, my husband straightened up and smoothed his soiled waistcoat. He kissed me fast, like a shy child, and lifted two of his sacks. And then, while the world burned, he strode from that garden, that life, while I stood over an empty grave.

*H*e had paused long enough to kiss Abigail's begging lips as well, and to stuff her tiny hands with coin. I might have flung those guineas into the street, but I knew how much we would need them. There were a goodly number, though it could never begin to repay the portion of my trust, and my mother's bequest, that I'd lost by law to my marriage. Together with the money in my private pocket, those coins would keep us—for a time. I was too stunned to lament my losses or pity us. With the fire threatening, we made our way north with the thronging crowds in the streets to Moorfields.

I thought Abby's grip would break the bones of my hand, and the baskets and sacks knocking against our legs kept us from moving with any stealth. It was now the fire's voice, more than the smoke and smell and shrieking, that terrified me, for never in my life have I heard such a roar. Punctuated by the great thunder of buildings collapsing behind in the conflagration, it might have been the sound of the devil's own bliss.

"Look there!" Abby called, and gestured to an alley where a cat—pink and shiny as a mousling with its fur burned away—went padding into the dim recesses with her scorched kitten in her teeth.

I pulled Abigail on.

"Need a porter, Miss? A porter?" asked a wild-eyed man who elbowed his way through the crowd. Muscles throbbing, I nearly relented, but something told me not to, and a good thing too—for I learned later that many a thief made his fortune from that flame, whether making off with goods outright, extracting unheard-of sums for use of a cart or wherry, or later charging exorbitant rents.

The opportunist in *me* wished only to find a willing captain, but after three days of pestering in the encampment at Moorfields, I found my father instead. Or he found me. And took up our bags and, at long last, our burden.

Where the earth isn't

What I best remember of those last days in London, where we lived shifty-eyed among hundreds of soot-black refugees, was a lone voice, a stranger's voice. One night, a woman accompanied by a recorder sang a ballad so sweet that it seemed a lullaby for the masses. It was very late, and the little cooking fires had all been carefully extinguished, but there were candles glowing here and there in the tents. The fields were riddled with these tents—makeshift bed-sheet shelters that caught the blue moonlight, ragged little huts pieced together from burned timbers. Rich and poor lay side by side in that field like the lion and the lamb. We were at best a joyless throng, with children, including my own child, ever whimpering, some woman always weeping, and many a searching soul bent in prayer. But that one night, that one voice was so gentle and serene, so forgiving of fate, that I will carry it always in my heart. She was a mother for us all, that singer, and—as my mother was much in my thoughts in those days—I was grateful for her gift.

Daniel Devlin found a captain by week's end—one bound for Salem Town and willing to brave the onset of winter at sea for the sake of the restorative wares he would be the first to return with. For London would begin again. All things do.

. . .

$\mathcal{R}$arely did my eyes leave Abby on that sea journey. Her limbs were long now, and her curiosity well advanced. Though she had not half the eleven or so years I could claim on my first such trip, she was, I think, alert to many of the things I was alert to then. The way the creaking deck seemed to shift beneath her and the wind-blown rigging slapped against the wood. The muffled cries of goats and cattle in the hold. The sound and smell of retching when the sea was troubled; the unholy stillness when it was becalmed. Tangled heaps of ladders and coiled rope, pitchforks, lanterns, and bellows. Mildew and scurvy. The pugnacious cockerel that strutted about ship like a foul-mouthed seaman. Monstrous sleek whales splashing and spouting. There is wonder in a journey like no other.

But we were both—all, perhaps, for I saw it reflected in the faces of my fellow passengers, nearly all Londoners on that journey—plagued by dreams of fire. In fact, one evening we lurched on a wave and a coal rolled from the cabin's little hearth, which was always attended by one or another boy, and bounced over the low grate. It found nothing to ignite before the boy scooped it into a nearby shoe and threw it back, but the collective gasp in that closed space was eloquent.

"Abby—?"

She moaned as I stroked her hair through that long night of many, and shivered under the thin blanket we had managed to procure along with a few other necessary things from generous strangers at Moorfields.

"Do you know there are paths on the sea the captains follow? Great paths of starlight that lead from one bit of rock to another. Only the captains can read them. Do you know that Mother came once on a path like this to England?"

"Will Papa come away too?"

"He won't, Abby."

"But why not? Where is he?" She sat up drowsily. "What have you done with him?"

"I've disappointed him." I stroked her hair, whispering, "And worse. But in any case, Abigail, he is not your father. I'll tell you that now. There's no good in keeping it from you."

Her brow creased. Her nostrils flared. Without warning she sat up and with an ugly stare shrilled, "Liar!"

Liar.

The noise was so startling to me and to the other passengers that I sealed a hand over her mouth. The weary strangers who lay on mats and quilts all around, like so many kittens curled together in a basket, stared while I rocked with her and hissed in her ear. The sloshing motion of the ship struck me. We were adrift on an endless plane of water. I felt the surging pressure of her tooth against my thumb. "Stop your racket, Abigail. Stop. It's true. I'll not sift the truth for you as my mother did for me." When her throat ceased throbbing, I let my hand fall.

"The truth stinks." She spat at me or mimed as if to. "Like a bad apple."

I yanked her up and dragged her away from scores of stern, expectant eyes in the cabin. We found a shadowy corner behind some barrels and knelt there together. "Be still now," I threatened, "before they lay you in bolts."

"I'm still."

"And listen."

She pouted resolutely. "I'm listening."

"You are fatherless now," I hissed, "though God has given you a grand-papa to help you bear it. There is nothing more to say."

She bowed her head and seemed to crumple, and though I felt hardened again, I pulled her close.

"Why?" she begged into my dress.

"Because of me."

"Why have I no Papa—"

"Because you are mine." I lifted her heart-shaped face and saw Simon there. "Mine own."

She relaxed against me or gave up, slumping, I know not which. But I could little help but wonder, with a kind of grave amusement, if this child would come sailing back across the ocean in the other direction one day, with her own history in tow, her woes.

While Dr. Devlin set himself the task of winning Her Majesty over, bouncing her on his knee or riding her up on his shoulders to view the waves, I read and reread his strange notebooks, fingering the soft paper, wondering at the spidery, half-familiar tale that was neither truth nor a lie.

I remembered Nehemiah's love for the sea and for once, though I am a creature of earth, I understood it. Time is rocked to sleep by the waves, propelled only by weather. Like Jonah in the belly of the whale, the passenger at sea is swaddled in expanse. It is all light and blindness there, where the earth isn't.

But instead of offering overboard the red letter, as Mother once dreamed of doing—as it might have pleased her to see me do whilst my chastened father looked on—I resolved to bring it ashore to Salem Town. I would keep it close as I stepped to earth again, and use it well and often, to barter for the life he had left.

Acknowledgments

I am grateful, of course, to Nathaniel Hawthorne, without whom Pearl would not exist; to Samuel Pepys for his lively diaries, which instructed me in countless ways; and to Quennell's *A History of Everyday Things in England,* Volume 2, from which I filched the irresistible (to me) love letter that appears on page 143. Special thanks to my husband, Courtney Wayshak, and our children, Clyde and Michaela, who as always weathered my distraction with affection, patience, and good humor; to the Ragdale Foundation, for precious solitude; to Bill Reiss, who helped so much with early drafts; to Lisa Goodfellow Bowe, dear friend and first reader; to my phenomenal agent, Jill Grinberg; and to everyone at Unbridled Books, especially Fred Ramey.